Praise for Marcella Bell's *The Wildest Ride*

"Marcella Bell brings grit, spark and brilliance to Western romance! Marcella Bell is one to watch!"
—Maisey Yates, *New York Times* bestselling author

"[T]horoughly charming, with strong cowboy flavor, fascinating family histories, and female empowerment front and center. True to its title, this wild ride is sure to sweep readers away." —*Publishers Weekly*

Also by Marcella Bell

The Wildest Ride

For additional books by Marcella Bell,
visit her website, www.marcellabell.com.

MARCELLA BELL

The Rodeo Queen

HQN

ISBN-13: 978-1-335-63985-1

The Rodeo Queen

Copyright © 2022 by Marcella Bell

Recycling programs for this product may not exist in your area.

For questions and comments about the quality of this book, please contact us at CustomerService@Harlequin.com.

HQN
22 Adelaide St. West, 41st Floor
Toronto, Ontario M5H 4E3, Canada
www.Harlequin.com

Printed in Lithuania

MIX
Paper from responsible sources
FSC® C021394

To Conar. I love you, little brother.
You *can* make things better.

The
Rodeo
Queen

PROLOGUE

Las Vegas, Nevada

DI-A-BLO—DI-A-BLO—DI-A-BLO!

The arena chanted his name in rhythm with the beat that thrummed in his veins, but Diablo Sosa ignored them. Instead, he focused on the near three thousand pounds of rage and muscle that shivered and snorted between his legs.

Memories flooded him as the old, familiar, preternatural calm took over, the world and all of his concerns boiling down into an imperative, issued, as always, in his nana's voice: *don't let go.*

His mind funneled down into a universe with a population of two—himself and a bull.

Every other input was muted, even as its data continued to process in the back of his mind: a crowd loud enough to add to the bull's agitation, his name on their lips, the ache of his ripped-out heart.

Front and center now, however, it was just him and the bull, his right arm raised in the air, the left bearing responsibility for his entire life as he gripped a tornado. His body was no longer muscle and bone but an overstuffed rag doll whipping in time to a bull's frantic efforts to unseat him.

Whether or not that occurred was really up to him, though.

To all the world, it would look like he wrestled for dominance—and found it—with a creature more than ten times as massive and a million times as mean as he was.

Looks could be deceiving.

Diablo never beat a bull by control. He'd never beat a bull by strength.

He beat a bull by release—releasing every pent-up emotion, every ounce of heartbreak that weighed him down, every encounter that reminded him he was a Black man who had never learned to hide his strength, everything that reminded him that he was a man who had once lost control of that very same strength, every time he'd had to swallow an insult, every time a woman had refused to love him in public, every time he'd had to give up a fight, all of the setbacks that a man named after the devil had experienced on his way to the top. All of that had to have been enough practice for now.

He'd unleashed everything each time he'd climbed on top of a raging beast, and it had always worked because everything that he held inside was too much, even for a bull.

That was true now, more than ever.

Should he give it all to the bull or should he let the bull tear him apart?

His nana would slap him for even pondering the question.

But there was no nana in this world with the bull; there was no time, no rules and no requirements—just a man with far too much to hold, a name that was too big to carry and a gaping hole inside that could never be filled, meeting a furious beast head-on.

He'd never wanted to cry while riding a bull.

He'd never worn a suit to ride a bull.

It had been a night of many firsts.

As he burrowed into himself, searching for everything he wanted to release at the bull, the creature itself seemed to disappear, leaving only himself at fourteen years old, reliving a memory he'd thought long processed.

"You can change it!" he'd screamed, chest puffed, neck straining, spittle flying. "All you have to do is sign this paper. All you ever had to do—and you could end it." He'd been hot and wild and thrumming with so much that he didn't have the words for back then.

Rage. Confusion. Loneliness.

He knew the words now. Back then, though, all that had mattered was that he shed the curse of his name. That, and the desperate need that his nana keep the secret that there had been tears in his eyes when he'd asked—no, pleaded—with her to change it.

"Can't you see, picarito?" The hand she had laid on his shoulder had been gentle, and somehow that made it worse. "Your name was her apology. 'I'm sorry that I couldn't live up to the name you gave me, Mama. Take care of him. Raise him better.'" His nana's eyes had been like charcoals in her face, her hair still dark then, though streaked by the long sections of gray that had widened with each year of his adolescence. "Your name and your eyes are the only things she gave you. They're gifts."

But he had not seen them as gifts. Instead, he let out an unholy screech, ripped the stack of papers in his hands in half and punched a hole through the plaster of their wall.

Like now, he wasn't a liar back then, and he wouldn't lie even in his memory.

He'd disappeared again, just for an instant, when hitting the wall.

Just like he had on skid row the evening he'd almost ruined his life.

But only for an instant.

Less than an instant.

The out-of-body experience lasted just long enough to miss his nana's gasp at the foot of the stairs, but not long enough to miss her long sigh. Not long enough to miss the way her eyelids fell, and her shoulders drooped, slightly.

She had looked exhausted, worn-out.

He had finally succeeded in exhausting the inexhaustible. She had only ever looked so tired once before.

His throat had closed around stuck tears, the knot of them a salty burn in desperate need of release.

He had thought she was going to get rid of him, that he had wrung her dry and she was going to get rid of him. She was going to kick him out on the streets. His mind filled with a reel of the homeless faces he always scanned—searching for a familiar set of eyes.

He couldn't live like that.

He knew them all, knew they had names and individual backstories. And they knew him. And they knew of him. The proximity and reminder of it was enough to make him panic.

Breath escaping him, throat tightening, chest refusing to do the usual thing of expanding and contracting, he had done what any fourteen year old would have done—he had turned around and run into his room.

And in the process, he had missed his nana taking

a deep breath, straightening her spine, squaring her shoulders and recommitting—as she had always done and would continue to do, every other time he tested her—until they both made it through.

She never did give up, and she never did let Diablo change his name.

And because he loved her, he never told her the reasons he wanted to.

He never mentioned the target it painted on his back, nor how it gave his teachers an impression of him before he even stepped into their classrooms, nor how it dared other boys to challenge him and girls to chase him—but only in the shadows.

He didn't tell her how some of those boys were enraged to the point of violence or that the girls played games to find out if certain rumors about him were true but refused every one of his requests to go to dances.

Like he'd told her, Sierra wasn't the first but the last in a long line of women ashamed to call him theirs. But at least he'd finally learned how to stand up for himself there.

Sierra…

He never had gone to any dances—never had dressed in an ill-fitting suit and rode around in a rented limo.

He rode bulls, instead.

Even back then he'd known that bulls were the only force powerful enough to take the full strength of his emotions without his having to worry about holding back.

And so now he let go; he released the biggest grief he'd ever experienced, until there was nothing left—no sorrow, no pain, no massive loneliness—just a weapon of a name and the knowledge of how to use it.

CHAPTER ONE

Houston, Texas

DIABLO ORDERED A rum and Coke at the hotel bar, mildly alert to the booth full of men who kept looking at him before turning back to each other to whisper. They didn't know he watched them through the mirror behind the bar, and they were therefore so obvious he almost smirked.

At four o'clock the bar of the downtown Houston hotel was quiet. The bulk of its clientele was still tied up in the work that had brought them to the city in the first place.

In fact, it was only the bartender, Diablo and the group of men—all of whom wore suits—in the whole place.

It was possible that they stared because of his attire.

Wearing a plaid button-up, his rolled sleeves exposed muscled forearms that had been drafted in rodeo and revised through self-discipline at the gym. Beneath that he had on jeans and cowboy boots. He was dressed down—for both himself and the hotel.

There were subtle signs that he belonged there, though.

He wore his favorite Rolex, a timepiece that cost as much as some people's cars, as well as his three chains—one platinum, two gold, all thick. He wore them every day, even beneath his three-piece suits in court, because some things remained meaningful even when class hopping.

His boots, broken in though they might be, were another expensive sign that he was exactly the kind of man they catered to in this establishment—especially here in Texas, a state in which millionaires were just as likely to have stock in the fields as they were to have stock on Wall Street, and where cattle and oil remained extremely relevant currency.

In fact, most passersby wouldn't bat an eye at the sight of a man in Wranglers ordering a drink at one of the most expensive hotel bars in the city.

But Diablo was not like the men who frequented this establishment.

While most stayed here for business, he was here for personal reasons.

While most came from money that stretched back to the time before the US took the territory, Diablo had grown up worlds away, if only miles, in Houston's third ward.

And while most were lily white, Diablo was Latine and Black, and of a complexion dark enough that no-body ever bothered to ask him where he was from.

The bartender handed him his drink, and Diablo dropped the rest of the bar patrons from his mind.

Diablo wasn't sitting here for them.

He was sitting here, nursing his rum and Coke alone because the Old Man had asked him to make the trip out, for reasons that he said he would "explain in person."

The old man had never been one for games or beating around the bush, so Diablo had booked his flight from Phoenix immediately.

And now he waited, while the group of men paid their tab and left the bar.

As it had been when he'd arrived, thirty minutes earlier, once again the bar was empty and he didn't mind one bit.

Diablo wore three chains because there were three people he cared to spend his time with.

Outside their company, he preferred to be alone.

To those three individuals, he was committed and loved them fiercely. It wasn't that he was against close bonds or connection; he simply didn't play around when it came to them. It was just that relationships required honesty, compassion and respect, and with a life story like his, he'd only ever encountered the kind of person who had those traits in sufficient enough quantity and quality three times.

Though he supposed Lil, the woman who'd stolen the heart of Diablo's best friend, was fast carving out a fourth spot in his stone-cold heart for herself.

The Professional Bull Riders Association's first female rough stock champion, Lil possessed the requisite qualities of honesty, compassion and respect in spades, and she was good for AJ.

Perhaps he should contact his jeweler… He pondered it, toying with the idea of making room for one more in his tight circle of care until the Old Man showed up a few minutes later, and Diablo rose to greet him.

"Diablo," he said, his voice like smooth whiskey in a gritty glass, with a nod and tip of his hat before opening his arms.

Embracing him easily, Diablo smiled. "Old Man."

Henry Bowman, or Old Man, as he was affectionately known to Diablo, AJ and all the other boys he'd turned into men through his years leading CityBoyz, the rodeo program he'd begun for boys who didn't have access to the kinds of lessons learned in arenas and on the range.

"Thanks for coming to meet me like this," he said as they sat at the bar together and he ordered himself a scotch, to Diablo's eternal dismay. The man was a cowboy to the core and always had been—drink preferences included. Diablo only wished, for his sake, that he would branch out someday and try a little real flavor.

But it seemed like if it didn't taste like a mouth full of dirt and peat, Old Man wasn't interested.

How else could one explain volunteering to train a bunch of teen boys how to ride bulls? And keeping at it, day after day, for the twenty-plus years that followed?

A lifetime spent cowboying—one that had begun long before cowboying had become a quaint relic of a bygone era and then a new nostalgic trend—had apparently given him a taste for eating hard ground and wading through shit.

However, though the ground and shit he himself covered now were of the metaphorical variety, Diablo could understand the drive, because it lived in him, too.

"Anytime," Diablo said, taking a drink from his rum and Coke. "Ready to tell me to what I owe the pleasure?"

The old man looked away, his eyes darting toward something behind Diablo just as the bartender arrived with his drink. Taking a sip, he let it slide down and paused, his five o'clock-shadowed Adam's apple and weathered skin bobbing with the swallow, while he closed his eyes. Opening them, he looked into his glass, a half smile on his face as he said, "It seems I have a favor to ask."

If Diablo didn't know the man like a father, wasn't absolutely certain that he was the kind of man who didn't bother with lies and evasions because never did a lie achieve an aim that a truth couldn't hit better— and without the collateral damage—he might have interpreted the old man's body language as suspicious.

But the old man was nothing if not forthright and direct—it was that trait that had convinced the young, wild and lonely version of Diablo to listen and look closer and see that there was something more to the dusty Black cowboy than simply a skinny old man in a stupid costume.

"It's as good as done," Diablo said.

The old man chuckled, but hidden in the dry sound, Diablo detected a faint discordant note of sadness. "While I appreciate the readiness, you might want to hear the terms before you go making promises I know you won't want to keep. At least, that's the general advice of my legal counsel," he said, the note of teasing sweeping away anything else Diablo thought he might have picked up in his voice.

With a smirk, Diablo said, "I know for a fact that there isn't anything you could ask of me that your legal counsel would advise against."

He was the old man's legal counsel, and there wasn't a thing on God's green earth he wouldn't do for him.

But damned if the wily old man didn't nearly call his bluff with his next words, saying abruptly, "I want you to ride for CityBoyz in the next Closed Circuit."

For a moment, Diablo said nothing. He reached for his glass and took a sip of his drink. Then he set the glass back down on the bar and said, "Didn't expect that."

It wasn't a no and it wouldn't be a no.

Diablo meant what he said and he kept his word— if Henry Bowman needed him to derail his entire life, Diablo would do it, even knowing that was the analogy that came to mind because riding rodeo again would be damn near doing just that.

Yes, he'd held on to his saddles and gear, just like he'd retained the know-how that was buried in the dust of his brain, but he'd had no plans to revisit that part of his life. Rodeo had saved him, but that didn't mean it hadn't hurt along the way. He and Rodeo had loved equally and learned equally and then moved on with their lives, like young lovers were supposed to do.

He was a lawyer now for Chrissakes, not a damn cowboy.

The old man laughed and the sound was filled with the body and warmth that Diablo was used to, and was free of the guilt that'd been dogging his mentor since he'd entered the bar.

Diablo knew firsthand that the man had a lot of pride, and had, in fact, only recently learned to accept help from the people whose lives he'd made possible.

"Now, see, you already said yes," the old man said mischievously, "and I should hold you to it just to prove my point about lettin' your mouth write the checks before your butt knows if it can pay 'em," he finished with a cackle.

"If it's money that's needed, I could just give it to you," Diablo offered, though he'd be surprised if Henry said yes. He might have learned to accept a little help, but he was still a ways away from accepting cash from his mentees. That was the whole reason AJ had gone above his head to compete in the first season of the reality rodeo show *The Closed Circuit* in the first place.

"I don't need your money," the old man snapped, offense lifting the tone of his voice. "Between AJ and Lilian, and the team they hired to run the office, City-Boyz is doing just fine in that respect."

He didn't add *these days*, but Diablo knew he thought it.

"So what's behind this unusual request, then?" Diablo asked, nudging the subject away from the thing he knew the old man was still ashamed about. Last year CityBoyz had almost gone under—it would have, had it not been for AJ, and to a lesser extent, Diablo. AJ, a world champion bull rider, had competed on behalf of the program and taken home the hefty second-place prize, not to mention reunited the old man with the daughter he'd never known he'd had in the process. Diablo had secured nonprofit legal status for CityBoyz.

In terms of repaying the debt they owed to their aging mentor, AJ was a lot further ahead than Diablo.

But perhaps he wouldn't be after Diablo granted this current request and made a fool of himself on national television.

Henry glanced out the tinted window that allowed patrons to look at the passersby but didn't return the favor, before he looked straight ahead to catch Diablo's eyes in the bar mirror.

"Publicity." He stretched the word out with his distaste, the country in his voice turning each syllable into a long slow damnation, PU-BLI-CI-TY.

Diablo laughed outright, his shoulders shaking as his eyes crinkled with amusement. It was more joy than he shared with most people. The old man wasn't most people, though. He was special. "Now, why do I think this idea came from the new team?"

Eyes darting down into his drink, the old man allowed a grumbling chuckle, saying, "Something like that," before knocking his glass back. He picked back up with, "We got more money than we know what to do with now. It's time to expand the program, but I don't have enough participants. We got a huge boost while AJ was out there hawking us, but since then it's petered off."

"You couldn't just build a second gym?" he asked.

"Already did that. Got a real cowboy sleepaway camp experience up at Lilian's ranch now, with brand-new facilities and all. But it's not my pockets burning. I need more kids because we got invited to put together a group for the Thanksgiving Day Parade, too. I want to put out a good showing, give the kids something to feel proud about, but we need more of them to really take up some space."

CityBoyz had certainly come a long way from the run-down gym he and AJ and the old man had formed an unbreakable bond within.

And Diablo was glad of it. Shaking his head with a smile, he said, "If you really need it to be me, I will make it work, but you know I'm not the best choice. My caseload is exploding at the seams at the moment and it's been over fourteen years since I've ridden a horse, let alone rough stock for points. Claudio or Marcus could both do it, and likely a better job than I could because they still at least dabble."

"Claudio is working with me to get the kids trained

up for the parade, and Marcus just had that little girl of his."

It was strange to think of Marcus as a father. Diablo hadn't kept up with Marcus or really any of his peers from CityBoyz other than AJ. Claudio he hadn't exactly kept up with as much as continued to interact with because he had stayed local and continued to help the old man out through the years.

Making an uncharacteristically impatient noise in the back of his throat, the old man circled back to his original request. "So are you going to do it or not?"

Mirroring his mentor with his own sound of impatience, Diablo said, "I told you I'd do it. I just don't see why you want it to be me when you've got a whole roster of cowboys better suited to playing show pony."

The old man looked at him directly again, saying, "Now, you know the answer to that, D. Every boy that comes through those doors matters to me, but you and AJ are different, and you know it. You and I both know that AJ'd do it again in a heartbeat, but as a former contestant, he's not qualified. Thankfully, too, since you and I both know that riding in one more rodeo is the last thing he needs. But you—" he paused, eyes narrowing as he examined Diablo, head to toe "—not only are you the second-best cowboy to go through the City-Boyz program, you've been out of the game so long we could make a story of it."

Diablo laughed outright. "I'm willing to argue about who's more successful, AJ or me, but I know that's not what you meant."

The old man smirked, sly savvy coming into his gaze. "It's not. CityBoyz is proud of how you turned out, but we're talking about cowboying here, not lawyering."

Diablo took another drink of his rum and Coke, surprised to find it the last one. "Not as much difference between the two as you might think," he said after he swallowed.

"Close only counts in horseshoes and hand grenades," the old man retorted. "I need you to cowboy up."

Diablo snorted, but there was less humor in the noise this time. Signaling for another drink with a lift of his glass, he said drily, "Well, when it comes to cowboying, close is all I ever got."

Flicking him in the shoulder, the old man scoffed. "Now, I don't want to hear any of that shit. You were one of the finest cowboys I've ever trained."

"Was," Diablo pointed out, grateful when the bartender arrived with his next drink.

He'd cowboyed his way through college, and hadn't just skated by doing it.

He was a three-time College National Finals Rodeo champion. His freshman year had been the only time he didn't take home the top prize—and even then, he'd still placed.

But as good as he'd been, he'd come late to the game and never had the right kind of address to be a real cowboy—at least, according to his competition.

"Could be again. We're proud of you, D. Just as proud that you laid down the lariat and went to law school as we are of your rides and records. You didn't need to tell me that CityBoyz had a part in that, but you did, and that makes you to my mind exactly the face I want to put out there right now. AJ used all that flash and flair to keep us afloat and he brought me my Lilian, and I will always be grateful for that. It's you, though, who I need to convince all those parents and boys—or kids, rather—that rodeo could be their path to achieving success, not just inside the arena. I'm not trying to sell them anything that isn't true, Diablo. You know that better than anyone. You're who I need to do this for me."

The old man could lay on the pressure just as thick as Diablo's nana and had never been shy about exercising the power. Why should now be any different?

The whole thing was turning into a ball of a headache.

Rubbing the back of his neck, he asked, "You gonna change the name now that there might be some City *Girlz* in the future?"

It seemed like a non sequitur, but the old man didn't comment on that, instead saying, "No," with a dug-in note to his voice. "I'm all for opening the door for girls, but we got tradition with that name. And it's what people know, since AJ was on TV."

"So the CityBoyz will just have girls, then?"

The old man nodded. "Yep. And I don't see a problem with that, either."

Diablo didn't say anything to that. "And you need me to ride for you in the next season of *The Closed Circuit* to rustle up more recruits," he confirmed with a long sigh.

The old man grimaced, looking away, saying, "Seems I do," and Diablo immediately regretted the sarcasm.

While trying out for, and God forbid, getting into *The Closed Circuit* wouldn't exactly be convenient, Diablo had meant what he said earlier—it didn't matter what the old man asked of him; he'd do it.

"There's no saying I'll get in, you know," he said.

He hadn't stepped foot in an arena as a competitor in almost fourteen years.

"If you want to, you'll get in," the old man countered. "There's never been a wall you haven't been able to knock down."

Diablo frowned even as he warmed under the praise. "How long till the qualifier?"

"Three weeks."

Dropping a hand to the bar, Diablo looked at the old man sideways, saying, "Three weeks? That's no time at all. How long have you been thinking on this? Or did it just pop into your head that day you sent me that message?"

Not meeting his eyes, the old man looked away again. "Something like that."

Diablo settled himself down and took another drink, finishing the second even faster than the first. While his size and experience meant he had no problem holding his alcohol, he'd never been a fan of being drunk and tended more toward nursing rather than chugging. This situation called for something a bit less restrained, however.

Finally, he said, "I'll clear my calendar for the qualifier, and if I make it in, I'll compete. I'm not making any promises, though," he said. "I haven't even been on a horse in over fourteen years, let alone rodeoed. Three weeks isn't a lot of time to train."

The old man's eyes were sad, even as he smiled and gave his jean-clad knee a slap. "It's plenty when you are the devil at the heel."

Diablo shot the wily bastard a cool glare and said nothing to that. He might be willing to do anything for the man, but he still wasn't going to laugh at his devil jokes.

Reaching out to place a warm palm on Diablo's shoulder after he'd stopped chuckling, the old man looked him directly in the eye and said, "Thank you for doing this, Diablo. It means a lot."

Brushing the words off as he pulled a face, Diablo broke eye contact first. "It's not like I had anything better going on."

The old man laughed at the bold lie, but wasn't ready yet to let Diablo shrug it all off. "I'm serious, D. Thank you. You're doing it for more than just me. You know it stands to change lives."

Diablo of all people could not deny the truth of that. Even if three weeks later he was dealing with the fact that some truths hurt more than others.

He'd finally made his way out to visit AJ and Lil in Muskogee—and he regretted every minute of it.

Excluding the home-cooked meals Lil's grandmother prepared every night because, regardless of however much pain he was in due to training, the woman could cook.

His own nana was many things, but a cook was not one of them. Cooking well took time and practice— two things his nana's life had been in particularly short supply of with becoming a single mother at nineteen, raising her daughter and then turning right around and raising her grandson, too.

Growing up, Diablo's childhood experience had been more of a ramen and eggs in front of the TV than a made-from-scratch around the dinner table situation, as it never took his nana less than two jobs to make sure there was enough ramen to eat, a TV to watch and a roof to do it all under.

Diablo didn't hold it against her.

He just loved home cooking.

And Lil's grandma, with her overflowing gravy and

biscuits, slow-cooked roasts and chicken and dumplings, was an excellent home cook.

With complete seriousness, he asked her, "Will you marry me?"

Across the table, Lil gave a low growl.

They both ignored her.

With complete seriousness, Gran patted his hand that rested on the table and said, "I could never love again, but not to worry. Your bachelor days are numbered—you've all the signs."

Shaking his head, Diablo denied it. "If I can't have you, I don't want anyone."

This proved to be too much even for the canny woman, and she broke with a cackle. "Careful before you wear me down, young man. Then you'd be stuck with me!"

Lil opened her mouth to protest even the joke, but AJ beat her to speaking.

"I'm happy to officiate. I've been saying he's overdue for settling down for at least a year now."

"That's pot calling kettle from a man permanently on the verge of retiring," Diablo noted.

Lil snorted, and AJ protested, saying, "Not me, my friend. My rodeo hat is solidly hung, now that the little lady's gone and made an honest rancher out of me." He wrapped his long, muscular arm around the woman who was genuinely small, with a pat of his gut.

Gran and Lil made the same noise in the back of their throats at that, and Diablo was struck by just how much change their little tableau represented.

A year ago AJ had returned from his farewell-to-rodeo world tour seemingly incapable of giving up the competition, and now, as he'd joked, he was a married man and an honest rancher. It was an ending neither man would have predicted for the city-boy son of two college professors, but Diablo knew it was right and was happy for him.

Both AJ and Lil remained involved in rodeo as official mentors for the CityBoyz program, as well as running CityBoyz's brand-new two-week ranch camp at Swallowtail Ranch. But as opposed to before he met Lil, AJ finally seemed content now—at peace in a way that only chasing rodeo had ever made him.

AJ and Lil spent most of their time at Swallowtail, traveling to Houston to do coaching intensives once a season. The space gave Lil and the old man time to build the relationship they'd both missed out on without too much pressure, as Lil was wont to spook.

Her resistance to bonding with the old man was one of the few things Diablo couldn't relate to about Lil—despite the vastly different backgrounds they came from. She was intelligent, honest and strong enough to break most men—everything Diablo would have asked for in a sister had the idea ever crossed his mind—but she also baffled him.

He would have given an ear for the right to call the old man Dad.

But for the most part, Diablo was overjoyed for his friend and glad of the presence of sisterhood that Lil had ushered into his life. Though she'd only been around for just over a year, she was worming her way into his inner sanctum, proving she was rare in more ways than just in rodeo.

AJ was the brother of his soul, and Lil was exactly the kind of woman he'd wish for him. Their love story, inexorably intertwined with the things they held dearest, was a neat little circle, just like *The Closed Circuit* promised.

Diablo had different expectations for his own experience.

In agreeing to go to the qualifier, he had signed up to climb back on top of a bronc for the first time in over fourteen years, and as the old man was so fond of pointing out to AJ, he wasn't a young man anymore.

And while some things were like riding a bicycle—mastered once and retained forever—riding a bronc or a bull was not one of those things.

So he had begrudgingly powered through his caseload, made arrangements for a sabbatical of unknown duration and traveled to Muskogee to train with Lil and AJ in preparation for the qualifier.

"Lord, save me from ranching," he said, remembering one particularly brutal round of practice, before nodding respectfully toward Lil's gran. "Not to disparage the life. I just prefer my wrangling be done in a courtroom."

"I'm here, too, you know," Lil said flatly, a dyed-in-the-wool, deep-rooted rancher, heart and soul.

As usual, Gran ignored her. Diablo thought it was only gentlemanly, not to mention riling to Lil, to take the older lady's lead.

"No offense taken," Gran said, smiling through laughter, "though if that's true then our love is even more doomed than I knew. I'm as tied to this land as old grumbles over there," she said, nodding toward Lil, unrepentant, while Lil rolled her eyes.

It was a family scene and Diablo, recognizing that for the precious and rare thing it was, was grateful to be a part of it. Even if he had to hurt like hell from a day of training in order to do so.

With his arm still draped possessively around Lil's shoulders—though there was never a need for such a possessive display as everything about the way the man's presence around the petite woman screamed to the world, *She's mine, back off!*—AJ grinned like a cat that got the cream. "I'd say it's long past time you found a partner and settled down. *The Closed Circuit* just might be exactly the thing you need. Think of all the fans you'll meet."

Diablo knew exactly the fans AJ meant and so did Lil, who elbowed him. "I'll thank you not to talk about groupies at my gran's table," she said with a huff.

At this, Gran, whose laughter had only recently subsided, picked up again. "We'll thank the stars your mama was a bit of a groupie, my dear. Otherwise, we wouldn't have the wonder that you are."

Lil, whom Diablo had witnessed opening and lightening up slowly over the past year, merely let out a long sigh rather than rising indignantly to her grandmother's bait. Diablo even liked to think he heard a bit of himself in her silence.

"What? I'm just saying that I met the love of my life because of *The Closed Circuit*," AJ continued, pausing to kiss the top of Lil's head before continuing with an evil glint in his eye, "and maybe Diablo will, too. Stranger things have happened," he concluded with a mischievous shrug.

Diablo knew that AJ expected a dry quip that nonetheless revealed the depth of Diablo's frustration.

Diablo loved to disappoint.

Instead of responding to AJ, Diablo turned to Gran. "Et tu, Brute? I thought we had something real."

Wicked humor bubbling in her crafty old eyes, she said, "When you really love something, you let it go."

"Well, I, for one, am on your side," Lil said. "I say you get in, get out and get on with life."

Diablo caught hold of Lil's all-too-familiar gray gaze, processing and promptly moving past the strange déjà vu that occurred every time he looked into the face of a woman and saw the eyes of the man who'd saved his life. To her, he said gravely, "Thank you, Lil."

Lil raised her small palms, as callused and tough as any man's, and Diablo spared another moment to marvel that this tiny woman was one of the greatest bull riders in the world.

"It's one thing to take your life in your hands for the cameras," she said, adding primly, "To my way of thinking, folks ought to have a little privacy when it comes to their hearts."

The Oklahoma and gravel of her voice lent a sweet note to smoky, but the thing that made her words impossible to ignore was their authenticity.

Just like her father, a person knew where they stood with Lil. She'd always give it to you straight.

Diablo didn't begrudge her the fact that the trait came naturally when he'd had to work hard to emulate it until it had become ingrained and interwoven into his psyche, hand-sewn by sheer force of will.

As was the case with Diablo, getting involved with *The Closed Circuit* hadn't been her idea, and like Diablo, she'd only reluctantly dusted the dirt off her gear and cowboyed up.

In that, the resolve to do whatever it took for the people they loved, they were true siblings.

It wouldn't be the first time he'd saddled up for reasons beyond the buckle.

No, riding a bull wasn't like riding a bike, but the reasons *why* were.

CHAPTER TWO

A WEEK LATER, he sat on the bare back of a bronco, waiting for the chute to open.

AJ, Lil, the old man and his nana crowded around the platform, as was the CityBoyz way.

CityBoyz never rode alone.

He tuned them out.

At the cusp of go time with a living, breathing animal beneath him was no time to be thinking about family.

And when it was time to go, his bronc virtually hurtled out of the chute, leaping out higher than Diablo had ever remembered a bronco leaping in his college days.

He gripped the riggin' with his left hand with enough strength that the shock of it jolted all the way up Diablo's arm to his shoulder. The burn far exceeded any hurt that had arisen in his body over his weeks of practice, and later, when he had room to focus on things like that, he would be grateful to AJ and Lil for how rigorous they'd been in their training. If they hadn't been, perhaps he would have lost his grip.

As it was, his body screamed and thrashed as he whipped to and fro on the saddleless back of a wicked bronc.

There was a strange serenity in the rhythm of the wild beating, like brutal waves in an ocean, flowing in and out to the pace of an animal hell-bent on shaking him off and stomping the life out of him, against the backdrop of noise.

Somewhere in the ride, he recalled a little trick he'd used to score extra points—his little added artistic flair. As the upper body flailed backward, to score well, a cowboy needed his spurs to roll up and over the horse's shoulders; the higher the better. Diablo was blessed with incredibly strong and long legs, so kicking his boots up as he crested the shoulders made him stand out, the little extra oomph gaining him precious height.

Recalling at the right moment, he executed the move on his next thrash.

Outside his world with the bronc, the crowd and announcers went wild.

The corner of his mouth lifted.

He didn't need to hear his score to know it'd be excellent.

The mental calculations that always operated in the background of the efficient machine that was his mind knew he'd had impeccable form and couldn't have asked for a better bronc—the primary combination one needed for a high score.

They announced his score—a more than respectable ninety-two—as he dismounted, the pickup men taking control of the bronc and the ring.

Ironically, it wasn't Old Man's happy hour request or the past weeks of training with AJ and Lil that flashed through Diablo's mind as he heard the result.

It was the burn of satisfaction that came with a good ride.

Diablo Sosa might have stepped away from the arena, left the boots and bulls and dust and mud behind like beer pong and all-nighters and the rest of college life, but he still had it.

What he was going to do with it, though, he didn't know.

As he walked, mind swirling, Sierra Quintanilla, the rodeo queen with more crowns than strands of hair on her head and the hostess with the mostest of *The Closed Circuit Rodeo* show, intercepted him.

Thoughts of his caseload fled.

It wasn't the first time they'd met, but as before, the woman stole his focus.

On the other side of her, greenies—*The Closed Circuit*'s small army of green-shirted minions who did everything from hauling equipment to making social media posts—local reporters, coaches, families and buckle bunnies crowded around, but as was one of her greatest abilities, she somehow created a moment and space in which it was only the two of them.

"What a ride, folks! Let's hear it for Diablo Sosa!" she said.

Sierra handled a mic like some handled a rope, expertly angling it toward him for comment amid the wave of cheers her words had ushered in.

Her smile, wide and pearly white, didn't reach her eyes.

Waiting for the beat when the crowd died down, she indicated to him with a look that it was time to answer.

Her every movement was calculated, timed to the instant, and because of it, she, a single woman, was in complete control of the entire arena with no one the wiser.

She would have made a killer lawyer.

She was the type to give a flawless presentation—

without a single strand of curled and highlighted hair out of place—each and every time, so consistently that even though he knew she didn't wake up like that, there was a part of him, and the rest of the world, that was willing to believe she did.

In certain contexts, he would be willing to believe anything those curves and sultry brown eyes said.

He would take a bet that her hair was naturally as straight as his was tightly curled, but big, shiny curls framed the oval face beneath her Stetson before falling down and over her shoulders in thick waves.

Her dress was subtle as far as rodeo queens went— not a sequin in sight—but her Western shirt was a glaring red with white piping and she certainly hadn't skimped on the fringe.

She wore a bright white leather jacket decorated with studs where a more traditional rodeo queen would have worn rhinestones, but the little hint of edge caught the light just as well.

Her chaps were white, too, decorated with Mexican embroidery patterns of flowers and birds around the hips and derriere, placed and designed, no doubt, to draw the eye to the thick, round thing with which she had been blessed.

She was a shark, alright, but her smiles and curves were all honey.

With her makeup and blinding smile firmly in place, not so much as a stray fringe out of line, she could have been preserved in amber.

Tipping his hat to her, Diablo answered, amplifying the Texas in his voice over the Dominican, knowing what this particular audience wanted and willing to give it to them to shore up his advantage. "Thank you, ma'am. There's a lot that can go wrong out there. I'm just happy that tonight everything went right."

Her eyes narrowed infinitesimally at the word *ma'am*, the movement too minute for anyone outside three feet away to notice. Again, allowing for the cheers and applause at his response to die down before she continued, she asked, "Rumor has it this is your first professional rodeo, but judging by that ride, I don't believe it! Where have you been hiding all these years?" Her voice was practiced, modulated to convey bright warmth, lively sweetness and innocent flirtation, even as she insulted him with the *first professional rodeo* jab.

Sweet even when she was nasty, and pretty about it—Sierra was everything a rodeo queen should be, delivered to a T.

As a well-known and well-established rodeo tradition, rodeo queens were the sport's rarified and virginal maidens, intended to be beautiful and unworldly and to ooze pure sucrose. They roped in the little girls and wives who were turned off by the rough and dirty elements of rodeo, with their pretty coordinated and sequined outfits and million-dollar smiles, and were the stand-ins for wives in cowboys' fantasies of going respectable after making it big.

As pretty, presentable and always friendly as they might be, though, good rodeo queens didn't fraternize with cowboys while they wore crowns—heaven forbid they provide a bad example for the youth.

And the practiced royalty that stood at his side was the role in its most complete iteration. One of the things Ms. Quintanilla was famous for was being the first queen to take something that everyone else aged out of by the age of twenty-four and turn it into a viable career.

Sticking with the humble act for himself, Diablo said, "I'd be lying if I said it wasn't true. This is the only professional rodeo I've competed in, and the only rodeo I've been in at all since I rode for NMSU."

A savvy light struck her eyes, her bright smile not budging an inch. She was putting the pieces of his story together at lightning speed—at least the obvious ones.

"A college star with all the makings of a pro!" she gushed. "Now, what could have lured you away?" Her voice dripped with romantic hints, and the crowd leaned in, loving it, eager for more.

Modulating his voice with the same warmth he used to charm a jury, he replied, "Well, my nana is sorry for me to say that it wasn't love. Quite the opposite, in fact. It was justice." Letting it out now that he was a lawyer was a risky card—this wasn't the crowd to be impressed by a suit—but he played it anyway, confident that his display on the bronc had established credentials strong enough to overcome any ingrained disdain.

It certainly wasn't because he wanted to impress her, even if he did feel a thrill of triumph when admiration lit up her expression.

He had her attention now.

Either that, or she liked the way he could play a crowd.

He had a sneaking suspicion she hadn't met many who could play the game like she could play it.

As good as she was, though, she remained a sweet young thing, whereas he was a grown man named after the devil.

Mesmerizing a crowd came as naturally to him as commanding a courtroom.

He gave her the smile that got him invited into bedrooms—crooked, bright white, with a hint of bite. It was a smile filled with the unspoken promise that, should they ever find themselves in intimate settings, he wouldn't be gentle and that she wouldn't want him to be.

And for all that she was professional and slick, she was still no match for the devil's smile.

He watched it do its work, sliding past her shields to bury itself in the place that made her heart beat fast and her breath catch.

A flicker of irritation flashed across her face, as if a part of her realized what was happening and didn't like it, but then it was gone.

Something in her recognized that a gauntlet had been thrown, and by a worthy opponent, even if her conscious mind did not.

But she was nothing if not professional, so she didn't miss her beat, the fleeting flicker the only evidence.

"He dares a bull and the bar, folks! Seems like this cowboy is one clever devil—I'm sure it'll take him far, as we certainly haven't seen the last of him tonight! Diablo Sosa, y'all!"

More applause followed her words, and then she turned back to the crowd, dismissing Diablo to the care of a slight figure in a green shirt.

Instead of giving Diablo time to find his companions, the greenie indicated that he was to follow them back to the green room. God forbid that anyone forget *The Closed Circuit* was reality rodeo TV.

A SINGLE CONTESTANT waited in the green room when Diablo walked in.

Wiry and compact, the man leaned against the counter, scrolling through his phone, the harsh lines of his face lit by the blue light of the screen.

Hard, mean and lean, he was a type of cowboy you could find in every arena—ready for a fight with something to prove.

Diablo sighed, mentally counting muscle kinks while observing that he was both too old and too cut to be this sore. He was certainly in no mood for a pissing match with a scrawny dude who had something to prove.

That Diablo would walk away from the encounter the victor was immaterial when he just didn't feel like wasting the energy. He'd grown past the need to prove anything in the arena. Maybe this man would grow past it, too. Diablo didn't care; he just didn't intend to be any part of the lesson.

So paying the man no mind, Diablo made a beeline for the refrigerator, out of which he removed a complimentary bottle of water, downed it in a few large gulps and reached for another, his neck, back and shoulders screaming all the while.

As the cool liquid flooded his system, he noted with a sense of remove that his blood sang in a way it rarely did in his life anymore.

Nowadays it was only after winning a particularly challenging case that he might feel even a hint of this thrill.

It was a feeling that had been hard to walk away from when he'd been a young man—and a feeling, he realized now, that might be all too easy to get used to again.

But to build a life around chasing this?

He shuddered.

That men could make this kind of pain and pleasure into a career—his best friend included—was really the only real difference between rodeo cowboys and addicts.

There were healthier ways to make a buck than rodeo, no matter how exciting it was.

Diablo's chosen pathway, for example—taking a fast-track course toward a black robe and a gavel— had merely taken years of long nights in school, standing for infamously arduous exams and wading through the politics of making partner at a good firm as a Black Dominican man. Give or take a few boring details.

Based on the feedback he was getting from his body now, compared to rodeo, all of that had been a breeze.

Or maybe he just wasn't as fit as he used to be. There was a difference between courtroom fit and rodeo fit, for all that Diablo had found the two were more alike than dissimilar.

Rodeo and the courtroom would forever be connected within him, so entwined that he didn't know where one began and the other ended. He wanted to be fit for both of them.

Feeling that now, he allowed himself to consider whether or not he might have made a mistake in walking away from the sport when he did. Should he have stayed? Should he have balanced and struggled as long as he could have?

He didn't revisit decisions; it wasted energy when executing long-game plans, but with his ride still singing in his system, there was no denying that there was a slim chance that he might have been wrong.

"Not a bad ride for a college boy." The other man had closed the distance between them and was now standing too close.

Rather than respond immediately, either to the man's proximity or to the way he pitched his voice just so to emphasize the word *boy*, Diablo took his time turning his attention to the man.

The baiting language was child's play—as juvenile as every early playground attempt to intimidate Diablo had ever been.

As Diablo had suspected, this man was a waste of time.

Adults didn't pick on or argue with children, which the man had clearly announced himself to be.

Unfortunately, Diablo had also never learned how to turn the other cheek.

Letting the silence stretch so long that the other man began to fidget, very obviously beginning to question whether or not Diablo had heard him or was ignoring him, Diablo finally responded, drawling with the kind of indolent lack of respect that this type of white man seemed to hate hearing most from a Black man. "Glad you enjoyed watching me. And you are?"

Eyes narrowing, the other man smiled with just one side of his mouth through which he forced out a chuckle. Reaching into the front pocket of his lambswool-lined jean jacket, he pulled out a round tin of chew and thumbed a wad of it between his lips and teeth.

Diablo held back from rolling his eyes, but barely.

The man could have at least tried to carve his own path, rather than simply let cliché have him.

If he kept with pattern—and there was no reason yet to suspect he wasn't going to—he would try again to get a rise out of Diablo, at which point, Diablo would once again rebuff him.

It was as if they were merely actors playing out a script.

"Name's Dillon Oliver," the man said, narrowing his eyes as he introduced himself.

If Diablo was supposed to know the man's name, he couldn't say he was sorry to disappoint.

There were some blessings, he suspected, to having walked away from rodeo for the past fourteen years.

Flashing him a vacuous smile with a vague tip of his hat, Diablo said, "Diablo. Friendly of you to introduce yourself."

It appeared bland geniality wasn't the response that Dillon Oliver had expected, and it threw the younger man off enough that a frown of confusion marred his brow.

Diablo almost sighed.

When you got paid a great deal of money for the express purpose of pitting your reason and logic against opponents with a great deal invested in lying to him, it was disappointingly simple to cross swords with run-of-the-mill bullies.

Dillon tried again, though, puffing his chest as he said, "Hear this is your first rodeo."

Diablo flashed an easy smile, casually stretching to his full height, increasing the impression of towering broadness that seemed to provoke men like Dillon. "In about fourteen years or so. It's gonna take a few go-rounds to get the rust off…" he mused lazily.

Diablo didn't know the other man's score, but he didn't need to for his statement to hit its mark. To Diablo, a ninety-two was rusty.

Bitterness lanced across the man's eyes, giving their army-green color a flatness akin to those of a feral dog in a bad mood. "That's right," he said, "you been dressin' slick and getting soft, protecting rich men's money. Well, it's good to see you getting back to your roots. It's never too good an idea to get above where you came from."

Diablo wondered where Dillon came from. It couldn't be the South—the guy was working too hard to keep his racism indirect for that—but it didn't exactly seem like he hailed from the North, either.

Racists from the North generally tried to ignore the problem of his presence.

"And where do you come from, Dillon?" Diablo used his stern courtroom voice, the one he used while pinning defendants' feet to the fire.

Dillon's shoulders straightened, unconsciously, Diablo liked to think.

"Riverton," Dillon said.

Wyoming. Diablo nodded. That seemed about right.

Riverton was cowboy enough to breed a rider like Dillon, and isolated enough that that rider might not realize he wasn't all that clever.

"Well, it's nice to meet you, Dillon."

The dismissal was obvious, and it appeared Dillon didn't know what to do.

Diablo watched the indecision battle out across his face, and it was all he could do not to laugh.

The interaction had been a waste of time, indeed, but there had been something oddly amusing about engaging in amateur hour.

Frowning, Dillon shifted his weight, apparently seeming to settle on backing off.

He'd begun making his way to the exit when the door opened.

The blare of the arena barged into the room, momentarily obscuring the figure who came along with it in its sensory overload.

Then the door closed, and there was no one else in the room but the newcomer, Dillon and Diablo.

Another contestant, the man stood at a height between Dillon and Diablo. His posture was upright, his boots worn in and easy, his hat broken in to his head. The scent of bronc lingered on him—as did the scent of old-timer.

It was an aura some riders got as they aged—as if the years of engaging raging beasts in pointless battles of wills had revealed to them the kinds of truths that couldn't be articulated but that showed up in the spine.

Old Man was like that, and because Diablo's nana was the only soul he respected more than Henry, Diablo found himself straightening his posture and taking off his hat in respect to the newcomer. The movement caught the man's eye, and he returned the gesture with a respectful tip of his own hat before heading to the fridge.

Moving to clear the way, Diablo found a seat at the edge of the table, his mind returning to a mixture of reminiscing and cataloging the aches and pains of the rodeo.

Stiffness was beginning to creep into his joints, and he wondered how much longer he would have to wait before he could leave the arena, meet Old Man, AJ, Lil and his nana for a late-night dinner, before getting back to his suite and the jetted hot tub that awaited him there.

Once again the *Closed Circuit* qualifier was taking place in Houston, so for the second spring in a row, Diablo found himself living out of a suitcase in the city of his birth—rather than using his vacation luxuriating in an exotic locale.

"And where do you hail from, Padre? This side of the border, I hope."

Dillon's approach to the newcomer was far more aggressive than his approach to Diablo had been, his voice laced with a layer of disgust, which it had lacked when he'd been speaking to Diablo.

Little old Dillon might not know enough Black folk to harbor a mature hatred, but it seemed the same couldn't be said for those of a more obvious Latin persuasion.

Tuning in to the exchange, Diablo kept his gaze on the old-timer, reflecting that, really, he ought to be offended that Dillon hadn't realized that he, a man with the name Diablo Sosa, was Latine, as well.

Dillon types never did. It required commitment to a one-dimensional outlook to maintain hateful ideas. Through that kind of lens, a man couldn't be both Black and Latine, and since Diablo was so obviously Black, the die was cast.

Upon closer examination, the old-timer was an interesting figure.

Boasting a wide-reaching and thick mustache out of another era—one that spoke of outlaws and territory grabs and outrunning the past—the man's thin face was a five o'clock-shadowed map of creases, liberally seasoned with salt and pepper.

It was a face that said its owner was no stranger to hardship—or to joy.

His demeanor remaining easy and unprovoked despite Dillon's aggression, the old-timer tipped back in his chair and answered with an easy shrug. "Oh, I've been around, here and there. Now you, you're Dillon Oliver. I hear talk you're the future of rodeo."

Diablo smiled. The response was a masterful example of deflection, not because it was subtle or clever, but because it didn't have to be.

Dillon types couldn't resist any opportunity to preen.

"Some say that," Dillon said, smirking.

Diablo snorted. Dillon might say that, but he doubted anybody else did. Especially not since Lil had rocked the world of rodeo down to its foundations with her debut.

Rodeo had a future. It just didn't look like Dillon.

But Diablo wasn't going to ruin the old-timer's trick by pointing that out.

The effort flew over Dillon's head, though, and nothing more so than his opportunity to exit the conversation without solidifying two new enemies, both of whom were more sophisticated than he was.

"Now, no disrespect, but ain't you a little old to be here?"

Irritation flickered across the older man's honey-brown eyes.

Diablo spoke up, "Seems to me the man might like a bit of quiet after his ride."

Dillon scoffed. "Don't see anyone here asking for your opinion."

"Call me a Good Samaritan. It's one thing if you want a picture with the guy. Otherwise, give a man some space."

Dillon shook his head, shaggy brown hair shifting with the movement like an old dog. "I'm just curious what a fogey like him thinks he's trying to prove out here—this some kind of cry for help, vato?"

Diablo sighed, voice dry and bored when he spoke,

"Your routine could use some work, Dillon. Maybe practice a bit more in the mirror?"

Whether it was the tone or the utter dismissal of his words, it was the spark the tinder needed.

Finding the fight he'd been looking for, Dillon made his move, leaping toward Diablo.

But he didn't make it.

Instead, he crashed into the iron-bar arm of the old-timer.

"Now, now. We're all friends here," he said, enough steel in his voice that it was clear the statement was a command rather than an observation.

Dillon bridled against the authority in the older man's tone, but couldn't budge the arm that held him back. With a noise of frustration, he threw his arms up, spun on his heel and stalked out of the room.

"Se un melon," Diablo said, borrowing his nana's favorite way to call someone an idiot as the door slammed behind him.

The old-timer gave an absent smile, but didn't agree.

Moments later the intercom speaker crackled to life in the room.

"The leaderboard is set, y'all, and it's filled with surprises!" Sierra Quintanilla's perfectly modulated voice radiated outward to fill the space. She continued, "Taking the number-one spot with a jaw-dropping ninety-nine-point ride, the surprise contender, Tio Julio! He's no spring chicken, folks, but he can sure as honey ride a bull!"

Sure as honey. It was almost sweet enough to choke on, but Diablo knew she wouldn't use it if it didn't work. He bet the crowd ate up Sierra's little teasing at naughtiness just as much as they ate up the way she dressed those curves.

"Second, and coming fast on his heels, is our court-room cowboy—the very devil himself—Diablo Sosa! He took a break from the rodeo, y'all, but with a ninety-two-point ride, it's clear he's still got the try!"

She played every angle like a model, though he supposed that shouldn't be surprising.

She was the only rodeo queen he'd known of thus far who'd been able to beat time. She was a professional.

And he couldn't deny he liked the shape of his name in her mouth, even if he was disappointed she'd fallen back on the devil trope.

"And rounding out our top three, the maestro of mean, the grit in your teeth, the master of man killers, the PBRA's regular-season champion, Dillon Oliver! Come on out, boys! It's time to kick off the second season of the *Closed Circuit Reality Rodeo Tour*! The rodeo unlike any other!"

The man he now assumed was Tio Julio walked to the door and held it open for him, a resigned half smile growing on his face. "Si," he said. "Pero me importa un pepino. Hombres como tú y yo tenemos que seguir la corriente."

CHAPTER THREE

THE CONTACTS WOULD be the first things to go.

That was, if she could get into her room.

Sierra Quintanilla slid the hotel key card in and out of the slot, watched the light turn red for the third time and puffed out a frustrated breath through her nostrils.

Steadying herself, she tried once more.

The fourth time, it seemed, was the charm. The light turned green, and she made a beeline for the luxury suite's bathroom.

Tonight was one of her last nights of civilization, or, more importantly, one of her last nights with access to a bathroom and a bed that wasn't attached to wheels. And she didn't plan to waste a second of it.

Cast members had invited her to paint the town red with them, greenies had let her know where the best underground parties were being held and the producers had tried to entice her to a black-tie gala celebrating the kickoff of the second season.

She had declined them all.

The Closed Circuit might be a rodeo unlike any other, but Sierra wasn't under any illusion that that meant the rules of the game had changed.

A rodeo queen had no more business at an underground function or bar hop than a nun did at a rave.

She had an image to maintain and it was rated G.

And while it might have been the teamly thing to do, she refused to spend any additional second schmoozing for the CC than she was contracted for over the next forty-five days or so. She was already going to have to be on nearly 24/7 for the duration of the tour—a woman was entitled to some rest.

For tonight that meant quality time with a bath and the finest delicacies the room service menu had to offer.

Still in her rodeo attire, she was a contrast of bright red and white, from her fire alarm–red shirt to her pretty embroidered, hip-hugging white chaps and jeans, and her well-worn red boots—and she was sick of it all.

She'd made the mistake of wearing unbroken boots once to a rodeo.

She never made that mistake again.

Sierra prided herself on only making a mistake once. But comfortably worked-in boots or not, it was time to get out of the costume.

For the second season of *The Closed Circuit*, she had demanded an RV upgrade. If she was going to live on the road for just over six weeks, she was damn well going to have a full-size mirror to change her contacts out in front of—especially because she was the only person on screen who was guaranteed to be there till the very end.

But upgrade or no, there was nothing like removing her contacts in a real bathroom.

Between her almond-tipped French manicure and eyelash extensions, the whole process was delicate business. Even with the upgrade, she couldn't say she was looking forward to the further complication of doing it in an RV.

Especially when compared to the suite the Circuit

had put her up in for the week and a half that spanned the lead-up to the qualifier and the week between that and the start of the competition, which was—ignoring the door lock—luxurious.

When her contacts were safely tucked away in cleansing solution and their travel case, she bent over to flip her hair into a messy bun on the top of her head and rummage through her toiletry bag. Coming up clutching a crinkling pack of travel wipes in her hand, the grin that flashed back at her in the mirror was infused with warmth and brightness that could make her the irrefutable queen of queens if she could ever figure out how to fake it. She wouldn't have made it this far in rodeo if she hadn't long ago mastered the perfect Vaseline-shiny, absolutely impenetrable and unfaltering smile of a professional rodeo queen, but the sparkle that lit her face now was as impossible to fake as it was irresistible.

If only she could somehow channel the joy she felt at the prospect of taking off her makeup in the arena.

Painted on as thick as a Broadway actor's, her stage makeup required a specifically formulated cleanser, infused with rose oil to protect her skin, in addition to the pile of extra-strong wipes to cut through the layers of primer, foundation, highlighter, shadow, blush, eyeshadow, eyeliner, mascara and setting spray.

Even with that, it took two rounds of sudsing and the sacrifice of two crisp white hotel face towels to dislodge the remnants of her cream smooth foundation in Kiss of Cinnamon. In the end, however, she triumphed—as always—left with a face so fresh that she looked about ten years younger than her recently achieved twenty-seven and even less sophisticated than that.

By this point in the process, strands of her bangs

had escaped the confines of the high bun and any curl she'd been able to beat into her thick, straight locks had fallen out, leaving wild little spikes of hair to poke out every which way.

In fact, with the unfortunately spiky hair, the face that stared blurrily back at her sans contacts looked much like it had when she'd been a senior in high school. Of course, looking in the mirror without her glasses she would have been able to say the same thing about her grandmother.

When she was young, before she'd won her first crown and was only just beginning her career, she had once timed her dress-down process, just to see if it compared to the multiple hours it took to create the complete look.

It didn't, but that didn't mean it didn't feel like it.

Everything felt longer when you were exhausted at the end of the day.

And she was exhausted.

Her face ached from smiling too hard, her throat was sore from shouting above the crowd—even with the support of the arena's PA system—and her feet screamed.

Dragging them to blessedly take a seat at the end of the California king-size bed, she searched through her luggage for the glasses that officially signaled she was in for the night.

Everything about them was thick—thick lenses, thick square black frames and all of it constructed out of thick durable hard plastic. Their lack of anything resembling grace, femininity and style was entirely intentional. No matter how beat she might be, their appearance ensured she was never tempted to skip a step or take it easy on her eyes and go without contacts—not if she wanted to protect the reputation she'd worked so hard to develop. She had put in too much work to squander it because of laziness or strain.

Perhaps that contributed to the decadence of delayering.

Her clothing came next.

The bright red Western shirt, unbuttoned with care, went onto a hanger to join the others in her sturdy, zip-up travel garment bag. The chaps were next, rolled carefully to protect the fringe and prevent creases in the leather before she placed them in a compartmented suitcase she'd found just for the purpose of storing her collection of chaps.

She removed and rolled her jeans next, having mastered the art of joyful packing organization on the real rodeo circuit long ago.

The control stockings came off next. She was blessed with the curves to fill them out, but blue jeans weren't nearly as forgiving as their reputation would have the women of the world believe—judging panels even less forgiving.

A little pudge and a few unsightly creases weren't officially against the rules, but you certainly weren't getting a crown until you took care of them.

In everything, a rodeo queen's goal was smooth perfection.

Standing in her bright red lace-front push-up bra and matching thong, free from compression for the first time in over twelve hours, she exhaled a huge sigh of relief.

If she stopped there, it would have been enough, but tonight she was going all out for herself.

It would be her last opportunity to do so for some time.

The bra flew off and the thong followed, replaced with a thin cotton T-shirt, long ago worn soft from years of laundering, and a pair of soft gray cotton boy-cut panties.

The shirt was pale pink and boasted a fanciful pony with a rainbow-colored mane and tail. At one time or another, it had belonged to each of the three Quinta-nilla sisters—Rosa, the oldest, Sierra, in the middle, and Linda, the youngest.

Sierra had swiped it the last time the family had gathered in Pensacola to celebrate their mother's six-tieth birthday. Sierra had had custody of the rainbow pony for approximately a year and a half since then.

And somewhere in her luggage, she had packed the greatest decadence of all: sweatpants.

Heather gray and soft as sin, her beloved sweats were a size too large and perfect in every way.

She would shove them to the bottom of the bag once they were on the road and she was on official duty again. As far as the public knew, a rodeo queen didn't even know what sweatpants were—she effortlessly slept, lived, ate and breathed in full rhinestone per-fection.

Tonight, though, was about indulgence. It was about decadence.

Tonight was about complete and utter comfort—the guiltiest pleasure of all.

After sliding her feet into a pair of fuzzy tie-dye socks, she moved across the smooth tiles of the floor toward the phone that sat beside the mini fridge.

The menu was extensive, and, more importantly, not road fare.

Anticipating a lot of grab-and-go from the microwave in her future, she ordered everything that sounded delicious, ending up with three appetizers, two entrees, a bottle of wine and two desserts.

Was it excessive? Yes.

But not too much as far as last meals went.

While the caravan didn't exactly leave in the morning, this was the last night she would have off until the end of the tour. She would absolutely earn every instant of her anticipatory R & R.

After placing her room service order, she made her way to the suite's plush sofa. She would watch a romantic comedy, eat and then take a long, slow bath before calling it a calm and quiet night.

She shivered in anticipation. Was there anything more exquisite to a professional pageant woman than a gourmet spread, a relaxing night in and oversize sweatpants? She was hard-pressed to think of anything.

She had just selected her movie when she heard the door. Leaping to her feet, mouth watering, she rushed to the door, overeager and unashamed, ready to devour the feast.

But when she threw open her door, it wasn't room service that greeted her.

It was Diablo Sosa.

Her heart thundered in her chest, panic gripping her throat. Coworkers, which he was at best, were not allowed to see the at-home version of Sierra.

As far as they were to know, the only Sierra that existed was Sierra Quintanilla, the quintessential rodeo queen.

She nearly slammed the door, her brain scrambling too late to stop or process the situation even as it took note of multiple details about him.

He was wearing a suit with clean, elegant lines, and a crisp white button-up, rather than the rodeo kit she'd last seen him in. The top three buttons of his shirt were open to reveal a vee of smooth deep brown skin, lightly dusted with short curling chest hairs.

Obviously, he had gone out after the show, and not to a rowdy bar, as she imagined the other contestants had. His suit was the quality and cut of someone who went to places that required them.

Closed Circuit contestants typically weren't going to be the suit-up-after-the-show types, but she supposed she shouldn't have been surprised Diablo was. He'd been wearing a suit when they'd met at the finale of the first season of *The Closed Circuit*.

Back then he had strolled over, liquid and rugged like a wild thing, wearing a white Stetson and a buttery-smooth black suit, a black button-up with a sheen to it and black snakeskin boots that hadn't just been for show. They might have shone, but the supple creases said he'd broken them in.

He'd been utterly cowboy, but refined; the grit that was so obviously deep in his bones turned creamy and rich, smooth with age, like a pearl—and all of it wrapped up like a fancy candy bar.

He had sauntered over to her, the corner of his generous mouth lifting in a manner that had hooked straight into her gut and encouraged her to make a fool out of herself right then and there by taking a step toward him. Something about him teased her, called to her and urged her to meet him in the middle when she had already given herself to rodeo.

His devil eyes had glinted with cocky awareness, as if her reaction was his due, filled with all of the entitled self-awareness that so many of the overly confident, incredibly handsome men she'd met in her life had.

So she'd decided to put him in his place.

Because she had to, for safety and sanity, and because if she didn't know how to handle an overconfident cowboy, she wasn't any kind of rodeo queen.

But just now, standing in her doorway, she wasn't a rodeo queen and she wasn't entirely certain she could handle him. She was in regular clothes, no shield of perfection, and his presence made her feel agitated and revealed.

What if he didn't like what he saw?

The corner of his mouth lifted, pulling his full lips into a smile wicked enough to match his name, fitting the bill all the more for being framed by his perfectly groomed facial hair.

How was it possible for one man to suddenly take up all of the room in a grand hotel suite?

And why was his face so magnetic?

He didn't have a full beard, but his crisply defined shadow emphasized the square cut of his jaw—and the model-like contours of his face. She was willing to bet he didn't have to spend twenty minutes every morning to get that level of highlighted and shadowed dimension.

"I was in the neighborhood and couldn't help but notice your door was unlocked," he said after it became clear she was only going to stare. "But now that I've been awarded this rare sighting of Sierra Quintanilla in her natural state, I must admit, I have questions."

The laughter in his voice and the cocky in his eye were finally enough to snap at least a little bit of sense into her, though.

Lifting an eyebrow, her perfectly shaped arch rising high over the rim of her glasses, she gave a nonchalant shrug and said, "Last I saw, this was a hotel, not a neighborhood."

Bringing his hand to his chest, his eyebrows rising to his neat hairline, he said, "Now, what kind of thing to say to a neighbor is that? I come by full of honor and good intentions and you deny my very existence."

And then that damn twinkle in his eye flashed again.

She snorted, not even registering that it was a sound rodeo queens didn't make. "I'm flush out," she said, bringing her hands to her hips, *"neighbor,"* she added.

"Between rodeo and Houston and the courtroom, I really thought I'd seen it all. But here I stand corrected because you ain't seen nothin' until you've seen Sierra Quintanilla in glasses. And to think this star-crossed occurrence only took place because I just happened to be rooming two doors down and on the right. Wonders never cease," he said, shaking his head as if it really was.

And though everything he said should have horrified her, she laughed.

It was a noise neither controlled nor ladylike—it was a real laugh, not a professional laugh, and therefore completely inappropriate to be sharing with a contestant after hours.

It was just so goofy, and Diablo Sosa being silly was as unexpected and intriguing to her as Sierra Quintanilla in glasses apparently was to him.

But she hadn't come as far as she had in the world of queening by letting fascinations distract her from the rules, so as her laughter settled, she said with more regret than she should have let out, "Well, mister, now that you've done the right thing, you can skedaddle on back to your room."

"No, no, no," he said, wagging a finger at her. "A real gentleman doesn't leave until he knows the problem is taken care of."

"How do you know customer service isn't on their way already?"

Looking her up and down drily, which was itself a feat as Sierra had never met anyone else who could make a look so arid, he said, "You're not dressed for it."

Sierra let out another loud laugh in response. "You know so much about me? Weren't you just raving about the rare sighting of Sierra Quintanilla in glasses? No me conoces," she challenged.

She didn't know why she'd slipped into Spanish. It wasn't her habit, but something inside, her inner voice or her inner amusement with the man, had urged her on.

He shook his head. "You don't think so? As a man of the law, I have become a master of reading people. I bet you'd be surprised at just how well I know you."

Intrigued and mildly amused, Sierra crossed her arms over her chest. "Oh, yeah? Pruébalo."

He leaned against her door frame, too large and comfortable there by a half, and held up his hands. "Sí. Bonita, rígida, peligrosa," he said, ticking them off on his fingers as he went. "Certainly not the type of woman to call customer service in her comfy clothes."

Smile freezing on her face, it was harder than it should have been to stop herself from frowning. Though he'd have no way of knowing, his words hit like darts, echoing accusations from former friends and each of her sporadic boyfriends.

In truth, it didn't make sense for her to be disappointed that he saw the same thing that everyone else did—she worked really hard for people to see just that—but she was. Maybe it was because he had seemed so delighted at seeing her dressed down, that she'd had the crazy idea that he might actually see through to the real her.

But really, she had no business even thinking like that. He was a cowboy and colleague and she was a rodeo queen.

Honestly, there was no reason to even have let him linger in her doorway as long as she had.

That he'd been funny and handsome and that she hadn't really wanted him to leave would be excuses that no one would care about if word were to get out.

Forcing a smile where the expression had been natural and easy before, she held her voice firm and said, "Alright, buddy. It's time to get you back to your room. Rodeo queen rules. Rusty though you might be, I'm sure you remember the drill."

Seeming to sense the shift in her, he kept his smile but didn't push, as she had been prepared for, but took an easy step back.

Surprised by the surge of disappointment she felt at his acquiescence, she still reached toward the door handle in order to shut him out into the wilds of the hotel, only to hear the shiny and fresh voice of room service arriving.

Diablo stepped aside, and the hotel staffer rolled dinner through the door on a cart before making a show of putting on the brakes and removing the lids that covered each dish.

Without missing a beat, they began, "We've got the sautéed mushrooms, the golden beet salad, cheese platter, the vegetable risotto and the grilled king salmon, the seven-layer chocolate mousse cake, the crème brulée and the bottle of Cabernet Franc. Will that be all, ma'am?"

Diablo let out a low whistle as irritation flickered across Sierra's brow.

There was that *ma'am* again.

She wasn't old enough to be anyone's ma'am yet.

"Yes, that's all. Thank you," she said impatiently.

"My pleasure, ma'am." The waitstaff gave a small bow with a flourish before turning to leave, closing the door softly behind them.

There was respect in Diablo's voice when he said, "A big eater wasn't one of the traits I would have put on the list."

Heat flooded Sierra's face, but it wasn't shame.

She could eat whatever she wanted, but as far as the outside world was supposed to know, rodeo queens only ate for promotional purposes.

It wasn't about the weight—entirely, at least.

It was about the chewing.

Chewing wasn't ladylike.

"Who says this is all for me?" she said.

He gave her the once-over and settled on a smile. "We've already established that you're not meeting anyone tonight."

"Where's your room again? You said it was on this floor, right? You were on your way back there, weren't you? And since when do cowboys stay at the Royal Carlton anyway?"

He snorted, reaching around her to pluck a saucy mushroom from her plate and plop it into his mouth.

The sound of his enjoyment was more sensual than it should have been.

She hated the sounds of eating.

If she wasn't allowed to be heard eating, why should she accept it in anyone else? Least of all this man who thought he knew her.

"Since this cowboy got on the fast track to circuit court judge appointment," he retorted, unbothered and happy after his bite.

It was her turn to scoff. "Ri-ight. I somehow doubt a man in line for a presidential appointment would be slumming it in *The Closed Circuit Rodeo*."

He brought a hand to his chest, looking wounded. "I'll have you know I'm included in the Forbes 40 under 40…"

Now she laughed out loud. "Of course you are, Diosa. Is there anything you can't do?"

"Go to bed hungry," he said definitively. "Now feed me."

"I don't think so. This is my dinner. And you just ate."

"You can't eat all of that."

"Who says I can't?" she countered, lifting a hand to shoo him away. "Off you go."

He didn't budge an inch, saying, "I'm eating with you. I like the glasses, by the way. They're cute."

Her mouth dropped open and he used her momentary distraction to step around her, grab a plate and the wine and make his way to the sofa.

Following him with the cart, she stood over him where he'd taken a seat. "I'm not sharing my dinner."

"From where I'm sitting, it looks to me like you are. Wine?" he offered, holding the bottle.

Crossing her arms in front of her chest, she gave him

a flat look and said drily, "Do I want some of my own wine? Why yes, thank you."

Smiling, he poured as if she had been all sweetness, handing her the glass with a magnanimous "Excellent."

And though she really tried, she could not stop the snort or the eye roll as she took the glass and joined him on the couch. "Why, thank you. So thoughtful."

Nodding sagely, he accepted her gratitude as if it was due. "I try."

Again, the noise that burst forth from her—somewhere between a bray and aspiration—was far from rodeo-queen behavior. "You're outrageous, you know. Nothing about you makes sense."

But rather than bristle, as a more insecure man might, Diablo had the gall to look proud, before saying, "We're good company in that respect, then. As I've always understood it, you are both too old and too brown to be the world's greatest rodeo queen, and yet, here you are."

Sierra's mouth dropped open in momentary shock as yet again he didn't take the expected course. She'd made a career out of wrangling any conversation in the direction she wanted to, her skill as honed as any cowboy's rope, but hadn't realized how much that depended on people following the script.

Diablo had a way of doing and saying things that social norms kept other people from doing and saying, and as a result, completely threw off her game.

Such as by casually remarking on things that were both obvious and true, but that most rodeo people found distasteful to talk about. But as unmooring as the experience was, there was something exhilarating about being thrown off center by Diablo. He freed her by breaking the rules himself.

If he could talk about it, then she was allowed to as well, and because it was her life and she didn't often get to, she wanted to.

So instead of deflecting, as a queen was supposed to do when "ugly" things came up, she said, "Well, if you're going to just call out the elephant in the room like that, then I take it that it's fine to mention the fact that cowboys and lawyers go together about as well as peanut butter and pickles."

Nodding casually, as if they discussed the weather and not the ways in which the sport they loved told them they didn't belong, he held a forkful of risotto out to her and said, "Some might even go so far as to say oil and water. And you didn't even mention that I'm Black."

"You're Black?" she asked, innocent confusion plastered on her face and threaded through her voice, before she accepted the bite to the sound of his laughter.

While she chewed, he nodded and said, still chuckling, "It's true. As a former rodeo champion and an ace attorney, no one expects it, but what can you do?"

Taking a risk, she continued to play along, shaking her head and weaving resignation into her voice as she shrugged in agreement and said, "What, indeed. I, of course, don't have that problem, as my blond hair and blue eyes so perfectly align with the rodeo queen archetype."

As she'd hoped, the risk paid off.

He laughed again and the sound of it wrapped around her and sank deep, because it wasn't predicated on how charming and pretty she was. He had opened the door for snark and invited her to play.

"So how did the blue-eyed beauty, Sierra Quintanilla, become the world's greatest rodeo queen?" he asked, but under the joke there was a real question, and one that, as much fun as she was having, she wasn't sure if she wanted to share the real answer to.

So she said, "Oh, you know. The regular ways, sleeping my way to the top and burning my enemies at every step."

His eyes narrowed only a fraction, giving her the impression that he saw things she would have preferred he didn't—beyond the glasses and makeup-free face—and what was perhaps worse, that he understood both that she was holding back and why. Then they lighted again with humor. "Ah, yes, the tried-and-true ways for success in this world. Not that different from my path, really."

The laugh that bubbled out of her was involuntary, his comedy thwarting her urges to retreat into more solid conversational ground at every turn.

She could sense that he didn't want her small talk. He wanted her real talk. He was both an audience for and a challenge to be the full Sierra, as opposed to just the pretty one.

Smiling, she teased, "So you slept your way to the top, too?"

Nodding between bites, he said, "First, I slept with the judge so that he would send me to rodeo instead of a sentence in juvenile detention, and then I slept with the college admissions folk to get a rodeo scholarship. Then I slept with the law school admissions folk to get a full ride into law school. Then it was the senior partners at my firm, and most recently, the producers of *The Closed Circuit*."

Unable to control herself, she laughed until tears came to her eyes and she had to take a drink of wine to calm down. "Seeing as how I saw your ride myself, I know at least one of those statements isn't true. But what about the rest?"

Grinning, he said, "Well, I did get full rides to NMSU and law school."

Intrigued, she pressed further, "And the choice between juvenile detention and rodeo?"

A new glint coming to his eyes, something she would have described as respect, he nodded again, though there was more seriousness in the firm movement this time. "That was true as well, though neither myself nor my nana, who was the one to insist something else be done, slept with the judge. Fortunately, that wasn't necessary. The love of rodeo, it seems, crosses all stratas, and this particular man of the law was a disciple with a deep and abiding belief in the gospel of rough stock, though I'd be willing to bet he'd never stepped in an arena himself in his life."

The last he'd said with only light derision, and it wasn't the sound of bitterness that it was tinged with, but something Sierra recognized all too well—the particular kind of cocky that a rough stock rodeo cowboy got because he willingly rode that which other men ran from. And that he was good at it.

"What'd you do?" she asked, but this time he shook his head.

"Not so fast, queenie. We've sorted through my truths and lies, but from where I'm sitting, your hair isn't blond and your eyes aren't blue. It's your turn."

Laughing, she said, "What could you possibly mean? I've never told a lie."

"Do you also like chopping down cherry trees?" he asked, and again she made the kind of noise that her contract frowned upon.

"Well, if you're going to be so uncouth as to challenge the word of a lady..."

"I didn't realize you were from the South," he teased.

Sticking her tongue out at him, she said, "Florida is the South, even if they try to pretend otherwise."

"Ah, so you're a Florida girl."

"Woman, but yes," she sassed, and was rewarded by one of his more sensual smiles.

"There's certainly no doubt about that..." he said, and there was also no doubt in Sierra's mind as to what he thought about it.

Heat coming to her cheeks, and other places it had no business being, she reluctantly acknowledged that she was going to have to rein in the direction of their conversation. As exhilarating as it was to flirt with Diablo Sosa, and that was exactly what they were doing, she was treading in dangerous territory.

Drawing back energetically, if not physically, without flirting, she answered him, hoping the reminder of all she'd gone through to get here would be a warning to them both.

"In all honesty, it wasn't easy. Especially at first. I'm competitive, though, so I won anyway, but the questions I got from the judges, the comments on my outfits, even the way they spoke about my horsemanship skills... they never talked to any of the other girls like that." She shuddered, the familiar feeling of shame mingled with injustice ready to rise up again alongside the memories, before she continued, "But thankfully, the writing was on the wall when it came to the public. They'd been hungry for something different for a long time before I came along, even if nobody wanted to admit it. And as it became clearer that I was the one the local media outlets were interested in featuring, the judges and rodeo organizations finally came around to treating me like I belonged. It took a while for the other girls to do the same, especially as I was beating them all the time, but eventually, even they came around, too." She shrugged, finishing with "It became better for them to be 'friends' with the most successful queen of all time, at least publicly, than it was to miss being in my group photo because they'd been racist to my face." She added a jolly emphasis to the end because she wanted him to know that even though it was the truth, she didn't hold it against them. Pageanting was dog-eat-dog, even if everyone pretended like they were pack mates.

Nodding his head, the expression in his eyes confirming that he knew all too well, Diablo said, "There will always be train jumpers on the rails to progress, and they'll be the loudest ones when it comes to saying they knew this was where things were heading all along."

Lifting her glass, Sierra added, "And say they had a hand in it."

Diablo closed his eyes to nod in solidarity, lifting his glass in the process, as well. "Hear, hear."

Sierra laughed once more, and in doing so, realized that she had become completely comfortable, more comfortable than she could remember being with another person.

Even her family.

They made room for her to be competitive and beautiful, praising her fierce determination, but they weren't the biggest fans of hers when she was silly or relaxed, finding those aspects of her to be unpredictable, weird and sloppy.

And her friends…well, she didn't really have friends.

For most of her life, the peers who had come and gone had either been her direct competition or off-limits. Cowboys were the wolves at the door, the female barrel racers tended to write off the queens as superficial and the girls who might have understood her the most were all hoping to win the very prizes she kept taking home.

But in this forbidden moment out of time with a man she barely knew, wearing no makeup and a pair of sweats, she felt utterly at ease.

So what would it hurt to dance with danger a little longer? Wasn't tonight her last night of comfort before the show really kicked off?

Of course, once the tour began, there would be no conversations in sweatpants and glasses—or hotel rooms for that matter—but what was the harm for now?

They were just eating and laughing. That was as far as anything would go, and there weren't any cameras around to catch him leaving her room—which he eventually would.

In the end, after they'd both eaten their fill, Sierra was still feeling good about the decision to relax and was even willing to acknowledge that she'd ordered the perfect amount for two—at least to herself.

Diablo, on the other hand, wasn't as circumspect when it came to his observations.

"You never would have eaten that yourself," he said.

She snorted. "That's not the point. I ordered it for myself."

"Well, you're welcome. Food wasters go to a special place in hell."

"You sound like my father."

"Sounds like a smart man."

"Humble, too," she grumbled. Could she remember the last time she'd grumbled?

Diablo chuckled, and the sound worked its way into a part of her that was deep and dark and, most dangerously, lonely.

Diablo leaned forward to top off her glass with the last of the wine, and once he was there, it would have been only a matter of closing the last few inches between them for their lips to meet. But did she dare?

Was this why he had really knocked on her door?

It would have been easier to believe if it wasn't true that her lock was acting up.

At the thought, Sierra reluctantly acknowledged to herself that she had wanted the answer to be yes, even as it was against all of the rules and she was contractually bound to rebuff him.

She wanted him to have come for the chance to kiss her.

She needed to get him out of here.

She shouldn't have even let it go this far.

Dressed down and laughing with him about her father, imagining what it might be like to press her lips against his—all of this would only make it that much harder to return to their respective roles when the Circuit began in earnest. That much harder to go back to pretending to not see what had been seen.

She was wearing her glasses for Chrissakes.

"Alright, acere," she said with a forced chuckle, attempting to create some distance. "This has been fun and all, but it's time for this queen to hit the sack."

Ignoring her clumsy segue, the corner of Diablo's mouth lifted up in that way that played haywire with her system, and he teased, "I can think of some other things in this room you could hit instead."

"Har, har," she said, rolling her eyes though her breath caught and her body clenched at the innuendo, refusing to release as if it were a child who could get what it wanted by simply holding its breath.

But wants and needs were different things.

She might *want* to give in to the magic of the moment, to forget the rules that existed outside this room, but she *needed* to do the opposite.

"The only thing I'll be banging is the snooze button in the morning, when my alarm goes off and I haven't had sufficient beauty rest."

It wasn't perhaps her best line, but she was proud of the way she'd circled around his naughtiness. She'd had to have at least earned some points for redirecting the metaphor.

Diablo was unimpressed, however. "Psh," he said, "entonces, si ya duermes más es como echar agua al mar. No podrías ser más guapa. Es imposible."

That he'd made such a bold and romantic statement as if he was simply observing an inarguable fact was outrageous. *He* was outrageous.

It was utterly ridiculous and in the face of it, all she could do was swallow. No extemporaneous speech came to mind over the sound of her heartbeat.

Others had called her beautiful—so many that she could barely count them at this point. But not when she looked like she did now. Not even her family.

No one had ever called her beautiful when she wasn't trying to be.

And because of that, she couldn't seem to shake the words off; wasn't even sure she wanted to.

Her contract could burn, and maybe her soul with it, because she was staring into the deep brown eyes of the devil, unable to speak for how his words had hit her.

And when her eyes darted down to his lips, it was because there was no way she could have stopped them.

Of course, he noticed.

He swallowed, and she noticed that, hyperaware of the bobbing of his Adam's apple for an instant before her eyes returned to his sculpted mouth.

And then they were moving into each other, magnetized and breathless.

To say it was a shock when their lips met would have been too mild.

The contact ground her to the spot and held her there while the rest of her disintegrated, even as she felt wrapped in cotton, every harsh and critical voice that lived inside her head gone quiet.

Sierra had kissed before; of course she had kissed before—she wasn't *always* on contract—but never had she felt fusion like this.

The pressure of his lips against hers was the final barrier between them.

His fingers came to her jaw lightly and she bloomed, her mouth opening for him like a bud that had been waiting for this exact moment.

She could taste him, not the food they'd eaten, nor the wine, but his essence, and the flavor of his desire for her.

Did he taste the same on her lips?

He growled, the low rumble its own form of answer, and the vibration drew a sigh from her as if her breath sought entry into him, trying to share the things that words would never allow.

Her energy, her tender heart, her desire to please.

She wanted him to taste that she wanted him.

She wanted him to taste her the way she could taste him, to know who she was from the pressure of her lips and the way that she had already shared more of herself with him—if not physically, then mentally and emotionally—than she had with anyone else.

She wanted him to know that he was special—that it had never even crossed her mind to take this kind of risk before.

There was no room for words or lengthy explanations between their mouths, though; no room for caveats and conversations as he probed deeper.

Their tongues danced, finding each other's rhythm with ease, and she marveled at the fit.

All at once she couldn't remember a single cowboy she'd kissed other than him, except that they'd all lacked the finesse of the man she was with now, that they'd been forceful and dominant as if they'd forgotten she was a living, breathing woman to be pleased in their desire to have her for a prize.

Diablo was commanding, but the command was that she lose herself in their connection, that she drown in the way he knew exactly what to do to keep her breathless.

He knew when to press, probing deeper, and when to pull back, teasing.

As if he could read her mind, he knew when to trace

his fingertips down her neck and shoulders, along her arms, leaving a shimmering, shivery trail in their wake.

He knew when to bring them to her waist, when to slide his rough palms beneath her loose T-shirt and caress his way up the sensitive skin of her ribs, his thumbs brushing the underside of her breasts along the way.

Every inch of her body lit. He was a catch—in her breath, in her plans, even in her understanding of right and wrong.

Leave it to the devil.

But was this so wrong? Perhaps she'd been the one in the wrong all these years, adhering so strictly to dictums of her career. She'd always considered the queens who snuck around to be reckless, but maybe she'd just been a prude. If this was what she'd been missing out on, the answer was obvious. Kissing Diablo made her feel fully alive and embodied, the same as rodeo and riding.

Yes, being here with him like this was risky, but did the risk outweigh missing out on feelings like this? Wasn't that an equal danger?

She'd thought this kind of thrill unnecessary before, but at the moment, she couldn't think of anything more necessary. Perhaps that was why, when they pulled back, staring at each other, breathless like teenagers, eyes shining, lips bruised, she said, "Don't leave."

The words slipped out before she really thought about them, about what they meant, and it was as if she could see them in the air, hanging like vapor between them.

Hunger and confusion flashed across his gaze, but disappeared almost as soon as she'd named them, replaced by a strange distance and an easy smile.

"I can't believe I'm the fool in the room saying this,"

he said before clearing his throat, "but I was under the impression that rodeo queens don't."

There was a strained pain in his voice that made him sound younger, a man desperate to do right while the hard edges of his body made other demands, and the power of being the one to put him there filled Sierra's mind with wild images.

Gone was the sardonic control that had clung to him since the very first time she'd met him, in its place earnestness and need and, though she imagined he wouldn't own it, goodness.

He wanted her, that much was clear from the angle of his body to the promise in the kiss he'd given her, but more than that, she felt he didn't want to get her in trouble.

It was as sweet as it was frustrating.

And it was right.

Easing back, she noted that, without his kiss, her lips felt dry. Breath stabilizing, she licked them before she said, "They don't. I apologize. I'm not sure what came over this rodeo queen, but you're right."

"It's hard to resist someone on the Forbes's 40 under 40 list," he said lightly.

Snorting, the sound not quite as boisterous as earlier in the evening but still genuine, Sierra said, "That has to be it. Just can't resist those young and successful types." And some of the embarrassment left her.

Enough that she finally had the wherewithal to stand.

Diablo followed suit.

Through force of will that was bolstered by lingering embarrassment, she managed to keep her eyes on his face. "Sorry again."

Shaking his head, Diablo said, "You don't have to be sorry. I would have, you know. If we could."

She knew he was smoothing out her feathers even as it worked. "I've never—" she started, only to stop and start again, "I've never broken the rules. Never even tried to with anyone else. I just want you to know that."

Her cheeks were hot, but she wasn't dead from the humiliation of saying the words, so maybe someday she would stop kicking herself for doing it.

But she wanted him to know she wasn't like that.

She wanted him to know he was special.

A look flashed across Diablo's gaze that Sierra couldn't name. He swallowed. Then he said, "You make me want to break them, too."

"But we can't." Sierra sighed her agreement. "My job depends on it, and you…" She trailed off, not entirely sure what Diablo stood to lose.

"And I won't be anyone's clandestine affair," he finished for her. Then he added, "But you sure make that hard, queenie. If *The Closed Circuit* were truly a rodeo unlike any other, if they broke the mold and set you free, we certainly wouldn't be talking right now."

Skin flaming at his words, she tamped down her body's explosive reaction with restraining words. "If only. But that'd be the same rodeo where a cowboy could ride in a suit," she said.

"Or a queen could show up in glasses," he added, regret in his voice at what they both acknowledged.

That would be a transformed rodeo, altogether, and while *The Closed Circuit* might have brought rodeo to reality television, it hadn't changed that much.

Rodeo was a sport that loved its traditions even more than it loved its events.

It was a sport that didn't take kindly to change. And they both knew it.

So he was going to leave and she was going to stay and they were both going to do their best to pretend like this had never happened. Because…rodeo.

She stretched out her hand to him, knowing it was dangerous to touch after what had already happened, but unable to just let him go without feeling him again.

Electricity jolted through her arm when their palms connected.

Then he was releasing her hand and walking past her to the door, turning when he reached it to tip his hat. "Enjoy your beauty rest, queenie."

CHAPTER FOUR

HE NEVER SHOULD have stopped by her room. Diablo admitted it to himself as he walked back to his room, hot and hard, his body clamoring for him to go back and partake of the lovely thing she had offered.

She had literally asked him to stay.

Who was he to act as her conscience or moralizer?

No one, that was who.

But he did have to act as his own. And it had taken only one taste of Sierra to know that she was the kind of danger that could make him forget his principles.

He had promised himself long ago he would never again be anyone's secret lover.

Sierra was a rodeo queen and the deal with rodeo queens was a deal breaker for him.

He wouldn't sneak around with her, even if it was the only available pathway.

Even *if* she tasted as fresh as a peach and sweet as a cobbler.

He wouldn't make an exception for this rule. Not even for her.

Christ, he should never have gone to her room.

He shouldn't have even known they were staying in the same hotel, nor that they'd been given rooms on the same floor. He couldn't help that he had been only a few patrons behind her in the line at check-in. She hadn't seen him—hadn't seen anyone, really, in her single-minded drive to get to her room. That she was frustrated and weary was clear without the all-business clip in her voice when she'd spoken to the concierge. Both rolled off her like waves, inspiring nurturing urges he rarely felt—to comfort her, to make her laugh, to help her unwind…

It was unfortunate, then, that after his evening out, which had coasted by on the adrenaline of a good ride, good food, top-shelf rum and excellent conversation with all of his favorite people in the world, that he'd been in a good mood, happy from a night that had been filled with the triumph of his first ride in over a decade.

If he'd been pissed and sore, he probably wouldn't have stopped at her door.

But he hadn't been.

Seeing his nana dressed to the nines at the restaurant, and Lil, in her simple little black dress, alongside AJ in his T-shirt and jeans, and the old man, in his cowboy go-to-towns of clean jeans and a crisp button-up—it drained the power and force from his general cynicism enough to leave him as close to peace as he ever came. And that was always when he got in trouble.

Good times cajoled him into giving his best to a world that more often than not gave him shit.

He recalled, as he returned to his room, that the last image he'd had of Sierra had been a glimpse of her red-and-white-clad behind stepping into the elevator, rooming on the same floor he was on.

When he'd noticed that her key box was lit green, signaling its unlocked status, he couldn't, in good conscience, simply walk by without letting her know.

She was a beautiful, single woman.

It wasn't safe.

He was honor bound to let her know.

It was the gentlemanly thing to do.

A questionable sense of chivalry didn't explain why, though, rather than simply let her know about the door and move on, he'd stayed for a while.

In the solitude of his own mind, he blamed the glasses…and the sweatpants…and the freshly scrubbed face.

All of her untouchable sophistication had been scrubbed off to reveal the woman beneath, and that was apparently his kryptonite.

And here he was still lying to himself.

Sierra in all her iterations was his kryptonite. There was just something about her.

Without the shine, she lost none of the perfection. She'd merely set aside the armor that she used to subdue the world to her will.

In doing so, she had undone him.

But still, that was only part of the truth.

The other part was more dangerous.

He liked her. She was pretty and funny and tough.

Now, in addition to this absolutely ridiculous competition, he had a situation with Sierra Quintanilla to navigate.

And she was a beautiful kisser.

He had a suspicion that his odds of coming out on top had been better with all of the bulls and obstinate judges in the world than they were with Sierra.

CHAPTER FIVE

DUE TO ITS incredible popularity, for the second season, *The Closed Circuit* had to map out a brand-new route for its caravan—and one that was twice as long—but as she was already endlessly satisfied with her new and improved RV model and they were just two hours into their summer of driving, Sierra knew she would be comfortable the whole way.

Already, the additional comfort features of the upgraded vehicle were proving worth taking the risk of asking for what she wanted. She got greater reflective glare protection from the slightly larger sunshades, a wider view through the oversize side-view and rearview mirrors, and a much clearer back camera picture and a more precise voice-commanded smart dash.

She felt like the queen she was called.

Years of carting her own horses to rodeos in her pre-professional days had cemented her ability to drive big vehicles, which she was especially grateful for now, as the super deluxe model was slightly larger than the last.

Her seat was all cushy leather and panoramic views, perched on a swivel that gave her near perfect sight to the road and environment in front of her and to her sides for miles and miles.

The experience would have been peaceful and picturesque, if Diablo Sosa wasn't still on her mind.

She certainly could have done with a little less time alone with her thoughts.

She just couldn't get over the mix of yearning and embarrassment that rose up in her whenever his face filled her mind. She usually made such winning choices.

He had a way of throwing that off. She rarely felt like she won in their encounters.

Having been a professional rodeo queen for the past nine consecutive years and having become the television face of rodeo queening was nothing if not winning—and winning a lot.

She made more money now, and at an older age than any rodeo queen who had ever come before her.

But when Diablo showed up, she stumbled.

Maybe he would get eliminated early? Maybe she wasn't really facing weeks of tension, stretched taut between all the feelings he stirred up in her.

Or maybe the driving and the demands of her job's full schedule would be enough to keep her too occupied to think of him.

Instead of circulating through a cluster of small towns generally centered in the mid- and southwest before saying goodbye to the RVs for the grand finale, this year the caravan was darn near traversing the full width of the lower forty-eight states.

Honoring the competition's roots, they'd kicked things off in Houston for the qualifier and kickoff, but immediately after that, the schedule changed.

Sierra was looking forward to the new route.

While she loved the rough delights of rodeo, her day-to-day tastes were a bit more varied than the kinds of entertainment and dining options they'd all encountered during the first season tour.

This season the caravan was stopping at major cities in Louisiana, Florida and Georgia, before looping back up and around to hightail it through Tennessee, Oklahoma, Colorado, New Mexico, Arizona and California. Like the first season, they would travel the last leg to Las Vegas where the even-grander finale would take place.

Though the CC schedule meant her tourism activities were limited to things that could take place in a single day off, and though she was contractually obligated to behave as if there were cameras on her at all times—whether she was on break or not—this year's route offered more opportunities to spend her downtime eating delicious food, exploring new cities and even visiting some museums along the way; all pleasures which—outside of riding—were joys she never tired of.

And if *The Closed Circuit* had increased the drive time for the second season, then they'd also kicked the camp and kitsch elements up a notch.

As decorated a rodeo queen as she was, Sierra was no stranger to or one to shy away from a little glitzy and campy showmanship, but the heavy-handedness of *The Closed Circuit* was at times enough to make even her blush.

Of course, she would never *actually* blush.

She was far too professional to ever do anything that could ever be construed as negatively reflecting on rodeo; she loved and respected it too much for that—whether it was the reality TV version or the real thing.

She had put off putting down roots or establishing stability and security for herself for that love of rodeo, pursuing crown after crown, and then again to audition for the hostess gig for *The Closed Circuit*; all the while the years raced by.

And she couldn't stop now, not if she wanted to keep what she'd earned thus far. There was no room for error in a career where retirement at twenty was a normal thing. If she wanted to keep going where no woman had gone before, she thought as she angled her neck from one side to the other in an effort to get the knots and cricks out of it, she had to remain perfect.

She loved rodeo and riding, and loved being center stage, and if she was beginning to tire of being a paragon, she could accept that it was just the downside of her job.

But then again, she usually didn't have Diablo Sosa swirling around in the same circles as her, either. He stirred up the kind of thoughts that spelled the end of rodeo queen dreams. But they were dreams she would have to be careful to protect, if she wanted to maintain the record-breaking career she'd worked so hard for.

It was just too bad that she couldn't do both.

It wasn't like her desires were anything but simple and normal. In fact, it would be considered utterly ridiculous—if not discriminatory—if she was in any other field and was forced to choose between the two.

But rodeo was rodeo, and if she'd learned anything in the years she'd been in the sport, it was that the harder you pushed it to change, the harder it dug its heels in against progress.

She'd seen girls try to fight it after losing their crowns and seen them lose every time, and she was no activist. It just didn't make sense to her to fight to change longstanding tradition. Instead, she just did her part and toed the line, putting her faith in the fact that things would change incrementally over time at a pace that the largely conservative audience could accept.

Hadn't her career up to this point proven just that? She, Sierra Quintanilla, was the most decorated queen the world of rodeo had ever seen, and her hair wasn't blond and her last name had a letter from a non-English alphabet in it. Didn't that prove that, when given time and reassurance that their entire way of life was not actually under threat, even people's most entrenched ideas could be changed and space for difference could be made?

Sierra certainly hoped so; she'd gone so far as to stake her faith in the idea deep enough that she believed she was doing something bigger than playing dress-up with ponies every time she went out in front of a crowd. She was proving to the world that the face of rodeo didn't have to be a white one.

So really, it wasn't even a sacrifice that her contract and his standards meant this attraction to Diablo could go nowhere. It was merely an inconvenience for a far greater, more important good.

Changing the world was more important than Diablo's lips, or jaw, or shoulders, or callused palms, or intoxicating scent…

"Play driving playlist," she said aloud, hoping to distract herself. Really, it was past time to distract herself from the man her mind seemed so desperate to circle back around to.

She didn't think about men. It was one of the things that had set her apart from the competition; in general, being rather oblivious to the distraction of men.

She thought about rodeo.

A rodeo queen was an ambassador, on at all times—

as the CC and years of representing local and national rodeos had been quick to drill into her—and appearance and poise were always something a queen was judged on, even when it just meant passing and waving on the road.

Nonfans often criticized rodeo queens for their open admission that looks mattered, but for herself, Sierra had always appreciated the honesty.

Navigating life in a female body meant that, whether you liked it or not, your appearance—and particularly whether or not you were perceived as beautiful—was going to play a role in your life.

Sierra's mother had drilled the fact into her daughters, unflinchingly acknowledging both the injustice and the reality of it in the same pragmatic way with which she approached everything else.

"You shouldn't judge a book by its cover, but everyone does," she would tell her three girls with a shrug. "The cover is the first thing anyone sees, and more often than not, it's the main reason they pick up the book."

Now, more than twenty years later, Sierra's mother remained just as beautiful and just as blond as she had been back then, and, as each day passed, Sierra realized, grew far savvier about how to keep it that way.

For the longest time, it seemed Sierra had been cut from a very different cloth.

She had been a horse girl and a sports girl and had generally looked the part as a child because she thought that a long, scraggly ponytail, scuffed tennis shoes, torn jeans and either a baseball hat or a Band-Aid or a smudge of dirt on your head were required if you wanted to show the world that you were committed to the athletic lifestyle.

She had had no idea that a person could go hard and be pretty at the same time.

But then she'd discovered rodeo queening, and it'd turned into the bridge to connecting with her mother and sisters that she had always craved. She finally belonged among them, having found her own place in their cloud of glitter and gel without having to give up who she was and what she was about—or even the core wild and competitive spirit that made her Sierra.

Her mother loved her interest.

Her father, whose pride in his three beautiful daughters knew no bounds, loved it.

And her sisters, with whom she had frequently been at odds in the past due to her rough and tumble and messy inclinations, also loved it.

Discovering rodeo queening had created a tidy place for a rowdy daughter, and one that didn't squeeze or hold too tightly and let her express her athletic prowess while also respecting the norms of her family.

She had entered her first pageant at the age of eight, won for the first time at the age of nine and hadn't slowed down since.

Until now, there had never been a reason to.

CHAPTER SIX

New Orleans, Louisiana

NEW ORLEANS WAS one of Diablo's favorite cities in the world, and even the nonsense and contractual obligations of *The Closed Circuit Rodeo* could not impede his enjoyment of the Big Easy.

The caravan pulled into the Smoothie King Center lot, by direction of the traffic manager, parking in the cordoned off lot according to competition rank.

Diablo laughed quietly at himself as he pulled into the second-place position as directed by the green shirt-clad guide.

He could scoff at *The Closed Circuit* for parading masculinity in every way possible while at the same time operating like an elementary school classroom, but that would just be deflection.

He was the one who had signed up.

It didn't matter that it had been at the old man's bequest. No one had had a gun to his head and as much as he would do anything for the old man, he wouldn't pretend they had.

With the rundown from both Lil and AJ, Diablo had gone in clear sighted and willingly.

So he had no one to scoff at but himself, and that he did, even as he smiled and waved at the young greenie outside who had been not so subtly eyeing him with hero-worship.

As a graduate of one, Diablo was a large supporter of youth programs, but the fact that *The Closed Circuit* had an intern program meant these kinds of wide-eyed moments were bound to be a regular thing.

Assuming he continued to perform well, that was, which was assuming a lot. It really had been a long time, especially in rodeo time. But he also knew himself and knew that even though the trait could be a pain in the ass at times, whatever he did, he did it hard and gave it his all—and his all was rarely not enough. He hadn't been lying about needing to get some rust off, but he was also a perfectionist—in every arena.

Some things were so deep a part of you that they couldn't be shaken.

So he'd just get used to smiling and tipping his hat to the youngsters.

And maybe it was kind of nice.

After they got settled in, he had the rest of the day free before the tour officially kicked off with the opening show that evening, and he would waste none of that time lingering in the RV he was likely to become very tired of over the next few weeks. No matter how luxurious it was.

For the opening night event, the showrunners were going to do an abrupt 180 from the rough and wildness of the bareback bronc ride qualifier to showcase the saddle bronc ride, rodeo's prettiest event.

Diablo had always been at his best on the back of a bull, but he could appreciate the saddle bronc ride for its aesthetic appeal.

It was the classic silhouette of rodeo, and its form

was the sport at its most refined, the ideal snapshot of the rodeo cowboy: hat cocked, one arm raised, balanced on the back of a jackknifing horse. Whereas Diablo had never really been a fan of the bareback bronc ride, which offered a whole lot of ass whooping without the satisfaction of having taken on the force that was the power and rage of a bull, he at least appreciated the saddle bronc ride.

He couldn't pin it to a particular feature, but facing off against a bull felt a lot like boxing—there was an understanding between both parties that the point was to try to kill each other through brute strength, but there was shockingly little that was personal about it.

Riding broncs was more like engaging in a fencing competition against an opponent who knew more about your people than you knew of theirs, and who was ruthless about utilizing that information in their pursuit of victory.

Audiences, and just humans in general, loved horses, and horses knew it—just like people feared bulls and bulls knew it.

Horses knew how to capitalize on the raw energy of a crowd, sensing the audience's ever-present undercurrent of desire to see them win out over a cowboy.

Time after time he'd seen the energy and the hopes and the expectations of the audience collide and dance with the intentions of the horse, infiltrating, breaking even the most stone-cold cowboy's mind. Horses were just too good at capitalizing on that force and shifting it to their advantage.

But that was a concern for tomorrow. Right now he had four hours to kill in New Orleans, and he wasn't going to waste them in a parking lot.

After calling a local ride service to pick him up and then drop him off in the French Quarter, Diablo made his way into a classic two-story, complete with elaborate wrought-iron railings and fading sea foam–green paint.

From the outside, the Green Deli looked like it could be one of the many boutique retail shops in the French Quarter.

What it actually was, though, was a small, bare-bones market and deli that had the honor of making the most delicious sandwich that Diablo had ever tasted. Part cramped corner store, part drippingly delicious lunch counter, the service was always excellent and the food even better.

Of course, he could only vouch for the food as far as the one thing he ordered went: a po' boy sandwich with grilled turkey, ham, two kinds of cheese, fried shrimp, sautéed mushrooms, caramelized onions and a secret sauce, all squeezed between delicious fresh sesame-paprika and garlic bread. It had been love at first bite and he ate one whenever he visited New Orleans, which wasn't nearly enough.

After taking his food to find a shaded place to sit and eat and people-watch outside, he attacked the beloved lunch—which included heaping piles of red beans and rice and macaroni salad—with easy joy until he was feeling happy and full.

Satisfied, he strolled without real purpose or direction, weaving through the heavy flow of pedestrian traffic and soaking in the comforting press and closed-in feeling that the packed and often pastel-painted colonial architecture created in him.

As he made his way toward the famous Café du Monde, the idea of following the large lunch he'd had with a café au lait sounded just right. And though he wasn't ready yet for beignets, he knew he'd appreciate them when his current full sensation dissipated.

Growing up, his nana would laugh, watching him eat and shaking her head with the words, "A beber y a tragar, que el mundo se va a acabar." She wasn't far off. Diablo attacked life with everything he had because he was acutely aware of how fragile it all was. She had always been able to see straight through him.

Thinking of his nana here, a city he'd meant to take her to time and time again but still hadn't, he realized he missed her.

He saw her every time he went to Houston, but didn't stay with her when he visited.

She refused to leave the neighborhood that he'd grown up in, and he could no longer go back there.

He couldn't bear to see the boys who were just like himself—his own peers having long ago moved or been taken on. Like it had been for him, there was an acute awareness of the fact that the world was unjust clear in the eyes of the new crop of young men and women, and one that he could do nothing to truly cure. No matter how hard he worked, or how much difficulty he had overcome in order to claw his way into a better future, he had not truly done anything to change the system or make it any easier for them.

Nor was one success story proof that the problems had disappeared, and Diablo refused to have his example used as evidence that they had or that these kids could make it, too, if they only tried hard. It was not a deficit in any one of them that kept them and would likely keep them where they started—it was the fact that none of them was yet desperate enough to leave everyone they loved behind.

It would be hypocritical to tell those kids that they had limitless choices and options because it wasn't true. Any choice they made would ask unconscionable trade-offs of them and would also cut off other options forever, and their experiences would hinge on how well they could identify and predict the consequences. Failure meant disaster; lives wrecked in ways that only the most determined came back from. Success meant forgetting where you came from.

Rather than pride at how far he'd come, or comfort at returning home, the old neighborhood was a stark and unwelcome reminder that as much as he tried, he'd done nothing to weaken the beast, and had instead simply abandoned others to it as he broke away.

His nana was different. She wouldn't leave her people behind.

He would have and could have moved her away in a heartbeat if she had let him.

But as with so many other things, she had out-stubborned him.

She flatly refused to leave the house that she had worked so hard to purchase.

Owning her own home, purchased with her earnings as an immigrant woman working low-wage jobs, was a point of immense pride for her, second only to her pride in her grandson.

But he knew it was more than that. It was her home, her neighborhood, her community. And, he knew, it was because it was the one place in the world where his mother knew to find her. His grandmother might have good reason to have given up on ever seeing her daughter again, but as long as there was breath in her body, she would continue to leave the porch light on for her every night.

It had worked once before. It was under that very same light that his mother had dropped off her infant son before disappearing for what had been the final time.

Diablo's nana was the strongest person he'd ever met, even stronger than the old man when it came to grit and indomitability, but she too had her blind spots.

To this day he knew her biggest blind spot remained her enduring hope to see her daughter again.

And he would never blame her for it. He respected her too much. And he understood.

It had taken the intensity of bull riding, the rigors of law school and practice and years with a therapist for Diablo to finally set down his own hope.

As his lunch settled, he considered dessert.

This late in the day, he walked up to a far less busy Café du Monde than most were used to the tourist trap being. Morning and early afternoon being the more traditional time for coffee and what were essentially doughnuts, that was the time of day it was busiest, so avoiding the crowd was nice.

Ordering, he waited half the time he normally did before he was ready to walk again, carrying his coffee and a bag of a dozen beignets.

Walking along Decatur Street toward Jackson Square, he watched the throngs of people cross to and from the large park in front St. Louis's Cathedral, until his eye snagged on a patch of vibrant red and purple. Before he could verify his suspicions for certain, a sharp lance of sunlight glanced off something reflective and shiny, momentarily blinding him.

When his sight returned, Diablo looked again to confirm that the source of the shock and awe was exactly who he thought it was. It was none other than his queen herself, Sierra Quintanilla.

Pausing in his tracks, Diablo watched her as she crossed through Jackson Square with long, determined strides, making a beeline for what looked like the cathedral.

Not only was she dressed in full rodeo costume, but on this bright afternoon in the syrupy golden sunlight and easy pace of New Orleans, she was particularly loud about it, too. She wore a bright red Stetson with a blindingly massive Closed Circuit crown affixed to it—the culprit behind the glare from earlier, he suspected.

Even from the distance at which he stood, he could tell she looked good—the kind of good that, as stunningly vibrant as her plumage was, didn't just catch people's attention. It made them stop and stare, long after she had passed.

Witnessing the phenomena was education in itself.

Everything about Sierra announced to the world that the rodeo had come to town, and, smiling, effervescent and endlessly patient with anyone who approached her—despite the fact that Diablo knew only too well how little time she had to herself while on tour—she was a perfect ambassador.

And, like always, something about all that perfection made him want to shake her up a bit, to lure her into admitting that she was just as human as everyone else around her—and that that was okay.

Even if she only admitted it to herself.

She was crying out to be shaken free of the shackles of her image and recognizing his utter lack of right to the position, Diablo wanted to be the person to do the rattling.

She knew what she wanted. Why did she let anyone get in her way of achieving her goals?

He found himself walking after her long before becoming cognizant that he had decided on the action.

With his own long strides, he closed the bulk of the distance between them with enough time to see her veer to the right, bypassing the famous cathedral's facade, to instead enter the Spanish Colonial-style building that stood to its right.

Frowning, he didn't know what the building was. He'd been to the city over a dozen times and never gone inside before. He preferred to spend his tourism time immersed in the parts of the city where the crowds and air were thick and barely restrained.

Following inside the more climate controlled and subdued atmosphere, he was surprised to find that whatever the original intended purpose of the structure had been, in its current configuration, it was a museum.

While Diablo'd had no problem imagining the hyper-controlled and traditional rodeo queen choosing to spend her precious free time attending a Saturday evening mass in one of the most famous cathedrals in the United States, he had not expected her to instead use that time to visit a museum.

She didn't strike him as the museum type—whatever that type was.

After paying the six-dollar ticket fee, Diablo finally caught up to Sierra a few steps into the museum, where she stood in front of a large Mardi Gras float.

"Fancy meeting you here," he drawled, announcing his arrival before he appeared at her side, lest he startle her.

As if she'd thought she was entirely alone in the space, she started at the sound of his voice before turning to him, a reflexive smile in place, and, cheer in her voice, said, "Why, Diablo Sosa, what a surprise to run into you at the museum of all places."

Pearly and bright though it all was, it wasn't her best smile, he mused idly, faced with it yet again. It didn't reflect any real emotion, just good training. Her best smiles were like those she'd shared in her hotel room, unguarded and authentic—and in glasses.

"I was thinking the same thing about you," he said smoothly, his words and posture filled with easy nonchalance that was forced. This close to her he could remember the way she felt in his arms, and his hands itched to feel her again.

Standing beside her, it was clear that the red-and-purple motif on her chaps and vest were actually large painted poppies floating on a purple background. Despite the breaks of purple, the overwhelming red of her outfit managed to feel both quintessentially rodeo as well as oddly haute couture for the sport.

Striking that balance was a feat he wasn't sure he'd seen any rodeo queens achieve in his time in rodeo, but then again, she was the best.

Just the idea of wearing full rodeo gear outside an arena himself was enough to make his spine stiffen, but seeing Sierra dressed like this in the middle of the museum had none of that effect. Or, rather, there was some physical tightening of his body, but it was purely because of the memory of her lips and how she filled out those jeans.

He might not need a Stetson to draw even more attention to himself.

But Sierra sure looked good in hers.

Beneath her hat, as he'd suspected it might, her glossy hair hung down straight as a pin.

"I'm no stranger to museums," she said, her voice library low, respectful of the social norms that said museums were quiet spaces. "I try to visit one in every new city I come to."

"This is your first time in New Orleans, then?" he asked. Would they discuss what had happened in the hotel? Or was that something best left out of the time and space of the actual tour? He could see her going either way.

In daylight, far from Houston, that night felt like a world away.

She nodded, setting off a ripple of motion in the shiny curtain of her hair. "It is," she said. "I've wanted to come for a long time, but the obligations of work haven't given me much time for leisure travel."

He lifted an eyebrow. "Your first time in New Orleans, and you make a beeline for the museum?"

A glint came to her eyes, and her voice lost some of its queenly sweetness as it dropped down a note and flattened for her to say, "Yep."

"Tell me that's not all you planned to do?"

Diablo wasn't against museums, although the incredulity in his voice might have suggested otherwise, but museums were like a fine cognac—they had their time and place.

One's first experience of New Orleans? Not the time and place.

A person could only have one first time in New Orleans, and it should be about food and flavor and people and sound, not an exhibit on the history of Mardi Gras.

Lifting an eyebrow herself, mirroring his expression with cute sass, she asked, "And what if it is?"

He might be a long way from his days as a latchkey kid in a neighborhood of latchkey kids, but he could still recognize a dare when he encountered one, so he shrugged and said, casually, "I would be morally obligated to pick you up, haul your ass right back outside and buy you a sandwich."

While it was clear that she had expected him to rise to her challenge in some way, the amused startlement that cracked through her rodeo-queen-in-public facade made it clear that she hadn't been expecting him to boil down all of the magic of the Crescent City into a deli sandwich.

If only she knew how serious he was.

Laughing in her lower register, the sound hitting him somewhere below the navel, she said, "While I doubt you would be as successful getting all of this out of this museum against my will—" she gestured to her body, the motion of her palm essentially commanding him to visually cruise the curves that all that red warned him away from, before continuing with "—you can rest assured that the first thing I did when I made it into town was eat."

"Atta girl," he said, offering her an approving nod.

"Excuse you," she retorted, her eyebrow lifting once more.

Grinning, Diablo said, "So you ate, and now you're at a museum."

"The Presbyter," she corrected.

"The Presbyter?" he asked.

"The museum we're at," she said. "It has two exhibits. One dedicated to Mardi Gras—" she gestured around them at the many pieces of Mardi Gras history as if she worked at the place, before continuing "—and the other, to Hurricane Katrina. That's downstairs."

The good and the bad, all mixed up together. It was as New Orleans as anything else, but still he said, truthfully, "That's an unexpected combination."

She nodded, a soft glow coming to her face. "I was curious to see how they achieved the balance, or if they even did," she said, adding, "I assumed they did. It's very well reviewed."

Laughing, he asked, "You checked the reviews before you came?"

Willing to laugh at herself, she smiled, saying, "I did," before continuing once more on her journey through the museum.

Walking alongside her through the space was yet another education in the ways of the rodeo queen.

She stopped in front of every piece, reading every placard, giving each and every artifact respect and attention. Before leaving any one section, she would stop and give it one more thorough and final scan.

And where he had assumed that it was the history of Mardi Gras that had drawn her to the museum—being what the city was most famous for and having many parallels to the rodeo lifestyle she'd dedicated herself to—she spent even more time in the lower floor's exhibit dedicated to Hurricane Katrina.

"Do you always read reviews before you go to a place, or just museums?" He continued to tease her lightly as they exited the museum, grateful her costume reminded him to keep his hand off the small of her back. They'd agreed that there was no future in that direction. Instead, they could tread a different, narrow path toward something near friendship as long as he kept his hands to himself. And, in this rare instance, Diablo was interested in walking that line.

He didn't have many people he considered friends, and certainly not many with whom he found it easy to balance the dance of antagonism and appreciation, rodeo and the rest of life that his exchanges with Sierra involved.

Nodding decisively, she said, as if it was a completely reasonable set of expectations, "Of course. I hate to waste my time or to pay for a mediocre experience."

"I'll keep that in mind," he said, wondering what his life might have been like if it had been possible to make a similar statement and live up to it.

Snorting, she said tartly, "I thought we established that that kind of information was none of your business. You don't sneak around."

Taken aback more than he would ever admit by her casual callout, he covered it with a smile and met her head-on. "Enjoying a museum with an interesting friend is about as far from sneaking around hotel rooms in the dark as it gets."

"What about playing tourist when you're really here to ride?" she asked archly, taking in his dressed-down attire of jeans, sneakers and a white tee. "Seems pretty sneaky to me."

"Claws in, kitten. Not all of us are on the clock all the time," he said, eyeing her. "At the moment I'm neither Diablo the lawyer, nor Diablo the cowboy. Just Diablo."

Lifting a brow, she asked, "Are you always so compartmentalized?"

Shaking his head with a laugh at her fierce tenacity, appreciating that she wasn't playing easy or nice, he said, "It's all part and parcel."

A triumphant light lit her eyes, which he understood as soon as she delivered the line, "Then you should be absolutely comfortable and at home riding a bull in a suit."

He didn't bother to restrain his laugh, though a few passersby turned in their direction.

And once they looked, they really looked, thanks to Sierra's attire, but he paid them no mind. He'd meant what he said about sneaking; they could look all they wanted.

"I'm sure I'd be a lot more comfortable in that suit than you would be in glasses," he teased, gratified to see the mild look of horror that crossed her face.

If she was going to dish it out, she'd better be ready to get a little back.

Outside and to their left in the square, the tall side-by-side towers of St. Louis Cathedral pointed toward heaven, catching Sierra's attention, and she stopped, eyeing the building with wide eyes.

Though his nana had made sure he was baptized—despite the protests of the presiding Father regarding his name—neither of the Sosas had ever been regular mass goers.

And while he suspected they had been better off for it, escaping a lot of well-intentioned intrusion into their lives, he could see that there was a pity in it, as well.

Crossing through Jackson Square and back across the street, Diablo didn't realize he'd been unconsciously leading them back into the French Quarter until they arrived.

He handed Sierra a now-cold beignet from the bag, which while not ideal was still delicious, and once again breathed in the city, to his surprise even more content in her company than he had been alone.

In that unexpected space, he made a rare, unprovoked confession. "This is one of my favorite cities in the world."

Offering him an equally rare unpracticed smile, Sierra nodded. "It's beautiful. I know it's French, but it reminds me a lot of Cuba."

"You've been to Cuba?" he asked, impressed again, though that told him he'd yet again misjudged her. Why shouldn't she have been to Cuba?

Boasting, she said, "Only every other year my entire life."

Laughing at her haughtiness on the matter, he said, "It's less impressive when you're Cuban," putting it all together.

Making a shushing sound, she waved his words away. "Tell me that after you've survived the gale of affection and food that is visiting family in Cuba."

Diablo laughed lightly, though his chest tightened at the casually tossed words. "I can only imagine. No large family back in the homeland for me."

"No?" she asked between bites of beignet. "What is your family like?" He noticed she didn't ask where he was from, and assumed it was because of his accent. No Spanish speaker he'd ever met had ever wondered where his family was from after they'd heard him speak. And he'd never even been to the Dominican Republic.

"Small," he said.

"Just you, mom and dad, then?" she pressed, oblivious to his reservation.

Shaking his head, he kept his answers short, like always. "Just me and my grandmother."

Startled, she stopped to look at him, her brown eyes going wide. "That is small."

"Yeah." He waited a moment before he started walking again.

"What happened to your parents?" she asked.

For a moment he didn't know what to tell her. He didn't share his origin story with just anyone.

After a beat, he offered her the canned line he gave to everyone, despite the fact that something felt wrong about misleading her. "My mother died when I was young, and my father was gone from the picture long before I knew what I was missing."

Empathy filled her eyes; not sorrow or pity, but compassion, and he felt even more like a tool for not giving her a more accurate picture.

"That's terrible. I'm so sorry. Family can be hard, but I'm sure you'd take that over the lack."

Her understanding was deeper and simpler than he'd expected, and because of it, guilt slithered in his gut like a constrictor, pressuring and prodding him to be more forthcoming.

And driven by its strange need to give her more, to not let the half-truth lie there and settle when that was what he would normally do, he said, "I don't know much about my father, but I like to imagine he was from New Orleans."

Sierra said nothing immediately, and he realized he was holding his breath. Had he misjudged? Should he have just let the conversation drift on to another topic? He wasn't used to second-guessing himself, and he couldn't say he appreciated the sensation.

After drawing in a long inhale, he let it out slow and quiet. This was getting ridiculous. He was an incredibly successful man and had made wonders of his life. So why was he suddenly so concerned and uncertain as to how his words would land?

"Why here?" she finally asked.

The idea of telling her that it was because of the way he'd felt when he'd first stepped foot in the city and inhaled its scent, the experience of loving it more completely and immediately than any other place he had been to, before or since, was absolutely ludicrous.

It was nonsensical and emotional—the exact opposite of what made him so successful in court.

And for some reason, he told her anyway. "Just a feeling."

Reaching out, she took his hand and gave it a quick squeeze before releasing it just as fast. "That's as good a thing to go on as any if you've got no idea."

"Or just some powerful wishful thinking," he said drily.

Flashing him a wicked grin, she shrugged. "Or that. Either way. I can understand why you'd want to belong here. It's a great city."

"You can tell from all of four hours?"

"Don't forget," she shot back, "I ate here. Speaking of…" she added mischievously, snatching the beignet bag from him. Once she'd plucked one out, she took a big bite and ended up with powdered sugar dusting her bright red lips.

"Mmmmm… Delicious." She virtually purred the words.

"Take note of how graciously I shared with you and recall that you attempted to kick me out of your room rather than share your dinner with me. There is a lesson there."

Snorting, she took another beignet before shoving the bag back at him. "This isn't sharing. This is a modest repayment for imposing on me yet again."

"Is that what they're calling it these days?"

Eyeing him imperiously, she said, "You're better than that, Diosa."

He grinned. "Do you want to find out how good I am?"

Without missing a beat, she reminded him with prim sass, "I will. Tonight, even. In the arena. And you're welcome. You shouldn't eat so many sweets before a ride."

Making a noise in the back of his throat, he said, "You shouldn't. Watching my figure isn't a part of my job description."

"Tell that to the bronc after you've beefed up," she retorted, before adding like the good ambassador she was, "And I'll have you know that—unlike other pageants—rodeo queens are not expected to meet unrealistic body standards. Rodeo queens come in all shapes and sizes, because a rodeo queen knows that true beauty is rooted in good health, hard work and a loving heart."

"Right," he said, side-eyeing her.

"It's true," she defended.

"Oh, I'm not denying what you said about rodeo queens coming in a slightly wider shape range than, say, Miss Americas, but it's hard to claim that something that includes gown contests and jean skirts and being contractually obligated to put makeup on are the characteristics that belie the idea that beauty is rooted in good health, hard work and a loving heart."

Eyes narrowing, she said to him with a *humph*, "I beg to differ."

Catching her eye with a quick grin, he said, "You've never had to beg for anything."

"And I certainly don't plan on starting with you," she retorted, deflecting his flirtation just as a rodeo queen was supposed to.

Behaving in ladylike and nonsexual ways was also a stipulation of her contracts, Diablo knew. He knew well enough that he'd stopped when he should have just accepted her offer back at the hotel.

But then where would they be? Sneaking around and trying to make sure no one found out.

And that was a pastime he was well and truly done with.

It had taken more than one experience of being good enough for a woman's bed, but not for her public life, to put him off operating on the down low.

Even if this time it was because of real external rules and not just the rules of her daddy or the effort to impress her superiors, he wouldn't walk down that road again, though it was clearly a pattern he was still drawn to.

The girl he'd lost his virginity to, whom he had been certain would accept his invitation after months of exploring each other's bodies, had refused to go to prom with him because she hadn't wanted to risk the repercussions of the school, and more importantly, her dad, finding out that she was seeing a Black boy.

And then there had been the woman he'd dated in law school. She had insisted they meet up outside Phoenix for dates because she hadn't thought it was good optics for a woman gunning for a spot as a top criminal prosecutor to be seen getting cozy with him.

Meeting him at hotel rooms throughout the city was a whole different story, though. *That* she had loved.

"Why do you do it?" he asked, dragging his thoughts away from relationships that he had already worked through, if he could not yet let go of the restrictive sexism of rodeo queen life. It was hard when it was that, and not her, that hemmed them in now.

"Do what?" she asked, startled, having had no access to his mental tangent.

He gestured to her whole person with his hand—the sequins, the fringe, the bright red and purple and, of course, the hat and the crown—and said, "Rodeo queen."

The way she did it, the words were verb, noun and adjective all in one.

She was savvy and professional and sharp—and he had no idea why anyone with all of that going for her would willingly submit to someone else's judgment for a living.

Her eyes widened, a series of emotions flashing across them: offense, pride and weariness.

The last one, utterly unexpected, was the one that interested him the most.

Which emotion would guide her response? And who would answer?

Would it be the ambassador queen, haughty and hyperaware of her contractual obligations and the constant presence of watching eyes and listening ears?

Or would it be the woman he'd met in the hotel the night of the qualifier, tired of being something she was not?

He got his answer when, in a voice that was low and wry rather than bright and enthusiastic, she said the last thing he expected.

"It was the horses, for me."

CHAPTER SEVEN

"YOU ARE A horse girl?" he asked, incredulous.

Diablo incredulous was as attractive as Diablo arrogant—and Diablo confident, and Diablo laughing. One of his straight black eyebrows lifted slightly higher than the other, his full lips drawing together and pressing tight into each other as if he was holding back just exactly what he thought of that.

He wore street clothes, the cowboy boots peeking out from beneath his jeans the only hint of the fact that he was in town with the rodeo.

There was nothing ambassadorial about Diablo. Nothing about his presence invited a passerby to ask him why he was dressed the way he was, or why he had come to town. Someone might even think he was a local.

Diablo's aura was one that gave the nonverbal suggestion to take him as he was or to leave him alone. It also assured that he didn't care which you chose.

Though she didn't begrudge the attention she garnered everywhere she went, the idea of being so loudly unapproachable was its own kind of thrilling.

He seemed to come by it naturally—not caring—when what little of the quality she herself possessed had been hard-won, like all of the other skills and abilities she had gained through queening. She'd worked hard for each and every one of them, all of which she had hungered for as the horse-loving middle child in a family of three princesses.

"All rodeo queens are horse girls," she finally said to him in response. "It's part of the job description."

And it was true.

Unlike the pageants in which her sisters had participated, which allowed for and encouraged a wide variety of talents, for rodeo queens, talent was synonymous with horsemanship.

"My mom and sisters have been pageant women since childhood, but I was an athlete. If I hadn't discovered horseback riding, I never would have given pageants a second thought."

"Why not just compete, then?" he asked.

"I do, thank you very much," she said, lifting her nose in the air. "Queening is as much rodeo competition as riding rough stock is, and I can barrel race with the best of them," she added, "but before I started queening, it was only my dad who took me to the rodeo. Just me and him. Away from my sisters and the need to show how different I was, I found the space to admit something that had always been true but I had repressed up until then." She was warming up to the part of the story she'd told many times now.

"Which was?" he asked, the warmth of humor and curiosity in his tone.

Grinning, she gestured to her ensemble with a sweep of her hand. "I love shiny things."

He laughed, smiling. "Who doesn't?" he said, meeting her eyes and holding them as his laughter died down. "Attraction to beauty is a natural human impulse."

There was no reason her throat should tighten, nor

her breath hitch, stuck fast, as if her body was trying to hold on to something while her stomach did a flip.

He'd said nothing inappropriate and there'd been not even a hint of innuendo in his delivery.

And yet, the words felt bold and heated all the same.

Or maybe it was just that the way he met her eyes as he said them, his gaze direct and almost aggressively open to her, made them a bald admission that he found her attractive.

He left her no room to doubt.

He still wanted her and he wanted her to know it, even after they'd made their choice.

A part of her, the part that was still stinging over his rejection, wondered at his nerve, to flirt and tease and make her want him more when he knew very well he wasn't willing to take things any further.

He was torturing them with what they'd missed, acknowledging that the thing that strummed between them was still alive and powerful as ever.

But she didn't want him to stop.

Thank God there was the distraction of rodeo.

Swallowing, she looked away, casting her gaze to the side, sweeping over the picturesque architecture of the French Quarter and the thriving hum of life all around her—anything but him—before she said, "Rodeo queens were the first ones to show me that you could be an athlete and be pretty at the same time. Growing up watching my sisters, seeing up close and personal all the effort and preparation and resources that went into being 'pretty,' or my concept of it at the time, at least… Knowing the sacrifices that it called for…not playing soccer, not running around, not going outside, not riding horses… While I knew that it was technically possible to be sporty and pretty, I didn't think you could do it at the same time until I saw rodeo queens. At best you could switch back and forth, but you would always have to choose, and when forced to choose, which happened early for me because of my mom and sisters, I had committed to sporty. But then rodeo queens showed me that I didn't have to choose sides. I could be my whole shiny, athletic, horse-girl self and express it for the world to see. I could be pretty *and* powerful."

For a moment, Diablo didn't say anything, and in that space, the edges of Sierra's stomach began to curl inward, tightening around the certainty that she had said too much and that her rambling, heartfelt truth would seem naive and simple to a man as sophisticated as Diablo.

But when he spoke, his words lacked any hint of sarcasm or derision. "Some people make it through their entire lives without learning that lesson."

His words had a soothing effect on her knotting gut, slipping in to loosen and untangle the unease like warm liquid.

Suddenly bashful—though she thought she had long ago forgotten the meaning of the word—she looked away to say, "So that's why queening."

"Sound like good reasons to me," he said, eyeing her with what looked like respect.

She shrugged. "Not really. At least, not reasons that judges like. For them, I say it's because I fell in love with the sport, each and every one of the events. I say I learned everything I could, stayed up past my bedtime at night to read about rodeo's history and present, and did everything I could to dedicate myself to Western living, despite the fact that I grew up in the suburbs of Pensacola. I tell them that I was determined that nothing stand in the way of me and my rodeo dreams and that story, they love. And it has the added bonus of also being the truth, just a different portion of it," she said, oddly sad for the side of the story that never got its chance.

Diablo laughed, saying, "It being true does tend to make it easier to persuade people to your argument."

Smiling with a decisive nod, she agreed before asking, "So what about you, lawman?"

Looking at her, he lifted an eyebrow. "Lawman? I kind of like that. Calls to mind Bass Reeves."

Rolling her eyes, she said, "I'll keep that in mind for the show tonight." Her voice was as dry as a drought-ridden plain, and he loved it. She continued with, "But don't evade. Why do you rodeo?"

"Do I rodeo?" he challenged her, "or do I lawman?"

Flatly, she said, "I have questions about both."

Pulling away from her as if he needed the extra space to get a good look at all of that audacity, he said, "Oh, do you, now?"

Ignoring him, she pressed, "Rodeo first."

"I'm not surprised you would say that."

"You're stalling," she pointed out.

"You would have made a fantastic lawyer," he observed.

"You're not the first person to say so, but that's irrelevant. Why do you rodeo?" she said again, pleased and stubborn at the same time.

"You sure you want the spoiler? I'm sure it'll come up in the profiles," he said, referring to the in-depth video profiles and interviews that *The Closed Circuit* produced about its contestants midseason so that viewers could "get to know" their favorites.

Sierra merely lifted an eyebrow, her expression a

mirror of her mother's when she had had about enough nonsense from her three daughters.

"Well, like I told you the other night, I rodeo because a judge ordered me to," Diablo said, a thread of a dare coming to his voice.

He dared her to ask more questions, and he dared her not to.

But if he thought that the cat he'd let out of the bag was a tiger, she wondered if she should let him know that it was really more of a kitten—at best.

"That's right, you're riding for CityBoyz, like AJ," she said.

At the mention of his friend's name on her lips, a frown dashed across Diablo's face.

He said, "Joining CityBoyz was my alternative to a relocation to a boys' correction facility."

"How old were you?" she asked, unsure why that was the first thing she wanted to know.

"Almost thirteen."

"Twelve years old…" she said, shaking her head. She couldn't imagine the successful and powerful man in front of her facing a judge as anything other than an attorney, let alone as a child. "What happened?"

He paused, staring at her as if assessing, before he said, "I assaulted a pimp." The truth abrupt and unembellished.

"You beat up a pimp when you were twelve years old and a judge sent you to learn how to ride bulls because of it?" she asked, earnest and serious in her synopsis despite hearing how outlandish it all sounded to her own ears.

When she had been almost thirteen, she had spent her time riding horses with her hair blowing in the breeze—either that, or practicing in front of the mirror to be the world's greatest rodeo queen while avoiding homework.

The audience-savvy part of her knew that with a backstory like that, he was destined to be a fan favorite this season for sure. The part of her that had remained acutely aware of him since the night in the hotel, though, wanted to comfort him.

"It sounds like a ridiculous soap opera when you put it that way," he said.

"I'm not sure *ridiculous* is the word I'd choose," she said.

"What word would you choose?" he challenged her, his voice even and serious as he eyed her with a gaze that was somehow nonthreatening and confronting at the same time. He was testing her and making no bones about it.

In response, she chose her words with honesty and care. "Brave," she said, after thinking about it for a moment.

His eyes narrowed and he looked at her for the span of a long breath before looking away again. "How do you know I didn't kick his ass because I didn't want to pay?"

Stopping in her tracks, Sierra growled. "If that's true, Diablo Sosa, then I'm not walking another step with you. It's not my place to judge what a person does for work, but that doesn't mean I'm going to keep company with a thief."

Stopping when she did, Diablo shoved his hands into his front pockets, still not looking at her, and said, "It's not, so you can release the pearls. The guy was a jerk and had roughed up someone I thought of as a friend.

I don't know what I set out to do when I approached him. I only know that it escalated."

"Oh, Diablo." She sighed his name.

Again, she came back to the fact that it would have been a lot for a grown man to experience, and he'd only been a child.

Shrugging, he said, "The judge was ready to send me away and throw away the key, but my nana was very persuasive in her request for another solution. The old codger who happened to be a fan of the rodeo had recently heard about a new program that supposedly reformed street punks like me through exposure to the hard knocks of the arena."

"I didn't realize that CityBoyz was a reform program," Sierra mused.

Diablo snorted. "It's sure as hell not. That judge had got word of it through the grapevine, and somewhere along the journey, the true story got picked up by its bootstraps. The old man never wanted to reform any of his boys. He just wanted to give them something to do after school and a taste of the Western lifestyle and work. He gave us an opportunity to connect to something that he still believes to this day is the right of anyone with the heart for it."

Letting out a little laugh to cover how much the sentiment spoke to her own heart, Sierra agreed. "He was right about that. Sounds like a smart man."

"One of the best there's ever been," Diablo said with a nod.

"It sounds like maybe you know a bit about your father after all," she observed gently.

His smile turned easy, easier than she might have ever seen it, and because of it, a little boyish. "The old man is certainly the greatest stand-in for a father anyone could have."

And like any good son, she thought, he was proud of his dad—had probably even set out to be just like him by the looks of it.

Diablo was proving to be more complicated and interesting than any other cowboy she'd ever encountered. And that was after the fact he was already the sexiest one she'd ever met.

Unwilling to let that thought go any further, however, she said tartly, "So that explains why rodeo, then. Your daddy was a cowboy, so you're a cowboy."

Whip fast, his finger darted out to tip her hat up—just a fraction, enough to dislodge its perfect placement, but not enough to knock it off her head.

"Excuse you," he said, infusing his voice with all of the *I'm a cowboy from Texas* he had in him, and she wished she could say that her body didn't light up in response. "I rodeo because I'm good at it. Not every CityBoyz participant rodeos, mind you. Most don't. One in every sixteen, maybe."

"Oh," she said, taken aback. "What do most of them do, then?"

Diablo gave a small shrug. "Ride in local parades, give lessons to kids, practice large animal husbandry, go on camping trips, develop interview skills, belong." He said the last as if belonging was a revolutionary idea, and she recognized that it was.

She'd wanted to belong so much that she'd become the evergreen rodeo queen. In fact, hadn't rodeo always been about belonging—in her family and in the world at large?

Pulling herself out of her thoughts enough to reply

with some sass, she said, "It sounds kind of like 4H for city kids."

Snorting, Diablo shook his head. "Yeah, I guess you could call it that. I mean, none of us did—but I guess you could."

"What did you call it?" she teased, echoing his earlier challenge.

"Cowboying."

She recalled that she had been guilty of thinking of Diablo as not being a real cowboy on more than one occasion now with a strange twist in her gut that might have been shame.

"Well, seeing you in the arena," she said, acknowledging what had always been obvious, "I don't see how it could be called anything else. You're a cowboy, through and through."

His eyes darted back to her and he said, "So now I've finally earned the rodeo queen's stamp of approval, then, have I?"

If she gave him an inch, he'd take a mile, so rather than apologize, she tilted her chin at a haughty angle and said, "There's more than one rodeo queen, but yes, you've earned this one's. Don't make me regret my decisions with a poor showing tonight, though."

The laugh he let out rang back at them as it bounced off the tightly packed buildings all around, the sound of it rounded and warm and strong enough to survive even passing the throngs of bodies all around them.

Watching him, she let the sound spill over her, filling her with a kind of warmth that felt softer and more enduring and deeper than anything else she'd encountered before.

Still chuckling, he shook his head, disagreeing with

an appreciative light in his eye. "One queen reigns above them all, and you're her," he said.

Regally inclining her head to mask how his words momentarily broke down her shields, drawing the sweet shock she felt to the surface of her face, she channeled the thickness of her voice into humor and deflection. "The one and only. But enough about me. You were good at rodeo and had the know-how and support of your family to take it all the way, so why did you walk away for law, then?"

At seemingly greater ease around her, he didn't lose his smile this time, or pull back as he replied, "That judge changed my life with the strike of his gavel. At the time I couldn't fathom the injustice of it all. All of these adults just standing in a room while a strange man wearing a black muumuu dictated my life, and all of them just went along with it... The guards were ready to control me, if need be, my lawyer and my nana steadily pleading and begging on my behalf...to my angry child mind, they were all complicit in what was an obviously rigged and morally defunct game. It was painful, but that experience showed me the lay of the land in a way that nothing else had before then. Some people have more power than others. I also learned, though, that there were specific pathways to that kind of power, and one of them involved wearing a muumuu."

She didn't mean to laugh out loud right after he'd revealed such a sharp and stark moment, but she did, and she suspected he had wanted her to. He wanted her to laugh and hop away from the subject quickly, distracted enough by the absurd image that she didn't pity or question him.

She was only willing to meet him halfway, though.

She would laugh with him, and she wouldn't pity him, but she definitely had more questions. "And what about now?" she asked as the laughter died down. "Do you still think they were all complicit?"

Eyeing her, his answer was measured. "I do, though I know better now that the only thing they were complicit in was the same social contract to which we're all expected to cosign, and none more so than the one in the muumuu. And I know that each one of them, particularly on that day, thought they were doing the right thing when they sent a boy to sit on top of bulls rather than behind bars. And I agree that they were."

"But you still want to be the one in the muumuu a little more than the one sitting on the bull," Sierra finished.

His eyes widened in surprise, but he nodded. "But I still want to be the one in the muumuu. I don't resent him for putting me on top of bulls anymore, though, or for sending me to the old man. In fact, I sent him a handwritten thank-you card for what turned out to be the greatest favor of my life."

Shaking her head, Sierra commented, "And people call me extra."

"Someday he'll be a reference for my judicial appointment," he said, grinning slyly.

"If he's still alive," Sierra shot back to keep him humble. The man was outrageous. "It's been a long time since you were a twelve-year-old boy," she said.

"We're here," he chuckled, ignoring her sass without shame.

Stopping alongside him, thoughts of small talk fleeing as she looked around, she was confused. She hadn't realized they were heading anywhere in particular, and from where they stood, it wasn't immediately obvious that they had arrived anywhere, either.

People walked around them on the sidewalk, where they stood in front of a green-painted two-story whose shaded rows of windows and lack of any obvious signage gave it an impression of abandonment.

Across the street other multicolored two-stories mirrored the building they stood in front of, but with bright and clear signage marking their lower floors as retail spaces.

"We are?" she asked, dubiously.

He opened the door for her with full confidence there would be something inside, and it turned out that his self-assurance was justified.

Inside was a tiny little market that reminded her of the corner store down the street from her childhood home in Pensacola.

Individually wrapped, perpetually fresh treats and snacks abounded, lining rows of white metal shelves tucked away in tidy boxes that spoke to her inner child in the language of its heart: candy.

There were people in the store but after looking up to smile in greeting when she and Diablo had walked in, they all returned to the conversations they had already been engaged in.

Diablo led her to the counter, which boasted one of the largest sandwich boards she'd ever encountered.

"I couldn't possibly eat again now. Not after all of those beignets," she protested.

Clucking his tongue, Diablo said, "Whoa, there. Settle down, queenie. Even I couldn't handle another one of these babies right now. They're for later. After the show. I promise. They keep well."

Unable to fight the belly laugh, she let it out, even if it was muted. It was a really small store, after all, and she was still an ambassador. "You walked me all around the French Quarter to get a sandwich?"

He side-eyed her. "I walked you all around the French Quarter for the enjoyment of your company and the scenery. We're not actually that far off from where I ran into you. I brought you here for an experience."

A darted look around the store confirmed that though the space was small, only an older woman, who smiled at them, seemed to be taking note of their exchange. Otherwise, no one paid them any mind.

She was losing her touch, though, forgetting, even for a moment, that her conduct reflected on *The Closed Circuit Rodeo*. Reality TV rodeo or not, regular old rodeo folk remained the primary audience for the show, and they had strong opinions about the way a queen should act.

"This must be some sandwich, then," she said, choosing her public voice rather than the private one while feigning ignorance to his baiting.

His eyes narrowed, a look of disappointment streaking across them, before he said quietly, "Only the best. I make a point to eat here every time I come here. It's my favorite place."

She hadn't done anything wrong, and yet she felt as if she'd somehow let him down.

Clearing her throat, she asked, "Really? What do you recommend, then?"

"Are you a vegetarian?" he asked.

"I don't think a rodeo queen is allowed to be a vegetarian," she said drily.

Still looking at the menu, he said, "I didn't say a rodeo queen. I said you."

She didn't say anything for a moment, pretending to read the board overhead when really she saw nothing.

Not for the first time had he suggested that the two were not one and the same.

"They're the same things," she said quietly, before adding quickly, "I'll have what you have. Best way to test your claim."

"What if you don't like what I like?" he asked, eyeing her in a way that said he was very aware of her evasion.

"Then I'll tell you you have dumb opinions and stupid tastes," she said matter-of-factly.

"I recall you mentioning siblings now..." he said, laughing.

"And what about it?" she asked, pushing the bad behavior, the tone and language that was inappropriate for a rodeo queen, because she couldn't seem to help wanting to get him to open up, and he only seemed to do so for her rawest self.

"It shows," he said, smiling at her again before turning to order. "Two Damn That's Goods, please," he said, declining the beverages but taking the rest of the combination meal components for both of them. He paid and carried the bag as they left the store, and she followed after him.

"There's no way I'll be able to eat all of that," she said, referring to the small mountains of side dishes that the market staff had heaped into pint-size to-go containers for them.

"After opening night? We're going to be ravenous," he argued. "You asked two questions earlier, which gives me the right to ask a second one."

"What?" Sierra asked, her mind still on the thought of late-night gorging.

"Earlier. Why rodeo, and why law. My second why is why a museum?"

As had occurred so many times in her conversations with the man, she found herself at a fork in the road with Diablo.

She could tell him the truth, reveal herself, to which he very well might poke and prod with cutting observations and sharp questions, or she could give him the easy, rodeo-queen response, and risk—and risk what, exactly?

Risk that he would energetically pull back from her once more, lessening the intensity of their connection enough so that maybe she wouldn't keep forgetting herself around him?

Wasn't that what she wanted to happen?

Wasn't that the most responsible course of action?

Opening her mouth, intending to give the canned reply, she surprised herself by telling him the truth. "Someday I want to start a rodeo museum, but one that—" She paused, uncharacteristically at a loss for words, searching for the ones she wanted without luck. The situation hardly ever happened to her anymore, as she had long ago mastered the art of extemporaneous speaking, but it felt important that she not use the wrong words with Diablo "—is muted and artistic, and not too serious, but takes it all seriously," she said, mentally cringing all the while. She had not found the right words.

He lifted a single, thick, dark eyebrow, his eyes casting down and back up. "Muted and artistic?"

Of course he would run into her on a day in which,

in preparing to be out and about in a city known for its color and flair, she had gone with one of her loudest ensembles.

Her outfit was an homage to Georgia O'Keeffe, and the West—and the ladies of the red-and-purple hat society—and she was nearly impossible to miss. A far cry from muted, though dead on target as far as artistic went.

"I adore the shine and glamour of rodeo—probably more than anyone," she explained, "but I know that the general public doesn't see what I see." Her mother and sisters didn't. They understood her pageanting but had only just given up trying to convince her that she was good enough to get into "real pageants." "Most people look at rodeo, and everything associated with it, and all they see is a two-dimensional collection of stereotypes. They think they know and understand what rodeo is all about and who loves it, but it's clear they don't because they laugh at us like we're idiots. It's not possible to understand something and mock it like that at the same time—in my opinion."

Diablo stared at her, his eyes narrowed for a beat too long before giving a small nod. "Mine as well."

Buoyed more than she probably should be, she continued, "I would want my museum to show the juxtapositions at the heart and beneath the surface of rodeo. All of the things that are so obvious to me, but that so many people can't seem to see."

"And what are those things?" he prodded.

"That there is beauty in the commitment to making a good show, even when it's some of the hardest, meanest and most dangerous work out there. I've been mocked so often for my makeup and clothing, called fake and worse, so many times over my career. I've never been asked how I managed to hold a ten-pound flagpole straight while racing around an arena on horseback, the wind whipping the yards of material this way and that. Cowboys get a little more respect, of course, but so often for the wrong reasons. Not because they practice and work hard like athletes, but because they're ballsy and cocksure like any teenager out there with a leather jacket. That's not even a real picture and it's really about as much as most people know outside of the rodeo world. I want to show people how stoic the clowns and pickup men are, how determined buckle bunnies are, the insanity of pageanting with live animals, the intelligence it takes to take on a bull. Rodeo is campy and over-the-top, but it's one of those grown-from-the-hard-ground-of-life things that churns with the promise that it can all still be a grand and exciting drama if you're willing to grab it by the horns and glue on some rhinestones. That's what I want to show."

He laughed softly at her joke, and the sound of it was a warm sensation in her chest.

After mulling over her words for a moment longer, he said, "And you went to the Presbyter because by showcasing Mardi Gras and Hurricane Katrina, it puts camp and grit together, too."

Startled, she stopped in her tracks to stare at him. "Exactly. Exactly! You completely get it!"

"And where do you want this museum to be?"

Her heart's happy leaps and bounds skidded to a halt, her eyes darting downward and away from him as she said, "It's more of a daydream than anything. I'm too busy with the CC."

Eyeing her, he asked casually, "So you're in it with *The Closed Circuit* for the long haul, then?"

Shrugging, she said, "I worked damn hard for the opportunity to rodeo queen forever. Everybody said it couldn't be done."

"Everybody, indeed," he said, eyes no less intent in their appraisal of her.

"And I'm not qualified to open a museum anyway. You need to go to school for that, to be taken seriously, at least, which is the way I would want."

"So go to school," he said as if it was as easy a thing to do as going to the store.

She laughed, though in reality she didn't find it funny. She'd made real sacrifices to get where she was. "I'm way too old for that now. No. The CC is a guaranteed win, and after a lifetime of being at the whim of capricious judges, that sounds about heavenly to me."

"So you're going to be the Vanna White of *The Closed Circuit*?"

"If I could be half the icon she is, it'd be an accomplishment. Wouldn't you say?" she retorted, eyebrow lifting.

Looking away, he shrugged. "If it's what you want."

"You and my mother should get together and exchange passive-aggressive techniques," she said, her tone flat.

"I'm open to the idea. You just let me know when she has the time," he said blithely.

Laughing, she shook her head. "I like a world in which you have never met."

"Well, I'm sorry about that, queenie, because she and I are destined to become two peas in a pod. You said it yourself."

"God save us all."

"God's not who you're dealing with today," he said.

Cocking her head to the side, she said, "When it's your own name, it's kind of like laughing at a joke you told."

Letting out another bark of laughter, he said, "Only you, queenie."

"This again?" she asked, bored, and he laughed again, though this time it was more restrained.

Looking at his watch, he let out a breath that would have sounded like a sigh if it had come from anyone other than the man at her side. "I hate to cut us short, but our time's just about up out here."

After pulling out her phone to look at the clock, she was startled by how much time had passed. It was later than she'd planned to stay in the city, in fact, which meant she wasn't going to have time to curl her hair before the show.

"I'll call a ride for us," he said, pulling up the number in his phone, but she held up a hand.

"No, thanks, but that's alright."

He stopped, looking up at her from his phone, eyes turning a strange mixture of flat and distant. "That's right. Rodeo queens can't be seen associating with cowboys."

Swallowing the strange knot of what felt suspiciously like shame that caught in her throat, she nodded. "Exactly."

For another beat, he didn't say anything, just stared at her with an inscrutable expression on his face. Then he looked back down to his phone and resumed dialing. "I'll order two."

Forcing a smile, she said, "Thanks," brightly, but inside she felt like she had let him down.

CHAPTER EIGHT

IN THE SMALL dressing room the stadium had provided for her, Sierra removed her chaps as quickly as possible, unzipping them down the legs before releasing the buckles at the back of her waist.

Stepping out of the pile of them at her feet, she quickly pulled them up from the floor again, shaking them out as she did so, before carefully laying them over a chair. Even folded in half and hanging, the huge flare of the batwing chaps and their beaded fringe took up quite a bit of valuable space in the room.

The bright white of the leather and the metallic shine of the embroidery and sequin designs made them perfect for setting the tone for opening night, but made them a liability, however, when it came to her performance.

Chaps, pronounced *shaps*, though most people didn't know that, were worn for many reasons. They helped the thighs grip the leather of the saddle, creating more friction and hold than jeans or chinos could. They also offered an additional layer of protection from the saddle and from everything else one might encounter while doing dirty, hard work.

They could even serve as a tool replacement in a pinch, with cowboys having been known to cut off bits of their fringe to replace broken loops on their bridles.

But a tight-gripped and protective ride was the last thing Sierra needed or wanted for her show.

Stripped down now to her show jacket and jeans, the picture she presented was less showy, but only marginally less shiny, thanks to the crystals, rhinestones and sequins caking her upper body.

The jacket had been worth every penny.

Changing out of her gold boots, which were garish rather than inspired when worn alone with the solid black jeans, she pulled on her old faithfuls—her most worn-in black riding boots. Shiny because she kept them up, and supple because she'd cherished them for a long time, they had been so polished and loved that they felt more like slippers than boots.

Next, she removed her earrings and her hat, placing them on the small table provided with respect, and secured her hair in a single low ponytail in the back of her head. Though it was nearly unheard of for a rodeo queen, she wouldn't be wearing her hat and crown for this ride.

A mentor and fellow queen had once told her that a cowboy hat should never hit the ground without a head in it—and Sierra had taken the maxim to heart. Like a horse, a hat was a partner—they were a team that rose or fell as one.

And because she planned to spend at least a portion of her performance upside down and did not intend to fall on the ground herself, the hat had to stay behind.

After a quick touch up of her makeup, she was ready.

Striding out of the room, the heels of her boots stomping a beat to the movement, she made her way through the crowded back ways of the stadium until she reached the staging area where Tony awaited her.

"There's a girl," she crooned to the mare, patting her

neck, standing close so the horse could reacquaint her-self with Sierra's scent in the instant of relative peace before they went before their public.

When the horse had reached the level of calm she wanted, Sierra hooked her left boot into the stirrup and mounted with muscled ease. Settling herself with a grounding breath, she tightened first one leg, calf to glute, and then the other, before squeezing both together around the girth of the horse, using her entire seat to alert Tony to the fact that their show was about to begin.

As her mount took its first steps forward, Sierra relaxed in her seat—though her upright and straight posture, her shoulders over her hips over her heels, ap-peared anything but relaxed.

She would start her portion of the night's show by leading her mount through a typical horsemanship pat-tern in front of the audience, guiding the horse through a wide figure eight shape in the dirt, throughout which she would showcase her ability, strength and control through maintaining a perfectly squared position on the saddle as she transitioned Tony through a series of gaits, left and right full circle turns and stops.

Positioning and placement were critical when being judged, and after a lifetime of being judged, she'd be-come expert, from her hands on the reins, to her seat in the saddle, to the height of her heels in the stirrups, to the angle in her forward lean as she went through turns.

In *The Closed Circuit*, there was no judging panel ready to give her a score, but she wasn't the type to let that make her sloppy.

If she had ever thought rodeo queen judges were harsh critics, then she had by now more than learned her lesson. Television audiences had proven even the harshest judging panels to be nothing but a bunch of lambs.

Only after she had successfully led Tony through her final two three-hundred-and-sixty-degree turns—one to the left and one to the right, and an impressive acceleration and stop display, to the applause and delight of the audience—did Sierra kick things up a notch.

Her performance music mix blasted through the speakers picked up tempo as Sierra and Tony raced around the perimeter, moving in fast circles around the arena. Clapping her hands, she smiled and yee-hawed while colorfully and ridiculously dressed rodeo clowns set up three barrels in the dirt, each one serving as the apex of a large triangle formation.

With the pressure of her legs and the weight of her heels, Sierra urged Tony to pick up even more speed while she waved her fist in the air, pumping it in circles in time to the music.

And when they hit the sweet spot, going very near twenty-five miles per hour, they attacked the barrels.

Because the barrels were merely the lead-up to a larger spectacle, rather than the whole performance themselves, Sierra's turn pattern was not a matter of choice and flexibility in the moment—as it usually was in the barrel race—but was one set in stone.

She had to go left around the first barrel, followed by right turns around the second two, before shooting out through the center of the barrel formation and straight into her first trick.

The reins she held until it was time to switch hands, cue her horse with her heels and hit the perfect lead. Shooting free on the other side of the turn, she slid her hands back up the reins, ready to take on the next barrel and turn.

Because she had been doing it for a long time, she was fast and accurate, coming in around three feet away from each barrel—the perfect amount of space to give both her and her horse room without knocking over the barrel—and accelerating out of the curve to get around all three barrels in less than twenty seconds. Coming out of the pattern, it would look like she and Tony were on their way to exit, but in truth, it was where things really got wild.

Rising in her saddle, her seat rising from the leather in a way that would horrify a horsemanship judge, Sierra lifted one leg, drawing it up and parallel to the horse's body before quickly twisting and spinning it over her pommel and transferring the rest of her body weight to stand upright in one stirrup.

The audience gasped, but she wasn't done yet.

Capitalizing on Tony's momentum, she swung herself back into the saddle to the cheers of the crowd before spinning once again in a circle around the pommel of her saddle, maneuvering her legs to avoid the horse's neck, as she spun like a top on the back of a horse that had only moments ago been doing its own spinning around barrels.

After four full rotations, all while leading Tony in fast circles around the arena to ensure that every section of the audience had its own spin to witness, she reveled in the energy the crowd fed back to her.

If, in general, she was beginning to find it exhausting to be a constant diplomat for the Wild West, at least in these moments, thrilling the crowd on the back of a horse, she felt energized.

Having completed another circle of the arena, she led Tony into what would be their final pattern.

It was a repeat of the same traditional figure eight that they had entered the arena with, only this time they wouldn't be showing off how smoothly they could transition from a walk to canter.

This time, rather than transition gaits, Sierra would show off her ability to transition her body position.

At breakneck pace—she would literally break her neck if she fell—she swung her body up and over, relying on her combination of strength, alignment and momentum to hold her first parallel to the moving horse, and then perpendicular, with her head upside down.

She did it on both sides, first on Tony's right flank, and then her left.

All the while, the horse's rock-star personality shone through, and Tony didn't miss a beat or spook at all as her rider spun and twisted around on her back.

For the grand finale, Sierra rose powerfully, her legs and balance fully engaged, to stand atop her saddle and ride out of the arena upright on top of Tony's back, to the screaming approval of the audience.

Dropping down only once she was well into the alleyway, Sierra slowed Tony to a walk, leading her through a controlled cool down to release the remaining speed and energy that swirled around them.

When she was satisfied that the horse was ready, she dismounted and offered pats of affection and a handful of coin-shaped carrots. Then it was time to say goodbye, with Tony's handlers collecting her. The horse had done well, everything she could have asked for in a partner, and now they would part ways forever.

Like every horse she rode for a show, the mare took a little piece of Sierra's heart with her when she went.

Like dancing or making love, when you joined so fully with another being it was impossible to walk away unchanged.

Her spirit marked by yet another horse, Sierra hurried back to her changing room, released her ponytail and fluffed her hair, touched up her makeup and then squeezed back into her embroidered chaps and golden boots before making a beeline back to the stage where it was time to announce the second round of riders of the evening—the group of riders that included Diablo.

She wondered if he had brought a saddle along.

Did he even still own a saddle? she wondered.

He didn't strike her as the type to hold on to a bunch of bulky old rodeo gear long after he had retired. That required a certain level of sentimentality.

But while it was one thing to jump on a bareback horse for the qualifier, it was a whole different thing to ride saddle bronc in an unfamiliar saddle.

Due to the performer's guild negotiations, none of the contestants were allowed to saddle their own horses, but they were allowed to use their own equipment—provided that they had any to bring along.

She really hoped he'd kept his.

Though she wasn't supposed to be rooting for anyone other than the best cowboy out there, she was looking forward to his ride.

Butterflies fluttered in her stomach, but outwardly she remained the smiling hostess she was paid to be. She wanted to see him ride. A part of her knew he'd do the event proud, but a part of her was terrified it'd been too long.

But none of that was what she needed to be doing right now. Right now she needed to be watching, not thinking about Diablo Sosa—at least, not until his ride.

Fortunately, the moment came soon enough.

"Just like a stone in your boot, folks—it's impossible to ignore Dillon Oliver when he rides rough stock! Another great ride from the meanest cowboy this side of the new millennium. He's the outlaw you love to root for, Dillon Oliver!"

Years of rodeo pageanting meant she never had to plan out what she was going to say about rides or contestants while watching—instead, she enjoyed the spectacle, and let her real impressions guide her commentary.

So while she always thought before she spoke, the segue wasn't premeditated when she referenced her earlier conversation with Diablo, saying, "And if Dillon is our outlaw, y'all, then who should come after him but *The Closed Circuit*'s very own lawman? Give it up for the lone champion of justice amid this crowd of dusty rogues, Diablo Sosa, y'all!"

The volume of the crowd kicked up a notch in the arena, and if it was due to the added warmth in her voice or because Diablo was already trending as one of the most popular contestants of the season—his connection to the previous season's champions only adding to the fact that he had proven handily that he had try—she didn't know.

The producers had their eye on him as one of the potential stars of the season, and she couldn't disagree with them.

It was one of her jobs to nurture seeds like that along.

To heighten the dramatic flair.

To see anything that might be grown and water it.

Diablo gave the hand signal and his chute flew open.

His mount leaped out and he marked out superbly, both of his legs shooting straight in front of him like a dual-legged kickstand, rigid and angled over the bronc's shoulders on each flank.

He held his mark for the recommended two bucks, before beginning to spur with a touch so light that even from the stage, it looked like a feather's tickle.

It took Sierra a moment of frozen delight—at his gorgeous flow and rhythm, at his massive body perfectly positioned and moving in ready meter with his horse, at the horse itself, who jumped and kicked and spun as if the two of them had worked out a backroom deal before going on stage—to determine what was different about the picture he presented, because as perfect as he was, something about his silhouette was unlike the other cowboys she'd watched throughout the night.

His form was flawless, ticking off all the boxes a judge looked for in a ride, as if his body merged with the horse's until both moved as one undulating creature, a kind of man-horse-sea creature chimera, and for all of that, there was something unusual about the way he rode.

And then it hit her: Diablo was left-handed.

A southpaw at the rodeo.

It wasn't a big deal, just made him stand out all the more.

If there was no one like Sierra, then there was also only one Diablo. As ever, he was a man apart from the rest.

As the buzzer rang the pickup men caught up with him to grab his horse, giving him both space and time to safely dismount, punctuated by his fist-pumping whoop and holler.

He was just too pretty for words. His powerful body thrummed with having done the job, the best job that anyone had done over the course of the night, throbbing and thick with his talent and skill—it was almost enough to rob a woman of words.

But she was too much of a professional to let that happen in the middle of a performance.

So though he was even more alluring in the triumph and celebration of it than he had been in the focus and strength of his ride, she maintained her steady flow of commentary, just as she had through all of those eight seconds.

It was her job to shove her emotions so far below the surface that nobody knew she'd been stricken with awe while he rode, nor how much she wanted to be down there at his side, shouting and hollering right alongside him.

For the first time that she could remember, she wanted to be chute side and not center stage, on standby to personally congratulate him, rather than over the loudspeaker.

"After another phenomenal performance, folks, I'd be watching my back no matter which side of the law I fell on! Our comeback king has proven once again that not only is he as good as he once was, he's still better than most of the rest! The lawman, y'all! Diablo Sosa!"

Roaring and stomping, the crowd took the cue she'd given them like practiced players, leaping to their feet to stomp and clap as they took up a new chant.

DI-A-BLO! DI-A-BLO!

And then, because it was her job and she would never let it be said that she didn't get the job done, she finally tore her attention away from Diablo as he'd walked out of sight and announced the final competitor of the night.

"Our final rider of the night may not be the youngest out there in the dirt, y'all, but he's the wisest and wiliest. The time he's invested has certainly returned, because coming into tonight with a score like Daddy Warbucks, our first-place rider, Tio Julio, is the one to beat! Give it up for Tio Julio, y'all!"

After the rush of sensations that had been Diablo's ride, it was a struggle to truly keep her mind on Tio Julio's ride, which was really a shame, as it was as near to technically perfect and aesthetically appealing as it was possible to get—beating Diablo's impressive ninety-point ride by a shocking three points, and Dillon's eighty-seven points by a whopping six.

At the end of the night's performances, it was only clearer that the top three stood high and proud in the spotlights in a class of their own, or, at least, the top two did, while Dillon persistently nagged from behind.

LATER, IN HER ROOM, Sierra realized that rather than the exhaustion she generally felt after a show and a performance, there was a hint of excitement in her veins that was completely at odds with what was going on a sixteen-hour day.

Still buzzing, sleep was the last thing she wanted. She wanted company, and of a specific variety, if she was being honest.

She was a rodeo queen, and a rodeo queen could take or leave any given cowboy.

A rodeo queen was in it for the horses and the lifestyle, not the men who tagged along.

A rodeo queen was an ambassador for the sport, a fan of each event rather than any individual competitors.

But like *The Closed Circuit*, Sierra was a rodeo queen unlike any other. Usually, that meant she had more discipline than the rest, but not tonight.

Tonight it meant she wanted a man.

And some food, having burned each and every one of her day's considerable calorific intake doing foolish tricks on the backs of horses and gnashing her teeth over a cowboy she had no business thinking about.

Unfortunately, in the bustle and commotion to ensure that the two of them were not seen coming back from the French Quarter together in the afternoon, Diablo had gone home with her sandwich.

CHAPTER NINE

As it was nearly one in the morning—the night's show well and truly over—Diablo was not expecting a knock at his door.

In fact, he was sitting on his bed, leaning back with his eyes closed, his head pressed against the wall behind him, breathing slow and even and wearing nothing but a pair of boxers and an ice pack.

It had been one hell of a night; enough that even the devil was tired.

There was a chance that if he ignored the knocking, whoever it was might go away.

As far as opening nights went, things had gone well.

His ride and score had been impressive enough that, just like the qualifier, he would've taken the top spot for the night if it hadn't been for Tio Julio.

The man was so good he called into question every maxim about rodeo being a young man's sport. It wasn't about being young or old. Rodeo was Julio's sport; the rest of them were just a bunch of amateurs and Diablo was happy for it.

A good ride made the blood sing, whether one won or lost.

As much as he loved the courtroom, it was only rodeo that did this to him.

The knock sounded again, surprising him after the long pause, but he still stayed where he was.

Unlike the real devil, after tonight he'd earned his rest.

He'd done good, pleased the fans and put on a pro-cowboy face through the whole thing. A little bit of peace wasn't too much to ask.

Sleep might be, though, as his body resisted his every signal and command to settle down and shut off for the night with the same determination that he resisted answering the door.

Like he was twenty-one all over again, his system craved the old familiar come down: an ice pack, a cold beer and company—preferably of the female and naked variety.

He had just one of the three—the weakest one, at that—and it just wasn't cutting it.

Everything was the same, but different.

It had been a unique experience, and a homecoming. He thought he'd walked away from rodeo square—he'd gotten as much good out as he'd put in before an amicable split. Tonight had showed him that he might have missed the relationship more than he'd let on. He had kept his saddles and gear, after all.

The competition and the seriousness of it, the thrill of a good ride, even just the pain involved in making whiplash look pretty—all of that had been just like it'd always been.

And, sore as he was now, and though he wouldn't go back and change a single choice in his life, he realized after having done it again, alone and grown, with no scholarship money on the line, that there was a part of him that regretted not taking rodeo all the way; that had always wondered what might have been.

A whole lot of hurt is what, he reminded himself, stern and uncompromising in dealing with the inner wistfulness. A career in rodeo would have been a whole lot of hurt and nonsense.

He was close enough to AJ and therefore had been close enough to the lifestyle to know the reality of it.

A rodeo cowboy risked life and limb every time he left the chute.

And as the sole relative of an aging loved one, he had a responsibility that most rodeo cowboys did not. He was all his nana had. Eventually, she would need someone to take care of her in more ways than simply financially, and he couldn't do that as a broken-down cowboy.

When that day came, he planned to take on the role himself and serve with honor. She deserved no less than a gentle way out of the world, her last days spent with the family she loved and the only family she had left.

He shook his head clear of the morose thoughts, then grimaced from the motion.

Adjusting the ice pack, he positioned it on the new crick he'd just created in his neck, when yet another knock on his door made him jump, dislodging the pack from its place.

This time there had been a different cadence to the knock, as if his discouraged visitor was finally about to give up. As if they were sad.

Diablo considered letting whoever it was slink off dejected.

He was in no mood for company.

But dragging himself up with a grumble, he grabbed the nearest T-shirt at hand and yanked it over his head while opening the door anyway.

That it was Sierra who stood on the other side was almost as unsurprising as it was surprising.

She wasn't supposed to be here.

Despite their afternoon together, they both knew there was to be no sneaking around to meet undetected under the darkness of night. He didn't want to be anyone's undercover lover and she didn't have the freedom to have a lover any other way.

But there she was looking up at him, her glossy dark hair pulled back into a ponytail, her face freshly scrubbed clean. His favorite version of her.

The look in her eyes was a combination of daring, energy and…relief, and for a moment all he could do was stare.

Closed Circuit staff crawled the premises, pretty much all the time.

Though the vast crew had their own block of RVs, bunking up together, their rigs serving as the caboose of the tour's large caravan—anyone from production and stage team members, to animal handlers and hospitality staff lived among it—they had staggered shifts. There was someone on active shift all day, every day, while the tour was live.

It was scandalously late, though there was never a time of day in which a rodeo queen had any business visiting a cowboy's private quarters. She shouldn't be there and he shouldn't let her in.

But since they were both the type to play with fire, they might as well do it together.

They'd been able to eat together without things going too far before. Sort of.

"It's dangerously late for a call, queenie," he drawled. He would not allow her the future possibility of plausible deniability. If she was dancing with him, he'd know she was going in with open eyes. He owed that to himself at least. Too many men who looked like him had been burned by women in this situation. He had to protect himself.

Nudging him aside, she pushed her way into his rig without so much as a by your leave, closing the door behind her before responding as if it explained everything from her presence to her willingness to take the risk. "You have my sandwich."

In any other circumstances, it would have been a comical pretense for coming over—as weak an excuse to get inside as offering a cup of coffee—and yet, his mind flashing with the memory of taking both sandwiches when they'd departed, he realized he might have gotten it all wrong.

The fact he experienced a moment of uncertainty over whether or not she was there because she wanted to be or because she wanted to eat was yet another ego check of the kind that he hadn't had since he'd been a teenager.

But she'd put in just as hard a ride as he had for the opening night. She might just be hungry.

And he had her sandwich because they'd taken separate rides coming back—separate rides because she couldn't be seen fraternizing with a contestant.

Feeling as if the powers that be were not willing to allow him the future possibility of denial, either, he faced up to the fact that he wanted her to be there because she wanted to be. He wanted her to cross his boundaries as much as it seemed she was tempted to cross hers.

Unless she just wanted a sandwich.

Laughing at both of them, he opened the mini fridge to retrieve her food.

Handing it over, still chuckling lightly, he said, his voice low and hoarse from a night of hollering at the rodeo, "I told you you'd be hungry later. Didn't expect you to be so hungry you'd risk being seen here after hours, but I am a believer in the power of this sandwich. You haven't even had a taste and yet here you are, desperate and begging."

Snorting, she lifted a brow, holding out an open palm. She didn't reach for it—that wouldn't be queenly, after all—merely waited for him to place it in her hand like the royalty she was. "I never beg for anything," she said.

Placing the wrapped sandwich in her hand with mock seriousness, he said, "Your eyes say what your mouth is too afraid to utter. You want it bad." His words flirted with her, for all that they were discussing a po'boy, but he couldn't seem to help it. "Enjoy," he said, unable to stop himself.

"I'm sure I will," she said, looking him in the eye even as she made impressive work of the sandwich's wrapper, her manicured fingers deftly demolishing the origami of the paper.

When one end of the long hoagie was exposed, she opened her mouth wide, her plump lips stretching to form an enormous O, and took a bite.

But what had begun as sensual teasing quickly turned into deep and real sounds of pleasure as she chewed, until there was no doubt that she was no longer flirting, but simply enjoying her enormous mouthful with gusto and verve.

"Mmm. You were absolutely right," she said when she finally took a pause between bites. "This is delicious. The best sandwich I've ever had. Hands down. And I've been to Cuba."

"We all know you've been to Cuba," he teased, voice filled with warmth for all that her interest in him had been overshadowed by a sandwich.

Watching her eat, watching her obvious enjoyment, was like experiencing it for the first time, refreshing memories as if he were living them all over again.

"Are you just going to watch me eat, or are you going to join in, too?" she asked after a few more bites, slowly becoming more aware of herself.

He had been so engrossed in watching her eat that he hadn't even considered eating himself—had not even bothered to remove his own sandwich from the bag.

Laughing softly to hide the fact that he'd been so obviously caught up in her, he reached into the bag to rectify the situation, then going one step further, reopening the mini fridge and pulling out two of the cans of beer from the six-pack that rested inside.

Drinking alone at one thirty in the morning was depressing, even if you'd lasted eight seconds on a bronc and delighted thousands of fans.

Drinking with company at one thirty in the morning, however, was just being a good host.

Their eyes locked again as he reached out with the can, though.

Offering her a beer was another test of sorts, even if he hadn't intended to press her to the line.

Just how far was she willing to push the boundaries of rodeo queen propriety?

It was one thing to stop by to pick up a sandwich.

It was a whole different thing to sit down and have a beer.

Queens had lost crowns for less.

She hesitated only for a second, resolution flashing

across her eyes, before taking the can from him with a firm grip and then going even a step further herself, sliding onto the bench of his dining table and making herself comfortable.

Following her lead, Diablo sat as well, taking his seat across from her.

"You looked good out there tonight," she said after they'd passed some time eating in easy silence.

The words warmed him, though he didn't imagine she meant them the way his body had taken them.

When she said he'd looked good, she didn't mean she liked his bone structure or the way he filled out a pair of jeans, as another woman might.

No, Sierra was a rodeo queen.

She meant she liked the way he'd looked thrashing around on the back of a bronco.

And somehow that made it better, that she appreciated his skill and try more than his body.

"Thanks," he said. "It's been a while."

"Couldn't tell," she said approvingly. "Tonight you showed that it wasn't just a qualifier fluke that got you into the second-place spot after so long away."

"Didn't know that was the rumor floating around," he said, taking a swig of beer.

Shaking her head, she replied, "Not so much a rumor as much a hunch I have about some of the folks up top."

She meant Dillon, of course, and though Diablo wasn't worried about the guy, he appreciated her looking out for him. "Well, it's good to hear it's laid to rest," he said, unmoved, he realized, by whether or not anyone thought he deserved to be where he was.

"Of course, good as you were tonight, you still don't

seem to be any closer to that number-one spot yet," she mused, a naughty light entering her eyes.

Taking a sip before he answered, he said, "Opening night is a long way from the finale, queenie, and you haven't even seen me on a bull."

All innocence, she said, "Yeah, but there was the qualifier, too, where you came in second, so really, I hear what you're saying, but the evidence seems to point a different way…"

Snorting, he shook his head as he said, "Bolder than a hungry dog."

Keeping it up, her eyes sparkling all the while, she said, "And with Tio Julio around, I don't know… You put on a good ride out there, but that man has angels on his side."

And because she looked like an angel saying so herself, sweet and innocent as she mercilessly ragged on him, a bark of laughter escaped him.

Not bothering to fight her, knowing he couldn't resist if he tried, he merely agreed, putting on his own front of pondering earnestness. "You do have a point there. Turns out his ride at the qualifier wasn't just a fluke, either."

Sierra laughed at that, cracking when he least expected it, and she said in full honesty and openness, "He really is an amazing rider, and nobody knows where he came from. Seriously, there's no history of rodeo in his background file, but obviously that can't be, not when he rides like he does. And at his age!"

Diablo smiled at the wonder and respect for the older cowboy he heard in her voice. Filled with a similar awe himself, he was even comfortable and willing to remain in the second-place spot all season, if it meant a tour of performances the likes of which had been coming out of Julio.

And that wasn't hero worship; it was just being a fan of the sport.

Anyone who claimed to love rodeo couldn't help but love what Julio did when he got out there in the arena.

But, unlike Sierra, Diablo was less curious about the man's background.

In his experience, the only people these days who didn't have pasts were the people who had erased them, and because he didn't get a predator vibe from the man, he was willing to respect that.

"There's a story there, alright," he said, but he didn't take it any further, as he'd also learned that digging around in people's lives—just getting involved, in general—usually ended with obligations to take action, either in support of or opposition to the person in question. "But what's this about background files?" he said instead, ears fine-tuned to the things people let slip.

Sierra scrunched her eyes closed with a face, before cracking one open again in a stage grimace. "There're files on each of y'all with your history, social media behavior, et cetera. Nobody's ever been kicked out because of what's in them or anything. Mostly it's to prescreen for anything with the potential to get the show in trouble for not knowing and to spice up the commentary."

"That explains the 'allow any data collection relevant to the contestant's participation in the competition' clause," he said drily.

Snorting at him, she said, "You *would* read the contract in full."

Looking at her as if she'd turned out to be the killer

in a horror film, Diablo said, "Are you saying you don't? Never sign a contract if you haven't read the fine print."

Raising her hands, palms up, she shook her head. "I don't. I'm not saying I do. I'm just saying most of the *Closed Circuit* cowboys I've met are more concerned with their score than the fine print in the contracts they sign."

"Most cowboys aren't lawyers—though the combination is far less rare than you might imagine. Especially in Texas," he said with a grin and a drawl for her, before he couldn't help himself and added, far less smoothly, "The show's lawyers are gonna want to be careful there, though. It only takes one cowboy pointing out the imbalance of power to cause real trouble."

Side-eyeing him, Sierra correctly guessed, "You just couldn't keep it in, could you?"

His cheeks heated mildly at the callout—it wasn't often someone pointed out that he got nerdy when it came to the law—but he breezed through it with a full smile. "It's impossible," he admitted. There was no point in denial. He was a man who spoke up.

"Well, I'll pass it on, though I'm not sure anyone up top is going to give much credence to the legal advice of a rodeo queen." She laughed.

"I would think that everyone from the top down would respect the word of rodeo's queen of queens."

"You would think that, wouldn't you?" she said before adding with faux sad flair, "But alas, it is the fate of a rodeo queen to be an expert whose brilliance is appreciated only by little girls."

She joked, but it was funny because there was some truth in what she said. Rodeo queens were a fixture of rodeo, but he realized that before Sierra, he had only ever considered them as a part of the backdrop—their presence part of the filler between the main events.

He would've certainly never considered consulting one about anything rodeo before meeting Sierra, though now he could see how foolish that was.

Sierra lived, breathed and dreamed rodeo and was an athlete in her own right—just as much as Lil, or AJ or the old man ever had been.

"Fate is so cruel, to deny such a genius her due," he said, happy to play along with this silly iteration of Sierra's.

But then she switched her focus on him again, her eyes narrowing just a fraction and going shrewd. "Almost like denying the pro rodeo world the genius of your talent for fourteen years."

She was adorable, disguising a compliment as a jab like that.

He laughed. "My rodeo genius pales in comparison to my legal genius," he said. There was no reason to be humble about something that was hard-won. "Rodeo was not my destiny."

"So why did you turn up for the qualifier?" she pressed, though with curiosity more than the intent to change minds. "As I understand it, with Lil and AJ's winnings, CityBoyz is doing just fine financially these days. Why ride again at all if you really gave it up so long ago?"

He paused before he replied. He didn't like to lie, but neither did he like to reveal his private business, especially to someone whose job it was, in part, to get the inside scoop. But something about Sierra drew him to open up.

"The old man asked me to. Said they got so much

money now that they need more participants. Last year they saw a huge spike in interest while AJ competed, so he was hoping to replicate that this season to spend all the cash burning a hole in his pocket."

Sierra laughed, shaking her head with mock disapproval. "So he's hoping to cash in on his little slice of rodeo being the hot new thing, just like everybody else."

Smiling, Diablo nodded. "Can you blame him? He's passionate about the capacity of the Western life to heal, especially for kids in the city."

Nodding, she agreed. "I believe in that, too. Horses are the best therapists out there. Almost as good as being surrounded by people you love. Where's the crew, by the way? I saw Lil and AJ and Henry at the qualifier, but they weren't at the show tonight."

Shaking his head with a smile, he said, "All tied up. It's CityBoyz's policy to be there in support, but with the extended programs and the ranch away camp, they're busy with kids and ranching. They'll be at the finale, though."

"Makes sense. It'd be hard to follow the tour the whole way," she said.

"And with everything televised, there's less to miss out on by not being here. And now that I'm a big boy, there's less worry about my getting jumped outside the arena."

Grimacing, she asked, "Has that ever happened?"

He considered lying to her because he knew she wouldn't like that the answer was yes, and not just for him, but a number of other CityBoyz program participants at Western events, but he didn't lie. And he remembered her at the museum. She might be sunshine and sparkle to the world, but she was willing to stare deep into reality, as well. "It has, and not just to me. But the old man took care of us and taught us how to take care of each other. But it lingers and shows up in strange places. Makes you want to keep some distance for your own safety. You should have seen how hard he had to work to get us to even put on cowboy hats back in the day. To this day, AJ will only wear one when he has to."

Looking aghast, Sierra said, "Had to convince you? I take it back. You're no cowboy, after all."

Perhaps it was because she was here in his rig, late at night, complimenting his ride and eating with him, that he could laugh when she said it this time, before responding, "You can rest assured, I am a true believer in the cowboy hat. Though there's a lot less money in it, going the college route, like I did, as opposed to going pro straight out of high school, like AJ did, gives you a better grounding in and respect for the traditions as they are."

"You sound like a rodeo queen," Sierra said, polishing off the last bite of her sandwich and washing it down with a long swig of her beer.

Briefly, he wondered if she charmed him on purpose.

Did she know the devastating effect that seeing her comfortable and at ease had on him, in the same way that she knew that her rodeo-queen charm could captivate an audience?

Realistically, he knew the answer had to be no.

She could have no way of knowing that she had seduced him with that swig of beer.

No, Sierra wasn't trying to seduce him. She just happened to be doing a damn good job of it.

Though it carried with it unwanted complications, her visit, their shared meal and her company—clothed though it may be—were having the effect that the ice pack alone hadn't been able to achieve.

As if it were a type of programming that only ran one way, his body had relaxed after she'd barged in, his muscles loosening as his body and mind unwound enough to let the exhaustion and tiredness slide in and start the job of shutting things down. Tilting his head to one side and then the other, he fought it to stay attentive to her.

As if she could sense the change taking place in him, she asked, her voice laden with genuine sympathy, "Sore?"

Nodding, he said nothing, but she made a sympathetic noise in the back of her throat.

"A good ride hurts just as much as a bad one, though," she said knowingly.

"Sometimes worse," he agreed, bringing a hand up to rub at the place where his left arm met his shoulder.

"I can rub it for you," she offered, quickly qualifying with, "I mean, if you want. I'm not a professional or anything, but I have seen and had enough PT massages myself that I could give it a go."

Once again, something shifted between them, though the words tumbling out of her mouth were clearly an effort to say that it wasn't like that.

The physical truth of the matter, though—that they wanted each other more than they didn't—would not stand for the lie. It was absolutely like that. That had been clear from the moment he opened the door.

But that didn't mean he was going to say no.

"I'd be a fool to decline," he said slowly. He didn't rush into disaster any longer. He walked to it slowly with his eyes wide-open.

Nodding with more vigor than simple agreement required, Sierra cleared her throat to say, "Absolutely. No problem," followed by a grimace.

Then, scooting away from the table, she stood, stretching her arms overhead for a moment before coming to sit on Diablo's bench.

He scooted in, turning his body at the same time, both making room for her and giving her access to his back.

While he had been the recipient of athletic massages in college, this moment marked the first time that an after-ride massage had been included in his post-show come down.

Her fingertips landed like butterflies atop his shoulders, his attention and focus immediately zeroing in on the delicate touch. Shivers radiated outward from the point at which each digit made contact, their pulsing rhythm sensual like the rumbling purr of a cat. Gripping more firmly, she began to massage, her strong fingers working their way through his hardened muscles, finding and making quick and merciless work of each knot she encountered. Though her touch had started light, she was neither shy nor gentle as she progressed, attacking points of tension with the intent to dismantle—and he loved every second of the abuse.

Her hands were large and strong, ideal for a woman of her height and inclinations, as well as his massage.

Riding the way she did—her trick riding and advanced horsemanship display far outpacing the choreographed prancing and patterns of most rodeo queens' performances—required at least as much strength and grip as any rough stock rider.

"Did you miss it?" she asked as she dug into a particularly sore and locked-up muscle.

"Miss what?" he asked through the haze of both painful and pleasurable sensations she was setting off within him.

"Riding," she said.

For a moment he was quiet.

Did he?

He hadn't thought he had. He hadn't thought about it—riding or rodeo—for himself in years, in fact. He had closed that door years ago, effectively ending a large chapter of his life when he went away to law school.

And yet, he'd kept his saddles all these years.

"I did. I didn't realize how much until recently," he said honestly.

He felt the motion of her nod behind him.

"It showed tonight. You tapped into something out there that was different even from the qualifier. If I didn't know you were a stone-cold lawyer, completely indifferent to rodeo, I'd dare say it was joy."

He said nothing to that at first.

Joy was not a word he had much experience with—not in the past, not in the arena and not as a word that described anything he did.

Forcing a chuckle, he said, "Well, if it was, it only lasted seconds before pain took over."

Softness and a smile in her voice, Sierra said, "There's many that would call those eight seconds a lifetime, and one well spent."

His own voice low, he asked, "Are you one of them?"

As soon as the question was out, he realized that her answer mattered.

He needed to know it now, before they made any decisions or compromises they could not go back from.

Did she see the value in him? In what he did?

Swallowing, eyes wide, she thought for a moment before she responded to the question and he wondered if her hesitation was because she didn't know the answer or if it was because she didn't want to reveal the truth.

He was surprised, then, when she said, her voice wry, "I wouldn't be here if not."

He hadn't expected the honesty. Certainly not that particular admission. Or was he just thinking that he heard acknowledgment of what was growing between them in her words.

But as was her way, she clouded the waters again with her next words. "It's a belief I've dedicated my entire life to."

Unable to stop the questions from flashing across his eyes, he managed to keep them from coming out of his mouth. Instead, he said, "That's right. You wouldn't be planning to Vanna White your way through *The Closed Circuit* if you didn't believe in it."

Letting out a laugh that didn't sound too happy, she said, "I certainly wouldn't have given up college and all the rest of it, if not."

"All the rest of it?" he asked, an eyebrow lifting. Becoming the best in your field required countless sacrifices. He knew that, but what were the roads Sierra had not taken?

Waving her hand, she said airily, "Oh, you know, relationships, general regular adult milestones, attending family events..." She was keeping it light as if the things she mentioned were minor inconveniences and not the kinds of things that caused people's lives to pivot.

She had been driven to get to where she was, focused so much that she hadn't let anything else in. She wasn't unlike him in that way.

But taking his cue from her, he didn't coddle or come down heavy on her confession, simply shrugged and said, "It ain't easy to be the best."

Inclining her head, she said in her work voice, "Thank you for the compliment."

"No problem, queenie. Where others try to woo and charm a crowd, you are a puppet master, a class above."

Her laugh and response was dry, though her fingers stayed strong. "I sound like a sorceress when you say it like that."

Shrugging lightly under her massage, he said, "It doesn't seem like a stretch to call the way you work both a mic and a crowd magic."

"Thank you?" There was laughter in her voice, but also a hint of doubt.

"It's a compliment," he assured her. "I love watching you work—on stage and on the back of a horse."

Unable to hide the preening in her voice, she said, "Oh, you liked my little show, did you?"

Smiling, Diablo said, "If you want to call hanging upside down on the side of a horse a little show then the answer is still yes, but I might disagree on the adjective."

"And what would you call it?" she challenged.

"Death-defying, perhaps? Daring?"

"That sounds more like the circus than the rodeo," she pointed out.

"It looked like it, too," he retorted.

Pausing in her massage, she gave his shoulder a light slap instead. "How dare you," she said, the rodeo queen in her voice out in full force. "I am a rodeo professional. I am not a circus performer."

"I don't know," he teased. "Seems to me you pal around in a traveling show putting on death-defying and daring performances in a shiny costume, standing on the back of a galloping horse... My nana always told me that if it looks like a duck and quacks like a duck... I'm sure you can see where I'm going with this."

Ceasing her massage altogether now, she said primly, "If you're going to resort to name calling, I'll just have to take my things and go."

"Pretty sure you ate the last of your excuse to be here, queenie, but if you want a trophy to take home, you can go ahead and have my T-shirt," he said, calling her bluff with a grin and a full load of Texas in his voice, his pearly whites showing.

"As wise as your nana is," Sierra said haughtily, "she doesn't seem to have taught you how to talk to a lady."

"Ooo. You better watch out, there," Diablo said with an exaggerated headshake. "Bringing my nana into things? Them's fightin' words."

Unintimidated, Sierra challenged, "So you're telling me your nana would be just fine with you mocking a guest?"

Laughing at how specifically she'd framed the situation, Diablo raised his palms. "I would never say such."

"Just like I thought, then," she said, one eyebrow lifted and her chin angled up.

Diablo sighed. "It's true my nana raised me to be a gentleman. Unfortunately, like so many of her generously imparted lessons, it just went in one ear and out the other. The poor woman ought to qualify for sainthood by this point."

Trying to maintain her hold on indignant while at the same time clearly resisting the urge to laugh meant that the strangled sound that came out of Sierra landed somewhere between a choke and a hiss.

Offering her his can, he said, "Whoa, there, killer. Settle down. We wouldn't want you to choke on your admiration. Yes, my nana is a saint, but she's not here right now, and I'm just a regular sinner. Unless you've got some other reasons for getting all choked up in my presence?" Waggling his eyebrows at her made the statement all the more ridiculous.

Still laughing, but settling down enough to roll her eyes, Sierra said, "None at all, thank you. And I'm sure you were a handful alright."

Looking away for a moment, he was serious when he said, "You can only imagine."

"Tell me about it," she challenged.

And whether or not it was the confidence in her—the utter expectation that her question would be answered—or simply because it was her doing the asking, Diablo did the rare thing of answering.

"My childhood was wonderful," he began, "in a lot of ways. It was also lonely and relentless. My nana is one of those people whose love is kind of scary—like the kind that would actually hurt something or someone in your defense. It's great to be loved like that, but fierce, as well. She's the kind of person who will always go to bat for you, but also the kind of person who wouldn't hesitate to beat your ass with that bat if she thought you were out of line."

Sierra smiled at that. "Why do I get the sense that you needed the latter more often than the former?"

Narrowing his eyes, he side-eyed her. "Now, what kind of thing to say is that?" Diablo said, bringing a palm to his chest in mock offense. "I have never been anything but easy and agreeable."

"And I'm the Queen of England," she said with a snort.

"Believe me, queenie. There has never been any doubt as to your royalty," he said without missing a beat.

Laughing again, Sierra said, "Tell me the truth, though. What was your childhood like?"

Diablo was surprised to find that he still had the urge to do just that. "From the beginning, it was just Nana and me," he said.

"What's the full story with your mom and dad?" she asked, apparently unhindered by the typical boundaries that stopped people from asking blunt personal questions like that.

He appreciated it.

For all that it was her job to masquerade and perform, Sierra was also straightforward.

Shaking his head, Diablo said, "My mother left me at my nana's doorstep a few days after I was born."

"Wait. Are you serious?" she interrupted, and he didn't blame her for the genuine confusion in her voice.

Abandoned infants were newsworthy because they were rare.

His own story, however, had barely caused a blip.

He had not been abandoned in any dramatic place, such as in a dumpster, or a fire department or a public restroom.

He had simply been left on his grandmother's doorstep in a cardboard box lined with an assortment of used clothing and a note.

"I am." His answer was simple because the truth usually was.

"You were an abandoned baby?" she asked again, clearly still unable to wrap her head around the concept.

It always took people a few moments for the information to settle in.

Like so much about his being, his origin story was confrontational without any effort on his part.

Hearing it reminded people that the things they took for granted were not as solid and unchanging as they'd been led to believe. His every anecdote, it seemed, served as an uncomfortable reminder that there was still a lot of work to do before anyone could truly call theirs a just and free country.

He was a hard pill to swallow, like the fact that singularities existed, imaginary numbers were real and sometimes mothers willingly gave up their children.

With the support of the small family he'd managed to hold on to, riding bulls and thousands of dollars of therapy, Diablo had come to terms with most of the facets of his life story. He understood it was harder for people who were just beginning to hear it.

He believed that it had not been a lack of love that led his mother to leave him on a doorstep, but that, after carrying him to term and delivering him, against all odds healthy and hale, her giving him up had possibly been the most unselfish act of love that she had ever performed.

He had had time to overcome the belief that it was something inherently lacking in him that had led to his abandonment.

When people first heard the story, however, they had to go through all of those thoughts for the first time.

Even the fact that she had named him Diablo was a demon with which he had wrestled and overcome. He could now find compassion for her through it. She had truly believed that it was because she was named Angela, she had been destined to fail. How could she live up to the angels?

"I was," he repeated after he'd given her enough time for the reality to sink in. And when she immediately followed up with a version of both the most common and most painful question that people had in response to the revelation, he was prepared for that, too.

"How can that be?" she asked, disbelief and confusion warring in her eyes.

Proud that the question stung only so much that he had to respond first with a single, measured blink before he answered her, he continued, again with more generosity of words and vulnerability than he was typically willing to share. "While I've asked that same question myself probably a billion times, with little exaggeration, the only entirely true answer I can come to is that I will never really know."

Though he shouldn't have been surprised by it, for the nth time of the day, she displayed far greater daring than the average individual with her next question.

"But what do you believe?" she pressed.

He answered because it wasn't morbid curiosity or clueless insensitivity that he sensed beneath the question, but an alertness to what lay unspoken in his words.

Sensing that, however, didn't make the words any easier to get out. His voice was hoarse as it wrestled and maneuvered around the jagged and salted edges of his truth. "I believe she did it because she knew that it was what was best for me. I think she was trying to be the best mother she could be, and that that meant giving me a chance to have something better than what she could give."

"Oh, Diablo," she whispered again, his name in her

voice becoming a single bleeding utterance, dripping with all of the emotions she felt on his behalf.

The heavy stickiness of it, the way it sought to wrap around him and soothe him, was too much, so he chased it away by taking another swig of his beer.

He focused his attention on the cold trail of liquid as it traveled down to his gullet, anchoring himself in its comfort, which was both impersonal and cool. The way he liked it.

Picking up the story once again, his voice took on a brusque quality that even he could hear.

Rather than soften or slow it, though, he simply hurried it on in an effort to put an end to the sob story and chase away some of the inevitable heaviness that this part always brought with it.

"The note she included had my name on it and asked my nana to take care of me. It gave her my birthday and an apology, and no contact information. No one saw her leaving me, so there was no one to say which direction she had taken when she'd gone. With no leads and a willing relative at the ready, there wasn't much effort put into finding her. Nana just got a second job to keep her house while covering the expenses of raising me and we did the best we could."

"That must have been so hard," Sierra said quietly, her eyes glistening, if not quite welling up with tears.

He looked away to swallow, nodding as he evaded the penetration of her empathy.

If he couldn't stop it, it would settle over him like something soft and warm. "I can't imagine how tired she must have been."

"And for you, too," Sierra said. "All the not knowing. Did you ever learn what happened to your mother?"

He gave a firm shake of the head. She was coming awfully close to the parts that wouldn't heal with her questions now. "We never heard from her again. She didn't leave any clues to who my father was, other than the fact that I must take after him."

She frowned. "How do you know that?"

"I studied every photo Nana had of my mother, could probably draw them from memory still, if I had been blessed with any drawing skills. I've got her eyes, but that's it."

Shaking her head in disbelief, Sierra asked again, "How could she do it?"

"Nana said life had always been hard for my mother after her father had left them. Nana worked all the time to get them a house and to put food on the table and clothes on her back, but that left my mother by herself a lot. With Nana always working and her daddy gone, my mother was that kind of lonely and hungry for male attention girl that's a beacon for predators. In her case, it was a recipe for the usual things."

Bringing her hands back to his shoulders, Sierra returned to massaging as she spoke, her movements more gentle this time, as she said with sympathy, "Some souls just can't handle being on their own."

In another era of his life, he might have shut her out or said something cutting, but now he merely closed his eyes and nodded, saying, "She couldn't," while tendrils of tingling sensation followed her fingers wherever they went.

As usual, he had brought the mood down with his tale of woe.

Seeking to remedy the matter, to lift her back to highs at least equal to that of the night's show and the world's greatest sandwich, he asked her about her family, sensing that, unlike himself, her memories and stories would be no minefield but the kind of bright prairie that no one need fear to tread.

"What about you, queenie?" Diablo asked, tilting his head to one side to give her better access to the place where skull and neck connected. "What was it like to grow up as the middle daughter of three in a pageanting family in Pensacola?"

What surprised him most about the question, he realized, was the fact that he really wanted to know its answer. Sierra made him curious about what it might have been like to grow up in the middle class—the strata where parents had time and resources to coordinate and attend every after-school activity, and bake things for the PTO and go on family vacations—for the first time.

"It was about as basic as you're imagining, I'd guess," she said, her hands keeping steady in their kneading. "My mom stayed home, always busy with three daughters in pageants. My dad runs a locksmithing business that he started with his brothers after moving to the United States. It was small at first, just him and my uncles and their one van, but now it's been years since any of them went out on a call themselves. He said he had to become successful because it wasn't cheap to have three pageant girls, nor to send two of them to college."

Noting that it wasn't the first time she had mentioned the subject, he asked, "Why didn't you go?"

She shrugged and the motion rippled down into her arms until he felt the pressure of it in her hands on his shoulders. "I didn't want to miss a second of what I knew would be my prime queening years. Even at the junior level, you are always so aware of the ticking clock. Most of us can only participate until we're twenty-four, twenty-five years old, at a maximum. That's the hard cutoff, no matter how many years you've put in on the job, and I couldn't fathom sacrificing two to four years at the peak of it to go to college, especially when I was doing so well at the time."

"As opposed to how terribly you're doing now, having become the unofficial face of the sport in its television renaissance at least a couple years past, forgive me, that twenty-five-year age limit." He was willing to be audacious for the sake of the truth sometimes, and this was one of them. She deserved credit for what she'd accomplished, even if he got the impression that it didn't satisfy her as much as she'd always thought it would.

Chuckling softly, she countered, "Whoever said anything about doing badly? I'm not humble. No rodeo queen has been able to accomplish what I have. I broke through a barrier and I'm proud of that. But back then I didn't know the greatness I would go on to achieve. Back then I was merely a bundle of dread at the impending end of something I wasn't ready to let go of and desperate to hang on to every minute. It's hard to focus on school with that kind of mind-set. And then I aged out of that, too," she added with a laugh.

Snorting, he said, "You can't age out of college."

Brushing him off, she said, "Of course you can. And besides, I broke the barrier, remember? I didn't have to give up the dream. I'm still here living it."

"With no end in sight," he observed.

"No end in sight," she repeated, a note of something that wasn't pleasure in her voice. He would have been hard-pressed, though, to say if it was sadness, regret, or simply exhaustion.

Shrugging again, she finished with, "So no college for me."

"You sound disappointed about it even though it sounds like you made the right decision for yourself," he pointed out.

Her fingers stilled. "When I was younger, I told myself I would go after rodeo was done with me..."

"But rodeo never got done with you," he finished for her, and she nodded.

"And instead, you became the most famous rodeo queen the Wild West has ever seen."

"Instead, I became the most famous rodeo queen the world has ever seen," she agreed, the uncertainty in her tone shored up.

Bolstering her further he added, "And you happen to be Latina. I'm sure there's more than a few little girls out there who want to grow up and be just like you."

"I am, though most of them forget all about both me and rodeo by the time they get to middle school."

"But not all of them, and it only takes a few. Hell, there's only room for a few. That makes you a pioneer of sorts, finding success in places most brown girls never go and leading the way. Plus, you ride upside down on horses. What's college in comparison to all of that?"

Laughing, though rather than being reassured, the thread of doubt seemed to have returned to her voice, she said lightly, "What's college, indeed?"

Hearing the waver in her tone, he shook his head, bringing his palm up to still the movement of her hand on his shoulder before he turned to face her. "Don't sell yourself short, Sierra. You're better than you think—just the way you are. Like you said earlier. You can be pretty and powerful, whenever and wherever you want."

CHAPTER TEN

SIERRA WANTED TO hate that he'd used her words against her, but irritation couldn't stand in the face of the heat that radiated from the center of her chest at hearing how he had taken them in and respected them enough to find the deeper meaning in them.

It was…romantic.

Like the night in the hotel room had been, and their walk in New Orleans had been, and the late-night sandwich and beer that she should never have stopped by and refused to stop knocking for had been. The way he listened to the things she said, heard what was on the surface of them as well as listening for what lay beneath, was romantic.

And just like she'd known from the beginning, that made it dangerous.

She had no business being in his RV.

But just like her academic dreams, it was too late to do anything about it.

She was here, and worse, she was happy about it.

Her belly was full, her mind at ease and her companion both gorgeous and intelligent.

It was no wonder that she had stayed longer than she was supposed to.

And now they were sitting too close together, both of them dressed too casually.

The beer pleasantly buzzed in her veins and he had just called her pretty and powerful and she realized she wanted to kiss him.

She had soothed the knots out of his muscles, in the process affirming to herself that she was both proud of his ride and concerned for his suffering, and now, as if they were something to each other, she wanted him to soothe and reassure her with his lips.

But in reality, they were nothing to each other.

Or, if not nothing, at best barely friends—certainly not a man and woman with the right and freedom to press their lips together and close their eyes.

She needed to get the hell out of here.

"I should get going," she said with a swallow.

Disappointment flashed across his eyes, before being chased away by shrewdness. "You should never have come by in the first place. Now that the *shoulds* are out of the way, what are you going to do?" he challenged.

He was a challenger and pusher. He was the kind of man who drew out either the best or the worst from everything and everyone around him, and she suspected he knew no other way to be.

But what did it mean that she didn't want him to be any different? What did it mean that she liked him just the way he was?

She appreciated that he was bold enough to just say what he really thought, and that he respected those he loved enough to trust they could handle whatever unvarnished truth he had to dish out at any given moment.

She liked it as much as she liked that his sarcasm and wit hid a spirit that was attentive to the most minute detail and nurturing enough to speak up when necessary.

She liked his integrity, and that he drew and demanded the same quality from her.

"I'm going to kiss you," she said, reveling in the fact that his eyes widened in surprise.

"Is that a good idea?" he asked after a beat, and because the blood was high and rushing in her veins, she could appreciate his unwillingness to have her with anything less than absolute honesty.

"No," she said, leaning closer, "but neither is riding upside down on a horse."

And then she pressed her lips against his.

His full lips were soft, warm and firm—an irresistible erotic combination that lured her to go deeper.

As if he could read the trail of her thoughts, he opened for her, allowing her to explore his mouth according to her desire, all the time beautifully responsive to her lead.

He tasted like Cuba at sixteen—salty but also sweet, intoxicating, like drinking on the beach with her cousins, a world away from everything ordinary but somehow *home* nonetheless.

She brought her hands to his face, her fingers tracing his jaw, rejoicing in the texture of his neatly trimmed facial hair, even as she basked in the sensation of touching him this way.

They were irrefutably in the realm of desire and attraction with the danger of taking things too far clear and present.

He let her have her way with him like that for a time, following her lead with the same easy self-satisfaction that both infuriated and intrigued her, kissing deeply when she went deep, teasing and flirting with her lips when she pulled back, catching her bottom lip between his teeth tantalizingly, his mouth following hers according to her desire.

His lips were soft and sensual but steel beneath. His hands, coming to her body to roam like rough silk, branded her through her clothing like delectable irons.

His scent—leather and pine and cocoa—threatened to overwhelm her, nearly carrying her away on a dangerous sensual wave.

And when she could handle it no more, he took over the reins.

One hand reached around her head to clasp the back of her skull, pulling her into his kiss, while the other came around to support the small of her back, as she arched her breasts up to press against his chest.

The grip of those rough hands, a grip that'd only hours earlier been the only thing standing between him and being thrown by a thousand-plus-pound beast, was gentle, butterfly light, as it traveled down the back of her head and neck and along her jaw to tilt her face upward and deepen their kiss.

He captivated her with his lips, no longer content to follow but demanding her full surrender, daring her tongue into a dance with his.

He was masterful with his mouth, directing her where he wanted them to go, leading her down avenues that left her blood rushing and body pulsing to a rhythm that didn't originate in her heart—until she found herself straining toward him, arms clinging to his upper body, fingers twisting and tugging at his shirt.

If she'd been carried away by the sensation and power of kissing him before, now she was submerged in the flood of being kissed by him.

His body was large and warm, but he could have

been rangy and slight and it wouldn't have lessened the energy he exuded now. This was expertise, utterly assured and confident—a thrumming aura of power that clung to him in the arena and, she imagined, in the courtroom.

It struck her that there likely wasn't a force on earth that was truly a match for Diablo Sosa.

It crossed her mind that straddling all that power would not be unlike riding a bull and she adjusted her position, rearranging her body ever closer to the reality of it, testing and pushing the boundaries in eagerness for what would be an entirely private performance.

He was a hurricane, and like the good Florida girl she was, she was well aware of the fact that the only thing to do in the face of a hurricane was to batten the hatches, buckle down and hang on.

Not throwing caution to the wind so much as ripping it to shreds with gale-force winds, she pressed into his kiss, surprising herself with a moan.

Caution was no longer any match for what blazed between them.

No one had seen her creeping to his place, and they wouldn't have recognized her anyway if they had. The risk was taken, so why hold back on the reward?

He smiled into her mouth and it knocked the wind out of her.

Tasting his joy, wicked and playful, was easily one of the most erotic experiences of her life.

Finally, she gave in to the urge to rest her weight on him, her body not collapsing so much as melting into his, with a sigh.

He held her close, arms wrapping around to squeeze her in an embrace that was equal parts comforting and arousing, enveloping her even more in everything that was him—a tidal wave she was eager to be lost to.

And then he stopped.

Abruptly set adrift, it took her mind precious minutes to reset, minutes he spent gently rearranging their bodies, so they once again sat separately on the bench.

He'd come to his senses in the nick of time. The bastard.

Heat and irritation warred with embarrassment throughout her system. Here, at least, was a sensory experience she was familiar with. As a middle sister, she was well practiced with the experience of irritation and anger mingling with shame and embarrassment.

Narrowing her eyes, she opened her mouth, but he beat her to speaking.

"As good as you taste, queenie, I don't think now is a good time to take this any further," he said, his expression serious. "Now, don't get me wrong," he said, "after today I'm tempted enough myself that if you want to revisit this after some thought by the light of day, I'm your man. But let's not let it be said that the sandwiches carried us away. If we're going to do this, it's because we've thought it through."

She was grateful he told a joke because it gave her a reason to force a laugh, releasing at least some of the tangled tension and pressure trapped inside her.

He was right, of course, and it was thoughtful and measured of him to even pump the brakes and point it out.

Honestly, she should have been the one to point it out.

But his being a gentleman didn't seem to matter when it came to the mortifying sting in her eyes.

And if she should have never stopped by in the first

place, then she most definitely should be on her way back to her own vehicle now.

"It's way past my bedtime, that's for sure. I'm going to sneak on back," she said once she'd gotten a better handle on things. She didn't use the word *should*. She had learned her lesson on that already tonight, and though she couldn't seem to stop herself from playing with fire with him, she was normally pretty quick on the uptick.

"Thanks again for the sandwich," she added, standing and adjusting her clothes.

Shaking his head, he said, "No problem. It was my pleasure."

The words hit the air rather bluntly, but Sierra suspected that had been his intention. It wasn't her, he was saying, it was her job.

She'd heard that one before.

And, really, she appreciated his attentiveness to that. She did.

Or maybe she would. Tomorrow.

Right now she wished she were already back in her own RV.

As it was, at least her walk of shame to his front door was only going to be a few steps. Turning once she got there, she gave an odd little side wave and said, "See you around."

Eyeing her, his eyebrows drawn low and slightly together above, he gave a single nod. "See you around, Sierra."

And then she hurried outside, shutting the door quietly behind her.

A glance at her phone told her it was past three-thirty

in the morning now, and all of a sudden she could feel it—along with the rest of her overcrowded day.

She'd toured New Orleans, ridden her heart out, MC'd a great opening night and enjoyed a late-night clandestine sandwich with a cowboy.

She'd also come on to a coworker in violation of her contract. And she'd thought she'd grown too old for firsts.

Closing her eyes as she crossed the last of the distance between the competitors' parking area and hers, she sighed and unlocked her door.

It wasn't only well past her bedtime, it was well past her time overall.

She was too old to be sneaking around parking lots and cramped quarters late at night and for standing on top of horses. And she was too old to be scuttling away from a man she wanted because her job said she had to be a perpetual virgin.

She was grown and, at the moment, tired of it all.

She could do what she wanted.

But that wasn't true.

And if tonight had proven anything, it proved that she needed to shape up and get a little more careful about Diablo Sosa if she didn't want to see her long and illustrious career go up in flames.

She had no business getting involved with Diablo Sosa—not his rides, not his wit, not his suits, not his sandwiches and certainly not his kisses.

So she would keep her distance moving forward, and everything would settle down just fine. Decision made, she smiled. It was only a matter of time before things snapped back to normal and Diablo was nothing more than another *Closed Circuit* contestant to her.

THE NEXT MORNING the caravan hit the road at 9:00 a.m., which was painfully early to the opinion of Sierra's still fuzzy and tired eyes but actually counted as sleeping in to the rodeo queen.

Hauling horses and ass around the country required a lot of early mornings.

Because of the late night, coupled with the wake-up time required if she wanted to hit the road looking like a rodeo queen and not a long-haul trucker, she had gone with her most low-maintenance look for the day.

Blue jeans, brown boots and belt, a red-and-white gingham Western shirt with mother-of-pearl snaps and red piping, a low and curled ponytail and her white hat with the *Closed Circuit* crown. She looked simple and sweet enough to take back home to mama.

Perfect for hiding the fact that her compression garments were holding in a bit more bloat than usual this morning because of her late-night sandwich and beer. Her concealer and Nude Attitude lipstick hid the dark circles under her eyes and the impressions of Diablo's kiss.

They set out beneath an overcast Louisiana sky, on their way to Miami, another town, and another show.

By the light of day—hidden though it was behind hot, wet clouds—what Diablo'd said the night before now seemed at least equal in importance to the pulling back itself.

Unlike the night in the hotel, he hadn't closed the door on the possibility. No, this time he'd said, *If you want to... I'm your man.*

I'm your man.

If she said go, Diablo could be her man. They'd have

to sneak and hide and never let anyone know, but they could have each other.

The idea had never been appealing before. Why take on the risk and put in all the effort for a shadow of a relationship? No man had ever been worth endangering her career before.

A rodeo queen, particularly an active one, was to be a sexless maiden—utterly removed from the carnal pleasures of life in her dedication to horses and rodeo.

She'd followed that maxim to the T in her career, dating, and unsatisfyingly at that, only during the brief interim periods she'd had between crowns.

Yes, she'd seen countless queens balance and navigate their clandestine relationships *and* maintain their careers, but she'd seen just as many go down in shame.

And this wasn't just any rodeo. It was *The Closed Circuit*, the rodeo unlike any other.

It was one thing to pull off a secret relationship when her rodeo duties were confined to individual events that were spaced apart by business days and seasons, rather than round-the-clock duty broken up by short blocks of time off and long stretches of road.

Meeting with Diablo would require a level of creativity and recklessness unlike anything she'd ever attempted.

Was she willing to deal with all that resistance and aggravation to have him? Was it worth it?

Having tossed and turned for a few hours in a poor impression of sleep, her mind returning again and again to the sensation of Diablo's hands on her body, she acknowledged that she didn't have much of a choice. Even now, halfway through the longest drive of the tour, she remained completely unable to get Diablo off her mind.

At this point it was a matter of either nurturing a real thing, or walking away completely. When it came to Diablo, she realized, she had neither the time nor the patience for a crush. It wasn't enough to watch him from a safe distance while toeing the line of her job. She wanted the mess and the risk of going all the way with him or she wanted to leave him alone. And since her mind wasn't willing to do the latter, it only left her with the former.

"Message Diablo," she said out loud, and the RV smart dashboard came to bright, back-lit life.

"What message would you like me to send to Diablo?" the cheerful computerized voice asked in response.

Sierra hesitated, strangely shy and a little paranoid, to have a witness in her exchange with Diablo—even just an electronic witness. What if she accidentally messaged the wrong person?

It would be all too easy to make a mistake like that.

Second-guessing herself, she hesitated.

Was the reward worth the risk?

But Diablo understood rodeo. And he understood contracts, and the expectations of her job. He understood all of that, and he'd said he was her man, if she wanted.

Diablo was a grown-ass man.

And not just a grown-ass man but a gorgeous one with a razor-sharp mind who knew how to ride and didn't seem to mind a powerful woman with her own interests.

When she put it that way, pursuing him didn't seem so much like taking a complicated risk, as it did being pragmatic. Diablo knew the score and was willing anyway. Diablo was a safe bet.

"Say, 'after some thought, I would like to revisit,'" Sierra instructed the RV smart assistant.

"Message ready. Shall I send?" the automated voice asked, flashing the text across the display screen in the center console.

Reading it, seeing her words reflected back at her in bold white typeface and large print, brought heat to Sierra's cheeks, and her stomach did a somersault.

What would it do to him?

What would he think when he read it?

What if the light of day had not brought him renewed interest, but regret?

There was only one way to find out.

"Send," she said, and the word had a period at the end.

Moments later the animated voice returned. "Diablo has sent you a message. Would you like to see it?"

Realizing her palms were clammy, Sierra laughed at herself. It wasn't the first time in her life that she had expressed interest in someone, so why did she feel like she was thirteen years old all over again?

"Yes, please," she said, making a token effort, at least, to sound normal and nonchalant about it—even if there was no one but an automated assistant around to hear her.

Where're we meeting? his message said.

Sierra's heart rate increased and she realized she was squeezing the wheel a little too hard and grinning maniacally.

Unwinding her fingers, grateful for the cushioned grip of the wheel, she pursed her lips, exhaling through them to steady herself.

Then she said, "Reply, 'Crandon Park, carousel. I planned a hike for the day off.'"

"Reply ready. Shall I send?" the RV asked.

Nodding, Sierra said, "Send."

The tour was headed to Miami, where the first challenge show would take place.

After the fiasco that had been the final teams coming in from the first overnight challenge last season, the showrunners had reconceptualized the challenges into events that could be presented in a single night like regular shows on the tour. This season the challenge shows were scheduled to take place between each rough-stock presentation, and the whole thing was a lot more streamlined.

"Message received from Diablo," the RV chimed.

"Display it," Sierra said quickly.

It read: I assume this hike is well reviewed?

Laughing out loud, Sierra said, "Reply, 'in fact, it is. Remember what I told you about wasting my time,'" and the RV did just that.

His next message came back quickly after hers went out, and she snorted reading it.

My hourly rates are exorbitant, but rest assured, I have the customer satisfaction ratings to back them up.

If his kiss from the night before had been any indication, she was willing to bet that he did.

She wondered if there was anything that Diablo wasn't good at. Her sneaking suspicion was that the answer was no.

As if the proverbial seal had been broken, accepting that something between them was going to happen unleashed her mental floodgates, and the cascade of impressions and thoughts about Diablo, which she had been repressing and denying, washed over her in full force.

The way he'd looked the first night he'd sauntered over to her, cocky and confident at the first season finale.

His one-sided grins, his unflinching integrity, his over-the-top physical perfection.

The way he made her feel beautiful in contexts in which she had only ever felt underdressed and plain before.

It stood out, she realized as she drove, that things with Diablo tended to be flipped.

Being in his presence in rodeo-queen attire had a way of making her conscious of the costume-like nature of it all.

Without ever saying as much, he drew her attention to the notion that regardless of the fact that it was all planned and intentional, and that she looked damn good, it was also true that she was, when it came down to it, overdressed and promoting, among other things, a few ideas that she didn't agree with.

He reminded her of the kinds of things that she had done a good job of ignoring and pushing to the back of her mind, or out of it entirely, because they didn't match with her idea of what she saw as an evolving rodeo world. Without trying to, he reminded her that her rodeo experience hadn't been all crowns and congratulations, but that it had also included smiling and conforming in the face of sexism and colorism, as well as retreating over and over again to the idea that—without effort or discussion—the prejudice and problems of rodeo were always "getting better."

Diablo made her see how naive that was.

For years she had said, with complete honesty, that she felt more like herself dressed up as a rodeo queen than she did at home on the couch, but when she was with Diablo, it was in her couch clothes that she felt most legitimate.

But if he flipped the world on its head, he also presented a backward picture himself.

He was a cowboy beneath his suits and dry swagger— through and through.

She might have missed it initially, but she knew cowboys well enough to know that he was not merely a weekend dabbler, but grit personified, encased and hardened into pearl.

CHAPTER ELEVEN

ALTHOUGH THE FOOD tonight was delicious, Diablo was pretty sure that he had gotten the short stick by participating in the second season of *The Closed Circuit*, as opposed to the first.

Whereas golden boy AJ had slipped in while things were fast and loose and made out like a bandit, Diablo was dealing with the fact that the showrunners had learned a thing or two from their previous mistakes.

For example, during AJ's season, the contestants' social excursion had taken place at an actual bar. It had been a particularly popular episode because the drama had been high and the sexual tension between AJ and Lil palpable, but the lighting bad enough that it had also become somewhat of a meme.

For the second season the show had decided to host a well-lit cookout. With assigned seating.

Having been assigned to the same campfire as Dillon Oliver, quality food notwithstanding, he would have much preferred a dimly lit bar with stale food, an out-of-date jukebox and weak drinks.

At least then they would've gotten to pick their own seat.

The *Closed Circuit* caravan had stopped for the night at a campground located between New Orleans and Miami, and in the group picnic area, the greenies had created one of the largest sets for the show that Diablo had seen.

This season they had a real budget, and it was clear they weren't pulling any punches when it came to spending it.

In the picnic area, lit up like it was an LA set, were three enormous chuck wagon replicas, each one laden with heaping piles of food. Dishes were laid out on every available surface, from ledges and stands, to the wooden prop-leaf tables that jutted out from the wagons. Each dish was served in some form of speckled blue tin, from plates to bowls to pitchers—with the exception of what awaited them in gleaming cast-iron pans and stew pots.

Large tin percolators full of what Diablo assumed would be stiff black coffee rested beside piles of folded red-and-white gingham napkins, which themselves were piled next to Mason jars filled with silverware and striped paper straws.

Fanning out in front of each of the chuck wagons were small campfires, the bulk of them set up with five rustic folding stools each. At the largest fire, however, there were just three stools.

The whole thing looked more like a Southern bride's chic cowboy wedding reception than the place where a bunch of bull riders were going to tuck into some chow for the night, but it was clear enough that the latter was what *The Closed Circuit* was going for.

Like AJ and Lil's rousing evening at the honky tonk during the first season, Diablo assumed that each of the intimate fireside chats would be filmed from excellent angles and broadcast for the delight of the fans.

Judging from the enormous silver buckets filled with

ice and plenty of beer, it didn't take a lot to guess the variable the showrunners considered essential for excellent televisual drama.

Diablo, however, did not intend to be the one to provide that drama.

Not only because he was riding as a representative of CityBoyz, but also because he was the type of man who liked to keep his mistakes private, would he take it easy for the evening.

Drinking with Sierra was one thing. Drinking with his competition an entirely different one.

He didn't trust them and he had no interest in them, with the exception of Julio. There was no reason to relax in their company.

When all the contestants were tidily organized at their assigned fires, they were encouraged to eat and drink to their fill, and to just go ahead and forget the cameras were even rolling.

Tonight everybody was friends, and anything could be edited later, if necessary.

Diablo would buy that as soon as he did oceanfront property in Dallas.

The bulk of the contestants appeared happy to do just that, though, including Dillon, who jumped into one of the lines around the chuck wagons and shortly thereafter returned with a mountain of food on his plate. Another second later he was cracking open a cold one with exaggerated enjoyment.

Like the other contestants in the lower twenty-two, Dillon ate and drank as if his masculinity was measured by how fast and much he consumed, and by how many beers he could knock back before losing control. It wasn't surprising they should behave so. It wasn't that far off from what went on in the arena. Whoever held on the longest and looked the best doing it took home the prize.

Whatever they were doing, these were men who wanted the world to know they were the best at it.

They just didn't realize there was a difference between showing and telling. Jostling for your place at the front of the food line was telling. Standing secure knowing that you had everything you needed to eat was showing.

Diablo and Tio Julio followed behind the rest of the cowboys at a more sedate, self-respecting pace, rounding out the end of the line at the same chuck wagon, filling their plates without hurry before making their slow way to the fire where Dillon was already gorging himself.

With Sierra's message fresh in his mind, Diablo would have much preferred to eat alone in his rig rather than share a meal with Dillon. Or, better still, he'd like to share another private meal with Sierra.

He hadn't expected her message earlier. He'd expected it even less than he had that moment when she had baldly admitted that she wanted to kiss him.

It astounded him that she somehow managed to meet every expectation of what a rodeo queen was supposed to be and yet she could still be surprising.

He'd stopped them in his RV because he didn't believe in stumbling into things when it came to physical intimacy. To his way of thinking, sex wasn't sex without clear acknowledgment of desire, absolute permission and knowledge of what was being gotten into on both, or all, parts.

He wasn't interested in sweeping a woman away.

He was interested in blowing the mind of the woman he wanted.

"Awful quiet over there, college boy," Dillon said, breaking into Diablo's pleasant thoughts with a classic lack of style and grace.

Diablo slowly lifted his face from where he had been staring absently into the flames to look Dillon in the eye, as usual taking too long about the whole thing, before waiting yet another beat to say, "What can I say? Guess I just keep my own counsel."

Dillon frowned in response, having been out-cowboyed after only one move.

Dillon talked too much to lay claim to the strong, silent cowboy archetype—having now established a pattern in the group of being a shit-stirrer—so he'd clearly decided to just go ahead and dig in on being an aggressive ass.

After a moment, Dillon smirked, saying, "And here I thought lawyers were known for always having something smart to say." Clearly, he was feeling clever tonight.

Taking a bite of his food and chewing it slowly before responding, Diablo said lazily, "The best lawyers let the dumbasses do the talking. Why waste your breath when self-incrimination is so much easier?"

It was really too bad that Dillon had managed to hold on to his spot in the top three.

Everything would have been so much more pleasant for Diablo had Dillon been relegated after the first round.

Even more outclassed in their exchange than he was in the arena, however, Dillon didn't know when to quit. Narrowing his eyes at Diablo, he took a bite of the biscuit in his hand before redirecting his attitude toward Julio.

"And what about you, old man? What do you think about lawyers? You ever meet with one yourself, or'd you just swim the rio, Tio?"

Diablo bristled at the insult on the other man's behalf, but held back from getting involved.

Julio had made it more than clear the last time that he needed no assistance in dealing with the likes of Dillon Oliver.

And, indeed, Julio's indeterminate grunt could have been considered a response—if someone wanted to stretch the definition of the word.

When Julio then took a bite of food and started chewing, as if the matter was settled, Diablo had to hold back his laugh.

"What's that, hombre? I didn't catch it," Dillon said, leaning forward to add, "You ever hire a lawyer, is what I asked," before sitting back again and making a dismissive noise in the back of his throat. "Of course you've never hired a lawyer. You guys never do it the right way."

Sitting across the fire from Julio, rather than to his left, as Dillon was, Diablo was the only one who saw the older man's eyes narrow slightly.

Keeping his voice even, Julio cracked a small smile, offering a nod in Diablo's direction as he said, "My father told me that everyone needs a good attorney and a good mechanic at least once in their life."

Dillon sneered with a scoff. "An honest man doesn't need a lawyer."

Smiling with his teeth while his stare remained hard,

Diablo said, "Then you must have made the acquaintance of one a time or two?"

"You suggesting I'm a liar?" Dillon's volume rose as he spoke, his body tensing, though he remained seated.

Happy to facilitate the other man's apparently endless drive to reveal himself, Diablo's grin widened.

And that was when Sierra decided to stop by their fire.

Like a teenager, Diablo's throat dried as she settled in beside Julio, a new, much more welcome kind of tension replacing the fireside conflict.

For the picnic, she had dressed like the rodeo-queen version of Mary Ann from *Gilligan's Island*, her gingham Western shirt and blue jeans as all-American as the apple pie that awaited them for dessert.

He had never been one to go for the girl-next-door thing, but as was often turning out to be the case when Sierra was involved, he was suddenly open to reconsidering. She was a breath of fresh air, blowing away the building anger at their campfire, and he thought she knew as much.

"And how are our top three faring with the fare?" she said brightly, making flirty eye contact with each of the three men, landing on Diablo last and lingering only long enough to make sure he knew she meant it, then moving cheerfully on without giving any of them a chance to answer. "Are y'all ready for the next show?"

Dillon was quick to respond; his antagonistic greaser persona disappeared and, in its place, an oozing cowboy on the prowl. "Every shot to upset the order at the top is a positive in my mind," he said with a grin. "When you're good enough, a little competition doesn't scare you."

Hackles rising in his neck as he watched Dillon lay it on for Sierra, Diablo said, "Good to see such confidence in third place."

Eyes darting like lightning back to Diablo, Dillon glared. "Like I said, when you're a professional a little stiff competition at your heels only makes you stronger. But don't worry if you're feeling shaky in your spot, lawman. The pace of this level of competition takes some getting used to."

As usual, Dillon's magnificent wit filled Diablo with the urge to yawn.

But instead, he said lazily, "You're right about that. I definitely didn't expect to increase my lead so much and so quickly. And how 'bout you, Tio?" he said, respect entering his voice only when he turned to Julio. "Did you expect to leave the rest of us in the dust so quick?"

"Just happy to prove that age comes before beauty," Julio said with a smile of friendly deflection. He had a way of ending conversations without seeming to that Diablo found impressive.

Diablo had prosecuted a number of people who could have learned a few things from Julio.

"Well, let it be a lesson to all of rodeo," Sierra said, "because you get out there and prove that getting old isn't for sissies every darn time!"

Smiling in her direction, Tio Julio said, "My back certainly agrees." And everyone around the fire— Diablo, Sierra and the filming crew that followed her around—laughed at the rodeo humor, except for Dillon.

With the shared joke, the last of the aggression that had lingered in the air around their fire dissipated, replaced with an energy of friendly banter and competition—at least for everyone outside Dillon.

And Diablo was present enough to the situation to know that it wasn't by chance that it had happened.

It was Sierra's doing.

He was grateful, even as he was once again a little disappointed in the missed opportunity to just get the Dillon situation dealt with once and for all. Dillon was the kind of problem that should be nipped in the bud quickly—a boil best lanced quickly—otherwise he'd only fester.

It was obvious to Diablo that Dillon wouldn't let up on either Julio or himself until one of three things happened: he took the number-one spot, he got his ass beat or somebody got seriously hurt.

Option two was obviously the best solution for everyone involved.

It really would have been nice to simply take care of things and be done with it.

The cameras had caught and recorded every inflammatory word the man had uttered. Diablo and Julio were sure to have garnered the sympathy of the bulk of the audience.

But it had been sweet of Sierra to jump in and keep things from going in a direction that might not have reflected well on him, and he sensed that that had been her intention from the moment she'd joined their little group.

He was here to make CityBoyz look good, and she seemed earnest in her effort to support him in that.

Despite the immense artifice of her life, what made her a champion was actually her authenticity. She genuinely loved rodeo. She cared about nurturing the next generation of athletes and fans.

"So what do y'all get up to when not chasing around

big shiny buckles?" she asked, transitioning their conversation into personality-quiz territory rather than anything touchy, further cementing Diablo's assessment that she'd come to their fire with a peacekeeping agenda, rather than the drama-stirring angle the producers might prefer.

Dillon, as usual, rushed in to answer her first. "Seeing as how my mother was paralyzed from the waist down just two weeks after I won my first professional prize, my career has been tied to her and my sister from the beginning. It's always been a tough act to juggle everything—training and competing in rodeo, being a father figure to my sister and running the homestead—but I manage. Mama enjoys the views, but can't help run the small farm I bought with my prize money, and my sister works hard, but I'm putting her through college so I want her to focus on that. That just leaves me and just a few seasonals to keep the farm running, as well as to get all my training done. Fortunately, there's some crossover between training for rodeo and running a farm, but that means chasing buckles is the free time and the rest of it is the work." The last he said with a smarmy chuckle, and a look-at-my-big-heart grin, which he aimed at Sierra, causing reflux to rise up in Diablo's throat.

That the fool even thought he had a chance with a woman like Sierra was just further evidence of his mental density. Dillon looked at her and saw a pretty pair of tits beneath a shiny hat and crown. Dillon thought that he had common ground with Sierra simply because both of their lives revolved around rodeo.

The man had no sense of the contradictions and conflicts embedded and inherent in her participation as the daughter of Cuban immigrants in a sport that emphasized down-home American values and blue-eyed American beauties.

But none of that kept the idiot from trying.

Tio Julio gave an easy shrug at the same time as he made a clucking noise in the back of his throat, loud enough to snap Diablo's attention and glare away from Dillon, as well as to draw Sierra and the camera crew's focus to him, and said, "Whether the arena is rodeo or everything else, I always do the same thing. Hold on and enjoy the ride."

Unable to refrain from it in the face of such a perfectly scripted line for unscripted television, Sierra let out a warm and wistful sigh. "Now if that isn't a nugget of rodeo gold, then I don't know what is," she said. "You heard it here around the fire, folks. Rodeo wisdom at its finest."

After Julio's redirection, their little tableau took on a warm glow, as if the exchange between Sierra and Julio had layered a Hallmark feeling over the scene, turning the situation from a powder keg ready to blow toward more family-friendly programming.

And, because in that moment there wasn't a centralized space for him, and because the feeling was not a result of his intention and because no one had gone out of their way to include him in it, Dillon couldn't let any of it stand.

"We all know what lawyer boy over here gets up to in his spare time. In fact, it's a wonder he even has time to hobby around with rodeo at all," he said, his voice acidic and overloud.

With an energy of reluctance, both Sierra and the camera crew turned to Dillon.

Without rising to Dillon's bait, Diablo smiled easily, keeping his voice even and cordial, as opposed to just scathing and dry, and said, "It's true that rodeo is more therapy than work for me. It takes a special kind of activity to balance out seeing the carriage of justice through, especially when it can be as thankless as it is in my line of work. As important as justice is, it doesn't undo harm. Nothing can do that. So when I get out there, it's not shiny buckles that I'm chasing down, but demons of the times I've lost and ghosts of all the work still yet to do."

For a moment everyone around the campfire was simply silent. Sierra's eyes sparkled in the dancing firelight, glistening, dark and wide, the expression in them not her typical show face, but wide and open and bleeding an emotion so complex he couldn't name it.

Dillon was disgusted.

There was a glint of new respect in Julio's eyes, mingled with a spark of laughter.

Though nothing about what Diablo had said had been false or exaggerated, and though he had not intended his words as a joke, Diablo found himself also fighting back the urge to laugh at their result himself.

He hadn't meant to hand out truisms, but he had.

Everything in rodeo was always deeper than it looked, which was a fact that had been easier to forget with time and distance away from the sport than he would have liked to admit.

But that was a minor disappointment, particularly in the face of the fact that while they might not have had a fistfight with Dillon, he and Julio had done their part to put him in his place.

"I've been in rodeo a long time, lawman, but I've

never met a cowboy like you," Sierra said softly, pausing
before adding, "When they say *The Closed Circuit* is a
rodeo unlike any other, they aren't lying!" The last she
punctuated with a tasteful and perfectly tuned *whoop*,
and the cameras turned to her, recentering as she seg-
ued into her next line, but Diablo's ears were too busy
replaying the first line to tune in.

*I've been in rodeo a long time, lawman, but I've
never met a cowboy like you.*

Hidden in plain sight, folded right into her performance, she had been speaking to him.

And he knew she'd meant what she said.

No compliment had ever struck him quite like Sierra's
statement.

Getting involved with Sierra any further required a return to everything he hated about his early relationships—
secrecy, sneaking around, shame—he knew that.

But he wanted her and he was a grown man.

He'd decided what he wanted a long time ago when
it came to Sierra.

"Well, I suppose it's about time that I let you three
in on what your fellow contestants already know," she
said with a nod toward the other fires she had already
visited. "Are you ready to find out what the first challenge of the rodeo unlike any other will be?" she asked,
her voice bright and playful, the private bomb she'd
dropped for him now just a warm echo in her eyes
when they landed on him. "It's easy to forget it amid
the screams and screens of the arena, but everything
in rodeo originated in the activities of a cowboy's regular day's work—and that's what these Closed Circuit
challenges are all about. We know you know how to
get it done in the arena," she said, her words slowing

and deepening with the faintest hint of suggestion before her eyes met Diablo's, "but we want to see if you can do it in the wild."

Her words shot straight into him and rooted, as visceral and physical as if she had run a single manicured fingernail down his spine. Again, she spoke to him, brazen because they both knew what was really being said, but slyly, because she delivered the line to a crowd.

"Circumstances out there on the range can get pretty hairy, but everyone knows that necessity is the mother of invention, and that's exactly where some of rodeo's most popular events arise out from.

"It's not enough for us to get you boys out there on the range if it's all smooth sailing once you get there, though." She paused here for dramatic flair, before continuing. "So for the second season, *The Closed Circuit* has kicked things up a notch. Rather than a sleepy overnight challenge, each one of you will have to make it through an obstacle course of simulated ranch emergencies—and the cowboy with the best time wins!"

Knowing the cameras were still rolling, and that the reaction shots were a particular favorite of the editors, Diablo held back from closing his eyes or sighing, but couldn't manage much more than that as far as hiding how tired the idea made him.

And it was only the first challenge.

But then Sierra smiled, the firelight enhancing the glow that was all her own, her eyes locked on his and she said, "May the best man win." And he knew he would go out there and try to be the man she was talking about.

CHAPTER TWELVE

Miami, Florida

IT WAS IMPOSSIBLE not to see parallels to *The Hunger Games* as Diablo led his horse into the arena the following evening.

Rather than the large circle of dirt that rodeo fans knew and loved, Miami's Hard Rock Stadium had been transformed into a small version of the Everglades, re-creating the dramatic landscape Florida was famous for outside with shocking and undoubtedly expensive realism inside.

Wet and hot and filled with foliage, the set's creators appeared to have actually drained the swamp right into the arena.

From Sierra's announcement the night before, Diablo had deduced that, even in the face of all of the drama and set effects, the first challenge was essentially a team-roping exercise.

His suspicions were confirmed when, upon arriving at his assigned call time, the greenies had informed him that his task was to enter the arena, find his partner and with them, both rope and guide a set of four steers into a designated holding pen that he had been assured "he could not miss."

It wasn't not being able to locate the holding pen that he was worried about, however.

It was the partner part.

Most roping teams worked together for at least weeks, if not years. He and his college partner had been paired up as freshmen and had competed with each other exclusively in the team-roping event for the next four years.

Thank God *The Closed Circuit* was obsessed with rank—in terms of both bulls and scores—and his partner for the challenge was Julio.

Somewhere in the fake swamp, he would find the older man as well as what he guessed would be some stressed-out steers.

Observing the mini Jurassic Park in front of him as he tuned out the sounds of the audience around him, he supposed that *The Closed Circuit* had also included a few booby traps.

Like all summer reality shows, they could hardly resist booby traps.

Why should they? Slapstick made good TV.

As far as roping went, though, Diablo was confident in his skills.

Years as a star college rodeo athlete had ensured that not only did he have the necessary know-how and precision, he also had had the benefit of four years of intensive rodeo education and training from one of the best college programs in the country. And if occasional coaches and teammates had been resentful or reticent about working with a Black Dominican kid from the city, Diablo compensated for it in the same way he always had—by taking the shit they dished out and spinning it into gold—or, more specifically, shiny buckles and college records.

Gingerly leading his horse into an environment that very clearly made it nervous, he could also acknowledge that as a collegiate athlete, he had also always benefited from competing in so-perfectly-controlled-and-cultivated-that-they-were-almost-sterile environments—nothing like the wild cacophony he made his way into now.

But having had the precollege experience of riding in atypical urban environments with the CityBoyz—environments that were just as prone to unsettling a mount—he was more than prepared to manage a nervous horse.

The sights and sounds of a city, the hard ground and cars and loud noises and heckling of the neighborhood kids might not constitute waving plants in an artificial swamp, but it prepared a cowboy for riding in an environment that nearly begged a horse to bolt.

Any cowboy worth his salt knew that a horse felt its rider's feelings and that that had about as much to do with how well you did and how hard that horse was willing to work for you as practice and conditions.

As Diablo and his horse picked their way through the narrow-cleared pathways in the created swamp, searching for Julio in an artificial world, he was careful to keep his muttering internal.

The contestants were mic'd for the benefit of the audience.

Because a significant part of the challenge was locating both the team member and the steers, it would have defeated the purpose for the contestants to hear how close or far away they were from achieving their aim via the announcers' commentary. So while the audience and Sierra could see and hear everything the contestants did, beyond cheering and the general amorphous noise of the crowd, the contestants in their artificial swamp were cut off from the outside world, which only added to the dystopian and gladiatorial nature of the challenge.

It was going to be interesting to see how the circuit managed to create a roping event with all of the clutter in the arena.

Traditionally, like other rodeo events, steers and cowboys burst through the chutes at high speed, tearing into a wide-open arena with enough space to build up momentum and power. One team member would rope the calf around the head, and the second would then catch it from the back legs and the clock would stop.

However, with the arena filled with vegetation traversable only by narrow pathways, Diablo wasn't certain there was room for either steer or horse to build up speed, let alone get going with enough speed to make it hard to rope.

Having nearly made his way across the length of the arena now, though, treading cautiously through the overgrown set for the sake of his horse, Diablo could only marvel at how transformed and fresh the event felt.

He had already been riding for multiple long minutes in an event that typically lasted fifteen seconds if you were slow, and far less than that if you knew what you were doing.

All in all, it had a strangely disorienting effect on the experience, making it feel as if he was truly searching for lost cattle in a swampy range, rather than competing in a staged competition in an artificial forest for a million-dollar cash prize and a shot at fame and glory.

Halting with a steady, "Whoa, there, girl," to his horse, it also occurred to him that he and Julio might be committing the oldest crime in the book as far as searching for someone went: moving around.

If they were both on the move, even seeking out each other, it was highly likely that they were just circling the arena, retracing ground behind the other's back while never making a connection.

Diablo had never been lost in public or separated from his nana—she had never allowed her grandson to wander when they were out and about—but he had watched enough television growing up to recall that the standard maxim of behavior when you were lost was to get to an easily identifiable place where you could call for help.

And then you were supposed to wait.

Considering that they were in a relatively small enclosure, rather than moving to high ground, he simply stayed in place where he had stopped.

That part down, he moved on to the second.

Transferring his reins to one hand, he gently placed both hand and reins against the warm body of his horse in order to reassure her through his next move. Then he placed his other hand's thumb and forefinger in his mouth and let out a shrill whistle.

Even with his comforting hand on her neck, the horse still startled, but she quickly calmed as the noise died down.

Then, like a good pair of lost children, they waited.

Just moments later a sound ahead and to the left of them alerted Diablo to the approach of Tio Julio and his mount. Cautiously rounding the bend of an outcropping of vegetation, the man was a sight for sore eyes.

"Ah. Ahi está," Diablo said, allowing the warmth and respect he felt for the man to infuse his voice.

Julio inclined his head toward Diablo with a smile. "Y aquí estoy. No pude encontrate. El sibato fue una buena idea."

Shrugging with a smile, Diablo brushed the compliment off. "Lástima que no podamos usarlo para encontrar las vaquitas." Though, if any operation would have trained its steers to come at a whistle, it would have been *The Closed Circuit*. They seemed to find the most docile stock on the planet.

"No sé. Podría funcionar para las vaquitas si estuviéramos un poco más cerca del mar," he said, making a joke in reference to the tiny gulf porpoise, a silly lightness coming to his eyes.

It was a dad joke if Diablo had ever heard one, so he said with a snort, "Creo que deberíamos llamarte Papá Julio si vas a hacer chistes así."

But instead of a smile, as Diablo had anticipated, a shadow crossed Julio's face before it closed off entirely once again. "Tío, papá, todo es lo mismo para mí. We'd better get started either way. Las vacas no se van a encontrar a sí mismas."

"Tienes razón, por supuesto. ¿listo?"

Humor returned to the other man's face and Diablo wondered what storylines played out beneath the man's weathered surface as he replied, "Los papás siempre están listos."

And this time it was Diablo's face that the shadow crossed.

But then it was time to move.

They set out together from there, Diablo taking the lead as he said, "Vamos a buscar en un patrón de cuadrícula. De esa manera, si los encontramos, estaremos listos para atarlos de inmediato." Looking in a grid pattern would save them time in not recovering ground while making sure they didn't miss anything.

Nodding, Julio agreed, "Me parece bien."

And they did just that.

Together, they systematically searched the arena, both men's eyes and ears and noses alert for the signs of the cows they still had to catch and rope once found.

And, of course, because it was *The Closed Circuit*, when they finally found the first of their four steers, it wasn't simply a matter of roping and wrangling it back to the pen.

No, when they finally found the cow, it was buried chest deep in a perfect steer-size mud pit, surrounded on all sides by an artful arrangement of fallen logs. Each log was laid out in a manner as to ensure that the riders could not walk their horses up to the bovine and wrap a rope around its head.

Obviously, it had to be harder than catching and freeing a steer from the mud in narrow swampy confines. One or both of them would have to maneuver their horses into one of two positions from which they would be close enough to try their hand at roping from a distance. However, each of those positions was set up with enough vegetation to make a horse feel boxed in and half-blind.

From there, hemmed in himself, a skilled cowboy with luck on his side could, theoretically, rope the distressed steer and then slowly reverse his horse back down the narrow swamp path they had taken to get into the position in the first place.

Seeing what it was intended that they do, Diablo sighed and reached for the rope at his hip, as if the idea of taking on such an impossible task didn't thrill him a little bit inside, lighting a fire that only burned when he found something actually hard to throw himself against.

Silently, he and Julio split, each going to take one of the roping positions.

With a quick series of movements, Diablo cast his rope out first, sending it sailing up and over the steer, its loop catching around its head.

When Diablo had the cow secure, Julio muttering reassuring noises from its opposite flank, he then commanded his horse to slowly reverse, nice and easy so as to ensure no injury to the young steer or his horse.

Another minute or so later the steer was kicking its legs free of the last of the mud and mooing plaintively in the square of logs.

Diablo continued to guide it until it reached the perimeter of logs whereupon it refused to budge another inch.

When Diablo attempted to pull it farther, encouraging it to help out by trying to get over the logs, the steer began to struggle as if, rather than the one to save its life, Diablo was now the devil trying to eat it. Convinced that it faced a life-and-death battle with both Diablo and the logs, it mooed plaintively and began to toss its head.

Staring at the now wild and struggling calf and roadblock with an expression not unlike that of a new father—helplessly contemplating his tantrum-throwing child while considering and weighing his options—Diablo was unsure of what to do.

But then Julio's rope sailed out to catch one of the steer's flailing back hooves.

It was abruptly clear to Diablo what *The Closed Cir-*

cuit had intended with this challenge—beneath the fake swamp, it was just classic team roping with a twist.

With its back legs caught and lifted, the steer settled, its panic subsiding, and when it was finally calmed enough, Julio loosened the slack of his rope, allowing the steer to stand on all fours once again.

Diablo guided the once again calm steer by the horns, this time leading it toward the one perimeter log that was more than low enough that a cow could step over. It was the obvious path that the producers had intended for them to use, which meant there was probably another catch.

As soon as the steer's front legs cleared the log, the log itself moved, the set piece rising upward from beneath the middle of the steer's stomach and pushing the beleaguered bovine just high enough that it could no longer easily make it over with its hind legs.

But this time they were ready.

Once again, Julio's rope sailed out, catching both of the rear legs and pulling taut to lift the animal, elevating them enough that they could clear the log as Diablo and his mare pulled forward from the front end. Shortly thereafter they had the satisfaction of bringing their first steer in, leading it into the pen where they locked it away inside, accompanied by an extremely loud gong sound and a wave of applause.

They had one down.

There were just three more to go.

Briefly, Diablo wondered why everything about *The Closed Circuit* had to be as exhausting as it was exhilarating, but he knew the answer: he was too old for this.

But it didn't matter, because he still loved it.

Returning to the portion of their grid search where

they had found the first cow, Julio and Diablo continued on in their search pattern until they located the second cow, standing in what looked to be a relatively open patch of ground, surrounded by picturesque flowers and grasses. But the catch soon showed up in a hissing sound that cowboys, horse folk, back-country hikers and Australians alike, knew to fear—the hiss of a snake, or in this case, the hiss of a thousand snakes, or perhaps just the largest snake in the world.

Blasted through the loudspeakers, the primal sound of danger set off a burst of terror and rage in the steer. But it didn't take long for Julio and Diablo to immobilize it, for it to settle down, and it took even less for them to lead it safely back to its pen to join the first.

Diablo had no sense of how well they were doing—beyond the knowledge that the thing had already taken far longer than the standard less-than-fifteen-seconds team roping events that he was used to.

As the first team, they had the added disadvantage—or advantage, depending on their performance—of establishing the first time. It would either be a high bar or easy to beat.

But Diablo was simply ready to be done, and judging from the worn look and his weathered expression, Julio was in the same boat.

Because their grid pattern had worked so well thus far, and because they were halfway through it, they kept it up, immediately returning to the place they had left off. They lost a few minutes in search; however, Diablo was surprised when they came upon the final two cows.

Expecting to find them one at a time, as had been the case with the first two, Diablo considered the situation with care.

Like the second cow, neither of these appeared to be in obvious distress, besides the fact that one stood inside a wooden cage. The other was tied in place, a thick black rope around one ankle.

Both men squinted as they scanned the terrain for a mechanism or device that might release the cows while they cautiously guided their horses nearer to the steers.

"Cuidado," Julio said as Diablo got within arm's reach of the seemingly happily caged cow, and Diablo nodded.

He wouldn't override his instincts a second time, regardless of how obviously calm things appeared. "¿Los liberamos?" Diablo asked, still eyeing the captive cows like they might jump the two men on horseback if their backs were turned. "¿O crees que este es otro truco?"

"Otro truco," the other man said without hesitation, confirming what Diablo was already inclined to believe.

"Entonces…" Diablo said, trailing off before continuing with the question, "¿Dónde está el tripwire?"

Idly, he wondered if there was a specific word for *tripwire* in Spanish.

His nana had always nagged him when he threw an English word into his Spanish because he either didn't know or was too lazy to come up with the right word en español—to the point that he had been driven to take private lessons with AJ's mom in order to improve and put an end to his grandmother's disappointment.

Through those lessons, he'd learned to accept that there were some words that permanently resisted translation, just as there were others that required creative thinking to communicate.

Which of those categories, he wondered, did *tripwire* fall under?

Near enough to the cage now to examine the chain it hung from, he searched for a clue. It would have to have something to do with roping, he assumed, as each of their previous cow encounters had and that was the point of this whole nonsense. But where?

"Es aquí," Julio said heavily, his weighted voice traveling slow and low on its journey to Diablo's ear.

Turning, Diablo looked to where the man stood beside the other cow, staring up a tall tree above the trap that held it. Following his gaze, Diablo's eyes climbed the tree, a tall palm so big that it had to have taken quite a bit of time and effort just to transport into the arena, until he saw the relatively large wooden peg that was stuck into the trunk.

Looped through a hole in the peg was the other end of the black rope that held the cow nearest Julio.

"It's a lever," Diablo noted before turning to check the caged cow's prison for any similar mechanism. Finding nothing, he returned his attention to the snared cow, this time following the long black rope all the way down past the cow it held, to note that the black rope actually stretched across the distance between them to connect to the cage.

One lever to free them all, Diablo thought from a strange place of exhausted remove, as he realized exactly what it was they were supposed to do.

As weary as the whole thing made him, a part of him was impressed by the showrunner's ingenuity.

Team roping was all about showcasing skill, partnership and speed—and for these final two cows, he and Julio were going to need to employ all three.

Pointing to the peg in the tree, Diablo said, "We're supposed to rope and pull that lever, pero—" he paused, tracing the line and the black rope from the lever, past the ensnared cow and all the way to the caged cow with his finger, before continuing "—cuando hacemos eso, ambas vacas salen libres a la vez."

Julio sighed, seeing exactly the problem embedded within the system.

It was going to take some clever roping to pull the lever in the first place, but once they did, it would free both cows at the same time. Meaning that the two cows would bolt while the initial roper lost precious time retrieving his rope from the lever. The other partner could only choose one of the cows to rope, inevitably leaving the other to go free, leaving them with one caught and penned cow, and another running panicked through a fake swamp.

Diablo searched the artificial landscape for anything that might help.

"El tocón," Julio said from behind him, and Diablo turned his head around to see what he was talking about.

Pointing to a large stump lying on its side on the ground, Julio continued, "If we pull that over the rope, we can keep one in the cage while we deal with the other. Then we move the stump and take care of the last."

Nodding with a grin, Diablo said, "Bueno. Hagámoslo."

And they did.

Rather than roping a cow, Diablo cast his lariat out and over the stump, catching the rope around a branch and guiding his horse forward, pulling and dragging until it sat atop the black cord that connected the ensnared cow to the caged cow, holding it firmly in place.

Julio then sent his own rope high into the air in order to snag the lever and pull it down.

Sure enough, in pulling the lever, the black rope went slack from above, freeing the ensnared cow.

But just as they planned, the stump that Diablo had dragged over the rope stopped the mechanism from completely releasing, so the cage and the steer inside stayed exactly where it was.

Because his own rope remained free, Diablo was ready to catch the released steer by its horns before it could even decide on a direction to go, and Julio had plenty of time to retrieve his own rope and catch the steer's back leg, ticking off the roping requirement with ease.

Because *The Closed Circuit* had gone all-out with their *Hunger Games* thing, as soon as the third cow was officially roped a loud bell rang through the loudspeaker, and once again, they could hear the audience cheering.

They made quick work penning the third cow then raced back to retrieve the one in the cage, ready to be done.

Julio dismounted quickly to push the stump off the rope.

After a heave and hissing grimace, the rope whipped free. Julio mounted with a quick leap just as the cage shot into the air.

Anticipating that result, Diablo had been prepared, his rope sailing out to hook around the newly freed steer's horns.

Pulling against the rope and upset about all the commotion, the steer gave Diablo and his mare a run for their money, but an instant later that was all over, as Julio caught a back leg with his lariat and the bell rang for a fourth time.

Minutes later their fourth and final steer penned, the arena buzzer blared, signaling a successful end to the challenge, as they exited the created environment, coming out to a post-challenge staging area that looked a lot more like the rodeo arenas Diablo was used to. The crowd went wild.

Willing to give them what they wanted, Diablo raised a triumphant fist in the air and shook it, and the volume kicked up another notch.

Then, gesturing with an open palm toward his teammate to give credit where credit was due for their success, Diablo turned to Julio and his grin faltered.

Julio's posture was also one of triumph and success, his own fist lifted high in the air and pumping to the delight of the fans, but from it a sizable trail of blood darkened the man's sleeve.

Diablo continued to eye the other man through the process of exiting the arena, dismounting and handing off their horses to the handlers, and continued to follow him all the way through into the greenie-filled, cordoned-off arena halls that constituted backstage.

Stopping abruptly, Julio whipped around to ask with an edge to his voice, "De acuerdo, ¿qué quieres?"

Raising his palms and keeping his voice steady and even, Diablo replied, "Alguien debería echar un vistazo a eso," nodding toward the other man's bleeding fist.

Shoving the hand in question into his pocket, Julio shook his head in a quick negative before drawing in a slow breath and letting it out to say, "No es de preocuparse. Es solo una herida superficial."

"It'll give the medical staff something to do," Diablo pushed gently.

But Julio only shook his head again, another absolute

definitive no, this one more final. "Aquí no hay nece-
sidad de molestarlos. Estaré bien mañana. Verdad. No
necesito ayuda."

In response, Diablo spoke low and slow, watching
the man's reaction with his lawyer's eyes on, "Sólo los
fantasmas no necesitan ayuda."

A new level of stillness came over Julio's body, as if
he had frozen not with fear but an incredible attention
and focus. Then he gave a perfectly cultivated chuckle
and answered with a smile, "Oh soy lo suficientemente
carne y hueso. Pero esta vez no necesito ayuda. Gracias
por su preocupación. Buen trabajo por ahí esta noche."

Diablo knew a dismissal when he heard one, and
sure enough, following his words, Julio took the opportunity to walk away.

This time Diablo let him.

If their score was good enough, they would reunite
on the winner's podium at the end of the show. In the
meantime, Diablo had a new concern to add to his list.

In Diablo's experience, there were only a few reasons
why a person would reflexively refuse medical care, and
some of them could become problematic when there
were folks like Dillon sniffing around.

"AND OUR FIRST-PLACE TEAM, folks, coming in at 21.5
minutes—a full fifteen faster than the next closest
team—our lawman, Diablo Sosa, and everybody's favorite uncle, Tio Julio! Let's give it up for the boys,
y'all! You've never seen team roping like you did tonight!"

Diablo was all smiles and victory on the platform
beside Julio, but his mind was still on the man's hand
and its implications.

When it wasn't getting snagged on Sierra.

She wore white tonight, like a regular rodeo angel. How fascinating, then, that she had upcoming plans with the devil.

He and Julio had been the only team to have figured out a way to prevent the caged steer's escape and, as they'd suspected, it had saved them a lot of time not having to hare after them through the bushes.

And, based on the highlight recaps playing on the jumbotron, it had saved them from looking like a pair of absolute fools in the process.

The same couldn't be said for Dillon's team. In a mildly surprising upset, his team had not come in nipping at Diablo and Julio's heels, but instead had taken third after the team made up of the fifth and sixth place contestants slid in to steal second.

Unsurprisingly, the highlights showed that young Dillon didn't play very well with others, wasting a good amount of time arguing with his partner at each trap. Not only did Dillon set both of the steers free at the double trap with his hasty roping of the lever in the final trap, he'd unwittingly chased it back to the mud pit, where it got stuck.

He'd had to rescue two steers from the same trap.

And because he'd taken so much longer than Diablo and Julio, there'd been plenty of space for the team from the bullpens—which was *Closed Circuit* lingo for all of the cowboys in shared RVs—to squeeze on up into the top three.

There was something poetic about that to Diablo.

And while the results weren't that surprising to Diablo, as the contestants exited the stage, making their way back to wherever the night was going to take them, it was clear that the final standings were a surprise to Dillon.

And, if the waves of piss and vinegar rolling off him were any indication, it was not a welcome one.

"The two of you are nothin' but a bunch of dirty cheaters," he growled as Diablo passed, his voice low and venomous.

Without pausing to stop, Diablo tossed him a lop-sided grin and said, "I think you mean *pair*. A grouping of two is called a pair."

Passing beside them at that moment, the second-place team shot looks toward where Dillon stood and laughed before continuing on.

Dillon's volume lifted a notch when he said, "You think you're clever, but just keep it up, college boy. Your luck's gonna run out and then neither of you will be laughing. Your friend's gonna get what's coming to him. He might play innocent and humble, but he's not, and neither are you, and I'm going to make sure everyone knows the truth of it."

Lazily tilting his head to take in Dillon, who walked with larger strides than appeared comfortable in order to keep up with Diablo's long strides, Diablo said, "From where I'm standing in the ranks, which is admittedly a solid point gap behind our good friend Julio here, it looks to me like what's coming to him is a big, shiny first-place buckle."

Dillon narrowed his eyes and opened his mouth, doubtless to say something he thought was pithy and clever, but that would be tired and mean-spirited in reality. But Diablo was done with him, so rather than stay to listen, he stopped abruptly and turned in another direction.

Dillon would have had to chase after him to continue their conversation and would have looked like a puppyish fanboy in the process, and because that would have been a kind of face the man couldn't stand to lose, Diablo knew he wouldn't.

Just as intended, Dillon didn't follow, and Diablo finally had the space to think that he'd been looking for.

And even if he had to walk the long way around the stadium, he at least had the extra time to consider Julio, and what to do about him.

CHAPTER THIRTEEN

FOLLOWING THE ENSEMBLE of the night before, Sierra's afternoon outfit was simple, to say the least, and yet she felt as confident as if she wore a sash and crown.

In reality, she wore a cropped white cotton T-shirt with a left breast pocket and simple blue jean shorts.

She'd begun to pick up, however, on the pathway to Diablo's heart, and casual was his kryptonite.

The fact that dressing to impress was one of her superpowers did nothing, though, to dilute the novelty of feeling the full power of it in nothing but jeans and a T-shirt.

Getting ready had been a shockingly straightforward matter of contacts, a little light makeup, pulling her hair into a ponytail and donning a denim baseball cap.

She had tossed a swimsuit into her day bag in case the urge to swim struck them—which one always had to be prepared for at the beach and was now standing in front of the carousel in Crandon Park, where she waited for Diablo.

As a Florida girl and one of three shopaholic daughters of a woman who herself loved to shop, Sierra had been to Miami more times than she could count throughout her life—enough that exploring the city itself was less interesting to her than taking advantage of the rare opportunity to get away from the bustle and prying eyes of the tour and recenter with a little time in nature.

At least, that was what she had been thinking before inviting Diablo along to join her.

So now, instead of solo trekking through her favorite beach trails, she waited at the carousel.

She was having second thoughts.

What had seemed urgent as recently as the night before—when she lay in bed replaying her personal highlight reel from Diablo's performance in the challenge and thinking about today while she tossed and turned—felt more reckless by the light of day. She'd achieved a level of success she'd only dreamed was possible. Did she want to risk that for a fling? Did she want to put the job on the line?

She would be fired if they were caught, and it wouldn't take much. Even this far from caravan and crew they could get outed—all that was required was a photo. Enough people tuned in to the show that it was feasible they could be recognized and snapped, even dressed down as she was.

There were people everywhere.

While it was an easy meeting spot in a massive park, she should have thought of something more subtle. Throngs of families and active photo shoots took place all around her.

What if they showed up in the background of someone's vacation selfie?

She had planned to visit Crandon Park long before she'd known she would have company, though, and of all of the Miami area's beaches and natural spaces, it was her favorite.

Encompassing eight hundred and eight acres, which

included a surprising diversity of settings, from near-white sand beaches, to hiking paths through coconut palm groves, to the developed carousel area she stood in now, the park also had some of the best cheap food you could find in the city if you were willing to walk for it.

Crandon Park was a place that regular people went, as opposed to a place just for tourists and Miami's wealthy to see and be seen and offered a laid-back experience that was hard to find elsewhere in the area.

It was the kind of place where you had to worry about sawgrass and whether or not your sunscreen was reef safe more than the thoroughness of your bikini wax and the depth of your tan.

When she had planned on a solo experience, she'd thought she would bring along a book, a towel, her wallet and a change of clothes—then she could swim or hike or simply read beside the beach should she so desire and according to her whim, but now she was going to spend the day with Diablo Sosa instead.

Which she could lose her job for.

If he showed up, which he hadn't yet.

She'd never been stood up before. What if Diablo was her first?

Her palms clammed up in her pockets as she looked around.

In her romantic experience, he fell somewhere between the plethora of men she'd gone on casual and harmless one-off dates with, and the two more serious relationships she'd tried in the off-seasons between crowns. None of which, however, had prepared her at all for the idea of being stood up.

If he didn't come, it would be a rejection of a kind she'd never experienced before, and as she scanned the crowd around the carousel once more, she was forced to acknowledge she might not handle it well.

At all.

"Come on, Diosa," she said under her breath, watching another wave of transition as the carousel came to a stop and one set of riders disembarked so another could get on.

"You called, mi reina?" His voice wrapped around her from behind, like a pair of arms curving around and enveloping her in a warm embrace.

Jumping, she turned, her smile brighter with relief than it might otherwise have been.

"Careful there, queenie," he added, a strange, somewhat stunned expression on his face. "Somebody might think you were waiting for me," he continued, smiling easily now, the corners of his dark eyes crinkled with mirth as he took her in with an appreciative light in his eye.

She used the moment to peruse him, as well.

She didn't know what she had expected but it had not been for him to show up looking every inch the fashionable south Floridian.

His apple-green shorts were crisp and slim fit, cutting off just above the knee, revealing his muscled and well-defined thighs and calves.

He had ditched his cowboy boots for the outing, and Sierra realized it was the first time she'd seen him in anything else—even the times he'd been wearing his suits. Today he wore slip-on canvas sneakers in a bright orange-yellow that was perfectly coordinated with the large hibiscus motif of his tropical-print button-up T-shirt. He'd managed to arrive appropriately dressed for their afternoon, as well as to look good doing it.

Uncommonly, Sierra could not say the same.

With her plain T-shirt and shorts and yellow day-pack, it occurred to her she might look a bit like Dora the Explorer by comparison.

But when his eyes returned to her face from scanning her, his gaze heated in ways that said more than words, he said, "You look beautiful." And she knew it was true.

And though it was by no means the first time that he had made it clear that he was attracted to her, the words ignited a new tension between them, because there was no ambiguity about it now. They were on a date.

"Thank you," she said, lifting a hand up to pinch the bill of her hat between the thumb and finger and tip it at his compliment. "I was going for low profile and in-cognito, though."

His own smile lifted one corner of his mouth, a new look coming to his eyes. "You did a good job disguis-ing rodeo queen Sierra Quintanilla, but it would take a lot more than a casual outfit to make you incognito, queenie. You've got the kind of shine that resists hiding. However, perhaps with a prosthetic nose…"

She laughed like the light compliment was some-thing she easily brushed off when, really, his words sank down into her to stoke embers that were already glowing with a healthy red heat.

She was never quite as in charge of the ways things went when she was with Diablo as she was around ev-eryone else.

In fact, intentional or not, he had a way of throwing her off her plans like nothing ever had.

She was goal oriented and had big dreams and there wasn't a man out there who could make her change her mind. And yet, he compelled her to drop the reins, without even having to try.

A natural blush warmed her cheeks, but Sierra waved his words off rather than reveal how much they'd impacted her. "Well, in that case, it's a good thing there won't be many people around once we get going. The last thing we need is for rising *Closed Circuit* star Diablo Sosa to be photographed tromping through the mangroves with a shiny woman at his side."

A shadow crossed his eyes, but it passed like faint gray clouds across a clear and deep night sky, to be replaced with intrigue and more than a little surprise. "Tromping?" he asked.

Cocking her hip to one side and bringing a hand to it, she lifted the opposite eyebrow and asked, "You didn't think I was the tromping type?"

Laughter dancing in his eyes, he shook his head. "I'll admit that I did not," he said.

Making a tsking sound, Sierra shook her head. "Diablo, Diablo," she said, "when are you going to remember that underneath all of this pretty is a woman who's never been afraid to muck out a few stalls?"

Bowing his head in the worst impression of contriteness that Sierra had ever seen, he said, the Texas heavy and loaded in his voice, "It might take some time, queenie, but I assure you, by the time I'm done with you, I will have thoroughly gotten to know every inch, nook and cranny hidden beneath that gorgeous shell."

The combination of his tone and the promise in his eyes sent shivers dancing across her skin. Going a little breathless and shallow, her voice lifted to float airily in her upper chest as she said, "We've only got the afternoon."

The intensity shifted in his eyes, deepening, darkening and thickening alongside his voice as he said, "We'd better get started, then."

Swallowing, Sierra nodded before casting a furtive glance around, recalling for the first time since he had arrived that they were surrounded by people—children, families, couples—standing in the middle of one of the most crowded places in the park.

Diablo made her feel so safe and comfortable that it was all too easy to forget the constraints within which they were supposed to be operating.

If they were going to do this, they needed to keep it a secret. Her job depended on it.

But it was so hard to remember that when he looked at her with open laughter in his eyes and an easy smile on his lips.

"Let's," she agreed with a mildly dazzled smile of her own and reached out a hand for his.

He looked at it first, casting his eyes back up at her, a question in his gaze, before he took it, capturing her entire hand in his large calloused one.

Holding hands, she led him around the perimeter of the carousel pavilion, guiding them toward the entrance of the Osprey hiking trail, which would take them as far as they wanted to go up the near two-mile stretch of beach.

More importantly, though, it would take them away from the crowds where they needed to watch their behavior and into secluded areas where they'd find privacy for chatting…or whatever else they might get up to.

Neither spoke for a time, each simply walking and holding hands.

Sierra reveled in the normalcy of it all, the unexpectedly homey realness of it. It wasn't a sensation she had expected to feel in a secret affair.

Walking together through the familiar terrain, with no passersby staring and no strangers approaching them for photos, it was a taste of what things might have been like if they had just been a pair of regular people, rather than rodeo people. Would this have been how her life might have turned out, had she never discovered rodeo and instead done something different with her life? Was this peace what investment bankers or architects experienced in their daily lives?

Is this what Diablo experienced?

He had a regular life, after all. His return to rodeo was merely a temporary blip before he returned to the kind of lifestyle where strolling hand in hand with a woman he was interested in would have been far less complicated and furtive.

The thought of him holding another woman's hand tightened her stomach. Though she was the one committed to the rodeo lifestyle, he was the one who was just passing through.

When the season was over, she would stay with *The Closed Circuit* and he would go back to his regular life, a life in which he had every right to go on dates that he didn't have to keep secret.

He had the right, and unlike herself, he had the freedom.

She had no right to keep him to herself.

But she wanted to.

And she couldn't even regret that it was her fault that they couldn't behave like normal adults, because if they could—if they'd been architects and investment bankers and able to take a stroll without fear of being seen—they wouldn't have found each other. They'd be normal, but they wouldn't be together; she wouldn't have this specific man at her side.

And that made all the difference.

Diablo Sosa was a rising-star attorney and a fiercely determined Texan from a poor neighborhood.

She was a beloved and pampered daughter from an upper-middle-class business-owning immigrant family.

Rodeo was the bridge that connected them—the only one strong enough to cross the gap between their respective backgrounds and carry them over.

In a world without rodeo, they would have missed each other entirely, and so as good as it felt to be out with him like this, free from the pressure of being "on" for *The Closed Circuit*, and even though it meant a foraying into the torture of stolen moments and secret feelings, she couldn't even bring herself to resent the ways her job hemmed her in.

Without it, how else would the two of them have ended up here?

"This is nice," he said, his voice slipping into her thoughts as if he had heard them. "It wasn't what I expected from a museum-loving rodeo queen, but I like it. Peaceful. Easy."

Feeling a greater sense of accomplishment than was probably warranted, Sierra smiled. Foliage arched above over their heads, enclosing the sandy path they trod.

A narrow window of sky remained open directly above them, itself bright blue and illuminated by the Miami sun, which bathed everything in a warm golden glow. "I love it out here. It's one of my favorite places," she admitted.

It struck her that in New Orleans, he had gotten to

show her his favorite place, and now here, in Miami, she got to show him hers.

"You didn't by chance bring a swimsuit, did you?" she asked, eyeing his attire and lack of bag doubtfully.

Reading her thoughts in her eyes, he grinned, canines showing, and patted the small bulge in his back pocket with a nod. "Sure did," he assured her.

Her mind raced with the possibilities implied by the fact that his swim trunks fit in the back of his pocket like that, offering her a number of intriguing images that once again revved the rumbling engine within. Hiding her reaction with a snort, she said, "Well, don't worry, I brought enough sunblock for both of us," mirroring his patting action with one of her own on her beach bag.

"I've got all the sunblock I need," he drawled.

"Spoken like a true Texan," she said, rolling her eyes. "Everyone needs sunblock. I don't care how dark you are. SPF is the true key to everlasting beauty."

Smiling with his eyes, he said, "given that the statement is coming from you, I'm willing to buy it."

Another blush rising to her cheeks, Sierra looked away, filling her eyes instead with the beloved sights of tropical Florida, palms swaying in the breeze, the turquoise blue of the Atlantic and long stretches of sand broken up by patches of beach grass.

She hadn't expected him to be so casually sweet. She had expected intelligence, yes, and courageousness, of course, considering he was brave enough to climb on top of bulls and broncs—but not sweetness.

Each time she encountered a new dimension of Diablo it triggered a nagging sensation in the back of her mind that he was the kind of man she could spend a lifetime with and never fully know.

She would never get bored talking with him.

And as much as she enjoyed cowboys, that most definitely was something that couldn't be said about every one of them.

Walking with Diablo, sneaking glances at him when he wasn't looking while a storm of sensations swirled within her, she wanted to put in the time exploring. In his presence everything she didn't want became clear, because what she wanted was so obvious.

She didn't want to live her life as a virginal paragon.

She didn't want to be the greatest rodeo queen the world had ever seen but be lonely.

She wanted to go to museums, and hike at Crandon Park and ride horses with Diablo.

She wanted a man who respected her enough to engage with her intellectually, to challenge her whenever the situation called for it and to enjoy sharing time and enthusiasm with her.

All of this time these had been the invisible criteria guiding her selections—or more accurately, her rejections—and she hadn't even consciously realized it.

She had been looking for Diablo the whole time.

No wonder, then, that she hadn't put the effort in in the past, nor was it strange that her list of noes was so much longer than her list of yeses.

She had been searching for a one of a kind.

"So will there be any swimming on this excursion?" he asked, drawing her out of her thoughts and into noticing his lips.

She needed to get a handle on herself.

Shrugging, she said, "If the water is nice and the

mood strikes. Otherwise, walking is great, and there're a couple places to eat in the park if we want. Or we can head farther into Key Biscayne when we get hungry. The afternoon is ours."

"Did you always plan to come here on your day off?"

Sierra nodded. "I did," she said before a mischievous note came to her voice and she added, "I've already been to most of the museums."

With a chuckle, Diablo said, "I was going to ask."

"I don't only go to museums, you know," Sierra said. Gesturing around them with her open palm, she added, "I also enjoy long walks on the beach, Ovaltine with marshmallows and historical fiction."

Laughter in his voice, he added, "And large meals, riding horses and rodeo."

Snorting, Sierra entirely agreed, repeating, "And large meals, riding horses and rodeo."

"What was it like?" he asked, a leading note in his tone.

Automatically hedging, Sierra asked, "What was what like?", suspicion laden in her voice.

"Growing up spoiled," he teased.

Lifting an eyebrow, Sierra asked, "Who says I was spoiled?"

Mirroring her expression, he raised his own eyebrow and asked, counting the points on his fingers along the way, "Do you mean besides the pony, and the feed, and the gear, and the entry fees and the sisters in pageants?"

Laughing, Sierra nodded and said with all seriousness, "Yes. I do."

"Ovaltine with marshmallows," he said. "Having either one in your house borders on fancy, but to have both?" Making a disapproving noise in the back of his throat he shook his head. "Mimada."

"Solo un poquito," she acknowledged without shame. Her family was comfortable enough to meet the needs of three daughters with expensive hobbies, but not so well-off that the answer to every request had always been a yes.

"You wear it well," he said, a new heat coming to his eyes as he took her in.

Shrugging, she said, "One can't help being loved," tongue in cheek, and he laughed.

Shaking his head at her, he said, "I don't imagine you can. I bet you're loved everywhere you go."

He was teasing, but there was also real observation in his statement, and so she felt compelled to respond truthfully. "And hated. Lasting friendship has a hard time rooting in the soil of ruthless competition," she said, attempting to soften the reality of her words with a light laugh.

Eyeing her, Diablo said, "It's a good thing you had your sisters, then."

Agreeing, Sierra said, "It's true. It might be lame to admit, but I don't think I'd have any real friends without them." She appreciated that he could accept what she said without pity or the urge to convince her otherwise. And that he was astute enough to pick up on the silver lining of it all.

Shrugging, he said, "Friends are overrated. There's nothing wrong with having good relationships with your family. It's clear yours is warm. That's a good thing."

"Thank you," she said. "It is. Between their schedules and being on the tour and doing promos before and after, I don't see them as much as I'd like anymore. Life is like that, though."

He nodded. "The time passes before you realize it.

My practice is located in Phoenix and between my case-load and the miles, it always shocks me how long I go between visits back to Houston. She wouldn't ever admit it, but I know my nana gets lonely." He looked away and Sierra could feel his inner tension and conflict.

She had no real sense of how old his nana was, but the woman was his grandmother and he was a grown man, which meant she couldn't be that young.

It was hard to age alone.

"Would she move out to where you are?" Sierra asked.

Shaking his head in a short negative, he said, "She bought her house and said she's going to die in it."

Laughing, Sierra said, "It sounds like she knows her mind."

Pausing to take in the scene around him, he smiled. "She does, if not her limits."

"What are limits?" Sierra asked as if she'd never heard the word before, eliciting a full laugh out of him.

"You remind me of her in more ways than one," he said, a warning in his voice.

"Oh?" she asked innocently. "She likes to hang up-side down on horseback, too?"

"If you'd talked to her twenty years ago…" he said.

"Only twenty?" Sierra asked, eyebrow lifting again.

Side-eyeing her, he nodded, adding, "If only to re-mind me that I wasn't the only one ballsy enough to rodeo beneath our roof."

"It doesn't sound like there was ever any doubt."

Shaking his head, Diablo agreed. "Not from me at least. I know better than that."

"So you're broken in, then," Sierra said with approval.

Shooting her a charming grin, he said, "She raised me right, if that's what you mean."

"I'll be the judge of that, thank you very much."

"Between the two of us, I'll be the one to be the judge, thank *you* very much," he sassed.

Frowning, she asked, "Do you really want to be a judge?"

For an instant he stilled, as if no one had ever asked him the question before. Then his fluid ease returned once again and he answered, "Since the day I heard the gavel fall."

"But is it because of spite or genuine desire?" she pressed, urged on by a need to understand combined with an unfamiliar blend of concern and compassion that demanded she make sure he wasn't acting from a place of pain.

His smile turned introspective. "Where does one end and the other begin? At first, I was angry and hungry for a kind of power that I'd been subject to but never had myself. Even then, though, what I was really concerned with was justice—or the lack thereof. Hell, that's what put me in that courtroom in the first place. I've always been deeply concerned with justice. Though it's what I do now, and I do it well, it has never been my dream to argue what is right and wrong in front of a bench. I know what's right and wrong without arguing. I had to accept that my petty and my drive have always been two sides of the same coin. Growing up, I saw injustice all around me, in the addicts and unhoused whose gateway crimes had been being dyslexic or wild or born poor, and in the women I saw persecuted, by cops and members of the neighborhood alike. These women were just trying to survive and protect themselves. Watching the black and brown people work twice as hard for half as much only to be labeled as lazy and worse also took a toll. Injustice was everywhere I looked and I thought there was nothing to do but rage and rage until one day I snapped and all the rage boiled out. And even after that, I was still angry for a long time, but the difference was that after I walked out of that courtroom, I had learned that there was something that could be done about it all, which, for me, was a form of hope. That hope, and the old man, and AJ, and Nana and the bulls and everything else all conspired to get me here, so I'd have to say it's both."

"Desire born of spite," she said.

"And spite born of desire," he concluded with a self-recriminating half smile.

"It makes sense to me. It's not that far off, really, from making a career out of being competitively pretty," she said, giving him a light punch on the shoulder.

Eyeing her with a shrewd look, he said, "Excuse you. Rodeo queens are competitive horse riders who happen to be pretty, thank you very much."

Letting out a bark of laughter that was not at all ladylike—and therefore against rodeo-queen rules—Sierra was still smiling, her eyes glistening, when she managed to get out, "Forgive my mistake."

Her stomach chose that moment to gurgle loudly, and whether or not it was because of the existing levity of the situation or simply because no matter how evolved human beings might get, body noises would always be that unique combination of embarrassing and hilarious, it nearly threw her into another fit of laughter.

Observing her with humor in his eyes, Diablo lifted an eyebrow to ask, "Which direction to food?"

His practical question was enough to hold on to amid the wave of giddiness still swirling around her. Checking her watch, she was surprised to see that an hour and a half had already passed. Though she was famous among those who she knew well for her type A adherence to a schedule, it was all too easy to lose track of everything when she was in Diablo's company.

They hadn't made it as far as she typically did in the same time frame, and that, coupled with the early arrival of hunger, meant they were nowhere close to the place she normally went when she came here.

They weren't, however, far from Jake O'Malley's—the kind of generic beach restaurant that existed the world over.

This near to the lunch hour and on a sunny day, the patio was packed, without a single table free, and as they made their way inside, the situation was not much better.

It was certainly not the casually intimate and insanely delicious Cuban food that she had hoped to share with him. But as he grabbed and perused a menu, giving her a chance to simply observe him while not actively engaged in conversation, she realized it didn't matter.

She didn't care that circumstances had conspired to have them eating at a basic restaurant with mediocre food instead of the unique hole-in-the-wall that would have been her opportunity to return the favor of his introducing her to that amazing sandwich.

She was having too much fun with him to worry about things not going exactly to plan.

"Hi there! I'm so sorry about the wait. We're slammed. It's going to be about a forty-five-minute wait for a table and about twenty minutes for a couple seats at the bar," the harried hostess said to them in a rush as she returned to the front booth.

Doing the mental math, Sierra frowned. If it was going to take that long to get some Jake's, they might as well make the walk farther up the trail.

"What about takeout?" Diablo asked, face and voice overly serious.

He was a man on a mission, and he was the kind of man unwilling to accept anything less than success. That his mission was feeding her warmed her in a way that was more tender than any of the other fires he'd stoked in her thus far in their acquaintance.

Smiling, the hostess's sense of relief at both lack of frustration and the idea of one less party to seat clear and obvious in the ease coming to her shoulders, she said, "No wait at all for that! I can take your order right here and have it out for you in about fifteen."

Looking at Sierra, Diablo asked, "That sound good to you?" and when she nodded, he turned back to the hostess with "We'll do that," his voice all firm and decided and take-charge, and Sierra found herself holding back a smile.

This might be her planned date, but it was clear that when it came to caring for those around him, Diablo took orders from no one.

Infuriating though she could imagine it might be at times, she appreciated that he was as fierce and immovable as an unbeaten bull.

They ordered and, sure enough, fifteen minutes later were heading back down the narrow path of sand that connected back to the larger trail, a bag containing two entrees and silverware swinging from Diablo's left hand.

"I know a spot where we can eat," Sierra said.

"I follow where you lead," Diablo replied.

Another ten minutes later they were once again leaving the main trail, this time headed east along a narrow path that was overgrown in multiple places and required a little creativity to navigate.

"You didn't tell me we'd be cutting trail today," he said in his characteristic dry tone.

A tad breathless from both the company and the bushwhacking, Sierra laughed airily. "Sometimes you have to deal with a little bush to get to the treasure on the other side."

As soon as the words left her mouth it was as if the invisible thread that connected them stretched taut.

A naughty note coming to his voice, he said, "Never let it be said that Diablo Sosa was intimidated or turned off by a little bush."

Heat coming to her cheeks, Sierra didn't back off from their flirtation as she had been compelled to before.

On the key, it was just the two of them—no cameras, no fans, no one who even knew their names. "How do you feel about a bare landscape?" she asked wickedly.

Stopping in his tracks, Diablo's eyes shot to hers, the intensity and focus of a hunter in them, and she couldn't say that it didn't thrill her to have thrown him.

"I wouldn't know," he said slowly, his voice thick and low, "but I'm always up for new experiences."

Her bare landscape in question sparked to life at his words. The idea of being a first—any first—for a man like Diablo, a man she was certain had come out of the womb knowing and seeing too much, was one of the most powerful aphrodisiacs she had ever encountered.

Her moment to respond with something equally suggestive, however, was lost as they stepped into the secluded beach grove that Sierra had discovered years ago.

Ringed neatly by vegetation on one side and a long stretch of beach on the other, the sandy spot was tucked far enough back from the water and low enough that it was out of sight from the main beach, hidden by a small dune that was still just short enough to see the ocean over.

Thankful that the spot was unclaimed, Sierra dug into her bag and pulled out the blanket she had packed. Laying it out on the sand, she made quick work of setting up a small picnic area.

Eyeing her as she worked with a half smile, Diablo said, "What else you got in that bag?"

Grinning and incapable of being ashamed over being prepared, Sierra pulled his bottle of water out and tossed it to him. "That for starters."

Catching it with the reflexes of a cowboy, he tipped an invisible hat to her and said, "Why, thank you, Ms. Poppins."

Laughing, Sierra said, "I am supercalifragilisticexpialidocious."

Giving her a once-over, he said, "I think you mean bodacious."

Pausing in her setup, she lifted an eyebrow and cocked her head to one side. "How old are you again?"

He threw his head back with a bark of laughter, his neck stretching long and thick, his Adam's apple bobbing, and all traces of sauciness and silliness left her.

She remained where she was, completely arrested, while rays of sunlight kissed him with a freedom that set off spikes of jealousy within her.

She tried to swallow through a suddenly parched throat.

Did he know he was beautiful?

She didn't think he did.

He led with his strength and intelligence and dared the world to challenge him, but did he know he was a work of art?

With his laughter dying down, he straightened his head, and as he did their eyes locked.

If she had been entranced by his glamour before, she knew she would never fully recover now—not after seeing his eyes so open and unguarded, filled with laughter as well as desire for her and an ease that only seemed to exist when it was just the two of them.

"Old enough to know what to do with a woman like you," he said, his eyes filled with a light that sent shivers along her skin.

"Oh, yeah?" she challenged, filling her voice with bravado to cover the breathlessness in it. "And what's that?"

With a wicked half grin, he lifted the takeout he held. "Feed her, of course."

Snorting, she rolled her eyes at him and shook her head. "Well, then, come on over and get to it, Diosa."

Leading by example, she plopped down on the blanket and patted the ground beside her.

Chuckling, he joined her on the blanket. "Your wish is my command, reinita."

"Then get to giving me what I need," she said, the slight catch and huskiness in her voice the only outward signs of the rushing sensation inside.

Moving with the easy grace of a cowboy, Diablo crossed the small patch of sand to join her on the blanket before taking out her order and handing it to her with aplomb.

She received it regally, which meant she gave him a cool nod in acceptance before laughing again.

As expected, the food wasn't particularly remarkable—a straightforward burger and fries for her and a halibut entree for him—and yet she knew she would remember this meal for a long time to come.

She had wanted to impress him with food that she was proud of loving in order to repay him for introducing her to that divine sandwich in New Orleans. Their meal from Jake's nowhere near met that bar.

It didn't matter. The company did.

When Diablo was around, everything she put in her mouth tasted delicious—especially him.

After they'd finished eating, she leaned back on her arms, taking in the man beside her and their private grove.

Then she asked, "Ready for that swim?"

Checking his watch, he said facetiously, "It hasn't been thirty minutes."

"Old wives' tale," she challenged.

"I don't see any old wives around here," he observed.

"My point exactly," she agreed. "The water looks just fine."

In reality, it looked more than fine.

On a perfect day like it was, the water was sure to be fantastic, and Sierra was smitten enough to push the issue just for the chance to see exactly what kind of swimsuit Diablo had brought along with him.

Eyeing her as if he could read every prurient thought in her mind, he said, "You just want to see if I really brought a swimsuit."

Rolling her eyes, although he was uncomfortably accurate in his assessment, Sierra denied it with, "You wish. I could care less whether you have one or not. I have mine and I'm going in."

A light of interest entering his eyes, he asked, "Are you wearing it now?"

With a snort, Sierra shook her head and said, "No. It looks like we both need to change."

Looking around them, noting the obvious lack of facilities, he said, "Public nudity is frowned upon."

Laughing, she said, "Ever the lawman."

"You know what they say," he said with a smug shrug. "A law is not valuable because it is the law but because there is right in it."

"Just turn around," she said as she stood, her swimsuit balled up in her palm.

Obliging, he looked away, and she made quick work of disrobing and reclothing herself in the tangle of strings and triangles of fabric that constituted her teeny-weeny yellow-and-white polka-dot bikini.

Of all her entire swimsuit collection, it was her favorite. She assumed Diablo would enjoy it as much as she did.

"I'm decent again," she said, and couldn't hold back her laugh at the quick way his head snapped around to take her in.

Seeing herself in his face, noting his obvious appreciation, was better than any mirror she'd ever looked in.

His pupils dilated, turning his eyes into big black pools, and he swallowed, the muscles of his throat moving making the action obvious.

She'd hoped to look good. His gaze told her she looked better.

"You're more than decent, queenie. I'd say you're out of this world."

Fielding compliments was part of her job and had been for so long that, like any addict, she'd built up a tolerance to them. But whether or not it was his way with words or the intensity with which his eyes devoured her, there was something different about them when they came from Diablo.

Or, she thought, as hooked into staring at him as he was with her, maybe it wasn't either of those things, but the honesty with which he spoke?

In all the time she'd known him, not once had she heard him utter an empty word.

Unlike herself, Diablo didn't appear to be impaired by the same social inhibitions that drove people to small talk and white lies.

When he spoke, he said what he thought, with no sugar coating, apparently impervious to concerns about what people would think.

Sierra cared all too much. She cared so much that she had crafted a life out of anticipating what people wanted to hear and delivering it, regardless of how it aligned with her inner truth. She was good at it, too—so good that she had become one of the most decorated rodeo queens of all time.

So good that these days she wasn't entirely sure where what she wanted ended and what they wanted began.

But when she was with Diablo, exactly what she wanted became crystal clear—even if it was in direct opposition to what everyone else wanted from her. She wanted him, like this, in as many stolen moments and for as long as she could get, right up until the tour was over.

Just the thought of the word *over* cast a shadow over

their sunny grove, filling her with a desperate urgency to hold on to as much of the brightness as she could, to magnify and increase it, for as long as she could.

"Your turn!" she demanded, a trace of overenthused panic edging her voice.

Eyeing her for a moment longer, Diablo was slow to nod, his own focus still clearly—and flatteringly—locked on her swimsuit.

When he made no move to change after another second had passed, however, Sierra snapped her fingers at him, saying, "Appurate, acere. We're wasting daylight."

Laughing at her impatience, but finally moving, he came to his feet and retrieved the tantalizingly small square of folded black fabric that had been tucked in the back pocket of his shorts.

When she made no move to turn, he cleared his throat, saying, "Ahem?" before making a little circular turning motion with his finger.

Feigning innocence, she said, "Oh? You want me to turn around?"

Casting her a knowing grin, he said, "I wouldn't want to ruin the surprise later on. What fun is a present if it's not wrapped?"

Heat thrilled in her system at the confidence in his words, but she obliged his request, turning around to look at the foliage that provided them privacy, rather than impinge on his.

Like most cowboys, he was lacking in neither cocksureness nor the body to back it up. Unlike most cowboys, however, he seemed to know how to draw out the delicious torture of anticipation.

"You can turn around now," he said. His voice, thick with both the Texas and Dominican in it, was its own form of seduction, but nothing compared to the broad expanse of his bare chest and the muscled trunks of his thighs.

He wore the simple pair of black swim trunks, which were fitted and shorter than most men dared to wear while not qualifying as a Speedo. Looking at the thin fabric she could understand how he'd managed to fit them into his back pocket.

He was every bit as sexy in them as she was in her own swimwear. It was a good thing she wasn't intimidated by a little competition.

She didn't know how long she stared, but when he cleared his own throat, she realized belatedly that it had been too long to be labeled anything but lust.

"Ready to swim?" she croaked, unable to disguise the hoarse irregularity of her voice but comforted by the fact that, as he swallowed again, he appeared as affected as she was.

"More than before," he said cryptically, moving to close the distance between them.

As he neared, she could feel the heat that radiated from his body and smell the leather and spice scent of skin.

The man was sensory overload on legs.

But she wasn't expecting him to suddenly dash past her and run straight into the ocean.

Nor did she anticipate that she would be filled with the urge to follow, screaming and laughing with glee like she was twelve years old again as she did.

They swam and splashed and body surfed and tried to dunk each other like they were teenagers dancing on the line between play and flirtation, eager for any excuse to touch each other, until they were both waterlogged, happily exhausted and ready to warm up in the sun.

"You're a strong swimmer, queenie," he noted as they made their way back to the blanket and towel that waited for them in their secluded grove.

As sensitized as her skin was from the water and salt and sun, and his company, her body alive from its many brushes with his, his words ran over her like a caress, even when they weren't anything particularly poetic.

"Comes with the territory when you grow up in Florida," she said. "Ocean safety and strong swimming."

"And sunblock," he added with a teasing smile.

"And sunblock, which reminds me..." she said, trailing off, though her implication was clear.

"Only if you rub it on my back for me," he said wickedly, and she laughed, though the idea of getting her hands on him—even just to rub sunblock on him—was far more appealing than it should be.

True to her word, she dug her SPF out of her bag as soon as they'd both dried.

"Lay down," she directed him, pointing toward the blanket.

Obliging her with a catlike smile and hooded-eyed expression, he all but purred in anticipation, and she found herself suddenly very aware that, in both of their cases, only thin fabric separated their bodies from each other.

He lay on a towel on his stomach, his incredibly muscled back still glistening with drops of the sea, and her mouth watered in anticipation, as if he was a meal waiting to be devoured.

Given how much she wanted him, the description wasn't that far off.

His glutes were perfectly rounded and defined in a way that some people were willing to go under the knife to achieve, though she knew in his case the perfection wasn't bought but the natural result of riding hard and not shirking leg day.

She had the sense that Diablo didn't shirk in anything that he did, and the knowledge set off a wave of shivers along her skin.

But even the thrill of the idea was nothing compared to the sensation of placing her cool palms against his hot skin to rub in the thick mineral sunscreen.

As she massaged his back and rubbed it in, blending away the cast of the sunscreen in the process, he made sounds that sent her mind to the kinds of pleasure best not enjoyed in public settings.

Diablo lit the sensuality within her, driving her to make the first move—or second, or third, or fourth move—because in his company it was abruptly clear that games and ought-not-tos were a bad way to waste precious time.

"Other side," she said, her voice hoarse but her command firm. Here was a test of sorts. He didn't exactly need her help to put sunblock on his stomach. Would he turn?

He did, and what was more, he did it without callout or comment.

She supposed they were still playing some game of sorts. Theirs just wasn't the game of pretending.

And if his back had been an experience, rubbing the sunblock across his corded and defined chest and abs was downright overstimulating—and watching his face while she did so? A simultaneous exercise in pleasure and pain.

His eyes were dark and endless and today was expressly and purposely about them, for this.

To be together, out loud and in the open, mutual feelings acknowledged between the two of them.

Sitting up with a contraction of his gorgeously defined muscles, Diablo leaned forward to brush the sand from her shoulder and once he was there, it was only a matter of closing the last few inches between them for their lips to meet.

She sighed into his kiss, eagerly surrendering to a sensation she was coming to crave.

This was mastery, utterly assured and confident—the same thrumming power that clung to him in the arena and, she guessed, in the courtroom.

And then he was everywhere at once—over her, his palms slipping her swimsuit bottoms down and over her hips, the calloused strength of his palm traveling the length of her leg in a rough caress against her hypersensitive skin as he pulled them down in an exquisite friction until he reached her ankle. Wrapping his hand around the delicate bones, with gentle pressure he pushed her leg up and slightly open, moving her body into the kind of wanton position she'd only seen online.

Cheeks hot, her breath caught, then released, and on it, his name slipped out.

He looked up, a crooked smile and wicked light in his eye, and she knew it was too late for her.

This was what mothers had been warning their daughters about since the dawn of time.

He knew it, and she knew it.

Then his hands were making quick work of the strings of her bikini top to bare and cup her breasts, and she didn't know anything but the urge to cry out softly, the contact sweet relief against the heavy, tender weight she hadn't realized had been so burdensome.

He rolled his thumbs over the hard buds of her nipples and she moaned, arching into his hands.

"Quieres eso?" he asked, leaning in close, brushing his lips against her neck, before trailing kisses along her jawline toward her ear. *"Y eso?"* he continued, his voice a low thrumming vibration entering her ear before shivering through the rest of her body like a sweet secret.

"Mmmmm." The mumbled affirmation was all she could manage, her mind taxed enough, split between paying attention to what he was doing with his hands and mouth.

He still had his swimsuit on, though it had become more constricted as a result of their activity.

Greedy to do some exploring of her own, she brought her hands to his chest.

He was magnificent in the flesh. Deep brown and smooth as silk, she wanted to taste and touch every inch of him that she could see, the cannibalistic language of love making sense to her in a way it never had before.

He was…delicious. And that was just without a shirt on.

To her gratitude, he leaned back to let her have her fill of looking, though her breasts pouted at the loss of his attention.

He did his own studying as well, however, his eyes lighting on hers before lowering, lingering on her lips, her exposed breasts, and then his eyes trailed lower, down the soft swell of her stomach to the nuclear core of her.

When they landed there, the look in his eyes shifted, more intent, his energy pointed in a way it hadn't been before.

Her breathing went short, and she froze, somehow

resisting the urge to cover herself, grateful she was just high maintenance enough to shell out for professional grooming despite the fact that there hadn't been anyone to see it in years.

Had it really been years? She wondered briefly with a kind of horrified awe at how that much time had passed since she'd been with a man, before circling back around to the reason.

The answer was the same as it always was: rodeo.

There was no time for men in a schedule like hers.

And yet, she had made time for Diablo. Forced it where it shouldn't be and didn't belong.

And what a reward she had gained.

Abruptly, the space between them disappeared again.

He cupped her mound with his palm, the warm, steady pressure of it teasing for all that it rested still.

And, as if he performed some titillating sexual magic rather than simply held her most sensitive core, she felt herself opening for him, her inner folds going slick, beckoning his fingers inside, even as her hips ground against his palm, driven by primal instinct.

He ran a finger along her most intimate crease and the world stilled. She welcomed him with joy, sending tremors in a wave from the epicenter, but he did not press, simply caressed, up and down, each stroke gentle and deliberate.

Her breath hitched with every pass, each one shorter than the last, as she watched him touch her, a somewhat out-of-body erotic experience almost for watching and feeling at the same time.

The air rang out with a series of strange whimpers and sobs and she was surprised to realize the sound was coming from her.

Her eyes screwed shut.

"No. Look at me, Sierra. I like it when you watch." His voice was utterly commanding. He spoke with the authority of a man who not only knew his orders would be followed, but also expected his followers to be grateful for the direction.

She looked at him, cheeks flushed, eyes bright, moist and large. And she was grateful she did.

He was a masterpiece. Hard planes, shadows, velvet and steel—perfection, unmarred by the scars that marked so many rodeo cowboys.

But she knew he could still ride.

The thought struck her at the same moment his finger slipped inside her, and the combination thrust her over the edge she'd been skirting. Her body locked around him, clenching before releasing in waves of pleasure that radiated from her center outward, erasing everything in their wake.

They had not yet subsided when he slipped his shorts off, nor even when he aligned himself, hot and sheathed, against her still-pulsing entrance, though they both shuddered on contact, a strange fluttering of awareness sparkling through her veins before dissipating like stardust in the face of more earth pleasures.

He adjusted her ankle, angling her hips for that much more access, his eyes reading hers, the tendons in his neck as rigid as he was.

And then, in a single stroke, he thrust inside her on a growl and stopped. "Dios mio, Sierra, this is criminal." His voice was strained, sexier for all of its leashed control, even as her body stiffened in reaction to the pain of stretching.

It had been a long time.

Neither of them moved.

His breathing came in ragged breaths, the sound harsh for all that she felt each one in her core.

Pleasure building again, growing more insistent the longer he remained within her—the more her body adjusted to the incredible size and length of him—she began to undulate her hips.

His muscles quivered, but he showed no signs of fatigue.

If he was indefatigable, however, she was feeling a growing sense of urgency, her hips moving faster according to instinct and primal design rather than any sort of control.

A strangled sound escaped his throat, but he held still, allowing her the freedom to explore him. When she experimented with lowering her hips, drawing him out before inching forward to slide back in, however, he took control of the reins.

Slowly, then with greater intensity, depth and speed, he thrust, drawing her nearer and nearer again to the gnawing edge of oblivion. She was eager to follow, eager to jump with him again.

As she kept his pace, her hips finding his rhythm, meeting him with each thrust, he spread her legs wider, the motion somehow possessive. And she was surprised by how much she wanted him to claim her, how each withdrawal brought a pinch of sadness and each return took her a step closer to bliss.

And then she was tumbling over the edge again, but this time, when she went down, she took the devil with her.

CHAPTER FOURTEEN

Atlanta, Georgia

IN ATLANTA, THEY WERE riding saddle bronc again, and there was something fitting about the fact that they were revisiting an event that was all about style in a city that was known for it.

After the challenge, the gap between Diablo and Julio and the remaining thirteen contestants—the bottom five having been eliminated after the points were tallied—had only widened.

The distance between both of them and Dillon, though, had grown into the kind of thing that was a numerical insult—at least, it would be to a man who touted himself as the future of rodeo.

But that being said, even after the challenge upset and subsequent eliminations, Dillon remained firmly enmeshed in the third-place spot. The likelihood of his catching up to either Diablo or Julio, however, was getting slimmer and slimmer every time they competed.

And if things kept along in the trajectory they'd been headed, with Diablo surprising even himself each time he got on the back of an animal, and Julio pulling out the kinds of rides that people called perfect, Dillon's game was going to turn from one of catch-up to one of trying to just hold on.

Disgruntled and hopeless wasn't a combination Diablo imagined would look good on a man like Dillon, so even though he had things he would much rather be doing in his free time, namely spending it with Sierra, he took some of the extended stop they had in Atlanta to approach Julio.

Knocking on the older man's RV door, Diablo hoped he was inside. Julio wasn't expecting him.

The tour was staying in Atlanta for longer than any of their other stops, in part so that they could shoot promos and specials while they had access to full production facilities. Because of that, they had also scheduled the contestants' private interviews and photos throughout the weeklong pit stop.

Julio answered on the second knock, greeting him with an easy smile though Diablo noted he opened the door only wide enough to reveal his body and not far enough that a visitor might see inside.

"Hola," he said, before asking with friendliness that didn't result in his opening the door any farther, "¿Qué tal?"

"I was hoping I could come in," Diablo answered seriously.

Something flashed across the other man's eyes, but he nodded and moved, opening the door to allow Diablo to step inside.

Closing the door behind them, Julio asked, his voice newly guarded, "So what'd you want to talk about?"

Eyeing him, Diablo considered the best course of action.

His training and experience at the immigration law firm he'd volunteered for in the summers between law school had taught him the best practices when it came to asking people about their immigration status, but applying those standards to his current situation felt oddly disrespectful to the man he was speaking to.

Julio was not in a state of duress or under direct threat—unless one considered Dillon's attitude a threat, which neither man actually did.

Dillon was a blowhard who thought he was tough. Really, he was just sheltered.

Julio didn't have a language barrier that could create confusion or lack of clarity around terms, and Diablo had witnessed him in action enough times to know that the man was a master of deflection.

Regardless of his status, it was clear that Julio was a man who knew the ins and outs of the world he walked in.

He wasn't confused or in distress, he was a cowboy, down to the bone, and he didn't need to be handled with kid gloves.

Hell, the man was older than Diablo was, and comfortable about it. He'd earned Diablo's respect from the first and Diablo wouldn't patronize him by delicately dancing around the issue with questions about the route he'd taken to get where he was, or his work permit or refugee status. Neither would he take an administrative approach with questions about this program or that program, his visa or green card, or, God forbid, his marital status.

Julio was a cowboy he respected, and he was going to treat him as such.

So rather than employing tact, Diablo chose to be direct. "¿Es usted un inmigrante ilegal?"

For a long moment—long enough for his eyes to go hard and flat and for him to take a long, slow blink—Julio said nothing.

And then, the tension popped and he nodded.

The movement was short and simple, businesslike even, and accompanied by no verbal confirmation, and yet, it spoke volumes.

Gesturing toward the bench of the RV's dining table, Julio said, "Sit. You want some coffee?"

Taking the seat, Diablo gave his own nod, adding, "Sí. Gracias."

Neither man spoke again until they sat on opposite sides of the Formica-topped table, steaming cups of black coffee in front of them.

"So," Julio said finally, a heavy acceptance in his voice, "why do you want to know about my immigration status?"

"I wanted to offer my services."

Instantly on guard, Julio lifted his hands and shook his head in denial. "I don't need that."

Rather than assure him that the offer came free of charge, which it did, Diablo instead asked, "Is that why you're doing *The Closed Circuit*?"

With a self-deprecating laugh, Julio shook his head again. "No. Well, yes. Not exactly."

Lifting an eyebrow, Diablo asked, "Which is it?"

"No," he reiterated, before adding, "my daughter is sick."

The non sequitur wasn't what Diablo had expected, but people's stories never were, and so he simply stayed quiet and let the man continue.

"She has leukemia. Her treatment is scheduled to begin in Mexico in the fall."

"And you need the money to pay for it?"

Julio laughed. "It wouldn't hurt, but no, that's not it. I need the money because she wants me to go with her."

Nodding, Diablo said, "So you need it to get back?"

Again, Julio shook his head. "No. This time I'm not coming back."

Diablo frowned, cocking his head to one side.

"I'm old and tired," Julio said. "I've been sent back and returned enough times to know how it works, but I'm just tired. Aurelia was born here. She's free to come back if she wants, but my wife and I are tired of it, and with the way things have been lately..." He shrugged before continuing, "Why stay in a place where you're not welcome? We decided that this time we're going back to stay. After Aurelia's treatment, we're going to take our money and retire in Cancún, just like the gringos." The last Julio said with a dry chuckle that couldn't help but bring a smile to Diablo's face.

"So that's why you were willing to risk *The Closed Circuit*," he said, and Julio nodded.

"We have enough money for Aurelia's treatment, but having extra never hurts," he said with a grin, "and after all these years, I'm tired of living on alert. I came here because there was no work for me in Guadalajara. At twenty, I thought the most important thing in the world was the freedom to buy a nice truck and there was no way I could do that back home, so I came here. But then I got the truck, and along the way a wife and daughter, and we stayed because Aurelia had a citizen's rights to schools and opportunities and we wanted that for her, even if there was no way for the two of us to get legal status without leaving the country and then waiting for years in the hope we might be the lucky ones who made it through. Aurelia is an American, she was born here. But my wife and I are Mexican. Neither of us had ever meant to stay here this long. When each of us was younger, we thought earning more cash, and faster than we could at home, was a risk worth taking for a short term. It was never supposed to be permanent. I wanted that truck, but after all these years here, I realize the truck wasn't the important thing. The truck was just what you had to show for the work you did. The work to get the truck, whether or not there was any pride in it, that was the important thing. At first, I worked at ranches and even competed in rodeo, nothing that could get me sponsored, but it was still good work. After Aurelia was born, though, that kind of work was too risky."

Savvy, Diablo eyed him. "You were too good."

An ironic half smile on his face, Julio nodded. "Too good gets the wrong kind of attention for a man in my position. But that was then. Now that I don't care, I'm free. I can be as good as I want to be, because what's the worst they can do to me? They can't make me go back and spend another ten years working in restaurants, that's for sure."

Diablo laughed, though the sound was weighted with the other man's story.

There was happiness in it. Julio had escaped from the oppressive net that had held him for what sounded like a huge chunk of his life, but there was no justice in his freedom.

"I'd still like to help. Free of charge. You have options, then, and rights, at least legally," he added.

He didn't say it didn't hurt to be prepared for retaliation from Dillon. There was no need for speculation if one was prepared for everything.

His instincts told him that the Dillon problem would only get worse as the score gap grew, and that Dillon was the type to lash out when he felt wronged.

Even if being wronged in this case was just being beaten.

Julio made a dismissive noise, waving Diablo's words away. "No. You don't need to do that. Your time is better spent somewhere else, getting your heart broken by pretty rodeo queens..." He trailed off, a knowing glint in his eyes.

"I can do both," Diablo replied drily, unwilling to be deterred, adding, "and it's not always so complicated as it's made out to be. The law works differently when you know who is responsible for what and who has clearance to make special decisions, the kind of people whose contact information I happen to have."

Chuckling, Julio said, "You're a funny man."

"Not a lot of people realize it," Diablo joked with a grin before going serious again. "I'm not promising citizenship or anything like that, which it sounds like you don't need given your plans, but I can get you a green card."

Smile shuttering, Julio shook his head again. "No, you really don't need to. The time for that has passed."

Diablo would not be moved. "I'll need some information about you, but it won't take long."

With a humorless laugh he replied, "I don't know how long is long in your mind, but I can tell you even the fastest, seven to eight months, is longer than we need. We'll be gone before that."

Scoffing, Diablo shook his head. "Try seven to eight days. I'm very familiar with the relevant law and have the right kind of contact at the USCIS. She has discretionary authority and can make things happen, and, fortunately, your case has a couple of things going for it."

Wariness stirring with frustration and hope in his eyes, Julio said, "And what is that?"

"A medical emergency and Hollywood," Diablo said, and though there was nothing just, right or fair about it, he also knew it was true and would make things easier.

Collecting photos and information about Julio before leaving, Diablo went straight to his own RV to complete the required forms and paperwork while everything was still fresh in his mind.

Having spent two summers in law school volunteering with one of the leading immigration law firms in Phoenix, filling out an I-485 form took him a fraction of the time it generally took an applicant, and his result was far more professional.

He kept things simple, brief and as general as possible while still fully addressing each field—just as he'd been trained to do.

Laypeople often thought that giving long, detailed answers was the key to success, but in fact, the opposite was generally true. Detail opened the door for denial. The key to success was to meet the requirement without going above and beyond.

Administrators didn't need or want life stories.

They needed their asses covered and the appropriate boxes ticked in case their supervisors checked.

When Diablo had compiled a complete application he contacted his friend Carissa, who worked in the Phoenix field office for USCIS. Having worked under her when she was still a young lawyer, one who had been particularly passionate about immigration as a key component of a healthy and thriving country, he had a good relationship with her. And in the interim years since then, she had made her way up the bureaucratic ladder within the citizenship and immigration services branch. As a GS-12, step level seven employee now, she also conveniently had the level of discretion he needed to get what he wanted.

There would be a few final boxes to tick through the process, there always were, such as securing official copies of documents, but he'd sent her everything she needed in the meantime in order to make a conditional decision, and that was all he and Julio needed for now.

Nashville, Tennesse

THE TOUR ARRIVED in Nashville a week later, the remaining contestants having completed their multiple press events and filming their personal profile videos during their long stint in Atlanta. But more importantly for Diablo and Julio, Diablo's contact in USCIS had confirmed that all of the necessary documents and approvals had been processed and completed and that Julio should be able to pick up his hot-off-the-presses card at the downtown post office here in Nashville today, shipped overnight via general delivery.

With the good news, Diablo breathed a bit easier, as he told Sierra the night before the Nashville show.

"Dillon's going to try something," he said into the top of her head as she leaned back into him, the remains of their shared meal of hot chicken and hushpuppies on the table. The instinct that told him to watch his back with the guy had only grown stronger in the time since his conversation with Julio. Diablo had learned a long time ago to trust his instincts.

"He ought to try to close the point gap if he wants any shot at winning," she retorted saucily.

Snorting, Diablo said, "That's impossible. That's why he's going to try something. When a man like Dillon knows he can't win the right way, he resorts to wrong. I've seen it time and time again."

Ever the devil's advocate, which he normally loved, Sierra said, "Well, it's still technically possible for him to catch up, but…"

And, technically, it still was, though the chances and trends didn't favor him.

"But not likely," Diablo finished the point for her.

With the weighted point potential for their show tomorrow, it was likely to be Dillon's last opportunity to catch up to and even possibly take a lead over Diablo, at least, though not Julio.

Conversely, the same was true for Diablo with respect to Julio because the Nashville show would be the first time they rode actual bulls for the tour.

Like the various point boosters that existed in the *Closed Circuit* scoring matrices—such as setting world records, as AJ had done in the first season, and getting perfect scores, as Julio had done this season—bull rides were weighted more heavily than the rest of the events.

It was just another way the show built excitement and fervor and kept the television audiences tuning in week after week.

And if Diablo's internal alarms weren't going off so hard about Dillon, he might have been able to enjoy it.

As the first bull ride of the season, each contestant would be riding a baby bull—brand-new to the arena and unpredictable because of it.

Last year the first bull rides had been all over the map, with some of the animals going wild—their fear, adrenaline and rage combining to make a bully ride—

and some of them, like Lil's, freezing up and choking in the face of a crowd.

A score was a combination of the rider's skill, the luck of the draw and staying on for the full eight seconds—which was harder on a bull than any other mount, in Diablo's opinion.

Thankfully, bull riding was Diablo's specialty.

And while rumor had it that Dillon was no slouch when it came to bulls, either, it would take more than skill to get him the upset he was looking for—it'd take luck. To beat out Diablo, Dillon would need a great bull, a great ride and for Diablo to get the opposite on both fronts.

Fortunately—or unfortunately given that Dillon was the only one likely to take underhanded action in the top three—luck hadn't shown herself to be on Dillon's side throughout the tour.

Honestly, if luck was on anyone's side, it was Julio's.

And that was why Diablo couldn't relax.

Smiling at his concern, Sierra said, "I wouldn't worry about it too much. Dillon might not have the most class, but he's got a comfortable corner of the rodeo market. Whatever happens in *The Closed Circuit* isn't going to change the fact that he's one of the sport's most successful riders. He's got plenty of money and great sponsorships and none of that is at risk if he doesn't take home the top prize here. Whether he does well or poorly in *The Closed Circuit* doesn't really matter in the long run."

But Diablo couldn't shake the feeling.

"It's not him losing money that I'm worried about, or even face," he added. "It's specifically Julio doing better than him. It's not about the money for men like

Dillon, or it is, but money's just a proxy. It's about their identity being predicated on being inherently better than people like Julio and me. Men like Dillon lash out not because their resources are actually threatened, but because their sense of their place in the hierarchy of life is threatened. When that happens, when brown people do better than them, brown people end up getting killed."

Turning to face him with an incredulous look, Sierra said, "Well, thank God no one is getting killed, then. Unless of course it's by a bull. We're talking about *The Closed Circuit* here, not a small-town lynching."

"I'm not so sure the two are as far removed as you might think," he said darkly, fully aware, if she wasn't, of how easily that line could disappear.

"You sure you're not just setting me up so that I feel bad for you when you get thrown before your eight seconds is up? We've been talking about Dillon, but you're no closer to that number-one spot, either." Her voice was light and mischievous and, though it wasn't the adjective he generally associated with Sierra, naive.

She didn't know to be worried because, despite the barriers she'd overcome, she'd never really been attacked.

The same wasn't true for Diablo. But because it wasn't, he knew to be prepared.

"The only number-one spot I'm worried about is the one in your heart," he said, turning his voice country and sappy and squeezing her tight to him.

Snorting, she retorted, "Then I guess you better stay in the top three because I like my cowboys to be of the winning variety."

"Aren't you getting a bit long in the tooth to have

such high standards?" he asked, to which she responded by jabbing him in the ribs.

"Keep talking like that and I might find that I'm a bit long in the tooth to be coming over so late. An aging woman needs her rest, after all."

Nodding as if what she said was perfectly reasonable, he said, "I have noticed you looking a little tired lately. Though, if you come over any earlier, we might as well go public."

Hitting him playfully again, she said through her teeth, "I meant I wouldn't be coming over at all, Diosa."

Which, of course, he knew.

Though, she had been testing the line recently, barely waiting for the dark of night to set in before skulking over to his RV.

And while he knew the deal and rules with rodeo queens, there was a thread of real desire in his joke.

As the competition intensified and the extras and promos ramped up, stealing daytime with her was becoming more and more impossible, and though he wasn't complaining about her midnight visits, he was getting tired of feeling like a teenager's dirty secret again.

They were both grown. That anyone outside the two of them should have a say as to what they did in their free time—and with whom—was absurd. That they were both willingly bowing to the arbitrary rules, sneaking around like they were doing something wrong, was even more so.

"You ready for tomorrow?" he asked, changing the subject rather than dwell on what he could not change.

"I should be asking you that. I'm not the one climbing on the back of a bull."

"Well, since you have now, I can assure you that I am."

Snorting again, the sound having quickly become one of his favorites that she made—after the way she said his name and the noises she made while they made love—she asked, somewhat seriously, "How long's it been since you've been on the back of the bull?"

Casually, as if it didn't matter, he said, "About fourteen years."

Gasping, Sierra bolted upright. "No. That's too long. How could you? You didn't practice?"

Laughing at her outrage, he shook his head. "They were all out of live man killers when I went to the store."

Unmoved and as unwilling to accept excuses as his nana was, Sierra said, "I've been to Lil's ranch. I'm sure she could have rustled up a bull for you."

Inclining his head in acknowledgment, he replied, "She could have, but I didn't want her to. Bull riding is my best event. With a little under two weeks' time to get ready, I focused on practicing the things that gave me a bit more trouble."

She eyed him doubtfully. "If you say so…"

Drawing her back down to his side, he pulled her close and held on tight, a part of him privately marveling at the easy fit of her in his arms, her form the perfect size and height to fit snuggled up against his, and said, "Thanks for worrying about me, but you don't have to. It's not bravado. I love riding bulls, and that's why I'm good at it. In all my years, they're the only thing I've met that I can throw my all against without fear for the consequences, and it's been a long time since I've had that chance. I've got plenty to bring to the table."

And it was true. Because it had been a long time, he did.

He'd quit riding before law school and before he'd

clawed his way into a good firm and dragged his way up the ranks.

After all of that, he had plenty to throw at a bull.

But he had something entirely different to throw at her, something that didn't have to do with Dillon or bulls or anyone outside the two of them.

Tilting her head toward his with care, he drew her lips to his, kissing her softly.

Tomorrow would be for bulls and blood and dust and mud and everything else that people came to the rodeo for. It could be for costumes and pretending to be nothing to each other, and for dealing with Dillon's petulance and performing for the *Closed Circuit* cameras.

But tonight, what little remained of it, would be for her—for them together.

And as if she not only sensed the shift in his need and mood but needed the reassurance of it herself, Sierra leaned in and opened, tender and receptive, the taste of her going as soft as her sigh.

He could feel her worry for him in the way her hands came up to grip and hold his shoulders, and he was touched by her concern. This queen who loved rodeo with her whole being, who had no doubt seen more tragedy and triumph in the arena than even the cowboys competing themselves and never seemed to tire of coming back for more, had trepidation thrumming through her body at the thought of him going out there unprepared.

But she had nothing to worry about on that front, and though he would prove it to her tomorrow, tonight he'd show her.

He was prepared. Life had prepared him by being more dangerous than a being made of muscle and horns and rage.

She was what he had not been prepared for, what had thrown him for a loop and had him questioning every vow and promise he'd made to himself up to this point.

She was what he'd been missing out on, what he'd given up by walking away from rodeo when he did.

But if he was using his touch and lips to tell her, then she had her own messages to communicate back to him—in the way she held and gripped and lingered, drawing out their shared breath in the kiss.

Maybe it was because of his misgivings about Dillon or hers about the bulls or the fact that with each and every performance they got closer to an expiration date that neither had been able to bring up, but this time was different than their first time together, or even the clandestine encounters since.

Tomorrow marked not just the milestone of the first bull ride, but the turning point of the season.

It was hard to imagine that the end of the tour spelled anything but an end to their affair—Diablo's law practice couldn't wait forever and her work would keep her tied to the circuit, the eternal rodeo queen.

But they could hold off eternity for a little while if they took their time.

So they kissed, soft and slow and then deeper, tongues mingling, until they were breathless and more than ready for the next step, but still they held off, extending the agony as well as the reward.

And when they could wait no longer, his hands came to her breasts, each one more than a handful, dense and heavy.

She moaned into him, leaning in as if she could press away the clothing barrier between them. And because he could give her what she wanted, because it was easy now to please both of them, he slipped his hands beneath her shirt, releasing the clasp of her bra with a quick pinch and flick of his thumbs at the center of her back.

And when his hands returned to the front, to the gorgeous mounds he knew would haunt his dreams ever after—the standard to which no others would be able to compare—she sighed into his mouth.

Handling her with care, not because she was delicate but because he wanted it to be absolutely clear that he valued her, that he was grateful to her for sharing herself with him, his thumbs made soft circles around the hard tips of her nipples until her hips writhed and she could take their pace no more.

Breaking their kiss, her eyes fluttered open, glistening and bright in the dim lighting of the RV, she turned her body around, angling herself so she straddled his lap, the hot center of her aligned with the part of him that was hard and pulsing and utterly impatient, before she recaptured his lips.

He loved the way she went for what she wanted, that she was as ambitious and driven outside as she was sweet and soft inside.

And, just like she'd wanted, their new position gave him even more unfettered access to her silken skin. He bathed her in attention, not only her breasts, but also the sensitive skin along her rib cage all the way to teasing along the line of her pants, until it was no longer enough to feel. He had to see. He had to fill his eyes with her, imprinting every freckle and line in his mind while he still had her because even though it was far from the last opportunity they'd have to be together, it somehow felt like it.

And what a sight she was.

For a time, she was content to let him look his fill, lips plump and parted, chest high and proud above the soft plane of her stomach. Her dusky nipples aimed directly at him and he gave in to the urge to taste them, leaning forward to lavish one with attention until her moans took on a slightly desperate cadence and her fingers dug hard into his shoulders and he switched to the other.

He remained fully clothed, but felt her voice like a caress across bare skin, each uttered sound wriggling past everything he wore to reverberate through a rod that was attuned acutely to her.

That she couldn't keep still on his lap, each movement exacerbating the effect that her sounds of pleasure were having on the part of him that felt like it had garnered every ounce of blood from his body, only enhanced his state until it became a type of pain he had no urgency to end.

Or rather, a kind of torture he had no intention of rushing to end.

It would be easy to rush, to take her when he knew she was ready and wanted it just as much as he did, but he wasn't looking for easy.

He didn't want easy. He wanted Sierra.

Not because she was off-limits, and not even because of her glorious curves. He wanted her because she fit, because she carried passion and intensity to rival his own and the intelligence to get where she wanted to go.

And he wasn't the only one wanting.

The grip of her hands eased on his shoulders, but only so that she could push him against the bench until his back lay upon it and he stared up at her topless form.

Leaning forward, she brought her lips to his once again, and her nipples brushed against his chest, tracing lines of lightning through the shirt he wore, demanding the return of his hands.

Were his palms too rough?

From the way she moved, he didn't think so, despite the fact that even years in law had done nothing to soften the hard calluses he'd developed as a young man.

She couldn't seem to get enough of them, and he couldn't get enough of her.

When she tugged at the base of his T-shirt, he obliged, shifting slightly to pull it off and over his head quickly, before she laid him down again.

Skin on skin now, it was a harder thing to control the urge to speed things up, to bring the forcefulness that thrummed in both of their personalities to the forefront and let it reign, but they managed, even as she abandoned his lips to trace kisses along his jaw and down his neck.

Interspersed here and there with tiny nibbles and licks, each plump, faintly wet, impression left by her lips felt like a bread crumb leading to paradise. Leading to home. And when her lips touched the skin just above the line of his pants, it was his turn to moan, the sound escaping as everything other than that single point of contact disappeared.

Her hands came to his waistline and he gladly lifted his hips for her to slide the clothing away.

Their eyes met, each flickering and wide, twin expressions gone nearly black from how large their pupils had grown.

She licked her lips and swallowed, as if she'd been starving for weeks and he was the first meal she'd encountered, and what little blood remained elsewhere rushed to his rod.

When she put her mouth around him, her hands coming to join, one cupping his balls, the other wrapping around to grip his shaft, her eyes still locked on his, something inside him cracked and broke, shifting in a way he could barely comprehend, let alone hide from his gaze.

And then her eyelids fluttered closed and she moaned like the taste of him was a delicacy, and he was lost to her. She had all the power, more than any bull or haunting memory he'd ever met or carried, and he groaned in surrender.

She worked him like that until he could take no more, until he had two options: to take her or lose it all.

But he wasn't ready to lose it—not before he took her with him.

The time for slow had ended, obliterated by her expert assault.

Sweeping her up, he carried her to the bed, thankful if only temporarily, for the barrier of her pants. It stopped him from taking her as they rose, gave him time to lay her down gently, to get what he needed to protect them both, before sliding the pants away to give her even just a fraction of what she had given him.

She had given him peace, turning herself into a living safe space for him as she demanded his surrender, holding him with care the whole time. It was the least he could do to make her come.

Only after she'd done that, after she'd cried out the name he shared with the devil as if she'd gleefully abandoned God, did he enter her, reaching down between them to bring her cresting over the edge again and again before he, too, gave himself over to the wave.

CHAPTER FIFTEEN

BY THIS POINT in her career, there was no real way to tally how many bull rides Sierra had witnessed, though the number had to be in the thousands.

"Coming up next in Nashville, folks," she said, her voice loud and diction clear, "is the one, the only, the bringer of law and order to this wild and rowdy *Closed Circuit Rodeo*, Diablo Sosa. We've seen him sentence broncs into submission, and we've seen him bring steers to justice, but now we're going to see if he's got what it takes to outlast an outlaw. We're about to see, y'all, because the sheriff's in town and he's about to take on Doc Holiday. It might be Doc's first rodeo, folks, but that also means he's never been beaten. Outlaw or lawman, man or bull, right or wrong—either way, it's grit that comes out on top in the justice of the West!"

The crowd ate up all of her heavy-handedness around the lawman angle, and the cameras cooperated, too, zooming in on Diablo in the chute as she spoke to broadcast his image across the enormous screens set up around the arena.

Around the mic, Sierra's palms were sweaty.

She smiled, red lipped and pearly white, and her eyes shone.

She didn't want to watch him. She had recognized it in herself as she'd reluctantly dragged herself away from him the night before and committed to avoiding just that tonight. It was self-care.

She'd even employed every one of her techniques to look like she was watching when she wasn't—casting the net of her gaze anywhere but where Diablo was loaded up in the chute—but thanks to the jumbotron, in every direction she looked the projection of him was already there.

In all her years, she had seen countless men absolutely dominate on bulls—both bulls that were new to the arena, as well as bulls that retired unbeaten.

And she had seen even more absolutely dominated by bulls.

She had seen one man sustain a head injury from which he later died, and she had seen countless other times in which it seemed only divine intervention that had stopped a person from getting killed in the arena right where they'd fallen.

She had gone through the thrilling agony of watching people she cared about climb atop bulls, as well as watching men that she'd had winter flings with flex their stuff during the regular season, and never once had had the urge to look away before.

She loved rodeo; she didn't look away from it.

She respected rodeo, knew it was dangerous and honored the daring it took to even do it by bearing witness to the very end, fair or foul.

But she didn't want to watch Diablo.

She had dedicated her adolescence and adulthood to rodeo, had committed to playing its pretty princess for all of time because of how passionate she was about the sport, but rather than excitement at the prospect of watching an excellent athlete perform, she felt dread.

In this moment under the hot stage lights and in front of thousands of people, she realized she adored Diablo more.

She didn't want to watch him, despite how good he promised to be, because there was a chance he could get hurt out there, and to the thing that pounded frantically in her chest, the chance alone was reason enough to cancel the whole thing.

A part of her was fully aware of the fact that the likelihood was that what was about to occur would not be the stuff of nightmares, but rather an example of mastery and brilliance. It would be the idealized performance of an incredibly skilled cowboy confronting an incredibly powerful force.

Because his try came from deep inside and had then been honed with coaching and collegiate competition, Diablo cowboyed with an aura that was somehow classically trained.

He was brilliant to watch.

Usually.

And usually, she loved to watch him.

But tonight, as he faced off against a real live bull for the first time in their relationship, she only felt terror.

However, whether or not she was terrified, *The Closed Circuit* didn't care. She had a job to do, a job that, as announcer, was integral to the show going on... and any professional worth their salt knew that the show must go on.

So she ignored the fact that her hands shook, unfocused her eyes so she could no longer make out every distinct detail about Diablo and stared at the camera to which she had been directed to address her commentary.

And so what if all of her tricks didn't work because the picture of him mounted in the chute was burned into her mind?

It didn't matter that she could visualize the wash of his blue jeans and almost feel his dark blue-and-green tartan flannel shirt against her skin, having noticed even the fuzzy faint halo of it along the sleeve of Diablo's lifted arm, the microscopic signal that it was made of an authentic material that hadn't been cheap.

Her cowboy had good taste.

He was strong and powerful and so skilled that he made most of his competition look like amateurs—and she still wished she could fast-forward through this moment.

She had never seen him wear a helmet to ride—only Dillon and a few of the other cowboys did—though the trend in the regular circuit seemed to be going in that direction. Her opinion had been neutral on the matter before, but suddenly, she was an ardent helmet supporter and thought Diablo should be wearing one. Though it wasn't much in a face-off against a bull, even a small protective barrier was a whole lot better than the nothing that a cowboy hat amounted to.

Diablo's right arm was raised high in the air, his left gripping his bull rope, her southpaw underdog ready to show the world what he had.

Sierra's breath stood still.

Time had never moved so slowly in her life.

Was it moving at all?

All of this was supposed to have been over in a matter of seconds, so why had it not even begun?

She'd been in rodeo too long to view eight seconds

as fast, but the eternity things were currently moving at seemed like a stretch as far as elongating time went.

Now she couldn't look away.

Why hadn't he started?

Then, Diablo and Doc Holiday shot out of the chute and Sierra's heart leaped all the way up into her throat, thrusting a tiny gasp of horror out from her lips as it did, proving her a fool for having wished he would just start and get it over with. Thankfully, the arena was too loud for the noise to be heard.

Time moved with no more sense of urgency now that he was in action.

If anything, it slowed down even further.

Watching was more terrifying than waiting.

Of course, Diablo was beautiful on a bull.

He was a work of art in everything he did because *he* was simply a work of art. Powerful, calm and controlled, he neither strained for dominance nor battled for supremacy.

He made it look easy, not because he was easy and fluid about it like Lil and AJ were when they rode, but because he so obviously knew what he was doing. He was confident and competent about it, a solid mountain holding the earth down in the middle of a gale.

Men like him were rare, and it showed.

He was a man who could dance with a bull—could lead one around like a partner on the floor—and make it look easy.

And he wanted her.

And she wanted him, more than she'd wanted any other person in her life.

She wanted to be with him, long after this season of *The Closed Circuit* and long past the summer.

She wanted to make something with him.

She couldn't look and she couldn't look away because she had fallen in love with him.

The eight-second buzzer sounded and time began again.

She had a job to do.

"And that's how you ride a bull, y'all, to the letter of the law," she shouted, the relief and excitement in her voice vibrant and real. "Diablo Sosa showing us all once again the kind of skill that a little hard work and dedication can build!"

The last part hadn't been her best as far as ad-libbing went, but she was still working on catching her breath, so she was glad to have just gotten the job done.

She had seen Diablo ride a bull for the first time and they had both survived it.

She could now check the experience off her anti-bucket list, though she knew she would have to go through it at least one more time, and that the next time it would be against a man killer.

Tio Julio was up next, the final rider of the night, and the necessity of transitioning her commentary to him was the final push she needed to anchor herself in her job of closing out the night's show.

Tio Julio's ride, technically perfect with that extra something that put him in a league of his own as far as *The Closed Circuit* went, was the easy anchor and reset Sierra's system needed after the havoc that Diablo's ride had wreaked.

And afterward it was relief that filled her voice when she said, "And once again, folks, Tio Julio has proven that even in the arena of brute and brawn, wisdom rules supreme! If that ride's not a perfect score, then I don't know what is, mark my words. I'm calling a perfect one hundred tonight, the first in Closed Circuit history, right here in Nashville!" She made sure to infuse an appropriate amount of awe and wonder into her voice, conscious of the fact that under any other circumstances, she would have had no trouble finding genuine awe and wonder at the kind of ride that Tio Julio had put on.

Through *The Closed Circuit*, Sierra had witnessed some of the most phenomenal rodeo of her entire career, from Lil's groundbreaking performances throughout the first season, to AJ's and now Diablo's in the second season, and none of them compared to what Julio could do. The man performed as if he had invented each event himself and was merely teaching it to the others.

His expertise was profound.

Yet, even though it was a stellar performance of a sport she loved, Julio's perfect score—about which she was shortly proven right when the score board showed a bright, flashing one hundred points—was nowhere near so profound as her new understanding about Diablo.

She was in love with him. She was in love and wanted to build a life together, love, with him.

IN WHAT REALLY did feel like the blink of an eye later, Sierra stood front and center stage at the night's winner's podium, the cameras trained on her star-spangled ensemble that she liked to call Old Glory.

Her shirt was sewn from shoulder to collar with stripes of sequined red, white and blue in a chevron pattern. Her collar and cuffs were red, white and blue, respectively, and also sequined. Embroidered on the breast was a detailed and light-catching motif, also in red, white and blue. It depicted sweet little flowers and horseshoes hand embroidered by herself, trimmed by metallic silver embroidering thread and even more sequins.

She wore her dark blue wash jeans beneath her white with red and blue accents fringed chaps. Her hat was bright red and her crown sparkling.

She had dressed to the patriotic nines for the first bull ride of the season. She had dressed to face love, and she hadn't even realized it.

But before she could do anything about it, she needed to make it through the end of the show.

"It's time to round out the top three for the night, y'all, and what a top three we have! Crossing over from the regular circuit to grind it out for the common cowboy, we've got Dillon Oliver, the grittiest buck buster *The Closed Circuit* has seen yet."

With a respectable amount of cheering, the audience ushered Dillon onto the podium where he smiled and waved with his particular brand of rough-around-the-edges charm.

He wasn't her cup of tea by any stretch of the imagination, but with his salt-of-the-earth persona and wiry strength, Sierra knew he was exactly what many women were looking for in a cowboy.

Sierra's interests ran more akin to the next cowboy in line.

Her chest warmed and her heartbeat picked up as she turned her attention to the cowboy who also happened to be everything she wanted and more in a man.

Her eyes locked on his the whole time, smiling for him instead of the crowd, as she said, "And leaping ahead to lay down the law like there's a new sheriff in *The Closed Circuit*, in second place, we have Diablo Sosa!" The light in his eyes, too, was for her alone.

As Diablo was the reigning fan favorite, Sierra had to wait for the crowd's cheers to die down before she could move on to announcing Julio.

When the moment arrived, however, she was ready, saying, "And, the years he has on them only reflected in the point spread between them, we've got the one, the only, Tio Julio! The first perfect score in Closed Circuit history! Give it up for tonight's riders, Nashville. They certainly gave it up for you!"

When Julio took his place at the top of the podium, once again the crowd's volume lifted to a crescendo. All three men smiled and waved, like good cowboys were supposed to, and Sierra took the opportunity to marvel and gaze at the one in the middle to her entangled heart's content.

He was stunning in his place among the top tier, confident and tall, taller than both of his companions, and comfortable enough with himself that his shoulders boasted only a humble acceptance of his own skill, neither self-aggrandizing nor self-deprecating.

He really was something else, the Batman to Julio's Superman in *The Closed Circuit*. That was why, in her opinion, he was more popular with fans.

Like Superman, Julio's accomplishments were perfect, inhuman and unattainable, whereas Batman, like Diablo, was a regular man who had achieved excellence via training and practice.

Her gaze skating briefly over to Dillon before bouncing back to Diablo, she felt a moment of pity for the man. He was a great rider—one of the most popular cowboys out there in the regular circuit—and, carrying a consistent twenty percent of the viewing audience in terms of popularity, he was as solidly popular among the fans as he was solidly third place in the scores.

But that gap between him and the other two was fast growing to be a thing insurmountable.

Dillon was a strong example of the same old thing at a time when rodeo's menu of options was going through a renaissance. He was the turkey sandwich on the menu at a Chinese restaurant, perfect for those who were uncomfortable trying new things, but if he was your pick, you were also kind of missing the point.

The point was the best and toughest. The point was Julio, and, more importantly for Sierra, the point was Diablo, who she'd once again returned her attention to.

So when Dillon cleared his throat, the hairs on the back of Sierra's neck stood up, her attention whipping back toward him, a sense of apprehension springing to life inside her.

As hostess of the show, it was her job to keep things running smoothly while the cameras were rolling but that didn't always mean heading things off at the pass. *The Closed Circuit* might be rodeo, but it was also reality TV, and reality TV loved nothing more than drama. Whether this would turn out to be the kind of drama they wanted or didn't want was always anybody's guess.

Bracing herself, she wasn't surprised when Dillon made his move.

Lifting his palms toward the audience at large to make settling motions with his hands, he said, "Now, I know we're all excited to see the first buckles of the season go out tonight, but before we get to that, before we get to all that celebratin' and settin' rowdy cowboys loose on this great town, there's something serious we've got to talk about," he said, pausing before adding,

"Now, settle down now," as if the noisy audience was a herd of unruly cattle he was dealing with.

Eyes narrowing, Sierra watched him. Nobody liked to see a woman interrupt a man, so she played her cards close, giving him time to get to the point so she could find out where he was going with this and how she should respond. Her own mic was at the ready, burning a hole in her hand.

When the audience didn't so much settle as become more confused and restless, Dillon simply pitched his voice a little higher to say, "After a few suspicious encounters, I took it upon myself to do a little digging. I hired a private investigator with personal funds, so as not to bother the folks who put on this wonderful program that all of us nice law-abiding citizens love so much." Here, he paused before turning to his right to look toward Diablo and Julio with a smug "gotcha" expression on his face, before turning forward again to finish with, "And folks, let me tell you, what they found out, it ain't pretty. I'm sorry to say, it will shock and sadden you, even as it finally starts answering some of the questions we've all had."

Instinct had told her she wouldn't like what Dillon was up to, but the reality was slimier and grosser than even that. Awash with an unfamiliar and sudden spike of heat in her face, it took her a moment to recognize what she was feeling as real aggression.

But she was the hostess with the mostest. She couldn't just push him off the risers.

Having really caught their attention now, Dillon had managed to wrangle the crowd's full interest, over which now hovered a ravenous hush.

They wanted to know every detail he hinted at.

If Dillon's news had the potential to sadden and shock, they were dying to know.

"There's a reason none of us have ever heard of our favorite little uncle over here." Dillon thumbed in Julio's direction and the insolence in the gesture made Sierra's stomach curdle. "And it's not 'cause he keeps a low profile. We ain't seen him around because he ain't been around. He's been laying low for the past twenty years or so. And do you want to know why that is?"

If Diablo was Batman and Julio was Superman, Sierra thought, then Dillon had chosen the role of the Joker for himself.

His face was maniacal, his eyebrows stretched too high for the over-the-top downturn of his frown.

He looked like an elementary school teacher reacting to a false answer.

Or a clown.

Sierra's eyes darted over to Julio to gauge how he was reacting.

He looked like he always did except he seemed to have lost the ever-present hint of a smile that usually lingered around his eyes and mouth.

They had been replaced with a hardness, both in glint and pressed line, that promised that regardless of how his little skit played out, Dillon had crossed a line tonight, and in doing so, had earned himself a real enemy.

Sierra shivered, though Dillon had yet to even realize his mistake. He was still too busy digging deeper.

"It's because, up until now, our little Julio here was afraid that if anybody knew he was here in the good ol' US of A they might send him right on back to where he came from, lickety-split, seeing as how he's here without permission, or illegally, as they say."

There was a collective gasp in the crowd against which Sierra gritted her teeth and held back from rolling her eyes.

Another thing her father had in common with rodeo was a penchant for conservative social views.

As a man who'd worked hard to bring his family to the United States, Sierra's father had only scorn for those who entered via different pathways, but to Sierra, there was nothing more American than welcoming all who came with open arms, however they arrived.

That was what the Statue of Liberty was all about. Give me your tired, your poor, your huddled masses yearning to breathe free…

If what she had learned in school was to be believed, accepting those who were looking for a better life—in whatever condition and state they arrived—was what America was all about.

Whether or not she was right, though, she knew from experience that one could argue the point for years, until blue in the face, and it still wouldn't change the mind of a stubborn man with a chip on his shoulder about it— and she now pegged Dillion as exactly that type of man.

But that didn't mean that words were entirely useless.

She might not be making a difference in Dillon's life, but she could sure as hell take back the arena and make a difference in everybody else's.

Testing the comforting and familiar weight of her hand-held mic, she sucked in a deep breath, her nostrils flaring the way her mother's did when she was angry.

Then she snapped her head up, her blinding promotional photo smile super-glued into place, her voice infused with honey and poison at the same time. "Now, Dillon! I just don't see how that could be! You know yourself just how thorough and serious the folks of *The Closed Circuit* are about their rodeo. It's almost like you're suggesting they don't know how to run a show, and we all know that couldn't possibly be true! Why, everybody up here knows that *The Closed Circuit Rodeo* is the greatest show there's ever been! It's brought the rodeo right into living rooms across America and started a real renaissance. You can't possibly mean they made a mistake, can you?"

He had thought he'd been careful to make sure his accusations didn't reflect badly on *The Closed Circuit*, but while he might be at the top in the game when it came to rough stock, he was an utter amateur when it came to handling an arena.

He might not realize it, but by taking her stage, he'd come for a crown that was held by a stone-cold professional who specialized in committing homicide with kindness.

He had entered her arena, guns blazing.

That Dillon was so obviously willing to threaten not just his competitor's success, but his entire life, and via seemingly any means necessary, just as Diablo had predicted, was enough to steal her breath.

It was glaringly obvious that Dillon's attack was motivated by the fact that, after tonight's rides, he had lost his chance to beat even Diablo, let alone Julio, but that didn't mean he couldn't do damage.

Eyes narrowing into a faint glare, he addressed Sierra when he said, "I know you're too sweet and simple to ever believe anyone would engage in such deception, but I can assure you, Miss Quintanilla, desperate people will engage in the most complicated schemes."

Diablo made a sharp angle toward Dillon on the podium, but Julio grabbed his wrist with an iron grip.

On her own behalf, Sierra was also outraged.

Beyond merely being condescending, there was a trace of real threat and warning in his words, the kind of thread of intimidation that some men felt equated to strength.

Dillon, however, was so far from the kind of thing that Sierra was afraid of that the idea was laughable.

She opened her mouth to say as much, when Julio chose the moment to speak, his voice low and effortless for all that it immediately captured the attention of everyone present—including the audience.

"While it is true, my friend, that I am not a citizen of this great country, I think you must have mistaken me for someone else, for I am perfectly legal to live and work here, though my wife would call you a liar for calling rodeo 'work.' For years it's been, 'stop playing around with bulls and broncs and get a real job,' but now that *The Closed Circuit* pays so well, she's changed her mind."

The audience laughed when he'd intended them to, and Sierra sent him a little nod. Like Diablo, it seemed there wasn't anything the cowboy couldn't do.

"That so?" Dillon challenged, his voice hardening even as the mood around him, as well as that of the audience, lightened and softened toward Julio. "And just what gives you that authorization? You got any kind of ID that can confirm that? And, no, I'm sorry to say it, but a social security card's not gonna cut it for me. That's easy enough to get for your kind."

Diablo chose that moment to enter the fray, his smooth baritone dry as a Santa Anna blowing in as he said, "First you suggest *The Closed Circuit* doesn't know how to do its job, and now you demand IDs? Careful there, Dil, you're starting to sound more like a grocery store manager than a cowboy."

Again, Sierra was impressed.

Like Julio, Diablo could work a crowd, playing what he knew about the world and people of rodeo against Dillon's baiting.

Hackles rising, Dillon said, "Nobody's suggesting nothing about anybody but a criminal. I would hate for the lovely folks of *The Closed Circuit*—" he nodded toward Sierra and missed her shudder before continuing "—to go handing out buckles they'll just have to take back when news with disqualification implications drops."

Dryness replaced by low menace, Diablo said, "Nobody is getting disqualified." And the hair on Sierra's arms lifted.

Diablo spoke with a kind of absolute authority that suggested Julio's actual immigration status was a matter of his decision.

"I wouldn't be so sure, lawboy. You'll notice that our friend here hasn't reached for any papers," Dillon said through his teeth, leaning into Diablo's space on the podium to make his challenge clear. "Unless that changes here in the next few minutes, to the way I'm seeing things, you and I will be moving up in the world here soon, and then I'm going to beat you, too."

"Careful, Dillon, your intentions are showing." Diablo's voice was near a whisper, but he was mic'd so the sound carried ominously around the stadium. "You don't have the authority to demand to see another man's identification," he added, his voice retaining the same thread of steel while his body remained rooted where he stood. Moved by neither Dillon's words, nor his posturing, Diablo gave the appearance of a parent who had about had it with their child's tantrum.

Sierra imagined that, like the jumbotron, the television cameras were also trained on the two men, zoomed in so as not to miss a moment.

Infuriatingly, Dillon just smirked harder. "Sounds like you're worried about your friend. Seems to me that if he had nothing to worry about, this all would've been over and done by now. 'Less he's got something to hide…"

Releasing an extended-to-the-point-of-insulting sigh, the universal sound of a person tested far past the point of no return, Julio reached into the breast of his vest and retrieved a wallet.

The audience sucked in a collective breath.

Diablo's face hardened. "You don't have to show him anything," he said, granite and justice in his voice, a lawman in every sense of the word.

Sierra longed to reach out and take his hand.

But she couldn't. Not in the middle of the stage with every eye in the building trained on them.

And that was…absolutely unacceptable, she realized with a strange, disoriented sensation. It was unacceptable to let anyone dictate how she was going to love her man.

Julio shook his head in response to Diablo. "No. No. It's alright. Sometimes the only way to prove to a child that there is no monster in the closet is to open the door."

The insult was devastating, so deep it rooted Sierra to the spot where she stood, and it hadn't even been directed at her. In so few words he had extremely, effectively, taken control of the narrative. Depending on what he pulled out of his wallet—and she had a good idea she knew what it would be—Dillon would walk away looking like not just a fool, but, as Julio had suggested, a child. A boy not fit to play with the men.

Regardless of how the scores played out in the end, even if Dillon was somehow able to close the growing point gap and prove he had the ability, being proven wrong in his accusations here and now would by default prove Julio right. It would reveal to the entire audience that instead of ballsy and confident in his abilities, Dillon was just a young man scared of being outclassed and lookin' for alternative means to win, and in the world of rodeo that was the kind of blow there would be no coming back from.

All of this was as clear to Sierra as if she had been tasked with narrating the scene.

Dillon, on the other hand, appeared to be unaware.

In fact, he seemed to lack even the good sense to know when to quit, let alone to recognize that he was dancing with men of an entirely different caliber than himself.

In all honesty, it was surprising that it was possible for someone to be so obtuse.

Just like during Diablo's ride, but for an entirely different reason, time had slowed, moving at a crawl as Julio pulled his ID out of his wallet for the world to see.

Sierra cringed, though she could not look away, standing in as the personification of the flag as she was, she was Miss Red White and Blue, bearing horrified witness to this insult to her principles.

And still, Dillon hadn't realized what was happening, didn't realize it was he who was in the wrong and about to experience a rude shake-up—not Julio and not the standings. He didn't realize that in making sure his moment was as public as it could possibly be, he was firmly establishing himself as *The Closed Circuit*'s first real villain.

Now that the question had been addressed in a manner that would satisfy most of the audience, timing-wise, it was the perfect moment for the producers—or their representatives, at least—to step in and bring the drama to its climactic peak, and so of course, that was what happened.

A scuttle of besuited individuals scurried onto the stage bearing handheld tablets and a scanning device. Upon arrival, their cluster broke apart, the men with the tablet and scanner attending to Julio while two others spoke quietly to Dillon and Diablo.

Sierra watched it all unfold at a complete loss as to what her role was in the situation for the first time since way back at the start of her career—when she'd still been figuring out what it was to be a rodeo queen.

The men with the scanners finished what they were doing with Julio and crossed the stage to speak with a man who had stayed apart from the others when they'd split, engaged in conversation on the phone.

The man paused in his conversation to listen to the men with the equipment then returned to his call. A moment later he nodded, then hung up the phone and flashed the thumbs-up signal to his compatriots who stood with Dillon and Diablo.

Feeling like she was watching some kind of government damage control force at work, Sierra noted that Dillon's quiet conversation with the man in the suit was becoming increasingly less quiet.

A fact that was only broadcast further by Dillon's still-hot mic.

"It's a lie. I'm telling you. They did something. He

pulled some kind of trick. I'm telling you that man is here illegally!" he shouted, his accusing finger now sweeping the stage to include Diablo and Sierra as the *they* in his testimony against Julio, but the man in the suit who spoke to him, his low words were neither close enough to hear nor loud enough for Dillon's mic to pick up, merely shook his head and lifted a calming hand, trying to gently disengage Dillon's pointing arm.

Then one of the men, none of whom she recognized as producers, caught her eye and gave her a nod. Because, of course, now that they'd showed up late and done the bare minimum as far as official damage control went, they wanted to volley it back to her to clean up.

With no idea of what they wanted her to do, she nonetheless remained a queen enough to smile and return the gesture, assuming it was the sign to take back over.

Thankfully, another individual in a suit, this one female, hurried up to Sierra, tapped her on the shoulder and gestured for her to lean closer, mic covered.

"*The Closed Circuit* is nothing without the talent it attracts and takes very seriously its management responsibilities thereof."

And then she and the rest of the black suits hustled off stage, having done too little, too late, leaving Sierra and the top three to clean up the rest of the mess and hand out buckles.

Turning to face the crowd once more, the structure of her professionalism held in place by pure muscle memory at this point, she beamed and projected the kind of affable shock that would make a Southern lady confronted with pure horror proud.

Her face transitioning from one of wide-eyed and wide-mouthed surprise to one of gossip and conspiratorial side-eyes with pursed lips, she blew out as much of the tension that had accumulated in her body as she could in the form of a high-pitched and country singsong whistle.

The she said, "Well, folks…" trailing off as she lifted and then dropped her hand back down against her thigh theatrically before swinging it back up and around to land on a cocked hip in a position that said, I'm sassy and determined, so let's get this wagon train back rollin'. "You ready to hand out some buckles?" She used her deep register voice and infused it with get-her-done energy, as if everything that had just gone down on stage was merely an embarrassing and regretful interruption of the real day's work—as opposed to an attempt to ruin a man's life.

And, because the audience had now had their fill of tension and drama and intrigue and fighting words, and because it was getting late, and really, all they wanted now was a happy ending and a good story to remember, the crowd eagerly took the lead she offered, roaring to life with the force of all the feeling they'd built up over the past ten minutes.

As she guided them all toward the safe conclusion they wanted, Sierra could only marvel that the entire interlude had happened so quickly. That kind of intensity crammed into a moment was impressive—even for rodeo.

Movement off stage caught the corner of her eye, and Sierra's smile grew, this time with genuine relief. The audience was behaving and greenies were getting the buckles ready. Soon, all of it would be over. Dillon could skulk off to his RV to lick his wounds, and she could get to the important business of anxiously watching the daylight fade so she could run over and be with Diablo.

CHAPTER SIXTEEN

DIABLO MAINTAINED HIS SMILE, waiting for the roar to die down and his opportunity to exit the stage before the rage that simmered inside boiled over and he gave in to the urge to direct it at the source that had stirred it up.

Things didn't go well for him when he gave in to those kinds of urges.

Or, he reconsidered, depending upon how long of a view one took on things, they went extremely well...

But that was as far as the thought got. Diablo had learned a long time ago that if he wanted to control the outcome, he had to control that drive to mete out justice via physical means.

Case in point, he had relied on his intelligence and instinct as far as Dillon was concerned, rather than fists, and as a result, he and Julio had been more than prepared.

Julio's position remained secure in *The Closed Circuit*, but only because of a combination of foresight, training and knowing the right people.

What kind of havoc had Dillon wreaked on the lives of those without all of that at their disposal?

Disgust curdled in Diablo's gut, swirling in a petty stew that demanded he make his feelings known in a more physical way.

It didn't matter that he and Julio had won the skirmish.

It didn't matter that they had been more than just a step ahead the whole time and had successfully headed Dillon off at the pass. The fact that he had always been a fool did not make him less dangerous. If anything, it made him more so. Some of the greatest ills of the world had marched under the banner of ignorance.

Anger roiled inside Diablo at the nonchalant cruelty embedded in Dillon's behavior—a reflection of the same nonchalant cruelty he'd run up against over and over throughout his life—and it wasn't the type to be soothed by the fact that they had correctly anticipated the man's capacity for aggression, malice and weakness.

It was the kind of anger that demanded restitution.

Dillon needed to be punished for his behavior, not given a buckle.

And it was nowhere near enough that his scheme had blown up in his face.

He had earned far more than a simple loss of face.

The man's behavior bordered on criminal.

Considering everything the man had revealed about his grand scheme, Diablo could see a number of pathways toward arguing that it had been.

He was mentally evaluating their strength, when the crowd finally settled down enough for Sierra to speak again.

"That's all for our show tonight, Nashville, and what a wild and rowdy one it was! Nothing like the rodeo to bring out the beast in all of us. Competition was fierce and tempers fiercer, but our cowboys proved they're ready to take anything on, inside or outside the arena!"

The crowd laughed as if they were recalling distant and silly antics right alongside Sierra, but really, they'd witnessed an attempted lynching, thwarted not because the producers had been ready and willing to act, but because Diablo and Julio had been.

Sierra went on, delivering the line he imagined they'd fed her when that woman had whispered in her ear. "We promised you a rodeo like no other, and we delivered, both with some of the finest bull riding seen in a generation, and some of the most intense drama and intrigue rodeo has ever seen. And for any of you sweethearts out there who might be worried, despite the extra flare-ups of the night, we at *The Closed Circuit* assure you that our talent is the heart and soul of our show and we take their management very seriously. All of our contestants are legally allowed to compete and each and every one of them wants that million-dollar prize, so stay tuned, folks. You never know what's going to happen!"

Sierra lifted her arm to wave good-night to everybody, her long dark hair swinging down her back, her bright red hat and crown and sequined arm catching the light from all directions, and for an instant Diablo caught his breath, the raging bull inside him calmed simply by the sight of her.

And then, from the step below him on the podium, Dillon let out a loud, phlegmy scoff.

The sound of it cast across the arena like a slimy skip in a record.

Sierra stilled, then gradually drew her arm down and turned, her eyes landing on Dillon.

Diablo would never believe that Dillon had intended to capture the arena's attention once more, but having it, he didn't waste it.

With a snort, Dillon said, "*The Closed Circuit* is a rodeo like no other, alright, because it's no rodeo at all.

Take it from a real cowboy, folks. This clown show is more like a circus than a real rodeo. I'm the number-one ranked bull and bareback bronc rider in the regular professional rodeo. This is what the top looks like in real life, Nashville." Gesturing with a thumb in his own direction like the angry primate he was, Dillon emphasized his point by near literally pounding his chest, before sweeping the hand forward to include AJ and Julio and Sierra on the stage. "Not this. Not this guy with fake papers. Not this aging queen who sneaks into cowboys' beds at night. And certainly not this guy," he said, eyes landing on Diablo. "He's nothing but an uppity suit who plays a cowboy during his summer break. That's not real rodeo. This is real!" His volume picked up at the tail end as he once again banged his chest, the force of impact audible across the arena through his mic.

The anger that had already threatened to push past the borders of his control was no longer possible to restrain, and in a strange wake of cool numbness, Diablo's forces of control beat a hasty retreat.

His mind flashed back to the warehouse district where he'd met Caleb, or as he was better known to Diablo at the time, Bumpkin.

Bumpkin probably hadn't started out a bad guy, but by the time he entered Diablo's life, he'd become one.

They first met at the Thursday night sandwich line.

Nana worked a double shift on Thursdays, so every Thursday Diablo had put on a black hoodie, grabbed his house keys and slipped out the front door, where he walked two blocks, turned left, then walked another block until he reached Our Lady of Perpetual Grace, the smaller and older Catholic Church in the neighborhood.

As far as he knew, only old, traditional people without families attended Our Lady of Perpetual Grace, which meant no one who might recognize him, or, more importantly, report back to his grandmother about what he was doing.

His bases and absence covered, he was free to spend five hours every week, from 4:00 to 9:00 p.m., slapping simple bologna sandwiches together and then handing them out to the unhoused community in downtown Houston.

It was on one such evening that he met Bumpkin.

Because he'd taken the time to look, even at the tender age of twelve-going-on-thirteen, he'd been aware of the fact that there was an inherent system of justice in operation among the citizens of the streets.

Like the mainstream justice system, while being true and consistent, the rules and mores of street justice did not, however, operate equitably among each of the classes and groups that lived therein. Humans liked to create class systems, it seemed, and among the unhoused—including the mentally ill, addicts, generically unhoused, sex workers, hustlers, gangsters, folks who had slipped through the cracks, entire families, runaways and more—it seemed not everyone was created equal.

That was particularly true for Bumpkin, who, as a chronically marauding interloper, by most of the rules of the street, should have been dealt with by those whose interest it was to maintain their territories.

But, in addition to being a dangerous outlier operating somewhat antagonistically in an established hierarchy, Bumpkin had the good street fortune to also be a dealer.

Because he had a hookup, he was allowed to act with

impunity by those who typically showed greater enthusiasm for rule enforcement.

The night Diablo met him had been a prime example.

Because it was Sandwich Thursday, there were some unspoken additions to the regular street rules that guided everyone.

No business or deals were allowed while the nuns and old folks and large Black boy were present.

Like an isolated watering hole on the Savannah, it was accepted Sandwich Thursday was neutral territory. And that everyone had to behave.

Occasionally, the community would cobble together some change to donate toward the purchase of supplies for the following week—and, as discussed among the nuns, their donations were always accepted, because, "it gave them a part in things beyond being charity."

But—and of the new rules this seemed to be paramount—under no circumstances were the volunteers to be given any trouble.

In part, this is what made it okay for Diablo to be there.

He could do good, and he could ask questions, questions that might lead him to his mother.

And, assuming that he was older than he was while at the same time perpetually losing touch with the norms of mainstream life, the unhoused of the Sandwich Thursday community answered all of his questions with unfiltered and unflinching honesty, including the questions in which it was obvious he was looking for information that might lead him to his parents. It was a special relationship, with them willing to stretch the rules of privacy and identity for a young man they knew had good intentions and a broken heart.

It was through that process, over months, that he learned how it all worked.

For example, after he had done it a million times, he learned that among the community it was frowned upon to ask about peoples' pasts, injuries, real names, location of origin, camp spot or criminal records.

But because he was respectful and earnest, he was forgiven for his trespasses and taught more acceptable ways of gathering information, including learning to read between the lines someone delivered and what they said with their eyes—especially when there was disagreement among the two.

But that wasn't even how things started with Bumpkin.

Things started with Bumpkin when the man took it into his head to harass one of the elderly women volunteers.

"You know," he said, out of the blue between obnoxious bites of his sandwich, "I've got a lot of clients looking for an old piece like you. What'dya say? I make all the arrangements and split the cash with you sixty-forty, me?"

A ripple of awareness skittered across the people gathered still in line, as well as those sitting in clusters with their sandwiches, and, attuned to it, Diablo's heartbeat picked up.

By that point, he'd learned the rules and even had a sense of what happened to those who broke them, but he'd never been around to witness it in action.

But instead of the menacing approach of Tinsel, the large man who was leader of the block where the Our Lady of Perpetual Grace volunteers set up shop, the man looked up, noted who it was that was crossing the line, then looked away again.

With a half-chewed bite in his open mouth, Bumpkin delighted in his impunity, only encouraged by being special. "I'm serious, you know. You'd be surprised how much a lady your age could make."

Without a word, the woman—Dolores—walked away from Bumpkin, not even bothering to acknowledge his vulgarity.

But his temperature rising and skin overcome with a tingling, not-quite-numb-but-certainly-not-normal sensation, Diablo looked from Tinsel to the volunteer coordinator, a nun and an elderly woman herself. And what he saw was nearly as stark as the life stories he'd learned since he began volunteering.

No one was willing to speak up, and no one would meet his eyes.

He didn't know what, if anything, to do.

The volunteers had nearly worked through the supply of sandwiches by this point, which was their weekly signal that it was time to pack up and go home.

And, though he might have been the size of a small adult, he was, as his nana constantly reminded him, still just a child.

So he, too, did nothing.

When the sandwiches were all distributed, Diablo began to fold up tables, and Bumpkin once again approached the woman he'd been harassing and propositioning.

Of course, harassing and propositioning weren't the words that had been in Diablo's mind at the time.

Back then, and later, to the police, he'd described it as "wouldn't stop messing with."

"You're a good-lookin' lady. I could make you a lot of money. I could take you out myself. I've always been fascinated by older women, you know. I bet you got a few little sexy tricks up your sleeve." Bumpkin held one end of the folded table while he prodded Dolores, pretending to lose his grip only to yank it back again, forcing her to stay within his sphere.

The two elderly nuns gathered to the volunteer's side but otherwise said nothing in defense. The Our Lady of Perpetual Grace rulebook instructed volunteers to remain silent and nonviolent in the face of confrontation. They were to reflect the Lord's peace in all situations.

But Bumpkin showed no signs of being moved by the Lord's peace, so once again Diablo was at a loss as to what to do.

Things grew more complicated when Sirenita, one of the young runaways from the pack of them, said, "Leave 'em alone, Bump."

Sirenita was new to the runaways crew and to the block, and Diablo liked her.

She dyed her hair turquoise and spoke Spanish like a Guatemalan and English like a kid from the Midwest.

Only a few years older than he was, it was plausible that—as she claimed—Sirenita was old enough to have graduated from high school at the top of her class. To Diablo, though, she'd seemed more like the age his mother had been in the photo that his nana had of her standing in front of their brand-new house—the same house Diablo lived in—which was just sixteen.

The picture had been taken just one year before she'd run away herself.

Like the stories he'd heard of his mother, Sirenita was full of spunk and swagger, but remained sweet enough to go out of her way to say hi to Diablo every Thursday, regardless of whose sandwich line she got in.

At the sound of her voice, Bumpkin froze and an uneasy stillness settled over the people gathered on the block.

Without a word, Bumpkin released the table and turned around, his narrow shoulders curved, arms hanging out loosely at his sides, body pulsating with kinetic threat.

The nuns took his redirected attention as an opportunity to shuffle their volunteers along and start up the van.

There was none of the usual small talk in the van on the ride back to the church that night, and when they arrived, Diablo said his goodbyes and hurried home as soon as he could.

The next time he didn't see Sirenita at Sandwich Thursday, though, he looked for her.

The time after that, she showed up, but she was no longer hanging with the runaways.

Instead, she stuck to Bumpkin's left side, one half of her face a swollen and discolored bouquet with blooms ranging in color from yellow-green to blue-black.

She didn't come through Diablo's sandwich line, nor did she come by to say her customary hello by the time they started loading up the folding tables for the night.

Diablo wasn't going to do nothing this time, though.

He was a week away from turning thirteen.

That was a week away from no longer being a child, a week from nearly being a man.

Doing nothing had hovered around him, like a fog of shame, ever since. He had learned from his mistake.

He crossed the vacant lot to where Sirenita sat beside Bumpkin. Conversation around them quieted.

"Hi," he said, his voice still high and light for all

of his imagined proximity to manhood. "I missed you last week." He had not planned out what he would say when he got to her, only built up the gumption to do it, and regretted that now.

"She was with me," Bumpkin said, speaking for her. "She's with me, and I don't tolerate other men talking to my woman, so mosey on back to your church ladies."

Ignoring the older man, Diablo continued to address Sirenita. "So, you're okay, then?"

"I said get out of here," Bumpkin tried again, but again Diablo ignored him.

To Sirenita, he said, "I'll go if you tell me to."

Immediately, she spoke. "Go. I'm with Bumpkin now." There was fear in her voice, true and urgent, and again he didn't know what to do.

"You heard the lady, kid. Now go. Get. Out. Of. Here." Bumpkin was getting angry at Diablo's lack of respect, the threat of real violence rising in his voice, but that was data that Diablo's adolescent mind did not have room to process while it simultaneously considered the dilemma in front of him.

What was the right thing to do?

Sirenita couldn't be with Bumpkin.

It didn't fit.

Diablo looked back across the street to where the runaways sat and they all looked away quickly.

Turning back to Sirenita, he said, confusion making him sound even younger than he was, "You can't be with Bumpkin."

Panic taking her pitch up a notch, Sirenita said, "With Bumpkin I can make a lot of money. He's going to help me save up and go back to be with my mom in Michigan. Everything's going to be alright. I'm fine. Now skedaddle, kid." She hit the last word hard and loud, as if she hoped to remind Bumpkin that Diablo was a child, but her attempt at cooling things down was marred when she tried to smile and couldn't quite achieve the feat because of the swelling in her face.

Dumbly, rage and confusion overpowering any instinct of self-preservation he had, Diablo repeated, "But not Bumpkin. Everybody hates Bumpkin."

At his words, the man in question came to his feet.

Lifting to her own feet, Sirenita had one palm outstretched toward Bumpkin in an inconsequential gesture to halt him and the other reaching toward Diablo, beseeching him to finally get his wits together and go back across the street.

From his position with his crew, Tinsel finally spoke up with a warning. "The kid's not one of us, Bumpkin."

But Bumpkin brushed the warning off. "A kid his size needs to learn a little respect."

"Bumpkin, no! He's a kid. No!" Sirenita was screaming now, alternating between trying to stop Bumpkin and warning Diablo away. "Get out of here, kid. I'm serious. Go. Nobody's going to help you. Nobody stops Bumpkin. Nobody even tries!"

Diablo watched Bumpkin advance on him, serious and ill intent written all over him, and still did nothing, Sirenita's words sinking and swirling around inside his mind.

Sirenita was spunky and full of swagger and had a crew—and no one had helped her.

She was young and smart and weak and whatever Bumpkin had done to her, no one had helped her.

Bumpkin came at him with an iron fist to the solar

plexus and it was only instinct that gave Diablo the intelligence to flex in time.

It still hurt more than anything Diablo had ever felt in his life, radiating outward from the impact point like his stomach had exploded and acid was attacking everything inside him.

For what would be the first, but not last time in his life, Diablo vomited from pain.

With bologna sandwich and bile down the front of his shirt, he rose unsteadily back to his feet as Bumpkin swung around a second time. It was pure luck—or possibly her slightly confused cousin, clumsiness—that had Bumpkin's fist connecting with Diablo's elbow.

Diablo's arm went instantly and inconveniently numb, but Bumpkin let out a howl of pain that gave him time to catch his breath.

"Run away," Sirenita urged, pushing him physically, but he did not budge.

"But nobody helped you," he said, the words a nightmare in his mouth.

She nodded, not bothering to deny it. "And you're too young to."

Diablo's dead arm recovered faster than Bumpkin's abused fist, regular feeling returning to it while Sirenita tried to get him to leave and Bumpkin's wailing petered off.

In hindsight, Diablo guessed that he'd broken his hand in the impact.

Bumpkin finally stood up, spitting at Diablo's feet as he did, and began to advance again, strong and wiry and deadly for all that he was skinny. Still, all Diablo could think was that just like nobody had tried to help the volunteer lady, no one had helped Sirenita.

And what if the same thing had happened to his mother?

The thought was the last thing he remembered before Bumpkin reached him.

Later, specialists had told him that the time he'd lost was a kind of conscious blackout, but as nothing of the kind had ever happened to him again—not even after heavy drinking—he could never confirm it.

The police report said that first the nuns had tried to pull him off Bumpkin, and then Tinsel had tried, but that, in the end, it had taken three police officers to finally pull him from the other man, mindless and wildly punching all the while.

The first thing he could clearly recall after the incident was the look on his nana's face when she met him in the detention center.

Her greatest nightmare had come true, nearly to the letter, and it showed in the crumple of her face when she landed on him in his detention center attire.

Never having known the love of his mother, Diablo had thought he understood heartbreak more than most kids his age. Seeing his nana's face like that, though, truly introduced him to the concept.

With his mother, he'd never known what he was missing.

He knew his nana better than himself.

He'd gone to Sandwich Thursdays for the same reason he had nearly murdered a man.

He was a little boy forever looking for his mom and dad, consequences be damned, and the consequences had damned him.

And in doing so, his nana's worst fears had come true. And he'd been the one to bring them to life. What made it worse was that it wasn't anger or fear or revulsion or blame in her face when she had seen him.

Her face cracked and shattered and it was as clear to him as if he felt it himself that she blamed herself, not him.

Out loud, she sobbed and held him and apologized and vowed to never again be so negligent.

His insides had twisted as much as she had twisted the reality of the situation. It hadn't been her fault. It had been him. His bad decisions had hurt not just himself and Bumpkin, but his grandmother, as well.

He'd made a mess for everyone.

Through the following months, his nana was a tigress in his defense.

She argued with and nagged his attorney, and she argued and nagged the judge, and then for the next nine years, she argued and nagged the old man to save her boy. By the miracle of her determination and willpower, Diablo did not become a statistic, despite the fact that in an instant he had nearly made himself into one.

He'd found bulls and law and he'd learned how to wield power that wasn't violence—learned deeply that violence was, in truth, the lowest expression of power, the kind of hallmark action that revealed to the whole world that you had no real power at all.

Real power was the ability to pull the kind of strings that could secure a green card in a matter of weeks.

Real power was scoring a ninety-three the first time you climbed on the back of a bull in fourteen years.

Having ridden a respectable but unimpressive by comparison eighty-six points, it was clear these were the kinds of powers that Dillon had not been equally blessed with. And because of that, and all of the other stories he made up in his small mind, he was jealous.

And because he was jealous, he was acting like a violent child.

Diablo knew all about children acting out violently.

For all those reasons, despite the fact that Dillon had earned it and more, and despite the fact that he didn't deserve an inch of ease for the shit he'd pulled, Diablo didn't find him and hit him.

He didn't cock his fist back and slam it into an infantile man's childish face with the precision of a machine engineered for that purpose, as he had apparently done the day he'd fought Bumpkin.

In a single evening, Dillon had tried to sabotage an innocent man's life and had jeopardized the career of the woman he loved. But knocking the dude out wasn't going to make a difference to Julio, and it certainly wouldn't lay to rest any of his accusations regarding Sierra.

Unavoidably, Diablo had been in fights since the day he'd beat Bumpkin—with his size, his darkness and the composition of his high school student body, fighting had been inevitable—but after the nightmare of losing control like that, of having done such incredible damage to another human with his body, the only place that Diablo would allow himself to feel the full strength of his emotions was on the back of a bull.

Anywhere else was too dangerous.

He was strong enough to hurt somebody, and even after Bumpkin, he kept that in mind.

Fortunately, as it was wont to do, his tendency toward extreme emotions had dropped off significantly following adolescence, and even more so in the years since he'd graduated from college and retired from rodeo.

What remained was mild enough to channel into his caseload.

But that had been before he'd gotten back in the saddle and fallen for a rodeo queen.

He was in love with Sierra.

In love, in *love*—not lust, or infatuation or contentment with her.

He loved her in the same way he loved rodeo, deep and abiding, steady and true, and regardless of the clothes he wore or how much he might try to deny it.

And like everything he loved, instinct urged him toward extremes when it came to protecting her.

But he had learned and evolved a great deal in the years since Bumpkin. He had real power now.

He knew there were better ways to protect her than with fists. Fists, in fact, would only prove that what Dillon said was true.

There were more intelligent ways to offer his strength and support.

It was time to conclude things with the walking spittoon that was Dillon Oliver.

As Diablo had suspected would be the case with Dillon from the start, his behavior throughout the night—the malicious audacity—had proven that he would only respond to violence, and so Diablo would show him a kind of violence he was not ready for.

He just wouldn't use fists.

And goddammit, it was really something that all of this bullshit had to go down after the bull ride was already over.

Turning suddenly, Diablo made quick work of grabbing Dillon by the front collar of his ridiculous faux wool-lined jacket, lifted him bodily from the podium he stood upon. Filled with the strength of a lifetime of working out and being entirely through with Dillon's obnoxiousness, he removed him from the podium, setting him on the stage.

While everyone watched—an entire arena's rapt attention on the two men in the spotlight, their faces close like they played out a love scene—Diablo leaned low to get in close to Dillon, exaggerating how far he had to bend to do so, and said low and quiet, his mouth near enough to the other man's mic to get picked up and broadcast throughout the arena, "You're up past your bedtime, Dillon, and it shows. Why don't you head on back to camp, little buddy. A snack and some rest will do that attitude of yours a world of good. You go on ahead and let the grown-ups finish up out here. We'll be right behind you."

He punctuated his patronizing goodbye by patting Dillon's head, harder than was translated via the jumbotron, through which, by the looks of it, he'd given him nothing worse than a buddy tap.

Looks were deceiving, though, and because Diablo hadn't been free to decimate the man, he at least channeled some of the depth of his revulsion and animosity toward the man into each of his paternalistic taps.

While the audience erupted in laughter, Dillon's hand instinctively came to rub the top of his head, and their roar grew louder, adding layer upon layer to his public shaming.

It was nowhere near enough or equivalent to the crime committed, but social justice had swept in to offer its comfort and condolence, and it was at least mildly soothing to the thing inside him that still wanted to see his enemy obliterated.

And though Dillon wouldn't be completely obliterated, if *The Closed Circuit* did what it usually did, it would at least take him some time to recover.

Rodeo didn't look too kindly on crybabies, nor folks who fell back on schemes, rather than skill, to knock out their competition.

Rodeo would be the judge of Dillon, and the man had better hope they went easy on him, because he'd shown his ass and it hadn't been pretty. If there was any justice in the world, it would cost him.

Karma could be swift.

Dillon had threatened two people's livelihoods in a single evening. There was balance in the idea that he ended the night with his own standing on shaky ground.

His face turning red, Dillon held back a stomp, but Diablo could tell it was a near thing. Instead, he spun on the heel that had echoed around the stadium, and stormed off stage.

The audience continued to cheer as he left, and when he was out of sight and Diablo had settled himself back into his place, casting a glance at Sierra, whose back was to him again, she said, bright and loud, "What'd I tell ya, folks? Only at *The Closed Circuit*! We had a wild night with you, Nashville. What a rodeo!"

And she gave the signal and the lights transitioned and cued the end of show music, and he and Julio and Sierra finally walked off the infernal stage.

That they did so to a standing ovation did nothing to lighten the weariness hanging over them.

Walking so as not to be in the way of the greenies whose job it was to break down the set, the three of them stopped when they'd made it deep enough into the recesses that it was no longer their job to smile and wave.

And that was where the staff in black found them.

However, this time they had someone highly recognizable among their number, *The Closed Circuit*'s executive producer, Boss Harper.

Julio was just as much an old-timer as the boss, whose gap-toothed grin was always at odds with his three-piece suit, but he was the executive producer and so there was no semblance of equality. And his face was uncharacteristically grim.

He did not bother with attempts at intimidation or beating around the bush, saying directly, "Outside of the bull riding, that was not what I like to see out there. We're going to be playing cleanup for a while now, and I tell you it's the last thing rodeo needs right now. It's damn near enough to stop the whole thing."

Diablo did not bother to point out that the one who bore the greatest responsibility in the matter was not present among them.

"Not to mention," the boss continued, "the goddamn fact you let him say that damn circus line. All the time, the circus. We're a rodeo unlike any other, but we're still a goddamn rodeo. That's why we have you, Ms. Quintanilla. You're here to remind everybody this is still the rodeo they know and love."

Sierra's spine stiffened in response and she winced, but she said, "Yes, sir," like a good little cadet, kindling the embers of Diablo's anger again. The man had no right to talk to her like that.

"Sierra handled things pretty well, I'd say. All things considered," he said, unable to help himself.

Attention landing on Diablo, Boss narrowed his eyes

and said, "Next time, less words and just throw the punch. We could have at least gotten a ratings boost out of this nonsense that way. And you," he said, turning his attention now specifically to Julio before pausing to look into his eyes.

They might not be equals as far as the *Closed Circuit* hierarchy went, but Julio didn't blink or look away from Boss's stare and finally the producer reached out and offered Julio a hand.

Silently, Julio took it, and they shook hands.

"Great ride out there tonight. Been a long time since I've seen rodeo like that," Boss said, and then he released Julio's hand and stepped back.

He then turned, apparently ready to leave, but stopped, spinning back to Sierra. "I wasn't kidding. I hope you're taking the clauses of your contract seriously. You're here to add legitimacy to the show, which means we expect you to act like a legitimate queen. You look good, you smile and you don't let anybody get in your pants."

Diablo's hackles rose, the fighter in him still close to the surface and eager to be set loose, but froze at Sierra's chuckle.

Light and airy, it was the sound of a woman who was absolutely innocent of everything she'd been accused of and was mildly perplexed to even have to address it. "They don't come more legitimate than me, and rest assured, God has yet to create a cowboy worth losing my crown over."

He knew she was covering her ass, had personally borne witness to the fact that her job was on the line, yet her words, coming so soon on the heels of his own recent revelations where she was concerned, dug across

his heart like spurs, leaving raw track marks on its surface in their wake.

This is what it was, and always would be, to love
Sierra.

Sierra was a rodeo queen—the world's greatest.

She got paid to be single and wholesome and dedicated to her horses.

Disdaining and discouraging cowboys was as much
a part of her job description as was respecting and re-
vering rodeo.

He was smart enough to know that the extra little
dig at the end, the bit about losing her crown, had been
added for effect—not because she was sending him a
special message about where he stood in her order of
priorities.

She hadn't been warning him to fall in line and back
her up.

There was nothing personal about it.

It was just business.

Frankly, he was surprised she hadn't had him sign
a nondisclosure agreement. A queen of her caliber and
prestige certainly warranted it.

And when she'd been in the hot seat, confronted by
the head honcho of *The Closed Circuit*, she'd had to be
convincing.

Her job demanded it—would likely demand it of her
again if they continued carrying on as they had been.

In truth, she had merely risen to the occasion—like
she always did.

Tonight the occasion just happened to be pretending
he was nothing to her.

He would have believed her performance himself, if

he had been cross-examining her in a courtroom. She was that good.

Boss's eyes flashed to Diablo and then back to Sierra before he said, "Keep it that way," and walked away, his train of suits following after him.

Watching them go, Diablo knew that things with Sierra were different than they had been with the girls he'd grown up around; that it was context and career that drove her—rather than shame and social pressure—and yet he could also recognize that, for him, the experience was the same. A promise to himself broken.

And he knew what would happen next.

Her shoulders would release the tension when the boss was out of sight, and she and he and Julio would make a bit of small talk before saying goodbye, and then she would come to his RV after the parking lot lights had gone out with an apology, a smile and need for comfort and reassurance in her eyes.

And then they would continue the second half of the tour the way they had started it—meeting in private and prepared to lie about it—until it was all over, and then what?

She would have a few months off before the next Closed Circuit season started and she had to be single again, and he would need to get immediately back to work in Phoenix.

And when the third season kicked off, what then? Would he watch her tour the country with another group of hopefuls wistfully recalling their summer of stolen kisses and sneaking around?

Was that future worth the reminder that despite everything he had done, there was still a large segment of the world that simply didn't believe he was good enough, and that it remained powerful enough to scare even the people who claimed to love him into compliance?

Sierra smiled, letting out a light chuckle as her shoulders released, the stars and stripes losing their buoyancy as her posture slumped. "Well, that was a train wreck. I'm so sorry, Julio. You handled it great, though. You could have a career in announcing, if you ever wanted."

A tingling sensation began in Diablo's fingertips and crawled its way up his hands and arms as she——her words were not exactly what he had predicted, because he had not thought she would so directly reference the drama, but presciently close——brought his prediction to life.

Julio, his face still hard from their scrimmage with Dillon, played his part as well, staring off in the distance with an unfocused expression rather than meeting anyone's eye, as he offered a grunt that was both assent and acceptance of what Sierra said before, adding, more to himself than them, "This is why. Years and years, for this."

Diablo knew what he meant, if Sierra didn't, and there was nothing to say to contradict it.

Julio was an old man, and an excellent rodeo cowboy. In a sport that liked to proclaim the only thing that mattered was how you showed up in the arena, Julio's experience was a case study to the contrary.

He'd shown time and time again that he was in a league of his own.

And they'd still tried to run him out of town.

The Closed Circuit might be revising things, but this was also a real story of rodeo.

It was the part that Diablo had been walking away

from all those years ago, and a part to which he had not given a backward glance.

And it wasn't something he had any intention of welcoming back into his life.

That was why, despite all the thrill and reclamation this experience had given him, his return to rodeo was temporary.

He'd begun losing sight of it, but this whole thing was supposed to have been a mere blip on the radar of his larger game, not some kind of life-altering rebirth.

The fact that he loved Sierra didn't change that.

That just made it more serious that he end things with her now.

It had been his choice to waffle in his convictions with her, but it could also be his choice to reaffirm them. His feelings for her only made his holding that line more important. He would not hide with a woman and he wouldn't lie about his involvement with one—especially not the one he was in love with.

He was the only person who could protect himself from those hurts and he had promised himself that he would in perpetuity.

It wasn't because anybody was wrong or bad; it was because most people were willing to do whatever it took to survive.

It had just taken Dillon's attack on Julio to remind him.

The world wouldn't change all at once, but an individual could, but only once they'd grown sick and tired of getting beat up on the front lines of evolution.

Rodeo might be slowly breaking open, but it had cracked Diablo in half long ago.

But while he had lived to see a rodeo in which men

like him and Julio could be recognized for the talent they possessed and the lineages they belonged to, he hadn't yet lived to see a rodeo in which men like Dillon didn't also get rewarded for doing half as much.

And, in his lifetime, he didn't think he would see the end to women treating him like the kind of man best kept a secret.

It wasn't in his power to enact that kind of large-scale social change.

But he could make it happen in his own life. He did have that power.

"I, for one, am beat. Gonna hit the sack," he said, halting the remaining flow of the evening more abruptly than it would have should things have played out naturally.

In a way, in this moment, he felt more like his regular self than he had in weeks, safely ensconced in the comfort of no longer being interested in dancing to someone else's tune.

As if reconnecting with his rodeo past had somehow required disconnecting from the man he had worked hard to become, he recalled that if life had dealt him a hard hand, he at least had learned to handle it.

He could do hard things.

He could even do multiple hard things at once.

He could love Sierra, and he could love himself, and because of the two, he could let her go.

Her eyes darted up to catch his as he spoke, and he knew she wanted the reassurance of eye contact after the hurt of denying him, but he looked back at Julio instead.

Nodding at the other man, he said, "Great ride. Never seen one like it." Then, to Sierra, he softened his voice, but did not offer the real thing that she wanted, did not speak to her with his eyes, gave her no promise to sort things out later. "You handled a difficult situation well," he said, and nothing more.

He looked away before hurt flashed across her face because it would be easy to fall back into old patterns if he thought it might alleviate some of her pain, and said, "I'll see you around." And because there wasn't anything else to say after that, he left.

THE QUIET THAT greeted him in his RV was deafening after everything that had happened throughout the night.

He had ridden a bull for the first time in fourteen years, and for the first time in a professional arena, and he'd been even better than he used to be.

And Julio had followed him up with literal perfection.

The rodeo gods had been good to Nashville tonight.

As had the devils, though this time, at least, it'd had nothing to do with him.

Dillon had reared the ugly side of rodeo for the world to see and he'd been set down because of it, but there were bound to be consequences and reverberations throughout the rodeo world.

If *The Closed Circuit* had set out to shake up rodeo, they'd done a good job of it in their two seasons, breaking the rules and norms left and right while at the same time taking its popularity to unseen heights.

In the wreckage of the moment, he realized that that, too, was one of the reasons he was competing. The opening up of rodeo had always been one of the reasons he had been there.

It was ironic that it was here and now, nearly twenty-five years after he had begun his rodeo journey, that he would recognize that trailblazing in this world had always been a part of it for him—that as much as he had resented it through his lifetime, he had chosen to be an ambassador in a world and sport where he was not and had never truly been welcome, precisely because he loved it.

It took rodeo at its most circus-like and over-the-top to show him a piece of the heart that beat inside him.

He had found love in an arena that was hopeless not because he didn't have the skill but because it had been incapable of seeing him as a worthy, valued and deserving human being, let alone one of its greatest successes. It hadn't mattered how much try he had or how well he showed up in front of a crowd.

And that was the real reason why he had walked away. He saw that now.

Eventually, it'd beat him down, as beaten down as he was now, he could finally admit that to himself.

He hadn't walked away because he wanted to, but because, just like now, he couldn't take being hurt by the thing he loved anymore.

But the defiance that lived in him hadn't been smothered. It had survived—it was why he'd kept his saddles despite everything he'd tried to convince himself of.

And all of it was also a part of why coming back had breathed as much life into him as walking away from Sierra was draining it.

He hadn't wanted to miss his opportunity to be a part of the revolution, even if it meant picking at old scars and walking away with a whole new set of wounds.

But wounded or not, and incremental it might be—

as Dillon's all-too-familiar persecution of Julio and the damning response of the showrunners had proved the transformation to be—if rodeo was finally changing, then Diablo would be a part of it. If rodeo was ready to acknowledge the people it had always tried to relegate to the shadows and the room it had to grow, he was going to be there. He'd earned his place in it and he refused to be just another anonymous Black man whose credits and accomplishments went unknown.

Fortunately, these days TV was ready for a more accurate picture of a cowboy, one that reflected the West as it actually was, rather than a whitewashed manifest destiny fairy tale.

Cowboy culture had been birthed by vaqueros, well before Texas ever thought of being a part of the United States. From there it had grown to incorporate enslaved stock drivers as well as the Indigenous peoples who had protected and held on to their own ancient horse traditions and lineages in the face of those who wanted to kill, replace, erase and take credit for them—traditions that had existed well before Europeans claimed to have introduced the horse to the continent.

The West was tough and gritty, not because brave settlers had faced the great unknown and encountered hardship in a vast and empty landscape, but because the people who already lived there, or who had been forced to come there, had retained their hard-fought-for footholds in harsh ground and survived every attempt not just to take it from them, but to erase the fact that they had ever even been there in the first place.

The West had never been white, and now that the world was ready to hear that truth, Diablo would not miss his opportunity to speak—with every single opportunity he got, whether his heart was shattered or not.

And though he had always had a way with words, he also knew that the best way to get his message across was to speak with his performance.

The Closed Circuit had given him an opportunity to show the world how a real cowboy looked and acted, and not just in the arena, and it certainly wasn't like Dillon.

It might be the same good old boys running things in the back room—perennially concerned with their bottom line over human dignity—but out on stage, *The Closed Circuit* had managed to repackage rodeo. It had given the public a rodeo that was culturally vibrant and diverse, and *that* was the image of rodeo that had gone viral. After tonight Diablo was willing to bet that they'd never intended it, but in just two seasons, the show had torn apart the myth of what it was to be a cowboy—including who could be one—and in doing so, had actually changed things.

That was why—and clearly only that, as the producers hadn't been too quick to jump in and do the right thing when given the opportunity with Julio—Diablo had no doubt that what had happened at tonight's show would be talked about in the rodeo world for a long time to come.

Just as there was no doubt that the Dillons of the sport would retaliate.

That retaliation would matter to the spate of girls that had been inspired by Lil's performance last season, as well as to all of the Black and Brown and Indigenous children who had seen the three of them and started to remember that it was their people who invented cowboying.

It shouldn't have been up to him to go to bat for Julio. *The Closed Circuit* had started this wave and they were responsible for it. But knowing that they wouldn't step in was also why Diablo had done it—maybe that was the reason he always stuck his neck out. The world might not be just and right and fair, but if he could make it a little more so, shouldn't he?

Whether it meant riding or filling out paperwork, he used his intelligence and strength to help protect those that needed it. That was what it meant to be a cowboy, and that was the truth he would continue to embody, through to the end of *The Closed Circuit* and beyond.

And that would be something, at least, in the face of the fact that there was no way he'd ever be able to look back at this time and not think of Sierra.

She was everything he had ever wanted in a woman without even realizing he'd been compiling a list.

She was the first woman he had met whom he knew he could walk into any situation with and remain confident that not only would she flourish, she might also steal his thunder.

She was the first woman whom he had introduced to every version of him—lawyer, cowboy, lover and friend—and though he was the one doing the walking, she would also be the one who got away.

But if he was going to love her, if he was going to let her get into the crack that she'd opened up inside him and settle in, inevitably making it bigger—breaking him open more and more until he was raw and exposed and vulnerable to her—then she had to treat him with care.

She had to recognize how hard it was for him. How much it hurt to trust, even when it felt good.

And if she couldn't, as she'd shown tonight, then he couldn't, either. He owed it to himself.

He would not give his love outside a space of care and consideration.

He would not willingly make himself vulnerable to someone who could be relied on to hurt him when their job demanded it.

And that meant that rather than stretch things out through the remainder of the tour, it was best to stop things now—before he'd confessed his feelings, before she had a chance to explain and make him forget his promises to himself once again, and before they did or said things that were irreversible.

Given the chance, she'd shown she had the power to wrap him around her pretty finger, so he wouldn't give her the chance.

He was a cold turkey kind of guy.

He just hoped he could withstand the real test when it came.

But even still, when it arrived hours later, in the form of a quiet knock on his door, it still came too soon.

She knocked, gradually increasing the volume, for a long time while Diablo lay on his bed, staring at the storage compartments overhead, gritting his teeth.

Throughout, she tried different means to get through to him. She called his name, quietly, urgently, then with more force and irritation.

She tried different rhythms and knock styles.

She talked to him through the door.

"Diablo. I know you're in there. I'm sorry about what I said. You know it's my job."

"Diablo, I just…"

"Let me in, Diosa. I—I have something I need to tell you."

She held her breath then; he felt it even as much as he heard it, and then she let it out in a loud and long exhale.

And he opened the door.

She wore jeans and a dull gray T-shirt. Her hair hung around her in a strange mix of curls, falling out waves, flat spots, volume and kinks. Her brown eyes were large and shiny in the parking lot lighting, each of them still bearing smudged traces of her eye makeup.

Diablo couldn't recall her ever looking desperate like this before, even after searching the countless saved images of her in his mind, and it chipped at his resolve.

He knew how she really felt. What did it matter what she said in public?

But it did matter. It mattered because someone who loved you prioritized your well-being over their reputation, even when it was hard.

She stepped toward his door, but he didn't budge. His will might be eroding, but he still knew what he had to do.

"It's over, Sierra."

Sierra gasped, the sudden inhale echoing across the parking lot, the glistening sheen to her eyes now threatening to well over.

"I'm so sorry, Diablo," she said in a rush on her exhale. "I had to nip their suspicion in the bud. You know that's not how I feel." She echoed his own thoughts as if she read them.

He did know, and it didn't make it okay.

"When I asked Mckenna Jean Miller to the prom in front of her friends in an elaborate setup, she laughed and said she'd rather go with someone she was sure could afford it, despite the fact that we'd been sleeping together for a year by that point and she'd told me she loved me."

"Diablo, that's awful. That's terrible, but that's not—"

He stopped her. "At a large firm's recruitment cocktail party in law school, I overheard a mentor advise my then girlfriend to break up with me before we graduated because it didn't look good for a woman who wanted to work for the prosecutor's office to be romantically involved with a Black man—"

"But that wasn't her fault. It was her mentor," Sierra said, and Diablo shook his head.

"To which she replied, 'I'm just getting the last of my wild oats out before I have to settle down with that one.'"

Sierra's shoulders slumped. "I'm so sorry, Diablo," she repeated. "I never should have said what I did."

Resisting the urge to comfort her, forcing himself to keep his distance, he shrugged one shoulder. "It's not your fault. You have to do what you have to do, and we both know it. Have known it from the beginning. I shouldn't have let things get past that night in the hotel. In truth, I shouldn't even have gone that far. We always knew the rules."

"Diablo—" Sierra's voice broke.

"I'm not angry at you, Sierra. It's just over."

"But Diablo," she started, until he held up his palms to stop her.

"It's past visiting hours, queenie. You don't want to miss out on any of that beauty sleep."

There was nothing for her to say to such a clear goodbye, and she didn't, just took a shuddering breath

and turned around. He watched her go until she made
it back to the area of her RV, and then he went inside
and closed the door.

But it turned out that leaving hadn't meant she'd
given up, not the woman he loved; she didn't give up
easily. So he continued to lie there, staring up at the ceil-
ing of his rig, certain that he'd had to have ground his
teeth into a smooth paste by this point, while his phone
vibrated on the bedside table, over and over again.

The calls didn't stop until the wee hours of the morning, and a perverse part of him was touched by her determination.

He had expected her pride to cut her off long before
it had.

IT FELT LIKE a lie to call it the next morning when he
woke up to his seven-thirty alarm, a mere few hours
after he'd gone to sleep, but it was nevertheless the start
of the next block of time over which he was expected
to be awake.

After yesterday's show and the night that had followed, however, tired as he was, he was still grateful
to be saying goodbye to Nashville.

Their drive to Oklahoma City had been broken in
half and spread over two days, and as exhausted as he
was, he could only be grateful for the reprieve. Two
days in a row where the biggest tasks in front of him
were all related to driving—as opposed to performing,
Dillon, Julio or Sierra—was exactly what he needed.

He was used to having a job that followed him everywhere he went and never really gave him any time
off, but *The Closed Circuit* was showing him just how
much alone time lawyering still left him.

He'd be more appreciative when he got back to it. At this point, that day couldn't come soon enough.

He felt like he'd drunk the sun up, when in reality, he'd been pummeled on top of a bull only to then have his heart stomped on before it even got a chance to beat.

He was bound to be a little sore.

But for the next two days he had nowhere to be but the road and no one to see him but people passing in cars.

He could feel as shitty as he wanted to.

It was almost like it was his birthday.

He brushed his teeth, ate a to-go bowl of Frosted Flakes and finally looked at his phone.

What he saw, however, rather than salt in the wound that was Sierra, confused him, because in addition to the many missed calls from Sierra that he'd expected, he'd also missed three calls from his nana.

She'd left him three voice mails, which was strange in itself—she typically called a few times and begrudgingly left a message only on her last attempt—but what was stranger was the fact that she had called him that many times from three-thirty in the morning. The only times in his life he had known her to be up at an hour even close to that was during the height of her working days, and even then, the earliest she'd ever awoken was 5:00 a.m.

And by this point she had been retired for longer than Diablo had been practicing law.

Like sweet little retirees the world over, she was usually in bed, sound asleep, well before 3:00 a.m.

The oddity around his nana's behavior was enough to lure his mind away from the fact that Sierra had left him eight voice mails and called more than that.

His and Sierra's affair had come to an end.

His nana was forever.

Playing the first voice mail from her, he frowned, a sliver of unease lancing its way through his stomach.

Something about her voice was off—not bad or wrong, necessarily, but off-kilter, as if she was feeling oddly light or silly—and maybe she was, to be calling so late in the first place.

"Recuerdo de cuando llegaste…" she said, pausing for a labored breath before continuing, a smile in her voice, "Empezaste a llorar. Me sorprendió tanto no podía recordar ninguna canción, pero, te canté, 'si se van la luna y obscuro todo esté, no me importa, tengo a mi picarito.'"

As much as she loved him, his nana had never been particularly sentimental or nostalgic, but Diablo knew from experience that 3:00 a.m. could do that to a person. Though it had been years since he'd thought about the day Nana had found him, himself, he'd spent many a late night replaying the story in his mind, as well as the special little song she'd continued to sing to him throughout his childhood.

She sounded steadier in the second voice mail, but the sweetness and wistfulness had kicked up a notch in a way that made his heart ache and his suspicions rise.

His grandmother wasn't sweet.

It started with, "Vi el programa y solo quería decirte que hiciste un gran trabajo ahí fuera—"

She didn't have to tell him for him to know that she was both watching and rooting for him, but it wasn't completely out of character, and he appreciated it.

It was where she went next that set off warnings in his gut.

"Sabes que estoy muy orgullosa de ti, ¿verdad? Cuando te busco, estás in todos. Tu eres mi corazón y alegria. Te extraño tanto. Te amo, siempre."

He did know she was proud of him, but not because they had a family tradition of talking about it, and while, if pressed, he would have said she loved him more than anything in the world, he'd never heard her speak in terms like heart and joy before. She was more direct than that.

Nervous after listening to the voice mail in a way he had not been after the first, he quickly instructed the device to play the final message she'd left. It was the most unsettling of the three.

As had been the case in her first message, there was an unusual wobble in her voice, as if she wasn't at full strength and fully in her right mind, but unlike the first two, her voice was neither cheerful nor nostalgic. Nor did it carry any notes of honey, just genuine uncertainty and regret.

But perhaps most concerning of all to him as he listened was that, more so than even a call to reminisce out of the blue, her words were slightly blurred and made no sense, as if a strong medication had kicked in over the progression of her leaving her messages, with the third one coming in after the payload had landed.

But his grandmother wasn't on any medications with those kind of side effects.

She didn't take any medications at all, in fact. She credited her health with working hard and eating right her whole life. Even in retirement, she walked every day, went to bed and woke early, ate a big lunch and light dinner, and napped in the middle of the day. Si quieres vivir sano, hazte viejo temprano, she'd say every time she came back from the doctor's visits with a clean bill of health—visits that he'd had to cajole her into making.

How many times had he teased her in response, saying that she would be healthy forever, then, because she'd been old before he'd ever met her?

But she had never sounded old.

She sounded old on the phone now, and tired. "Perdona te estoy llamando…" she said, trailing off before coming back with, "Lamento no haberte dicho."

Didn't tell him what? he wondered, his concern rising.

"—No me di cuenta que nunca habría una despedida. No pensaba con claridad. Solo quería verte una ultima vez, pero tarde o temprano estaré contigo otra vez…te amo, picarito, más de lo que te imaginas."

He played the message a second and third time before trying her number with no success, his sense of foreboding growing with each passing moment.

What was she talking about, wishing to see him one last time? If he didn't know any better, he'd say she was saying goodbye, and not the temporary see-you-around kind of goodbye, but the more permanent variety. But he did know better, and specifically, he knew that while his grandmother was old, she was healthy.

When she didn't answer the phone, he reassured himself that if she'd been up that late, she was likely asleep—ignoring the fact that she regularly complained that she couldn't sleep in anymore even if she wanted to. If she'd been up that late, it didn't even really count as sleeping in as much as just sleeping.

And really, for a woman her age after what seemed like an all-nighter, sleep would be the best thing for her now. It was a good sign that she wasn't answering, then.

He would try her again, later during the drive, in the afternoon.

She would be awake by then and could put his wild fears to rest.

He would feel like a fool for getting alarmed, but ultimately she would be fine. His grandmother was just feeling tired and sentimental and maybe even lonely—things that could be fixed with a few hours of shut-eye and a visit after the tour wrapped up.

He looked forward to feeling like a fool over his concerns at that point, because as he played her final voice mail one more time, he realized that the worst thing about it was that it sounded like she'd failed.

CHAPTER SEVENTEEN

Oklahoma City, Oklahoma

"How y'all feeling out there tonight, OKC?"

Sierra's voice rang out through the arena, carefree and filled with excitement, while the jumbotron projected her smiling face to those who couldn't make it out from their seats, and the audience's resounding and loud cheering in response confirmed that they were indeed feeling good.

It was her job to make sure they stayed that way. It was her job to make them feel even better.

And she wouldn't let anyone say she wasn't good at her job.

She wasn't just good at her job. She was stupendous at her job. She was interstellar at her job. There had never been anybody before her that was better at her job and no one yet out there with the skill and talent to come up from behind and usurp her.

She was the queen.

She was at the pinnacle of her career, she set the new high bar and it was only fair that she reign supreme.

And to get there, all she had had to do was give up everything else.

Her youth, education, future stability, having a family and her chance at love.

Heavy was the head that wore the crown.

Heavy were the hands that applied concealer to the dark circles under her eyes, dabbing a thicker-than-average layer of foundation to cover the wan and drawn flatness of her skin.

Heavy was the amount of makeup required to hide the feelings.

Heavy were the false eyelashes, every time she blinked, and the denim and leather and boots, weighing each step down.

Heavy was the winning smile.

Heavy were the Spanx and the push-ups, and the saddles, and the photo ops, and the contact lenses, and the Vaseline on the teeth and the hiding what she did in her downtime.

Serving as the living and breathing embodiment of rodeo had become a hard bit in her mouth, a painful and rigid reminder that she did not have full lead over the direction of her life.

That control of her own destiny was just another sacrifice to the process of turning her passion into her career was a hard pill to swallow. She'd given rodeo the reins and let it guide her into hurting the man she loved.

The damage was done and she had no room to complain about or bemoan it now.

Just because she hadn't known the true price when she'd signed on the dotted line was no excuse to renege now.

And if her life had turned out to be more rhinestones and glue than real diamonds and gold, she could at least still make it look good.

If she was a fool, then she would be one in private.

To everybody else, she was going to look like the best damn rodeo queen the world had ever seen.

She would bring her very best to each and every remaining show of the tour, regardless of whether or not she'd spent the night before crying over Diablo in her RV.

She would watch every moment of his performances, bearing witness to not just his excellence and beauty but also to his risk and threat, and she would comment and celebrate it like he was any other top-tier competitor, even as it tore her to shreds inside. It was part of her job and she could be counted on to do that right. She had sabotaged every other good thing in her life so that statement could always be true.

"Boy, have we got a show for you tonight!" she called out to the crowd. "This one is a brand-new, never-before-seen event coming from the one and only rodeo like no other, and you won't be disappointed. Tonight is all about the ladies, but because it's *The Closed Circuit*, that doesn't mean any of these cowboys are getting free drinks. Nope! Tonight we're honoring what we all know is true about us ladies—we've got to do everything the fellas have to, but backward and in heels. Well, tonight we're turning the tables on the men. We'll see how well they do, riding in our boots for a little bit. Our rough-stockers are gonna get a run for their money when they try their hands at a little barrel racing and horsemanship riding. We've seen them pit their brute force against bulls and showcase their suave power with broncs, but tonight we're going to see if they have the finesse it takes to ride like a queen!"

"A Boy Named Sue" began to play through the loudspeakers and the arena erupted into cheers made all the more buoyant for the sense of shared hilarity woven through it—cowboys riding like girls? *Hilarious!*—and Sierra smiled a brittle smile at the campiness of it all, her expression held up only by the cold comfort of having nailed yet another perfect segment.

She might not have been able to get through to Diablo, but she could still get an arena right where she wanted them.

There was that, at least.

The next segment of the night's schedule featured a performance by the clowns to allow the first contestant time for any final preparations before the show started, and to give Sierra a chance to have a sip of water, which she did, grimly aware that it was going to be a long night.

She would think about him the whole way through Part A of the evening—the portion that came before his performance—wondering how he would compare to his brethren and if he would fall on his ass as they were likely to, or if he would excel, as he was likely to do.

And for Part B—the time of his performance—she would have to force the kinds of words that she was paid to say to come out around the growing knot of her hopes and wishes that everything would go well and the world would see how remarkable he was, as well as the frayed cords of her fears that something could go wrong, that he could be hurt, physically or emotionally, that he might fail, and then back around to the fact that she loved him when he'd made it clear he was over her.

That knot was difficult to breathe around, let alone speak through.

But he would get it done and she would get it done, and then she would struggle, depleted, through Part C—

the rest of the night—until she could finally drag herself back to her RV, peel off her costume and think about him until she fell into fitful sleep.

She would be glad when this tour was over.

If he kept with recent tradition, he would deliver a performance that was executed almost to the letter of the law—which was no surprise, really, given who he was—and when it was all over, the pride that she felt in him, the pride that she didn't have a right to, would thread its way into her voice, so thick and obvious that it revealed that there really was something between them.

Even if it was over and had left her with nothing but the knowledge that there *was* a difference between Sierra the woman and Sierra the rodeo queen. There was a line where one ended and the other began even if she'd lied about it to herself and everyone else through all these years.

Diablo had seen it and seen that the part of her on the other side of that line, the wild girl who had wanted to ride fast and be loved by her mother and sisters, was dying under the weight of her Stetson.

There was a difference between the feeling she got when she rode horses for herself—not weighted down by her queen gear or the heat of the spotlight—and the feeling she got when she rode fully costumed for an audience.

There was a difference in the way she felt when she had queened with the dream of earning the next big crown and now, when she queened for the next paycheck.

There was a difference between the way she thought about her future with rodeo and the way she thought about her future with Diablo.

And in each case the difference was the same one that separated a calling and a daily grind, love and obligation, a fully realized existence and one that just looked good from the outside.

She had chosen duty when she thought she had chosen joy, in the form of a man who had come down in her life like a judge's gavel, but now joy wasn't giving her a chance to make things right.

Joy had shut the door in her face and now refused to open it up again.

Joy needed some sense slapped into it.

But if she was to be stuck with lemons, she was just Southern enough to make lemonade.

For that reason, tonight she wore nearly monochrome supple yellow leather.

If she couldn't have joy, she would be joy.

The ensemble was one of her rare fringe-free costumes.

Instead, what pushed this outfit over the edge, were the hundreds of small pieces of raw turquoise that she had affixed to both vest and chaps.

Tonight she had dressed in order to gather up what was left of her dignity and poise, and she looked fantastic.

She looked like everything Oklahoma loved in a cowgirl—nothing too flashy, but pretty and down-to-earth—and because of it, and her years of practice, she had them eating out of the palm of her hand.

But Diablo might as well as have been a brick wall to her.

CHAPTER EIGHTEEN

Fort Sumner, New Mexico

FOR SEVEN NIGHTS in a row, after days on the road and nights in the arena, Sierra knocked on his door, and for seven nights in a row, Diablo did not open it.

Nor had he answered the phone any of the times she called thereafter.

For the past two nights she had not come at all. Neither had she called.

In the same amount of time, he had not been able to get in touch with his grandmother.

Worrying about her, gnawing on the mounting certainty that something wasn't right, was perhaps the only possible distraction that could have dragged his attention away from Sierra.

If he wasn't so worried, in fact, he might have even been grateful.

But this was not like his nana.

He'd tried both the home number and her cell multiple times, every day, and each time it had simply rung through to her ancient tape-recorded answering machine, or gone through the automated voice mail inbox that she'd never gotten around to recording a personal greeting for.

There were challenges that came with having a family of two, and one person not answering their phones was one of them.

Diablo had no other kin, which meant there was nobody else to check on her, their visit welcome or not.

The old man hadn't been picking up, either, but that was more normal. With him, Diablo at least knew that he could trust him to check on her as soon as he got the message.

But over a week was a long time to go without hearing from both of them.

To no one's surprise by this point in the season, Diablo had placed second in Oklahoma City, as he had done again in Denver, just last night.

Despite the predictable outcome for him, however, Denver had been a wild night.

Denver had marked the final stop of the regular season, which also meant it was the last hurrah for all of the bottom-tier cowboys who remained in the bullpens. It was the last chance for all the remaining contestants to compete against each other as a whole group because after the points were tallied for the evening, only the top three would continue on.

Points were given, but even though it had been theoretically possible that one of the bottom scorers could catch up to and replace Dillon in the final three if he scored high enough, nobody had expected any real upsets, given how consistent the top three contenders had been this season.

In fact, going into it everyone had taken to calling it the filler stop—the episode in reality TV leading up to the finale in which nothing really happens.

The event was set to be a roping showcase, showdown style, in which cowboys pitted their ropes against each other to loop into hard-to-reach places, as well as aim and striking at finite points.

What no one could have predicted, however, was the fact that there had been a roping savant lurking in the bullpens.

Casey O'Brien from Idaho, a tenacious but oddly forgettable cowboy who'd advanced through the whole contest by the skin of his teeth week after week, it turned out, could have run away and joined the Cirque du Soleil with how good he was at roping.

With long-shot odds that Diablo hoped someone had made a little money off, Casey beat every other cowboy present—including himself and Julio—and by a wide margin.

Genuinely. He'd won by a shocking number of points.

Diablo—the runner up—had ended the event trailing him by a whole thirty points.

And in the process of his domination, *The Closed Circuit* got its second perfect score for the season, giving forgettable Casey his moment of glory.

Of course, nothing was more glorious about his moment than the fact that in having it, he knocked Dillon Oliver, the PBRA's current regular season champion, out of the final three along the way.

Diablo roping out a surprise victory over Julio for the event had given him just enough points to hold his sweet spot in second place.

In the end, Dillon was out, Diablo was in second, Julio remained in first place and Casey O'Brien from Idaho was going into the final challenges in third place.

While Diablo might have liked a little more pain in the going, being up close and personal to witness Dillon being dragged away from the arena by security after having launched himself at poor Casey was at least some form of karma.

And though Diablo knew it was a long shot, he held on to the fact that there might even come a day when Dillon realized that getting pulled off stage kicking and screaming was, in reality, more humiliating than getting knocked out of a competition by a "nobody."

After the roping, the rest of the show had been an opportunity for the cowboys going home—including Dillon—to show off in their best events one last time, and they gave the audience a rough-stock smorgasbord of bulls and broncs for their viewing delight, while the top three riders—now Julio, Diablo and Casey—kicked back, watched and rested up for the final challenges and the finale ahead.

This season *The Closed Circuit* had announced that, rather than being flown around the country for challenges in their home towns, the three of them were going to return to the road, Casey taking over Dillon's RV, and make stops for the final three showdowns before the finale.

Under normal circumstances, Diablo would have been grateful for that.

The idea of doing a special Diablo-themed challenge back home in Houston was asking to be insulted and tokenized on national television.

His grandmother's strange behavior and lack of contact, however, had passed the point beyond unusual and made their way well into concerning. A brief stopover in Houston under these circumstances would have been a relief at this point.

He would have at least been able to check on her.

According to the contract he signed, going to check on one's grandmother constituted forfeiting.

He couldn't do that to the old man.

And so he was on his way to New Mexico, Fort Sumner to be exact, instead of Houston, where he and Julio and Casey were supposed to chase each other around acting like outlaws, rustlin' each other's cattle in an arena that Diablo assumed would be some kind of southwestern desert simulation.

Yet another opportunity for a live audience to watch a group of grown men play cowboy.

It wasn't the most charitable way that he'd ever thought about *The Closed Circuit*, but it had lost some of its Back in the Saddle sheen as soon as the producers had waited for the fight to end before they stepped in to pick sides.

Before Sierra had denied him, not with an obvious lie but a painfully believable bit of acting.

Did it matter that they both knew it was only make-believe, if to the rest of the world they had to pretend like it wasn't? What percentage of a life was lived publicly, and if it was greater than half, did that make the lie the truth?

That the season and tour were rapidly approaching their end was a profound relief, nothing more.

By this point Diablo was more than ready to walk away from Sierra—this time, in more than just spirit.

He was ready to not see her every day, to not hear her voice.

He was ready for her not to be within arm's reach at all times when it was critical that he keep his hands to himself.

He was ready for the wound to scab over without being ripped off fresh anew each day.

He had more than fulfilled his commitment to the old man, having put in the best performance he possibly could, over and over again.

And if he hadn't inspired any new signups for the CityBoyz, then he had been the wrong man for the job.

He was ready to get back to real life. He needed to. His heart couldn't take any more of this.

He would figure out what was going on with his nana and finally just spend some time with her at home. It was something they both needed.

THAT NIGHT THE arena was as done up as Diablo had imagined it would be, but this time rather than a swamp, the crew had re-created the arches of Moab.

They could have perhaps tried something that looked a little more New Mexico, but he wasn't going to pooh-pooh the impressive feat they'd accomplished. It was a set that evoked the West, while also giving contestants plenty of place to hide their cattle as well as their intentions.

They had two options by which they could rustle: stampeding or sneaking up and separating from the herd. Their goal was to rustle the most cows while retaining their own herd of five. As with the first simulation challenge, each cowboy entered the arena alone, but this time around, instead of finding the cows, they had their own to manage from the start.

While Diablo preferred bulls to broncs, he couldn't say he was a huge fan of cows in general.

Yes, because of CityBoyz and college, he could rope and wrangle with the best of them, but he just didn't have an appreciation for cows bred into him like some of the folk he'd encountered in rodeo.

His current bunch were fine as far as cows went, but still slowed him down with a tendency to fan out that he wasn't thrilled with.

The challenge had a two-hour time limit, and once again in the style of *The Hunger Games*, the set designers had projected an enormous ticking countdown along the top of the stadium.

Casey, high on being promoted to the final three and seemingly cut from a genuinely eager and earnest cloth, had no doubt charged in, guns blazing, completely under the impression that he would be able to steal quickly and protect his cows—all at the same time.

Casey wasn't who Diablo needed to worry about.

His mind was full of concerns about canny Julio and suddenly moving set pieces, and the sounds of snakes and scorpions being projected through the loudspeakers—things that could really set him back.

Or so he thought. Because, of course, in the end it wasn't Julio or scorpions or snakes or the set that came back to bite him in the ass, but the thing he'd brushed off.

Once again, he had to worry about Casey.

With the same stealth he'd employed to push Dillon out of the top spot, the little shit made off with two of Diablo's cattle.

He'd turned his back for one second and, just like he'd warned them several times, the two stragglers at the back were gone.

And in the instant of bitter realization, Diablo was faced with the choice of killing time trying to find his lost cattle, or trying to find someone else to steal from.

In that instant, as corny and overproduced as it was, *The Closed Circuit* transported him back to the West of old.

Should he follow the law when breaking it was tacitly allowed?

Fortunately and unfortunately, it wasn't the kind of question that kept a man up at midlife.

He'd answered it long ago. He didn't follow the law; he embodied it, even when breaking it wasn't against the rules. He wasn't a thief.

In the end, Diablo neither searched for his missing cattle nor stole anyone else's. He maintained the three he had for the remainder of the time and, in the end, his choice served him well.

Casey might have made off with two of Diablo's cattle, but then he lost them, plus the rest of his herd to Julio—who wasn't playing against himself, as Diablo was, but for the real-life stakes of his family's future comfort and stability.

And at the end of the night, everything had settled the way it always did, with Julio far ahead in first place, and Diablo taking his easy time in second, while the third placer slunk in from behind.

"He might not have rustled any cattle, folks—and did we really think our lawman would?—but he sure as sugar held his spot in second place going into final challenge number two, folks! Will his rock-steady approach lead him all the way to buckle glory? It just might! Give it up for the *Closed Circuit* man of the law, Diablo Sosa!"

Hearing his name in Sierra's voice felt like tiny blades running delicately along his skin, first registering as shivering pleasure but leaving a trail of lacerations in their wake.

The audience loved it, though.

He loved it.

He loved her.

But there were some points that could not be compromised upon.

He didn't hold it against her; understood, even, that the world had set them up.

She couldn't do anything but deny him, while he refused to be anyone's secret lover.

And if his running away from her was cowardly, he at least admitted it to himself as he fled the arena after the show, deliberately chatting with a social media intern for his post-performance interview while Sierra was tangled up with Casey's flood of emotions, before quickly leaving the scene.

He retreated to his tried and true RV, his partner as reliable as his hold on his second-place position. The vehicle was an ideal partnership—a comforting friend he could count on being there for him, as long as he performed.

What more did a man really need?

He was glad that Sierra had stopped knocking.

Silence was better than enduring the urge to give in to her.

And because he'd so effectively exited the arena after the show, it was a great deal of silence that stretched out before him.

He tried calling his nana again, unsurprised when she didn't answer.

By this point, he realized, he would probably be more surprised if she actually picked up.

Maybe she'd gotten a new phone and hadn't gotten it set up yet?

And a new phone number, and an entirely new sense of phone etiquette.

At eleven, he decided to get ready for bed and lie down.

He was still awake at 2:00 a.m., long after Sierra would have stopped calling, but not so tired that he couldn't make it to the time at which his nana had called.

And by the time he got there, it wasn't a big thing to stay up a little longer, in case that was when she decided to call again.

Getting three to four hours of sleep a night—up to five on the tour's days off—was only as grueling as law school had been, and he'd made it through that just fine.

Of course, he'd been a lot younger then.

But he was making it work again.

As the tour dragged along, bloody and beaten, toward the finale of the show, Diablo knew an end was near.

Thank God.

He could catch up on sleep when he got back to his condo.

Thinking about his condo was almost as jolting as the ring of his phone.

Was a condo where he lived, and not in this moving ode to recreational travel? Did he have a home with furniture and mail service and a full-size television? It was hard to remember.

Scrambling into a seated position, he reached for his phone, hoping that his grandmother was on the other end, no matter how late it was.

"Alo? Digame." The words rushed out, only a fraction of the worry he'd felt escaping in them.

"Diablo?"

It wasn't his grandmother on the phone.

Pulling the device away from his face, he read the screen. Old Man Bowman.

Had he even looked at it before he'd picked it up?

Bringing it back to his face, he said, his voice dropping back down, "Yeah."

"Son, I—" the old man's voice broke, its rich baritone shaking and rumbling like a concrete crumbler when he picked back up with, "Son, I don't know how to tell you this other than to say it straight. Your nana died tonight."

It was the last thing he remembered before waking up on the floor of his RV the next morning.

His phone was dead and there was someone knocking on his door again, but it was broad daylight, and it wasn't Sierra.

CHAPTER NINETEEN

Thirteen Days Later, Las Vegas, Nevada

No one had heard from Diablo.

Sierra paced in the living room of her two-bedroom marquee suite at the MGM Grand and fretted, the hard-fought-for hotel upgrade forgotten in the face of her concerns around Diablo. For all she knew she was worrying about something that was a relief to him.

Given what was going on in his life, she wouldn't have put it past him to not show up for the finale, forfeiting because it simply didn't matter.

No one would blame him. His fans would be disappointed, but then they could always hold on to what could have been.

After he had missed caravan call the morning after Fort Sumner, the greenies had found him on the floor, dazed and confused.

When the producers learned what had happened they'd sent him home under special circumstances—and likely only because he was his grandmother's only kin—while also airing a few hastily thrown together promo videos explaining the tragedy.

She had ached for him, watching him as he waited for the cab that took him to the airport.

Desperate to go to him, she hadn't, because she'd

known she wasn't welcome. He'd made it very clear he no longer wanted her. But even in the face of that pain and rejection, it'd still been a hard thing. His need had been so loud, for all that he didn't say a word.

But all of that had been nearly two weeks ago, and time was running out.

Having not anticipated a situation like the one they faced with Diablo, the showrunners had no specific policy in place to guide the handling of it, so they'd fallen back on the talent management agency's guidance, which insisted that Diablo had fourteen days to go home and conduct whatever business he had necessary, without losing his place in the contest.

Easy-peasy, except that the amount of leave time he was to be given carried right up to the day before the finale and had him missing the final two challenges.

There was no way to account for the points he might or might not have earned through both events, so the producers came up with the dubious solution of awarding him no points for the missed events, but also not disqualifying him from the competition for his absence.

The compromise amounted to a loss of points with no recompense that essentially destroyed his shot at surpassing Julio, but as long as he remained up for riding in the finale, even with the points lost from the missed events, he still had a shot at beating out Casey for second place.

But for what reason in the whole wide world would he give a shit about any of that?

The only family he had ever had in the world had just died.

He was all alone now, in a way he never had been before.

Why in the hell would he care about *The Closed Circuit*?

And that was why she didn't think he was coming back.

And as almost no one had heard from him since he'd left, it seemed like she would be proven right.

The fact that she was even worried about whether or not he showed up to compete in a deadly event—an event that was usually advised that competitors be of sound body, mind and soul before they attempted—was honestly probably wrong or twisted or something else unflattering.

But in the same way that for way too many nights she'd proven her dignity and pride wrong by showing up to knock at his door, something within her insisted that she not leave him alone.

Maybe there was just something wrong with her, something broken and forever warped by rodeo and heartbreak.

She knew she wouldn't have stopped going to his RV at night if Julio hadn't been there to put an end to it on the last three nights she'd tried.

On the third night he'd sighed and said, "Stop tormenting him. You're too old to play such games." The older man's voice had been weary, but firm, his judgment cast but not nearly so damning as the truth in it.

After that she had stopped tormenting him.

But was that the same wisdom she needed to heed now?

There was no one to tell her.

He never answered her calls, and, as a tower of one, there was no one but Julio who knew him well enough to offer her advice.

As the thought rippled across her consciousness, though, a refutation hounded on its tail.

She did know someone who knew him. Two people, in fact. People who knew him better than he let most. And most importantly, two people she knew how to contact.

Like Diablo, AJ didn't answer her call.

Lil, however, did.

Never had Sierra been happier to speak with Lil Island—or rather, Lil Garza now.

Though neither was competing anymore, Lil and AJ had become rodeo's star couple, royalty without any need for a crown.

At one point that had been the future Sierra wanted for herself.

Now all she wanted was Diablo. She wanted him so much that she was no longer willing to let anyone's rule but her own dictate how she treated him.

She wanted to go to museums with Diablo.

She wanted to eat sandwiches with Diablo.

She wanted to go hiking with him and make love with him on the beach, and in recreational vehicles, and maybe in a real bed or one of their houses for once.

She wanted to take care of the special privilege it was that he had chosen her to be on the short list of people he opened up to—of people he trusted. She wanted to be worthy of that, even if it meant stepping away from her crown and all of the overreach that came with it.

But more than all of that, she wanted to go to him. She wanted to comfort him, because the aching and throbbing chord that lived and pulsed between them told her he needed her.

"Sierra?" The natural country grit in Lil's voice had

once annoyed Sierra—the other woman truly didn't try at all and still had a million-dollar voice and skin that looked like she didn't work outside—but now it was a lifeline.

"I'm trying to find Diablo. Nobody knows where he is and the finale is tonight."

"Oh, yeah." Lil's voice turned heavy over the phone, authentic sorrow filling it. "Last we heard he was headed to Houston, but no one's heard anything since. He's not picking up for AJ." Lil's voice grew quieter at the last, as if it was a sore point.

"Does he know where he would be?"

Lil asked AJ before relaying to Sierra, "His nana's house for sure. I'll give you the address. He said he's going to meet you there if you're on your way. I told him to give the man some space, but now that you're haring off there, I guess we are, too."

Sierra wrote the address down and thanked both Lil and AJ, feeling the rock that had fallen on her shoulders the night Dillon had blown everything up lighten for the first time since it had landed.

She had something to do. And she had reinforcements.

Grabbing nothing but her purse and a cardigan, Sierra hopped in a cab in front of the hotel lobby and headed for the airport. She would miss her last gown fitting for the finale, but if she was lucky, she would make it back in time with one of the finest cowboys *The Closed Circuit* had ever seen. And as she'd put on a few pounds eating a few feelings in the past couple weeks, she probably didn't need the last-minute tightening anyway.

Her curtain call was at seven thirty, which gave her

eleven hours, skipping the fitting, to get there and back again.

It was enough time to at least try—and if anyone tried to give her guff over it, she'd lie and say she was doing it for the fans.

She was doing it for Diablo, though.

And she was doing it for herself.

AJ and Lil, and Henry Bowman, the man they all referred to as the old man, met Sierra at the airport, each of them landing at the Houston airport within an hour of each other, where Henry picked them up.

It took only twenty minutes to reach the neighborhood where Diablo's nana's house stood, an adorable pink bungalow with white shutters and a garden filled with particularly riotous dahlias out front.

The curtains were drawn, all the lights off and no sign of movement or sound could be detected from within.

The house was so darling, she could see why his nana had been proud and unwilling to leave, but from its stillness she was not convinced that Diablo was inside.

The whole scene looked too bright and cheery. Diablo's grief, the intensity of his emotions, called for black clouds and storms and forces that made mortals tremble. Diablo would be as unrelenting in his sorrow as he was in his honesty.

His grief did not have room for dahlias.

Henry led them up the front porch stairs, opened the screen and knocked on the door.

Behind him, Lil made a noise in the back of her throat. "He's not going to answer for you. You knew she was sick and kept it a secret from him. You're the bad guy as far as I see it."

Though Sierra knew of the dramatic paternal history

THE RODEO QUEEN

between Lil and the old man, she didn't have any time for it now. Diablo needed them.

AJ put a hand on Lil's shoulder and said low and firm, "Settle down, Lil. He did what was right for D. It's hard to understand when you don't know him as well as we do, but it was right. Just like what we're doing now."

Lil looked up at her husband, doubt written all over her face, but leaned into him. It took Sierra a moment to recognize the body language for what it was—trust.

With her lips pressed into a thin line and the same fierce frown that Sierra had seen enlarged on the jumbotron so many times last season she'd lost count, Lil nodded before adding with attitude she clearly couldn't help, "If you say so."

AJ grinned, though his eyes remained sad, and said softly, "*The Closed Circuit* finale can go to hell in a handbasket for all that it matters, but right now Diablo needs a bull more than anything else in the world— that's the whole reason his nana set this whole charade up. No mother ever knew her boy so well as Nana knew hers, and that's counting my mama."

Sierra's eyes pricked with tears as more pieces of the story came together in her mind.

When there was no answer, Henry let out a noise of frustration. "He's in there, alright. But the door's locked."

The squeeze around her heart tightened at the sound of frustrated defeat in the old man's voice. He'd aged since the last time she'd seen him, no longer the upright old-school cowboy she'd encountered over the past two years, but truly an old man.

But relief came from AJ next, as a bit of his smile crept into his eyes despite the fact that they'd welled up and glistened. His voice was hoarse and thick with tears when he said, "Like that ever stopped us before," and then he was wiping at tears and turning to make his way around the house like he'd done it a million times before.

Lil and Henry and Sierra stood on the porch there, quiet and stiff and awkward without Diablo or AJ around to build a conversational bridge for them, none of them bothering to make small talk.

Of the three of them, it would have fallen to Sierra to get that ball rolling, and she found she just didn't have it in her to chitchat—and maybe didn't even care that she didn't.

This wasn't the time for talking and pretending everything was fine.

This wasn't a pageant.

It was a crisis of the deepest variety. Deeper than love rejected and mishandled, deeper than competitions and the sport she'd made all the wrong choices for.

She was dressed in her rainbow unicorn shirt and a pair of jeans and tennis shoes, with her hair pulled back into a plain ponytail and she hadn't even bothered with basic makeup because not a shred of dressing bore any importance in the face of what Diablo was going through. What he needed to be dragged out of.

It wasn't the rodeo queen Sierra Quintanilla standing on the porch, but a woman concerned with getting the man she loved the help he needed, and she realized with a start, standing in front of the childhood home of the man she loved, that maybe the rodeo queen didn't even exist anymore.

She had died, bit by bit in a Houston hotel room, and a hole-in-the-wall sandwich joint in New Orleans, and in Crandon Park and on the stage in Nashville. The rodeo queen was dead, and in her place, Sierra had become real.

And being real, in all senses of the word, meant admitting that the only thing that truly mattered to her anymore was Diablo.

He'd been left on this porch as an infant. She'd be damned if she didn't leave this porch today with him as her man.

When the front door swung open, AJ stood there, a grim smile on his face, a small swelling cut above his right eyebrow, and he had Diablo at his side, apparently untouched, but nowhere near what anyone would call in great shape, nonetheless.

Lil let out a gasp, her hand fluttering protectively to her abdomen before she darted up to her husband. "What the hell happened in there?" she demanded, no gentle concern in her voice but the same bristling irritation with which she reacted to everything. Sierra would have rolled her eyes if it wouldn't have meant taking them off Diablo.

His own gaze froze and locked as soon as it found hers.

A gale of emotions flashed across his expression—agony and defeat, utter loneliness, as well as what she knew he wished he could continue to hide, relief. He was glad she was there. He'd wanted her all along—before she'd even had the sense to accept it for the gift such a thing was. To be wanted by a man like Diablo Sosa, in times of wonder and in times of devastation, was worth walking away from the rodeo for.

She took a step toward him, her arms rising and opening to him.

Something in his eyes broke, crumbling every shred of resistance that remained in him.

Time slowed as if she had entered rodeo time, as if instead of crossing the porch to embrace the man she loved, she was about to exit the chute on the back of a raging man killer.

She noted every minute detail as if it were massive— the way his broad shoulders curved in as they lifted to meet hers, the way his body fell into hers, for all that he maintained his ever-present control, the way his arms wrapped around her, drawing her into a cyclone of sensations even as they held her safe and rooted in the calm center of the storm.

His despair, his being unmoored, his uncertainty and confusion, his care and the reprieve of their bodies returning to one another. And then there were her own emotions, her bottomless well of sorrow to see him with his heart so broken and raw, her resolution to protect him, to buffer him from the very world itself if that was what he needed from her, along with the undeniable and irrefutably selfish joy that ran through her system at being in his arms again. A part of her acknowledged that there would never be a time in which his embrace did not weave at least a thin thread of joy—regardless of what else was going on. Everyone had to journey into the deepest pits of grief and hurt in a lifetime. If it was going to happen anyway, she would rather do it with him.

No one spoke a word as they held each other, the sounds of the city neighborhood going on around their ragtag bunch on the porch.

They were Diablo's family, and now the only family he had left.

AJ, and Lil and Henry remained quiet when, after a long stretch of just staying clasped close to each other,

Sierra gently drew back to examine him, up close and personal, for the first time in nearly two weeks.

Dark circles and deep grooves hung below his eyes, faint creases etched a grimace into his face and he had grown a mildly unkempt beard.

The hair on his head had grown out as well, the crisp lines and streamlined look he preferred grown into something less polished, but nowhere near less attractive.

For the first time that she'd ever seen him, he now looked like the lawman from the Wild West of old she'd dubbed him. Haunted but no less resolute.

She was the one to break the silence, and when she spoke, the words were wholly unplanned and spontaneous.

"Diablo, will you marry me?"

She didn't look away so she would never know the reactions of the people who stood around them, the family he'd forged through a life that had been far harder than it ever should have been.

Silence continued to reign.

But while they'd not been intentional, as soon as they'd escaped she'd known the words were true. As inappropriate and unexpected as her timing was, and as far from her fantasies and plans of how this moment would go were—she wanted to marry Diablo.

She wanted to join the family he'd crafted, in all senses of the word.

She knew she could never replace his nana; that wasn't possible and that wasn't what she was offering, but she could make a promise to stick by him until the day she died—and she could keep it.

His eyes intensified as if all of his energy and fire

and drive momentarily condensed into the two points of his pupils, and then she was once again crushed in the circle of his arms. Again, the emotions swirled around them, but this time there was something in them even more profound than his relief at seeing her. This time, amid all the sorrow and conflict, she could swear she also felt peace.

When his voice finally emerged, thin and cracked and drier than she'd ever heard it before, not his usual silky sands of the Sahara sound, but reedy and torn like the broken remains of a lake, he said, "You don't even have a ring."

She chuckled, incapable of rustling up a show laugh even if she'd wanted to in the face of his pain and the momentousness of this moment.

Not since her father had taken her to her first rodeo all those years ago, had everything in her life changed so irrevocably in a single instant—because although he hadn't said it yet, she already had his answer.

Diablo wouldn't have joked his refusal.

He was too grave and earnest for that.

He only joked when he felt safe and nurtured, surrounded by the people he loved most in the world—at least those who remained.

And, fittingly, in the same way that the logic and reason of life only makes sense in hindsight, Lil was the one to break in with a demand for clarity.

"Well," she drawled, somehow stretching the word out into a threat even when she didn't mean to, "are you gonna answer the lady or not?"

At Diablo's side, AJ—whom it was becoming more and more clear had taken the first round of Diablo's emotional triage to the face—gave his wife a rueful smile and nudged his friend in the shoulder.

"Answer the cowwoman, D. She doesn't stop until she gets her way."

Pulling back to look at her in the face, he answered AJ without taking his eyes off Sierra's. "I know the type. But I've got a few questions first."

Doubt fluttering into her stomach, Sierra's eyes glistened, but she held her ground and hid none of her emotions. You didn't turn your back on a bull, and you didn't win a man like Diablo's heart with anything less than complete honesty.

"What about your work?" he asked and held his breath.

His question was simple, but by now she understood everything he meant. What about rodeo queening? What about the career and identity she'd pursued and crafted with single-minded ferocity for more than half of her life? He wasn't asking her to give it up, but he was gently reminding her that if he had not been willing to be the lover she wasn't allowed to have, then he certainly wasn't going to be the husband no one could know about.

And all of the doubt that had risen up to tangle in her throat disappeared.

None of this had been premeditated, but it was entirely what she wanted, she realized as the words left her mouth, as was her answer to him. "I've decided to apply to the museum studies program at ASU."

For a moment he said nothing, searching her eyes while she held still and wide-open before him.

He was scanning her to make sure she meant what she said, and she would have expected nothing less from him. Diablo didn't trust easily, nor did he easily open the door to his heart.

In the rush of being loved by him, she'd taken for granted how rare it had been for him to add her to his list.

Never again would she make that mistake.

And then he said yes, and the waterworks that she had been able to hold back from the moment of seeing his incredible sorrow until now, when he'd catapulted her into happiness, became too much for her to hold back.

He held her again while AJ said, the entwined happiness and sorrow in his voice at odds with the smugness of his sentiments, "Didn't I say you just might meet the love of your life?" Looking at his own wife, he added, "It's *Closed Circuit* magic."

Finally, Diablo stepped back from Sierra, this time to turn to Henry, who, though tears flowed freely down his weathered face, had remained silent through the entire exchange.

"I forgive you," he said.

The words lanced through Sierra's heart and came out the other side clean and pure—and she wasn't even sure who they had been directed at.

The statement was everything that Diablo was at his best—honest and direct, pure and true, full of compassion.

Henry let out a ragged breath, head and hat hanging and shoulders slumping for only a second before he looked back up to meet Diablo's stare.

"Your nana only ever asked me for two favors in all the time I knew her, and both were heavier than most. The first was when she asked me to save her grandson from a world that was doing its damndest to take him down, and the second was when she asked me to lie to him. When she found out how little time she had, the first thing she did was call me and ask me to talk to you about *The Closed Circuit*. We both knew we could never tell you the truth, though. There was no way you would've done it. You'd have been at her side at every waking moment, and she was insistent that was the last thing either of you needed. She said she didn't think she'd be able to get through what she had to go through with you there watching. Knowing she was abandoning you and there wasn't a damn thing she could do about it, was a second kind of death sentence for her. She did it for you. Don't you ever forget that."

Diablo's voice remained hoarse as longer sentences made their way through his throat. How long had he gone without speaking to another human? she wondered, another wave of heartbreak for his incredible loss mingling with gladness that she got to spend the rest of her life with him.

"She wrote it all down in a letter. Said the same thing about you," Diablo said, a soft smile coming to his lips even as his eyes welled over with tears, the first he'd let free since they'd been on the porch.

Sierra took his hand and held it, subtle and soft, without fanfare or squeeze. She had learned how to read people very well in her years as the most successful rodeo queen the world had ever seen, and while the skills would still not be enough to ever fully understand the mind and heart at her side, she intended to put them to very good use on him.

Picking up again, he added, "She said a lot of things.

It was a good letter. Would have been better to say good-bye, but it was a good letter."

Pain and shame slashed across the old man's expression and she felt for him, even knowing Diablo had not intended the statement as an admonition.

There were times when witnessing the truth of what you'd done was punishment enough; situations in which intentions mattered far less than results.

But they were family, and so they each reached out to each other.

Speaking with earnest spine, the old man said, "It was the first and only time I've lied to you in my life, son, and I'm sorry for it. If you still want me in your life, I can promise you, it'll never happen again."

As upright as he stood, he looked older in that moment than Sierra had ever seen him, perhaps closer to deserving the moniker that both AJ and Diablo used to refer to him more now than ever before.

Diablo frowned, giving a small shake of his head in irritation. "You're forgiven. I know you. I know Nana. She said a lot of good things in the letter. It helped. You both loved me enough to do things you never do. Her letter helped me see that."

He paused, giving a solemn nod that was more to himself than any in the group standing around him, the quiet sorrow of which set off another rush of tears in Sierra, before he continued with, "And both of you were right. I needed this season of the circuit and I need that bull tonight. I'm going back to the finale. I love you and you love me. She reminded me of that," he said to the old man, giving Sierra's hand a squeeze as he spoke. "But there have only ever been two things strong enough to let it all out with, and those were bulls and her. Only one of those is left now, and it was her last wish."

After a speech like that, come hell or high water, she was going to get him to that bull.

Digging into her purse through her lingering tears, she searched through the abyss to check the time.

Unfortunately, her contact fell out.

Jumping, she made a noise, and Diablo's attention fell to her.

"I lost a contact."

"Do you have a spare?" he asked at the same time as he checked his watch, for the instant, falling into the precision and goal-oriented focus that was autopilot for him. "There's exactly four hours until curtain and the flight is just over three."

Stomach sinking, Sierra shook her head in panic, her own autopilot mode of putting work first switching on even as she continued to search for her contact.

Her outfit for the night was at the stadium but her show bag, and her spare contacts, were back in her hotel room. There was no way she could get it and get to the show on time, no more than Diablo had enough time to pick up his own gear.

Woodenly, she said, "I only have glasses."

There was no way they were going to be able to pull this off.

There wasn't enough time, neither of them were ready and all she had were glasses.

But Diablo smiled. Turning to her, he leaned down to press his forehead against hers, a note of real and easy laughter coming to his eyes as he stared into hers. Gesturing with his palm to his suit, he said low, "Looks like the day when cowboys can ride in suits and queens can show up in glasses has finally arrived."

An only slightly unhinged laugh bubbling out of her, she gulped a deep breath, and nodded. "And it got here just in the nick of time. How are we going to get there? There's no way we can make it through the airport in that amount of time."

With his characteristic cocky bravado, of which she could not believe she had ever seen any appeal in— *why would you want fluff when you could have all of the deep and real of Diablo?*—AJ chimed in with a *tsk tsk*. "I know you're new to these parts, but you'll have to get used to the way we do things around here. This is CityBoyz territory, this is rodeo and this is Texas. It's never been a matter of a commercial flight to the show, not with this much on the line."

And abruptly, the only thing to worry about was getting him to the arena on time.

They pulled off the miraculous feat with the assistance of an eccentric Texas oilman by the name of Rick Jermaine, who was all smiles when he met them at a small private airport outside Houston.

He was an old friend of Henry and AJ's, a lover of rodeo and of making a splash, and happily offered the use of his plane for the small price of being a part of the action.

And in the face of such blatant fame-grabbing, Sierra didn't care at all. As long as they got Diablo on that bull, the man was a saint in her book.

CHAPTER TWENTY

IN THE CHUTE, Diablo secured his left arm and raised his right, gave the signal and burst through the gate, marked out and precise, because some things were bigger than any single person.

Some things were universal and primal—the roar of a crowd, the rage of a bull, grief…

Some things were capable of resisting the incredible willpower of a man who'd learned too much, and far too young.

Not many things, but some. His nana had been one. Bulls were another.

The crowd chanted his name, the three syllables becoming the sound of the people clamoring for a hero, and not a hero with a ranch in Montana, but him. Diablo.

DI-A-BLO—DI-A-BLO—DI-A-BLO!

In all his life, bulls were the only creatures he'd met that were strong enough to take the full force of him and end up standing.

It took three thousand pounds of primal rage to face off against the boy who had been left on his grandmother's doorstep, to become a family of two, then one, and then, miraculously, two again.

And it took three thousand pounds of focused and unbridled deadly intent to acknowledge just how much he'd lost.

Bulls had brought him everything good in his life, and his nana had brought him bulls.

The world—his world—would never be the same, could never be, but he didn't have to worry about hurting the bull as he let it all out.

And even though it all happened in the blink of an eye, it was enough.

His nana had left him a pink house in Houston and the gift of forgiveness—and the bulls. Everything she'd known he needed.

Nothing would ever be the same.

When the eight-second buzzer rang, tears freely streamed down his face, but he didn't wipe them away. The pickup men rode out to meet him.

He didn't know if he'd had a good ride or not and didn't care.

He understood why his nana had done what she had done, and he forgave her, he forgave the old man and he forgave Sierra, to his everlasting fortune.

She would be his wife. Or rather, he would be her husband.

Only she would have the audacity.

And he would be forever grateful for that—and for showing her exactly how he felt.

When Sierra's voice rang out over the loudspeakers, it was to sing his praises, infused with the warmth of a person who hadn't let love slip by them. "Now, that, folks, is how you ride a bull."

Her dress was slightly loose on her, only a bit off, but nothing like the perfect rodeo queen she usually presented. The dress was simple, all black with some fringe here and there and a few studs, a little big everywhere and intentionally big in the shoulders. He imagined she'd been going for some retro theme she'd planned to do more with. But it was actually cute with her thick black hipster glasses and pin-straight hair.

She'd been wearing sneakers to come for him and he wondered where she got the ivory boots she wore from. And the hat, too. Simple and plain and perhaps a size too big, they most certainly didn't belong to her.

Leave it to her, though, and she'd probably end up starting a new fashion trend in rodeo pageants by the end of the night.

She was glowing and captivating, and the audience wanted in on it.

But strangely, he could tell she paid them no mind. Her voice wasn't controlled tonight; it was filled with enjoyment for her favorite sport. She was thoroughly in the night, because as only he knew, she was going to be saying goodbye.

She hadn't been able to go back to her hotel room after they'd landed for a full change, but it didn't matter. She looked beautiful. And he'd actually ridden the finale in a suit. There wasn't a lot he wouldn't do for her.

Julio finished the season with an astounding ride, as usual, and in the end, the positioning of the top three endured, but of course with Dillon switched out with Casey.

Sierra called them to the podium, brushing her fingertips against Diablo's as she handed him his buckle, the contact a promise of more to come later—more talking, more laughing, more crying—and Diablo was under no illusions as to who the true winner of the tour was.

He was impatient to make up for lost company with her, and to get away from the lights and watching eyes to be raw and aching again.

But of course, it was the *Closed Circuit* finale, so everything had to be dragged out.

Good TV, and all of that.

But when Sierra raised her palm and said, "Now, just one more thing, y'all. I've got more news before *The Closed Circuit* closes for its second, records-breaking season! You didn't just think I'd let you go without a little peek and nibble of what you can expect from the new, always improving, renewed for a third season *Closed Circuit*, now, did ya?" It was a hard thing not to grimace.

The audience shouted back their deafening refutation and Sierra smiled at them before turning her face into a pout. "But before I get to that, I do have a little bit of sad news, my friends. *The Closed Circuit Rodeo* is going far, y'all, all the way to Hawaii, even, but this little rodeo queen won't be crossing the big blue with them for a third time around. Nope, y'all," she said with a crowd-pleasing shrug and shake of her head. "I've finally met a cowboy worth leaving the circuit for, folks, and it's none other than our very own lawman, Diablo Sosa!"

The audience ate her performance up while it was all Diablo could do but grin down at her from where he stood on the podium while the jumbotron zoomed in on the two of them.

He hadn't expected her to do that, hadn't needed it, even as he couldn't help but puff up his chest.

Like in everything else she did, she'd managed to make the announcement on her terms, and while her adoring fans would be sad to see their beloved queen go, it made a great story to lose her to love.

And when it did finally come time to exit the stage,

she rushed to him and grabbed his hand, setting off another wave of cheers, and they walked off together.

Julio, glowing with the pleasure of having won, but grave in his approach nonetheless, grabbed Diablo's shoulder, giving Sierra a pregnant nod before returning his attention to Diablo as he said, "Gracias. No hay nada más que decir."

And Diablo said, "No hay de qué," because there hadn't been, which was always the cruel part. All Diablo had done was be decent.

But somehow it had all turned out for the good anyway. In this very real *Closed Circuit*, a community separate from everything hard and cold waiting for their return in their regular lives, trying had worked out. It had more than worked out.

Here, when life had been preparing its greatest offense on him yet, he'd found the one person in the world who could face it with him. What were the odds of that?

Sierra stayed beside him for the barrage of reporters that met them outside the venue, and through the rest of the night, her hand looped tightly through his the whole time, for which he was grateful.

The grief continued to come, wave after thrashing wave, but Sierra was there, and the old man would be there, and AJ and Lil were there, and, with the deep sense that he wouldn't go over fourteen years without riding ever again, the bulls were there, too.

Things would never be the same, and they weren't okay now, but he knew they might be alright again someday, and that was something.

* * * * *

AUTHOR'S NOTE

BETWEEN WRITING THE first draft of *The Wildest Ride* and the first draft of *The Rodeo Queen*, the world completely and utterly changed. Not only had I just welcomed my second child, but far more drastically, COVID-19 and the murder of George Floyd swept through the globe, undermining the foundations of what most of us understood to be immutable and redefining our lives into the future.

Among other things, I am Black. I grew up deeply and thoroughly immersed in the "nice racism" of the Pacific Northwest. From there, I navigated a pathway through life as a bubbly, friendly, agreeable *Black Girl*. It was a path that was relatively free from aggressive encounters with racism and optimistically dedicated to being a *Black Ambassador*—living and breathing proof of the ignorance of racist concepts and beliefs.

Of course, there were obvious flaws and cracks in my rose-colored view of what I was doing, could do, and who I was. Those cracks had been growing and multiplying in the years leading up to the onset of the global COVID-19 pandemic and the summer of 2020. But it was truly the one-two punch of witnessing my community's refusal to make public safety a top priority paired with its expressed commitment to maintaining the racial status quo that drove me to confront my full experience.

What was seen could not be unseen, and what was

worse, it demanded a reconsideration of everything that I had ever believed or thought I knew. After that reckoning, I was left with shame, anger and loneliness.

I felt shame at all of the anti-Black ideology that I had absorbed, and how I had participated in my own denigration. In serving as an ambassador, I was furthering the harmful idea that it is the actions and behaviors of Black people that drive discrimination and oppression. It is not. It has never been about Black people and has always been about racist people. We do not need ambassadors. We need justice and reparations. We need to make things right.

My anger, while justified, was a mask for the fact that through this I realized how powerless and afraid I had always felt. From the moment I first learned about the enslavement of Black Americans from a white elementary school teacher as the only Black child in a classroom of white students, to the moment I painted and put up the Black Lives Matter display at Rebel Heart Books, I have been petrified by the prospect of white violence. I have lived a life driven by the need and desire to protect myself from it. I will never know how much of my success is a result of my personal desire or the result of the intricate defense system I developed to navigate this world as safely as I could, because they are forever intertwined. Fear drives many of us to strive and succeed—fear of hunger, of being without shelter, of death. In a moment long overdue, I learned the shape of the fear that drove me.

As a result, everything changed. We made the difficult decision to leave Oregon, where my husband and father and I were born and raised, and where we had chosen to continue to grow our family. Feeling like I was a part of progress and my deep sense of home were no longer good enough reasons to tolerate the psychological onslaught of living as a person of color in the Northwest. Realizing that so many of the people I knew and loved were unwilling or unable to acknowledge and sit with such a major portion of my experience showed me that it was time to leave.

I have never felt lonelier than I did when I recognized how much of my experience was invisible and unbelievable to so many of the people I loved and who loved me deeply in return. Racism is its most insidious and cruel when it weaves its way into love.

All of this came out in *The Rodeo Queen*. *The Wildest Ride* was an adventure written in stolen hours late at night, full of hopes and dreams and brightness. *The Rodeo Queen* was written while preparing to leave the home that had never made space for me.

Like everything I can no longer unsee, Diablo existed before the summer of 2020—his anger and frustration a slight hint of what lay on the other side of all of my hope and belief in the capacity for progress that was reflected in *The Wildest Ride*. Like all of the other revelations the past two years have brought, it was only a matter of time until Diablo boiled over into my consciousness.

This book reflects an important, if painful, point in my personal evolution. Like Diablo, I am tired of injustice and frustrated by how little power I have in the face of it. I hope, though, that also like Diablo, someday in the future there will be an opportunity to dust off the old equipment and show up stronger and wiser on the front lines of change.

ACKNOWLEDGMENTS

> Appreciation is a wonderful thing. It makes what
> is excellent in others belong to us as well.
>
> —Voltaire

SOMETIMES IT TAKES the courage, intelligence, talent and compassion of others to help us find our own. Sometimes we need to see examples of these qualities in others in order to have any sense of what or how to develop them within ourselves. Sometimes we need others to help us identify and define the shape of our dreams. In *The Wildest Ride*, I noted many of the people who loved me into being—the people without whom this book, myself and everything that led up to both would not be possible.

Continuing that tradition, I'd like to give thanks to the people who led by example, drew me out of my shell and encouraged me as I took some of the earliest steps to getting here. Shannon. Sham. You have talent, beauty and brains, and are confident and bold whenever it matters. You made it so much safer to put myself out there and to try—whether that be for auditions, competitions, clubs or just being more social. You're also the reason that I've got a soccer family, and that was honestly probably the longest shot of all. Nicole. Nico. You know this, but in my mental dictionary, your face rests as the definition of integrity. Like our girl, Shannon, you have more than your fair share of intelligence, beauty and humor. You have always been someone I aspire to be like, and someone I feel so grateful to have a relationship with. That we have technically known each other since fifth grade makes you my oldest school chum. Thank you for being my prom date (and your mom for her huge role in getting me there). Perhaps more than anyone outside my editors, you know what it is like to write with me and do the hard work of getting from a first draft to publication. I wish I could say it's better, but, honestly, nothing has changed ~_~. That is perhaps not much of a surprise. What was a surprise, though it really shouldn't have been, was that the two of you were two of the first people to reach out with congratulations and support following the release of my work. Our paths don't cross in the ways they used to, but I should not have been surprised. Of course you would be a part of it now. You've always been a part of it. Nicole and Shannon, together with George and Bryan and Alan and the rest of the crew, you ensured that high school, a time period that can be so fraught, was not just fun, but full of happy memories. Thank you for being my friends, for doing outrageous amounts of extracurriculars with me, for dragging me to hang out and for understanding when I wanted to stay home and read.

In addition to the people who have loved me into being, *The Rodeo Queen* would not be possible without the steadfastness of Nic Caws, whose editorial brilliance continually pushes me to be the best that I can be.

It also wouldn't be possible without George Floyd, the Black Lives Matter movement and all of the dedicated and daring protestors who refused to let the world look away in denial. Thank you for your conviction and bravery. In the face of disease and violence, you fostered greater awareness in the world. I owe the kind of debt to you that you don't pay back, you pay forward.

And to my family—especially Josh and Em and Xen and Dan and Patty—it was only with your understanding, support and patience that we made and survived the biggest move of our lives while I was simultaneously working on two books.

HARLEQUIN
PLUS

Announcing a **BRAND-NEW** multimedia subscription service for romance fans like you!

Read, Watch and Play.

Experience the easiest way to get the romance content you crave.

Start your **FREE 7 DAY TRIAL** at
<u>www.harlequinplus.com/freetrial</u>.